"The death of the world is imminent in Erica L. Satifka's short story collection *How to Get to Apocalypse*, which, flecked with cyberpunk details, explores its many possible endings . . . This insightful, unsettling book balances elegant storytelling with a black sense of humor. Unconventional comparisons create jarring images: in one story, a besieged city's walls are 'studded with endless fields of gemstones all cut into wicked facets,' while elsewhere, a full-time Florida sea god yearns for his family in the oceanless Midwest. Immersed in viable, plausible speculative futures, *How to Get to Apocalypse* is an unforgettable collection."

—*Foreword Reviews*

"Satifka is one of the most exciting writers around and still sadly under the radar. Her mordant stories grapple with technology and society in a way that brings to mind the cyberpunk greats. The tales in her first collection range from a grim story of dead children turned into flesh puppets for a TV show to an incredibly effective response to Ursula K. Le Guin's classic "The Ones Who Walk Away from Omelas."

—Silvia Moreno-Garcia, *The Washington Post*

"Satifka presents 23 strange and captivating stories about the end of the world. None of these endings call for rains of fire and brimstone. Instead, these apocalypses are most often brought about by extraterrestrials, and the tales explore a wide variety of human-alien relationships . . . displaying wide-ranging creativity. Fans of speculative fiction are sure to be pleased."

— *Publishers Weekly*

"The stories in Satifka's debut collection are inventive and gritty, bleak and satirical, hilarious and horrifying. Her work is reminiscent of Philip K. Dick at his best in revealing the struggles and resilience of everyday people caught up in the machinery of the future."

—Tim Pratt, author of *Prison of Sleep* and the Axiom series

"Erica Satifka has a knack for building unusual, strange worlds that are filled with horrifying wonders and characters. She writes provocative, thoughtful genre fiction that isn't afraid to challenge readers and push boundaries."
— Jason Sizemore, editor-in-chief of *Apex Magazine*
and Apex Book Company

"If you're like me you've been expecting the end of the world for a while now, and it takes a hell of a writer to make the apocalypse fresh anymore. Everything you'd expect is in this Pandora's box of dire scenarios—from aliens to ancient cryptids, rising waters to biodiversity collapse, drugs that make people inertly happy, to video games that drive them to kill. But, as familiar as these disasters may sound, each and every one of them is brilliantly twisted, quite different from what you'd expect. And at the bottom of it all, to complete the metaphor, there's a tiny bit of hope."
— Carrie Laben, author of *A Hawk in the Woods*

"These are electric, melancholic, and hilarious stories crafted from the ashes of our Big Tech future. If science fiction has any satirical zeal left, Erica Satifka is among its sharpest stars."
— Jason Ridler, creator of the *Brimstone Files*

"An uncanny chronicler of the human—and inhuman—condition."
—Jason Heller, author of *Taft 2012*

HOW TO GET TO APOCALYPSE

AND OTHER DISASTERS

ALSO BY ERICA L. SATIFKA

Stay Crazy
Busted Synapses

HOW TO GET TO APOCALYPSE
AND OTHER DISASTERS

ERICA L. SATIFKA

FAIRWOOD PRESS
Bonney Lake, WA

*Dedicated to my spouse and in-house editor Rob McMonigal,
who makes all my stories better.*

CONTENTS

INTRODUCTION
NICK MAMATAS

THERE IS A LIE, FREQUENTLY promulgated by editors of short fiction magazines, that there are just far too many good stories out there to publish, and that the work of rejecting stories and accepting just a precious few is difficult. Heartbreaking, even.

Most stories are awful and can be rejected after reading the first page. At best, the editors who promulgate the lie that the "slush pile" of unsolicited submissions are wheelbarrows full of diamonds being dumped at their feet, depend on volunteer readers who deal with ninety percent of the magazine's submissions, so they only see the tippy-top best ones anyway, and have to reject ninety percent of that top ten. When I was co-editing *Clarkesworld Magazine*, I made the extremely dubious decision to read most of the unsolicited fiction myself. It was not a wheelbarrow full of diamonds. It wasn't even a wheelbarrow full of coal. You know, dear reader, what fills the wheelbarrow.

The very first story I acquired for *Clarkesworld* was Lavie Tidhar's "304 Adolph Hitler Strasse." It had been weeks of reading before finding something good. Tidhar was already a well-known writer, and the story needed substantial revisions, but it turned out great and terrified everyone. As the months went by, there were a couple other pieces by fairly well known writers I was happy to see, and their stories were good, and we published them.

The first story I acquired for *Clarkesworld* by someone with no particular reputation was "Automatic" by Erica Satifka. I remember the moment well because it was shocking to find something so good in the wheelbarrow. *Clarkesworld* received many submissions every single day; enough to fill a year's worth of issues back then. So reading the stories had become something of an emergency, like dealing with a septic tank backing up into one's basement. It was two o'clock in the morning by the time I got to "Automatic" one Sunday. I was up, demoralized but determined. The woman I was dating at the time was up, trouserless, sitting on my couch and petting the two sleepy dogs on either side of her. The three of them were also demoralized, and the dogs couldn't even read!

When I finished "Automatic"—itself a surprise, as there is no need to finish most of the stories—I asked, "Ever hear of Erica Satifka?" and neither the woman nor the dogs had. "I'm gonna call this girl and buy this story," I said. Back in those days it was still de rigueur to put one's phone number on one's manuscript.

"Nick, it's a quarter after two in the morning," my dog-petting companion said. "You'll freak her out, even if she picks up. Just email her."

"It'll be her first publication though," I said. The woman on the couch was also a writer of short stories, and was a reader for another online magazine. "Wouldn't you be excited to get a call, even if it's 2:15?"

"No," she said. "Don't be a maniac."

Wise.

"Automatic" is a very good story. It did have one problem, and in the first sentence too: Satifka used the word "credits" to refer to future money. Speaking of ninety percent, I rejected ninety percent of stories that used "credits" out of hand, as it's a signal of the failure of imagination. (Hint: we still call dollar bills "bucks" a couple hundred years after animal skins stopped being handy trade goods.) But the rest of the sentence: "He rents his optic nerve to vacationers from Ganymede for forty [travesty deleted] a night"—oh my. Could have come right out of Philip K. Dick, or Kurt Vonnegut, or Kit Reed, or Joanna Russ. A throwback, yet thoroughly contemporary.

So, my email to Satifka was an acceptance, and also included a note to change credits to, frankly, anything else. And she didn't respond. And I moved from Vermont to Massachusetts and a month went by. And I actually did call the number on the manuscript, in the manner of a maniac, and left a message, and she called back and said she'd change "credits" to "skins."

(Aside: I was extremely happy to see "skins" reappear, fourteen years later, in Satifka's recent novella *Busted Synapses*, which I presume you'll be reading after you finish all the stories in this collection, if you haven't read it already.)

And I don't think I ever called any writer ever again. The twenty-first century had taken over, so we all just followed one another on Livejournal, and later, Facebook and Twitter. Satifka was also involved in the zine scene—another throwback!—and I ordered a couple. She stopped writing for a bit, because some people in an online writer workshop told her that her stories weren't any good, or at least they were unfashionable. I was very annoyed at this: why listen to those wannabes, no-hopers, and climbers trying to get the rub from Michael Resnick of all people, and not to me and my check for ten whole cents a word from five years before?! Thankfully, she got back into it. (I'll note that a couple of the stories in this volume were inspired by story prompts provided by the online workshop, so it must not be all bad.) Satifka also created the pages of a zine, *Fuck Tentacles*, for my novel *I Am Providence*, which was extremely handy as I write short and people buy books based on spine width. Satifka's been busy enough since coming back to writing to make a nice thick book of stories, so good! Be beguiled by the spine, and the stories glued to it, and then buy extra copies for all your friends.

You can differentiate a Satifka story from the mass of published work as easily as I could from the mass of unpublishable work. Who else writes social science fiction, with protagonists floating somewhere between proletarian and precarian, who engages with politics without being either tedious or imperious, who wears the influence of the New Wave and cyberpunk on her right and left sleeve respectively, who snickers at the future while obviously loving it, and and and . . . ?

Well, nobody does. The wheelbarrow is empty, except for traces of glittering diamond dust, tradable by people living in their cars, snortable by aliens, and consumable by you.

Enjoy!

Nick Mamatas
Oakland, California
July 2021

HOW TO GET TO APOCALYPSE

AND OTHER DISASTERS

STATES OF EMERGENCY

MONTANA

IN A NO-TELL MOTEL just outside Billings, the psychotic cattle rancher known as Paranoid Jack freezes when he sees the baby-blue eyeball glowering at him from the mouthpiece of the Bakelite phone.

"Hello? Hello?"

Jack swallows down the bile rising in his stomach. Nowhere is safe. He sets the phone back in its receiver and walks out to the motel lobby.

"I'd like another room."

The bored receptionist snaps her gum. "Is there something wrong?"

He gazes around at the tourist guides littering the cramped lobby. The eyes are everywhere. He closes his own. "The moon-light's keeping me up."

She rolls her eyes—normal human eyes, for now at least—and flips him another set of keys. Jack doesn't find the new digs any more comfortable. He blocks his ears as a begging man is whipped with chains, or perhaps alien tentacles topped with metal, in the room next door. It sounds like it hurts.

Jack's been driving all over Big Eye Country for weeks, warning of the coming infiltration of the Greatest Nation on Earth by the Alien Brotherhood League, but nobody listens to him. He goes to the parking lot where his truck, painted with a tableau of poked-out eyes, waits for him.

A hawk perches on the hood.

Paranoid Jack throws a rock at the bird, missing by a foot. He swipes another stone from the ground and prepares to aim again when the hawk turns its head. Within its beak is one bloody eye that stares right at Jack. It throbs, slightly.

Time to jet, Jack thinks.

FLORIDA

Atlantis rises in Tampa Bay on a baking hot Thursday without a cloud in the sky. Neptune, the King of the Sea, parades through the palm-lined streets of Tampa on a chariot drawn by oversized seahorses floating through the air. The people on the street might have been more curious about how the seahorses performed their locomotion had they not been distracted by the death toll wrought by the royal procession's swinging tridents. Though some of the onlookers have fled to temporarily safe locations, most are petrified to the spot, wide-eyed terror engulfing their gore-flicked faces.

Neptune frowns as his own trident comes back with a beating heart speared at the end of it. He sighs and shakes it away, then wipes the tines with his silken robe. *Just another day*, he thinks.

He's not the original Neptune. His parents, a triad of desiccated desert spirits, gave him the name ironically. They were disappointed when he took this job.

"I'll be back for the holidays," he'd said, and he'd really tried. But life under the sea had changed poor Neptune's physiology in such a way that he can never go home without suffering extreme physical distress. His parents asked him not to return after he'd run up their water bill by taking eight showers a day.

"I am the mighty water god!" he bellows, though he can't really claim the title. Another disappointment for his folks. If he'd stayed in the Painted Desert like they wanted him to, he'd have been at least a minor household deity by now, if not yet a true god.

Neptune bids his lackeys to set up his throne on the set of a *Girls Gone Wild* production, after flattening the director with a blast of his aqua-ray. He wonders if he'll ever be satisfied with his life, or if he'll just keep on running the same patterns over and over again.

He just wants to be happy. Is that too much to ask?

DELAWARE

The citizens of the Amalgamated Corporate State of Delaware are shrinking. It's the only way to fit all fifty million of them in a plot of land as large as some billionaires' backyards.

They've been hiding these extra people for decades, those crafty Delawareans. Each normal-sized resident of the First State keeps several dozen of the small people around his or her house: in the breadbox, in the closet, in the dryer. God help you if you forget to remove the small people before you run a load.

The small people are engaged in the creation of tiny tracking chips, which are installed in credit cards issued by the state to each and every red-blooded debt source in the nation. Day and night, they toil with their machines, creating chips no wider than a human hair.

Nona's getting sick of the small people who live in her sock drawer. The buzzing of the machinery depresses her. Once, they started a fire.

She wonders what the chips are tracking. She's asked the Grand Elders of the credit card company she works for about it, but she's just a lowly data entry clerk and these things are not for her to know. Nona's stopped using her own cards entirely, risking the wrath of the Corp Corps when she skips by them in her wallet on her way to the cash.

The small people are having a party. She can tell by their raucous voices. She taps on the sock drawer like it's an aquarium.

"Go away."

"But this is my house."

"And shut the drawer behind you."

Nona slams the drawer. She knows the small people's work is important, vital really, in some way she can't understand yet. She knows that some day soon, the small people of the Amalgamated Corporate State of Delaware will rise up and over the East Coast like an overflowing popcorn machine. As someone who's shielded and nurtured them, she will survive the coming revolution.

She doesn't know what to make of the fist-sized eyes she now sees in every reflective surface.

NEW YORK

I am the switchboard, the awake man thinks.

He's got ten thousand people jammed into his brain, this awake man, representing three hulking towers on a formerly-bustling Brooklyn block. Riding the thoughts like a cresting wave, he patrols the park with a truncheon in his hand, slapping it into his palm. The sound rings off the silent streets.

Behind a Dumpster waits an awake woman.

They fight, of course. With snarling teeth and clash of limbs, each awake warrior fights with the combined power of their burden behind them, guiding them in their maneuvers. Clumps of hair flecked with blood drift to the pavement. An ear bounces off a sewer grate. They fight for what seems like hours, the twenty thousand and two.

When it's all over, both the warriors are dead. Soft rain falls over their mushed bodies, cleansing and cool. Pungent steam rises from the offal.

In a building in South Brooklyn, someone wakes up.

In another building, somebody else does.

VERMONT

From this point on, nobody will die in Vermont, but they continue aging.

ARIZONA

The desert stinks of creosote, and it is full of voices.

In the ghost town of Phoenix, a lonely widow turns on the generator-powered air conditioning to get her through another desert day. Heat hangs around her like a too-thick blanket. Her leathery skin, dried by the sun's beating rays, is the same even brown as the foraged canned beans she uses in her stews.

Every night she inhabits a different apartment. A different bed to sleep in, a different kitchen to raid, a different closet to pick through. Tonight she wears a men's double breasted suit and a tie with birds on it.

Come out, says the voice of the desert. *Won't you please come out and play?*

The widow picks up her shotgun and cocks it, aiming it toward a cactus growing out of the barren garden of the complex across the road. This ain't her first day at the rodeo.

Everyone's here. We're all waiting for you.

She's far past reckoning how long it's been since the day she woke up to find Phoenix deserted. She opened her eyes, and everyone was gone: people, pets, power. The voices had started soon after.

You're the only one left.

"I know that," she growls deep in her throat. She sticks the shotgun out the window and fires on the solitary cactus. A rain of green flesh and pink flowers spatters on the asphalt.

The dead city sometimes shows her pictures in her dreams. It shows her friends and family, her husband, out frolicking in some oasis. Water flowing down their bodies, their mouths filled with breadfruit.

Are you scared?

"Yes," she says, aiming the shotgun at a graffito of an eye chalked on the bank kitty-corner from her borrowed apartment. She doesn't fire. She's already running out of shells.

Within the hour the air conditioning gives out. The widow tentatively steps through the front door onto the wide streets. The atmosphere wavers with heat like an oil painting splashed with turpentine.

The voices grow louder, speaking with the combined sound of everyone she's ever loved, competing for air time with their pitiable screeches.

She's been to the edge of the dead city, and she knows there's nothing out there. Not just empty space, not just blackness. There's *nothing* out there. Just a void.

We miss you.

"I miss you too," the widow says, as she looks for another dead building, another live generator. She lives in the city center now, far away from the void. But it's not enough distance for the voices.

We love you. Don't you like us anymore? Come back to us. What's wrong with you?

THE LINE

This isn't Paranoid Jack's first visit to the line that circum-scribes and contains the rapidly decaying American heartland, but it may be the one involving the most shoes.

They drop their shoes when they leave, these faithless emi-grants. Just slide right out of them. Rows of penny loafers, Mary Janes, high-tops, and cowboy boots line the border from Wash-ington to Maine, toes to the north.

(On the southern border they leave small bundles of hair lov-ingly tied up with string, which seems somehow much worse.)

Jack picks his way along the mound of shoes, which comes up to his knees. He's never left America before. Never wanted to. Everything he knows and loves is here. He's even grown to love the Alien Brotherhood League, for all that he's condemned them in his broadsheets.

But it's time. Jack unlaces his threadbare sneakers and places them atop the pile, pointing them in the correct cardinal direc-tion. Then he shucks off his socks and sinks his feet into the mushy loam.

"What are you waiting for, asshole?" says the little man who lives in his hair. He told Jack he was from Delaware, but Jack's pretty sure he's just a random misfiring of brain chemicals.

"Shut up," Jack replies through gritted teeth. "This isn't easy for me, you know."

So much of his life spent to chronicling the manifestations. So many of his warnings gone unheeded. Perhaps up there, people will understand. Out there. What was the name of that country again?

He steps across the river of shoes and immediately collapses.

UR-KANSAS

Professor Melody Zhang slides her camera into her satchel and calls it a day. She's been out at the site for the past two weeks, and her team is no closer to discovering the origin of the ziggurat that appeared out of nowhere forty miles due north of Little Rock.

"Hey Doc, wanna hit the town?"

Melody rolls her eyes. She's never been much for partying, and the closest town to the encampment is a little hayseed dump where Asians are almost as alien a sight as ancient Mesopotamian structures. "Pass."

"Well, if you have some free time tonight, take a look at these rubbings."

She takes the paper from her assistant. The cuneiform isn't the same as that used by the ancient Babylonians, not even close. They still haven't worked out the phraseology, despite the presence of linguists from all over the world. "Okay."

"And try not to work too hard. We're all worried about you."

"I'll be fine." She slips the paper into her satchel with the camera and walks to her scooter. Not for the first time, she wonders at how calmly the people here have taken this. When the ziggurat appeared, everyone had freaked out . . . *except* the locals, who regarded it as a sight no more interesting than the opening of a new discount store. They'd been more disturbed by the scientists sent here to study *their* structure, and agreed to outside interference only under duress.

Weirdos. Melody sticks her key into the ignition and turns it.

Then a warrior clad in bronze armor steps up behind her and slices her head off with his sword.

NEBRASKA

In a bunker buried underneath Chimney Rock, a man tortures another man until he dies. The first of these people strikes a fearsome pose, seeing as how he is nine feet tall, and his face has been replaced with a metal grate.

In fact, the first man is two people sewn into one body. The two men sealed up within the skin used to fight all the time, but now realize they must work together if they're ever going to find a way out of this mess.

Each one taking control of a trunk-like leg, the grate-faced torturer lumbers over to the phone bolted into the wall of the bunker. He/they place a call.

"The sparrow flies at daybreak."

A wet thick sound like spaghetti being dragged over a linoleum floor echoes from the other side. "Show me."

The grate-faced man angles the receiver toward the ex-human. An eye extends from the mouthpiece on a thin stalk.

"This is acceptable."

The grate-faced man knows there's no release from this place. Even if he/they were to escape from the bunker, where was there to go? Back to the streets of Omaha, to be stared at and taunted by young children? The reconstructed being can feel the utter wrongness of the fused body beneath the skin and the grate. Even if the grate-faced man separates, life will never be simple again.

The eye blinks, snapping the grate-faced man back to attention. "There is another."

There is *always* another.

NEVADA

The house always wins. So does the Autonomic SmarTrak DwellingUnit 3.0.

Step inside. Allow the polished servo-mechanisms to lift you up, float you through the air like a luck-kissed cherub. Spin the wheel. Roll the dice. Make merry. Have another scotch. Ante. Raise. Call.

Later, when the lights go dark and the thrill of winning is gone, sink into the luxurious honeycomb of the fully furnished basement. Order some room service. It's on the house.

In the middle of the night, you wake to find the meat of your legs stuck to the Egyptian cotton sheets. You pull, and there's a sick tearing sound.

You free yourself and head to the bathroom, but your steps are labored, as if you're stepping in tar. You pull the light cord and find small bits of sheet nestled in and among the raw muscles on the back of your legs, products of a fusion, a *melding* . . .

Above you is the unmistakable sound of digestive processes at work. You didn't notice it before. But now it's all you can hear.

KENTUCKY

Revival night. The line of sinners snakes like a broken ant trail into the tents pitched on the outskirts of Lexington. Unlike most revival meetings, there is no mention of Christ or God, no complicated hosannas. What there is, is the shredder.

Pastor Dan doesn't know where the shredder came from. He woke one day in his double-wide trailer to find it sitting at the end of his fold-out cot, one corner of his bed sheet in its gaping maw. Dan leapt from the cot, grabbed a yardstick, poked the shredder, all in one fluid motion.

It continued to chew the sheet, unabated.

Experiments were conducted. Through a series of increasingly bizarre coincidences, Dan discovered that one's sins could be erased from existence by feeding them into the shredder, allowing one's deepest shames to scatter at one's feet like confetti.

He doesn't charge for use of the shredder. Wouldn't feel right. The index cards and ballpoint pens to write down the sins, though, they'll cost you.

A young woman approaches the podium with her infant son in a sling. When the shredder pukes out the remnants of the index card, both sling and child dissolve into thin air. Pastor Dan has to concentrate to remember what was there before, and by the time the next parishioner comes up to the podium, it's already gone from his mind.

After the services are over, Pastor Dan sits in the green room with a bottle of vodka in his hand. Across from him sits the shredder.

"What *are* you?"

Of course, there's no reply. The sin-eating shredder is an inanimate object: it does not feel, it does not love, it does not care about its small amount of regional fame. It doesn't even acknowledge its frustrated owner. Dan has fed six hundred and twenty-nine scrawled index cards through the shredder's gold-plated teeth. He's become a rich man, all thanks to the shredder. It's not enough. He needs to *know*.

He places a fingertip into the shredder. The pain is staggering, immense. The white walls of the green room spatter with blood. He bites his tongue to keep from screaming.

"I'll figure you out," he says, focusing on the pale yellow light that sits square in the shredder's control panel. It looks almost like an eye.

He shoves the arm in up to the elbow, then the other one. The shredder almost seems to expand to accept him. There is so much pain that he has forgotten to even register it as such. He has been inside this moment forever, it seems, for in the pain of the sin-eater there is no beginning and no end.

Pastor Dan inserts a foot.

Now you see, the shredder says, *now you see inside.*

When Dan's agent jimmies open the door two hours later, she finds a foot on the ground and a star-shaped hole in the windowpane. She packs her bag that afternoon and moves to Germany, where things make at least a sliver of sense.

MICHIGAN

From his lair in the furthest reaches of the Upper Peninsula, the mighty Elf Lord defends his realm.

"Come on, Dad. Gimme my Nerf gun back."

The Elf Lord has no such time for such trivialities. He slings his weapon across his back and, listening to the voices so many people across this nation can hear now, strides down the gravel road to stake his claim of the Lower Regions.

"Mom? I think there's something wrong with Dad."

All across the Upper Peninsula, war rages. The Elf Lord, once a lowly insurance salesman named David Wright, hops the fence of his neighbor, the Cleric Prince. When they'd first started this divine mission, there'd been snickers from behind the fists of everyone who roamed the cubicle kingdom of Northeast Insurance, Incorporated. They'd thought the men in the office were playing a new sort of game. A nerd game.

It was not a game.

"Hark!" the Elf Lord bellows, rattling the screen door of the Cleric Prince's keep. "Dost thou wish to ride thy trusty steeds into yonder village? There is plunder there, and treasure."

The Cleric Prince's concubine answers the door. She sighs audibly, breath pluming in the crisp breeze. "Those are the *same thing.*"

"Vile woman, let me through."

"Sorry, Gary can't come out to play today." She starts to close the door, but the Elf Lord shoves his fist in the jamb.

"Play? This is not a *game*, wench."

"He's not here. I sent him away." She'd been begging Gary to get help for years, even before the game started. The Cleric Prince had never been a fully sane man. He'd filled his days with useless projects: resurfacing the blacktop on the driveway until it was perfectly level, organizing his books by smell, optimizing his health by taking all his sleep in the form of catnaps. He had seen no problem with any of this.

Honestly, when he'd started playing the game, the Cleric Prince's concubine had been *glad*. At least he was out of the house, with other people. But enough was enough. Better to kick him out than to allow the crazy to rub off on her.

She wonders if she should do something to help the Elf Lord. Even now he stomps and whines, certain that the Cleric Prince is within the walls of the keep, hidden from view.

"Hey," she says. "You want me to call your wife for you?"

"Temptress, do not vex me." He spins around suddenly, smacking her in the face with his Styrofoam broadsword.

She grunts, pushing the neon weapon away. "You're not even using those words right, David."

By that time, he's already halfway down the street. She rubs her belly, thick with life, and sheds a tear.

ALASKA

Paranoid Jack's had quite an adventure, but now it's nearly over.

He could have lived quite comfortably here in a land called Canada, a place where the Alien Brotherhood League has made only minor inroads on their quest for global domination. Hardly any strangeness here, aside from the occasional sound of crying babies emanating from prairie snowbanks.

As the months pass, the dispatches from home grow more crazed and urgent. Jack can't stop collecting the American newspaper clippings, pasting them up on the dashboard and windows of his new ride, a fuel-efficient sedan bought at below market cost from a desperate Saskatchewan salesman.

He has to get back. He has to *warn people*. It's just his nature. He peels the taped-up report of a man-eating shredder from his rear-view mirror and lights out for the most distant region of his shattered place of origin.

Jack might miss the Delawarean most of all. The little man couldn't take the cold. Or the sanity.

That makes two of us, he thinks sadly as he guns the sedan's practical motor as hard as he can.

In Whitehorse, he stops at a diner where the waitress takes pity on him and nestles a few extra strips of grease-flecked bacon onto his plate. She stares blankly when he talks of the aliens, the eyes, all of it.

"Haven't you heard what's going on down there?"

"All Americans are crazy," she says as she fills his mug with Bible-black joe.

Kilometers flip to miles, and now he's in Alaska. Denali National Park. In the shadow of the great mountain he brings out the clippings and spreads them across his lap.

No link between events, and no reason to believe that the aliens who have been on his tail for the past twenty years of his life are behind it, but he knows they are. He can feel them tear across the entire blighted nation, sparking chaos and seeding madness.

He sleeps fitfully and wakes with the sun. He kills a squirrel and eats it, roasting it over the charred remains of the last of the clippings. As he sucks the marrow from each and every tiny bone, he looks over at the great mountain that towers above him. It's already beginning to explode, long tendrils of liquid fire reaching toward his grizzled face.

Above him, the great eye winks.

HUMAN RESOURCES

EVEN A HALF-BRAIN LIKE me can see that Celia misses the hell out of her left index finger. It's a tiny loss in comparison to folks who've auctioned off muscles, organs, or whole limbs. Or those who, like me, wear the invisible scar of an absent chunk of frontal lobe. But it matters to *her*, and Celia matters to me.

"I just want to know what they're doing with it," she says, rubbing her intact hand over the stump.

I shrug. "Who knows?"

"Girl, I'm taking it back. They can't do this to me."

"You did it to yourself." Tough love, but it's true. "Besides, it's good for the economy."

"The *economy*," she mutters bitterly. "Like some rich asshole is going to need only a finger."

I drift, because that's what I do now, and find myself transfixed by the television bolted above our heads. The mayor's latest skin graft stands out in stark blue-black against his pale skin. He's saying the market is stagnant, and that we all have to dig a little deeper to discover those parts of ourselves we can live without. When I come to, Celia is shaking me by the shoulders.

"And that's what I'm going to do. Are you in?"

"Huh?"

"You're in," Celia says. "Get in the car."

I used to be vain. I didn't want my body carved up, so when things got rough I auctioned off a small piece of my brain for a luxury condo and free food for a year. *You'll never miss it*, the broker said, and most of the time he's right. I can't focus too well anymore, and my memory is shot, but it's actually kind of nice sometimes. Like living in a dream.

Celia only got a car. The economy really *is* weak right now.

She stabs the air in front of her with her remaining index finger, as if popping invisible word balloons. "This car doesn't even run that well. It stalled out in the middle of the highway just last week! Now, how is that fair?"

"Still, a car for a finger. That's not a bad deal, Celia. You're not even left-handed."

"That's not the point!" She slams both of her palms on the steering wheel. "Oh, why do I even talk to a half-brain like you?" The car squeals to a stop.

Like many of the affluent people of this town, the mayor built his house on the side of a cliff, in order to better appreciate the sweeping vista of the landscape. A young woman with a third arm reaching out of her chest is rappelling down the side, nimble as a spider. A lot of the rich are into extreme sports: rock climbing, sky-diving, wrestling with sharks. It's because they have nothing to lose . . . at least not permanently.

"Go in there," she says. "Get it back."

"How do you know it's with the mayor? It could be in any of these houses," I say, indicating the half-dozen manors dotting the horizon.

"Then get me anyone's finger. This is about *justice*."

As I ponder what stealing a finger has to do with justice, the familiar fog settles over me. What was I supposed to be doing? I look back at the car.

"Go. In. There. And. Get. Me. A. Finger." Celia waggles her mangled hand. I fix the words in my head. It's very important not to forget what she told me.

The mayor's throwing a party. A throng of many-limbed guests surrounds a little boy at a piano. The holo-screen in front of him displays a riot of notes and symbols, like five pieces of normal sheet music superimposed upon one another. He cracks his knuckles. There are at least eight fingers on each of his hands, including a pale brown one wedged in the web between the thumb and original forefinger.

If it's not Celia's finger, it's close enough to count.

I wait, unobserved, until the little boy finishes his piece and the crowd begins to disperse.

"Hey, that was pretty good." It really was.

The boy looks me over. I wonder if he's checking me for extra parts, to see if I belong here. "Thank you."

"I don't think I'd be able to play like that."

"You couldn't." He holds up his hands. The patchwork quilt of skin tones and sizes is both grotesque and oddly mesmerizing. I find myself drifting, thinking of the beauty such hands brought into being only a short while ago. "They were my birthday present."

Stay focused. "Hey, how'd you like to go for a walk?"

His eyes narrow. "Do I know you?"

"I'm your long-lost aunt. I have a present for you. It's, um, a puppy."

His face brightens. "Puppy?"

Celia's got the kid in the back under a blanket. She's mad I didn't just chop off the finger and make a break for it. But what if he bled out? I don't want to be a murderer as well as a thief.

We're stopped by the cops only a mile away.

They give Celia a choice: prison or a hand. She bursts into tears. I watch the scene, all of it, from my spot in the holding area. The police won't charge me with anything. I don't know what I'm doing.

I think of the missing sliver of my brain, lodged deep within some rich academic's skull. I think about Celia, about all of us. I walk up to the cops.

"Take mine instead," I say, after figuring out which hand is my non-dominant one.

I won't even miss it.

DAYS LIKE THESE

ON DAYS LIKE THESE, when the boredom reaches down Park's throat like a debutante's finger, it's all he can do not to hop on his board and hoist a hearty double-middle-finger salute to this crummy slice of consensus reality called Home Sweet Home. He'd do it too, if he knew the subroutines wouldn't reel him in, fish-flopping on the macadam.

No way in hell am I going through that again, he thinks, shuddering.

He'll give the neighborhood this much: it always knows who you want to talk to, which is why his front yard now directly abuts the front yard of his best pal Lynka. He feels the tiny frisson of energy that sparks when you walk into another person's domain, and slouches down next to her. Lynka's blonde hair reeks of vodka and sewage; it's a flaw in the program. Park doesn't mind it anymore, because it reminds him of her.

"Hey."

"Hey."

Together, they wait on Lynka's spacious porch for the familiar melody of the Jolli-Tyme van.

"You know, you don't smell that bad today."

Lynka sniffs. "Took them long enough. We put in that service call, like, six months ago."

Park plucks a blade of grass, rolls it between his palms. "Van's late."

"Maybe there won't be any more van. Maybe the neighborhood ate it." She gazes off into the distance, which ends roughly thirty feet away. "It eats everything else."

She doesn't have to spell that out for Park.

Park listens for the jingle-jangle of the van. You hear it before you see it, owing to various irregularities in the program, and for the five minutes it takes the van to enter Home Sweet Home, he and Lynka lick their lips, fidget their fingers. Park's toes curl within his Nikes. They need a fix, and they need it *bad*.

And here it comes, barreling down the cul-de-sac. And there goes Lynka, stinky hair flapping behind her like a ruined flag, always the first to step into the van's maw.

Nobody knows who really drives the van, or how it even manages to break the firewall set up by the Simulation-Owners' Association. Today the driver is represented by a piece of stock photography, a smiling brunette woman frozen in time, Bluetooth clamped to her jaw.

He taps on the window, but the piece of stock photography doesn't budge.

Lynka pops her head out. "Are you coming? You better get here before the rush."

Park needs the van. Not as much as Lynka, but then again, she's been here longer. How much longer? He doesn't want to know.

He goes to the back, jumps inside, puts his back to the wall, slides the pipe in his mouth. Before the door slams shut, he catches a glimpse of the sad sacks still out there in the cul-de-sac, denied their escape hatch for the day. *Suckers.*

*

When he's under the influence of the van, Park feels himself splintered. In one way, he's aware of the tube as it grinds against the walls of his esophagus, every uncomfortable inch of it. When he goes home after his time in van-space, he coughs out blood, so he knows it's not pleasant. But the bulk of his mind is shunted into a new reality, a world where time halts and you're treated to a rush of colors, sounds, and neurotransmitters which are a feast for the soul. You can't control the experience, but you don't want to. It's completely dialed in, especially for you.

There are six spots on the daily tour, and as Park waits for the chemicals to trickle down the tube and flood his fake body with real enjoyment, he briefly touches minds with Lynka and the others. There's a lot of bleed-through here, and he feels his simulated body melt into the mercury-like substrate that constitutes the beginning stages of van-space.

He doesn't feel his real body, the one in the refrigerator. Not even a little.

The only sucky thing about getting high in the Jolli-Tyme van is that before you can trip, you have to talk to something the simulation coughs up, a deep-voiced lady dressed in blue. Park and Lynka call her the Technician. She never looks at you directly. Park isn't even sure what her face looks like. Just that she's a girl, and she wears blue, and if she likes you then you'll have a good trip, and sucks to be you if she doesn't.

She likes Park. She and Park are tight.

"And how are you doing today?"

Park thinks. "Not good."

The Technician laughs, which is weird, but he's given up trying to gauge her reactions to things. "What could we be doing better?"

"I guess if maybe I had some different books to read. Or a

pet. What kind of a loser neighborhood is this where we can't have a pet?"

"I'm afraid that having a pet would go against the rules of your Simulation-Owners' Association."

Screw them, Park thinks. He can feel Lynka drifting close to him, embroiled in a conversation with another instance of the Technician. "Okay. But the books, at least?"

"I'll see what I can do. So, how's your father?"

Park shrugs. "Same. Still won't let me move out on my own."

"The world can be a scary place for a young man like yourself." Park doesn't know if she means the world of Home Sweet Home or the world outside. The Earth ravaged by climate change and acts of mob violence so bad that Park's parents had no choice but to contact a disrealtor and sign away Park's future. And their own, Park guesses.

"Is it any scarier than being *a piece of programming in a tin can?*"

The Technician sighs. "Please don't get excited."

Park can never figure out what the Technician's role here is. Is she his therapist? His programmer? His friend? He and Lynka never discuss their simultaneous conversations with the Technician. "I'm not. Can I drift, now?"

She smiles. "Okay." She exits the ghost of a room and lets the show begin, the swirl of colors and sounds that remind Park of what happened when he used to take too much cough syrup and crank up the drone metal. It's not a bad way to kill the boredom for a few hours. However long they *really* are.

Park's mother adjusted to life in the neighborhood the way eyes adjust to the dark. One day Park came home to find her lovingly subsumed in the subroutines, a mom.exe with no arms to hold him.

But a man of eighteen plus whatever doesn't need hugs as

much as a grown man, and his father had never recovered. Dad couldn't leave Home Sweet Home now, not with his wife's ghost haunting every mailbox, gutter, and microwave oven in the cul-de-sac. Dad's refusal to leave affects Park in a very personal way.

Because you have to be put back into a body when you leave Home Sweet Home. And Park's dad won't give up the keys.

When a bleary-eyed Park comes in with static in his hair, his old man doesn't even look up from where he's crouched against the wainscoting. Dad thinks that if he tries hard enough, he can get into the program, same as Mom. It's Park's job to make sure that doesn't happen. "Hey!"

Dad looks up. "Go to your room."

Park sighs in relief. *Good. Still here.*

Home Sweet Home's rendition of a teenage boy's room is heavy on Playboy and car posters, and light on anything that Park would have wanted. *They don't even drive on Earth anymore,* Park thinks. And he's never seen a real babe as luscious as these ones, not since the global food shortages.

A lot could have happened in however many real years he's been trapped here. By now it could even be safe out there. But he'll never know, not unless he gets his dad to turn over Park's right to inhabit his own body.

Park scans his bookshelves. There's the usual rows of neatly bagged Marvel comics and colorful manga, but a dusty old hardback is crammed in there too.

He pulls it out. *War and Peace.* Not something Park would ordinarily read, but he opens it hungrily, and is asleep before he hits page five.

Next day. 7:30. Almost time for Jolli-Tyme. Lynka reminds Park of a cartoon dog with a fork in one hand and a knife in the other. He can almost taste her saliva in his mouth, bleed-through from the program.

When the van stops and the hatch opens, she dashes forward, eager as ever to put the tube in her mouth and her back to the wall. Park hangs back, suddenly afraid.

"Why are you just standing there? Come on!" She waves her hand.

"Something's wrong."

Lynka shrugs. "Suit yourself."

Park walks around to the front. Today the driver's a humanoid bear with a friendly smile on its fuzzy face. Slowly, the unsatisfied members of the Simulation-Owners' Association are creeping out like ants after a rainstorm. He won't be able to get his fix if he doesn't get in the van right now.

But he can't. Something feels off. Park sniffs the simulated air again and winces.

"Lynka?" He goes around to the back of the van. "Lynka?"

She and four others are already deep in the tubes, eyes turned to the ceiling, hands splayed out behind them feeling the inner wall of the van. An old woman with hair like a hornets' nest pushes past Park like he's not even there and takes the last spot. He lets her.

Park leans against the back of the van and just watches for once. Mostly he watches Lynka, having never seen her go under the tube when he himself is stone cold sober. He's hasn't noticed it before, but her gums are bloody, like two slabs of bad meat. Her eyes are two punched-out clocks. The woman with the hornets' nest for hair sighs, and the back door of the van slides shut, and then it's Park all alone. Again.

Another day. Same Park. He doubts less now, as the hunger gnaws at him. He enters the van and jams the tube down his throat, feeling like a billion bucks.

The Technician's bare-bones office sketches itself out before Park. He can feel the enlightening playground of van-space straining behind the bars of the dull façade like it can't wait to get out.

Park slouches in the Technician's crappy chair. "Who are you, anyway? Do you work for the disrealtor?"

"I'm whoever you want me to be, Park."

He flips the bird. "Whatever. Anyway, if you work for them can you tell me how much longer it's gonna be? I don't care if Earth sucks. I don't want to be here anymore."

"But you signed a contract."

"That was *them*." The parental units.

She tosses her head, her pixels fracturing as she does, so that she's fuzzy in areas, a poor resolution. "Try to make the best of things. You've got it better in here than they do out there, trust me."

"I doubt that very much."

"You *do*."

He changes tactics. "So, my body. Are you sure it's still there? I'm pretty sure that you had to protect it as part of the contract." It was only a hundred and twenty pounds of teenage flesh, but he wants it back, anyway.

"Refrigeration is an inexact science." The Technician smiles.

Sometimes Park wonders if this whole "rebel teenager with a genuine cause" thing is a sham. This seems especially true when he interacts with the processing parental unit known as Dad. What else could explain the way he feels driven to protect the unit, the way he sometimes feels compelled to tousle Dad's hair, teach him to fish, et cetera and so forth?

Could it only be because Park *père* is so pathetic, so un-dad-like? Here he is, same faded "Best of the West" rodeo T-shirt that he's worn every day since Mom disappeared into the digital aether. Park doesn't care that it's only a program, that his father never actually owned a shirt like that, that the Parks weren't the kind of people who'd be caught dead at an event like that.

Sometimes, Park dreams of a city with massive bridges reaching to the poisoned sky.

And yet, here in the simulated reality of Home Sweet Home, Dad wears one, just like Park puts up posters of Ferraris. Dad tips his bottle of simulated booze (Park's tried the stuff; it tastes a little like Worcestershire sauce and doesn't even get you a fraction buzzed) into his mouth, but most of it lands on the curious shirt.

"Dad. *Dad*."

The man in the rodeo shirt looks up, eyes big in his specs, words slurred but it's not from the faux booze. "Wussat?"

"I need to borrow the car."

Dad thinks the code at Park. "Jus' don't wreck it."

But that's exactly what Park's going to do.

When he and Lynka aren't tripping in the Jolli-Tyme van or sloppily making out, they spend most of their time exploring the perimeter of Home Sweet Home. The simulation is surrounded by an ocean of dead land criss-crossed with highways. Park seems to remember from history class that real subdivisions of the twentieth century looked a lot like this.

How many times has he done this drive? He can't recall, any more than he can recall his precise age or his true relationship with the man who lives in his house or the identity of the van driver. More than two dozen, less than five thousand, roughly.

The boundary shimmers, a soap bubble. Park slams the brakes the instant he sees it, causing the car to whine and fishtail on the false grass. It should leave a mark, but it doesn't.

Park hunts in the shrubs for a rock, which he finds, because just as the neighborhood takes, so does it give. He drops the rock onto the accelerator and the car speeds past him, bursting the bubble, going into the distance beyond that Park can't reach. He wonders if the cars have stacked up beyond the gate in a digital automotive Stonehenge, or if they simply disappear, reduced to dead, dumb information.

He directs himself back into his front yard and collapses onto the lush green carpet, exhausted. *These are your salad days*, he thinks.

As Park sits at the kitchen table with a bowl of Lucky Charms, he thinks back to the day when all this went down. When he and his mother and father, or he and his two children, or he and his husband and some woman they found on the street, went to the disrealtor and signed up to be crammed into a pocket drive.

"There's no crime in the simulation," the disrealtor had said, giving them a knowing glance, as if to say *those people*. Park knew what she meant, and approved. "Everything is included: your food, your water, your entertainment."

"You still have to *eat*?" Park had said.

"Not very much. Just to keep you in the habit. For when you get out."

Everyone on Earth was poor now, but some were poorer than others, and that wasn't the kind of poor the Parks were. Either he or his father or his cousin or his fairy godmother had signed the paperwork, and Park's body was stacked with over a thousand others in a warehouse for the powerful and desperate. If Park thinks really hard, he can almost see the shape of his world, feel the other digitized humans in the other neighborhoods.

He can't feel his body.

Park dumps most of the cereal into the sink, because it doesn't matter, and goes outside just in time to catch the van.

It's full already, so instead he goes to the cab. Today's driver is a collection of writhing hands. Park looks away, disgusted.

This time, though, it's Lynka who comes up front to check on Park. "Here," she says, handing him her tube. "You go."

He doesn't want to. But yet he does.

"Haven't seen you in a little while," says the Technician.

"I haven't felt like coming."

She clucks her tongue. "You should really come every day. It's good for you."

Park huffs and slides further down into the large leather chair that's materialized underneath him. "*He* never comes. My 'father'." Park makes a set of air quotes, feeling like the bored teenager he's pretty sure he's not.

"Oh, so you've figured that out, have you?"

"I guess I always kind of knew." Park thinks back to the sad old man in the rodeo shirt, searching for his wife in patterned wallpaper. "Were they married, at least?"

"He thought they were. That's what matters."

No, it damn well is not what matters, Park thinks, bitterly. "Just give me the light show."

"Not at this time."

"Then let me go. For real. I have to make sure he's okay." The man in the rodeo shirt isn't his father, but even so he holds the keys to Park's body, and for some reason Park still cares about the guy.

But she just sits there with that grin on her face, and her eyes that never look at you straight on (diffused, as they are, among six or maybe hundreds of patients/clients/owners/prisoners simultaneously), and Park can't stand it anymore. He launches himself from the chair and at the Technician's face, hands full of her candy-floss hair, slamming her back into the walls of the barely-a-room.

He expects sirens, warning bells. Maybe a voice telling him he's beat the system. Perhaps he pictured the Technician's head opening to reveal a robotic interior, or that she'll be him. But instead she's just dead.

Distantly, he hears the Jolli-Tyme jingle, and then the rough sensation of the tube sliding out of his mouth as Lynka pulls him from the apparatus, saves him. Park gets a whiff of her hair and gags.

"I think you had a seizure," she says. "Are you okay?"

It's a stupid question even if she doesn't know it's stupid. Park looks back at the van. Surely his neighbors know what he's done. She was just a piece of code, but then again, so is he. And Lynka. And "Dad."

"Park." Lynka shakes him a little. "Wake up."

But there's no waking up from this, Park knows. No joyous reunion with his body, with his old life. No in-the-flesh Technician waking him up to tell him what he's missed during the last twenty, or two hundred, or two thousand years.

Earth could be burned to a cinder, or be elevated to a paradise. His body is almost certainly gone, and whoever or whatever lives outside now has no reason to plug in the time capsule that is Home Sweet Home. Someday, if these distant beings become curious about life in the twenty-first century, they might do that, if they can find technology compatible with this particular sardine can world. Park doesn't think they will.

The Simulation-Owners' Association contracts had planned for many things, but they couldn't plan for obsolescence.

Park says "I need to go home." And because this is Home Sweet Home, he says it and then he's there.

The man who could have been Park's father isn't home when Park steps across the threshold, though there's a stained T-shirt with "Best of the West" printed on it strewn across the pointless hearth. Park goes into his bedroom, pulls out the incongruous copy of *War and Peace*, and tries to go to sleep.

It's too loud to sleep, though, and he tosses against the pillow like he's having a fit. Park's not sure if it's the woman he's killed or the woman who probably wasn't his mom, but there are voices in the air, thick as chalk dust.

He presses his face against the wall and breathes in.

THE BIG SO-SO

WE'RE BOTH SITTING ON the rotting front porch one muggy July day when Dorcas asks me if I want to break into Paradise with her. I lace up my sneakers and we do the old huff-and-puff up Negley Avenue to the big Cygnian compound on the hill.

It's dark, which doesn't mean much. Most of the compound-heads are wired up to the pleasure-juice on a more-or-less constant basis, and who needs light when you've got that? Still, it only takes about three minutes until we're spotted climbing over the semi-permeable barrier that separates the Chosen Ones from the Not There Yet. And it only takes eight minutes until we're sitting in the bare-bones holding tank, waiting for an attendant to rouse one of the compound-heads from their ecstasy.

I look over at Dorky. She looks over at me. She mouths the words "play along."

And I mouth the word "what?" because for the life of me I can't figure out what the hell the point of this little stunt is.

The compound-head enters in a thick bathrobe that hides just how fucking *skinny* they all are. It picks up its slate and starts to write. The chalk squeaks.

Colorless ideas sleep furiously still.

"We want to stay."

Sonic results spiral within documentation.

The Cygnians say they're preparing the compound-heads for life on their homeworld, the *real* Paradise. For three weeks all of us were jacked up on pleasure-juice dialed to Max Effect, while the Cygnians ran tests to decide which of us got to live in the compounds. They shepherded their lucky few into one of the many squat nanofoam villages that dot the entire globe. Then they turned off the tap.

What happened next . . . well, at least some of us survived.

"We want to live here with you." Dorky does this every month at least, though this is the first time I've come along for the ride.

"That's enough," says the flabby, mealworm-colored attendant. She wheels the compound-head away.

"*Traitor*," hisses Dorky through gritted teeth, her voice corroded with jealousy.

I tap her on the shoulder. "Let's go."

The streets of Paradise on Earth (Lot #517) are filled with the bustling crowds of attendants at work. None of them look at us, the leftovers. The attendants are those who were judged good enough to wipe compound-head asses, but not good enough to get the drip. They're still human, but they think they're better than us. Maybe they're right.

"I hate them," Dorky says as we pass a clutch of attendants, their beige uniforms all glowy in the moonlight. She doesn't mean the Cygnians.

"You'll never get in if they hear you say that."

She drops her voice. "Bullshit. They've got murderers in there. Actual *serial killers*, Syl."

I shrug. I kick at some stupid overgrown hedges. "Just deal with it, Dorky."

Tears form at the corners of her eyes. "Just *deal*, huh? Like it's that easy. Maybe for *you* it is. You never felt it."

"I felt it a little," I say, bristling despite myself.

"Not like the rest of us. You're not *normal*."

I toss Dorky her bag and shoulder mine. "Let's just go. I'll make you some waffles."

"Fuckers," she says to the compound. "Empty heads."

The compound just looms there, dark and silent. The compound doesn't talk back. It just *is*.

Later, after the whole house has scarfed down the peanut butter and chocolate waffles I made for dinner, Dorky calls me out to the porch for a little "girl talk."

That's what she calls it. Like she actually sees me as feminine or something.

"I'm going to become an attendant."

I almost laugh in her face. Almost. "They'll never take you."

"Why? I barely missed the cutoff."

"You keep saying that." Dorky thinks the rationale for selection is genetic. Both her parents and all three of her siblings are in the compound.

"What else could it be? They can't look into our *souls*, Sylvia."

"Maybe they can. They scanned our brains, remember?"

Dorky juts her chin out. "A brain is not a soul."

I take a swig from my scavenged, chipped "#1 Dad" mug; Frank's bathtub hooch burns like acid in my esophagus. "Even if you do fit the criteria, they won't accept someone who's always crashing their party."

"They'll accept me," she says, looking straight ahead. I can see the sick lust for pleasure-juice boiling just beneath the surface of those baby-blue eyes. "Or regret it."

"You need to find someone to take your room."

She swivels to face me. "Come on, *really*?"

I shrug. "You signed a lease."

"Fine. I'll get some sucker to rent my stupid room, sell off my worldly belongings, then go plead for contrition to those assholes in the sky."

"We have a good thing going here." I gesture around me to the sidewalk no longer filled with wailing addicts, the scraggly garden Frank put in, and the intangible quality of our friendship. "Are you just going to throw it away so you can eventually have the hope of spoon-feeding a person who doesn't even know what planet they live on?"

Dorky sighs theatrically. "The sad thing about you, Syl, is that you're too stupid to know how stupid you are."

The pleasure-juice felt good. It just didn't feel as good as all that, at least not to me. More like a tingling, I guess, or maybe a little spaciness. Not something I needed. Not something I *craved*. It was in the water supply, so I couldn't stop taking it, but I spent many a night bemused as my friends and neighbors talked to God, fingerpainted the images in their heads on the walls with the food in their fridges, sang "Kumbaya" at every hour of the night. It was a twenty-four-hour hippie love jam, and through no fault of my own I couldn't get into any of it.

There's a word for what I am: *chemical insensitive*. And there's another term: *someone clearly not making it onto the mothership*.

I don't mind being left behind. It makes sense in a way; maybe the pleasure-juice is some sort of preservative, and all the insensitives like me would burst when we tried to leave the Solar System. Perhaps all the drug-reactions were just a side effect of something very boring, like temperature regulation.

Or maybe those aliens just felt like fucking with us.

It was me who seized this house from the selected family that left it behind, clearing out the rat nests in the closets and scrubbing the shit stains from the tile floor (when you're on the pleasure-juice, the world is your bathroom). I'm the one who assembled this little patchwork group of fellow leftovers and took care of them until the pleasure-juice voided their systems.

Pretty good for someone who dropped out of college after two semesters, if I do say so myself.

The Cygnians still take care of us, stocking our food and helping out where they can. They know they screwed up our world to get their chosen souls. Those aliens owe us, big time.

As for me, I tried to keep the momentum going. But after Dorky and Frank improved, after they were able to chew their own food and talk again, everything went south. My job as caretaker had been completed with not even an obligatory thank-you, and I was so tired, so jaded. I didn't want to rebuild the world anymore. The world was like one of those thousand-piece puzzles of a Tuscan fishing village where half the pieces were lost under the couch. It would never be put back together again.

I might have just walked the hell right out of there, if it hadn't been for Dorky. My friend, whose greatest desire is to run away from me as fast as humanly possible.

Frank's playing with capsules again, chasing the dragon. "Help me sort, Syl."

"Where'd you go this time, Frank?"

"Pharmacy on Ellsworth, near the Giant Eagle." There hasn't been a Giant Eagle there for two years and he knows it, but old landmarks die hard.

"Surprised that wasn't cleared out already," I say as I shuffle the OxyContin into one pile, the Ritalin into another. I wonder if the Cygnians keep stocking our drugs as well as our food. Maybe they can't tell the difference between the two things.

He shrugs and slides a bright red capsule into his slack-jawed mouth. "Don't care."

Frank used to care about a lot of things. He'd woken up from his withdrawal with big ideas and bigger plans: restarting civilization, at least on a limited basis. That enthusiasm lasted approximately one fortnight, then like everyone else, he'd allowed himself to be overtaken by the big so-so of our post-medicated existence. Either it's some kind of lingering side effect, or more likely, Frank is the biggest freeloader this side of the Mississippi.

We sort.

After fifteen minutes of this, Dorky comes tip-toeing down the rickety stairs on new stolen high heels, a too-small ladies' suit stretching over her belly.

"How do I look?"

It's a bit too Vice President of Systems Analysis for me, but I smile anyway. "Ravishing."

She loops a pilfered Coach bag over her forearm. "Well, I'm off."

"Off?" Then it's like, oh yeah, the interview.

"I'll be back for my things. Don't wait up."

Frank just glares at her like she's going to steal his horde. I swear I can hear him growling under his breath.

"One for the road?" I say, thrusting up a random pill toward her.

Dorky waves it away. "They want us pure. The pure product. That's the whole point. They want good people."

"We're good people."

"Good at swallowing pills, anyway." She leaves with a flounce.

Frank glares at me. I glare at Frank. Then I sigh. "She'll be back."

That night there's an explosion over in Shadyside. The telltale stench of sulphur points to an amateur chemist, one of the people trying to reverse engineer the pleasure-juice.

I'm buried under the cover of my bed, the enclosed space around me sticky with tears. My dad died like that, before the

Cygnians, while delivering pizza to a clandestine meth lab. Wrong place, wrong time.

I take deep breaths. I imagine my dad as a cartoon character with little explosion lines coming out of his misshapen body. I picture him waving to me from Heaven, which probably doesn't exist in reality, but it does in my head. Then the scene is over-written by Frank's wheedling voice, muffled by the afghan.

"We should start a band," he says. "Or a zine."

I steady my voice. "No we shouldn't."

"You could be the editor. Or the bass player. I bet you'd be real good at that, Syl."

"Shut up," I say, wiping the back of my hand across my eyes. "Just shut up."

"It could be power-pop-electroclash-funk-reggae fusion," Frank replies. "Or saddle-stitched. Depending on whether we do the band or the zine."

I don't respond.

"We could write an anthem. An anthem for the house. Or a manifesto."

I can't take it anymore. I throw back the covers, slam Frank's skinny ass against the wall. "Is *this* what you meant by restarting civilization, Frank? Making plans for stupid shit that isn't *ever* going to go anywhere so that you don't have to think about plea-sure-juice all the time? Because if it is, then you can just *get out*."

Frank blinks twice without saying anything, and I relax my grip. I slam the bedroom door behind me on my way out of the house.

Once, sirens would have been wailing, ambulances navi-gating the narrow streets on their way to the explosion. Now, there's nothing. Now, there's the mothership just watching us.

We can't even see the damn thing. It's behind the moon. Or Mars. One of them.

I look over to where I could have seen the compound if it was lit up. Smoke curls over the neighborhood like the largest question mark ever drawn. It's a little *too* apt, so I go back inside the house. Frank better not be messing with my shit.

A week later and Dorky's still not back. We get a new girl, just to keep the place balanced, so I don't kill Frank. The three of us are on the wide front porch of our humble home, splitting a pitcher of something that isn't at all like pleasure-juice, when one of the drab compound vehicles pulls up to the curb.

Neither Frank or Miss New look like they're about to move, so I throw them a sour expression and go up to the car myself. "Yeah?"

It's an attendant, maybe even the same attendant I saw the other day, though I can't tell for sure. They're all pretty similar. "I came to talk about your friend."

"Dorcas? Is she with you?" Was she taken, is what I want to say.

"You'd better come with me."

I don't want to get in the car, but when I look back at the porch, Frank's just jawing away on some stupid thing with Miss New, so you know, whatever. The attendant unlocks the door and I slide in beside her. She smells vaguely of ammonia.

"Are we going to the compound?" I bet we're going to the compound.

The attendant merges onto the potholed road, and I investigate the torn-up upholstery of the car, plumbing new depths.

"Please don't do that."

I unearth a chunk of stuffing and launch it at her. "Just try to stop me."

The attendant frowns, takes a hand off the steering wheel, and wrestles my fingers back into my lap. "Your friend's in big trouble."

All of a sudden, I'm not thinking about how boring this trip is, or where they get the gas for the car. I'm only thinking about Dorky. "What did she do?"

"You'll see."

And it's all tense and quiet like that, all the way up that steep, steep hill.

Crime dropped. The world stopped. Utopia, such as it was, lasted for three weeks. Then the tests began.

As we laughed and danced and pawed one another, silver pods emblazoned with strange symbols appeared in the center of all the world's cities. One by one we found ourselves herded into them, driven to the pods by a low subsonic hum that decreased in intensity the closer you got to the pod. You could feel it in your bones. You could hear it no matter how much tissue paper you stuffed into your ear canals. When you were inside it cut off completely. And then you were tested.

You'd think it would take a very long time to determine the fate of the entire world population, but the Cygnians were extremely efficient. After all, there were so many pods, and the test itself only took thirty seconds per person.

They put your head in a silver box.

There was a short, sharp snap.

They didn't show you the picture they took of your brain and they didn't let you know what it was they were looking for. It wouldn't have made any difference if they had told us.

Yet, as I stumbled out into the bright white-hot sunlight on test day, I knew I'd flunked the test. I stumbled against the silver skin of the Cygnian pod and heaved up everything in my stomach, half-digested microwave burritos festering on the dull green grass of Point State Park.

It was a bad day, even if I did live in Utopia.

*

The nanofoam structures of Paradise on Earth (Lot #517) are blocky, drab, and completely identical. The attendant picks out an unmarked building, seemingly at random, and ushers me inside.

"Wait," says the attendant as she locks the door behind her.

I sit at the desk, the chair groaning underneath me. Time passes and I start getting bored, so I build a mini-trebuchet out of paperclips and a gumband and start lobbing spitballs into the far corner.

What did Dorky do? Did she kill someone? Can jealousy tear a person up that badly, erode them so deep inside? I try to picture Dorky with a knife in one hand and a compound-head's throat in the other, and the image doesn't resolve.

Finally, the door squeaks open. I fumble with the trebuchet and a spitball lands smack-dab on the tip of a compound-head's nose.

Its attendant isn't impressed. "I told you this one was dumb," she says to an unseen person behind her.

I look at the compound-head lolling in its chair. A thick tangle of tubes flowing with the purest pleasure-juice is knotted at its arm. The attendant tries to untangle the tubes. She's really bad at it.

"Where is Dorcas?" I say to the compound-head.

Chalk on slate. *What has reverberated in this domicile shall never slumber.*

"What he *means*," says the unseen male attendant, "is that your shitty friend stole from us."

"Stole what?"

"Like you don't know," says the first attendant. "Like you're not involved in this."

They're grasping at straws, they don't know shit. I think that maybe this means I have the upper hand here, but since I don't know what they want, I'm not sure how to leverage it. My hands sneak back to the trebuchet. "I don't know what on *Earth* you're talking about."

The first attendant, the woman, snatches the mechanism from the desk and crumples it in her hand. "We need you to find her. We need you to bring her back."

Harvest the eternal singing that dances in the streets.

I look at the strung-out compound-head, its pink tongue raveling—or is it unraveling?—from its skull. I have to keep myself from rolling the slimy muscle back inside. Is this really what Dorky wanted out of life? "I don't know where she is. And even if I did, I wouldn't tell *you*."

"We'll pay you."

"I don't want money. Or your drug."

"Everyone wants the drug."

I shake my head and walk out. Surprisingly, they don't try to stop me. I'd imagined myself tackled from behind, hog-tied, forced to wear some kind of galactic space-wire and spy on my best friend. But there isn't any of that. I trudge down the gravel streets of the little village and down Negley Avenue. Alone. Un-followed.

I think.

The end of Utopia came with a whimper followed by a bang. Over the weeks that followed the testing, we noticed a slackening of the amount of pleasure-juice fed to us through the water supply, and an increase in hatefulness. In crime. In all the things that made humans human. Finally, tests were run that indicated a significant loss of the amount of "unidentifiable chemicals" in the water. Within two months, it was down to a trace.

And then not even that.

After the tap turned off, of course the compounds were attacked. Even though most people only had the vaguest sense of what went on in there, they knew that the compound-heads had what they wanted. What they *needed*.

"They've got factories in there," Frank said once, but he

might as well have been saying it today. "Factories where they make it."

"No way," Dorky had said. "They beam it down from the mothership. We could *steal* it." But they'd both been too sick to do any such thing in those few weeks after the shut-off, and I wasn't about to go get it for them.

So Dorky had finally stolen the pleasure-juice. Even if I knew where she was, I wouldn't rat her out to the freaks in Paradise on Earth (Lot #517). But that doesn't mean I'm not going to conduct my own investigation.

I roll out a map. In the post-Utopia world, travel between cities is dangerous if not impossible, so there's a good chance she's still in Pittsburgh. I stick pushpins in the map almost at random, hoping that they'll create a pattern. Twenty pushpins later, I'm no closer to discovering Dorky's whereabouts than I had been at the start.

"What are you doing?"

I look up to find the hollowed figure of Miss New. "Research."

She stretches out on my bed, languid and angry. "Frank found a bass."

"That's nice."

"We're going to start that band."

"Uh-huh." I jab another pushpin into the map. It still doesn't make any sense to me.

"He wants you involved."

"I'm busy." Busy replacing *you*, I should say.

"You're in love with her, aren't you?"

"*No*. We're just friends." I can't believe she'd ask that.

Miss New plucks the box of pushpins from the floor and starts sliding them into her fingertips, slowly. "If someone came into this house with a gallon of pleasure-juice, I'd kill them for it."

"I know that." That's why I need to find Dorky so badly.

There's no paucity of ex-junkies in this world who wouldn't straight-up murder someone for even a drop of juice.

"Anyway, we'll be practicing for the next couple hours. Just felt I should warn you." Miss New slides off the bed, and I return to the map. A few minutes later the music starts up, and it's more awful than I ever could have imagined.

Our lives, such as they were, collapsed into a single point the day we realized the pleasure-juice was gone. We became local. We lost the ability to plan for the future. We had seen the perfect chemically-assisted future, and we'd lost it. There didn't seem to be much of a reason to go on.

It wasn't even so much the physical withdrawal that killed people's motivation, but the shame and confusion of having been left behind. The horror of being stuck on Earth, even as others lingered in that strange waiting-room phase of abduction. Like there was no point to life if you had to go through it without pleasure-juice being poured continually into your synaptic cleft.

"I don't get it," I'd told Frank once. "We're no *worse* off." And he'd just smiled, because I clearly didn't understand.

I kick the map aside. I've been staring at it for days, trying to make sense of the patterns, all while the riotous cacophony of Frank and Miss New's "power-pop-electroclash-funk-reggae fusion" bubbles up from the dirty basement. I push my way out of the house and into the late-afternoon heat.

You know how you can sometimes find something the moment you stop looking for it? I see Dorky getting into the backseat of a rusty hatchback.

"Dorky!" I yell, hands cupping my mouth. "Hey!"

She gives me a look, the kind of look that shows she *definitely* knows I'm talking to her.

I run to her, my chest burning from the short-distance

sprint. I hold one finger out to the driver. "I've missed you," I say, the words catching in my throat.

She crosses her arms. "Does this have a point?"

"The house hasn't been the same without you. Come back."

Dorky smirks. "So they can arrest me? So they can *kill* me? I know what I'm doing, Syl. We're going to start the world over."

"By addicting everyone again," I say. I think of the compound-heads wired up in their beds, of the way Dorky licks her lips when she talks about the pleasure-juice. "What gives you that right, Dorky?"

"You're never going to get it." She opens the door and swings herself inside. "It's not your fault."

"What don't I get?" By that point the car's already started moving, so I jog alongside it. I can't possibly keep up, but I don't want to let her out of my sight. "What don't I get, huh?"

Her mouth forms words I can't make out between the sound of my own breath and the hum of the motor and the twittering of birds overhead. I want to think she's saying "sure, I'll reconsider" or "you're so *right*, Syl."

Then the driver guns the accelerator, and the car slips into the distance. I collapse to my knees. The tears don't fall right away, but when they do, they don't stop.

Somehow, Frank and Miss New's band gets a show. I didn't even know people were really putting on shows anymore. Yet I find the fliers all around Shadyside and Bloomfield, in apartments that used to be student housing but that are now the world's largest halfway house.

They make a zine, too. I frown as I look at the pictures of all of us—pictures of *me*—that litter the Xeroxed booklet.

"Nobody cares, Frank."

"Someone has to do it. Someone has to start the world over. Are *you* going to do it?" In my mind I see Frank pointing at me accusatorily, a strung-out Uncle Sam.

"Your band sucks."

He shrugs. "It's a start. You're the one who told me I had to better myself."

I'm not sure how to tell him that this wasn't what I meant, so instead I help them unload the audio equipment from the wagons they've used to cart this stuff over here, on foot. It occurs to me that Frank has somehow conned me into joining the band. Maybe a part of me hopes that Dorky will be here, that she saw one of the fliers and wants to visit her former housemates.

She's not. Nobody else is, either. The warehouse is as empty as a slaughterhouse after the vegan revolution. "Some bitchin' party you got here," I say, talking extra loud so my voice echoes off the concrete walls.

"They'll come," says Frank into the microphone. I don't even want to think about what Dumpster he's pulled it from. "Let's jam."

As they start to play, people trickle in, folks I've seen around the neighborhood a time or seven, *before*. Once they were businesspeople in crisp clean suits, old ladies in fancy church dress, toddling youngsters with candy in their pockets. Now they're sharp-angled scarecrows, for the most part, heads crowned with unruly thatches of hair. Their clothes are ratty and smell of rot.

It took an alien invasion to do it, but I'm finally the best-dressed one in the room.

Our neighbors don't dance, but then again, it's not really that kind of music. They lean against each other, nodding in time to the crazy sound. By the end of the first set, the garage is almost full.

I still hate the music. And yet, I find myself dancing along, moving my feet to the rhythm. Maybe some others join me, or maybe they're just trying to get out of the damn way. Maybe Frank's managed to jump-start society, or maybe he's just given people something to focus on for one afternoon besides their missing pleasure-juice.

It's not a lot. It's a little. But it's something. And I want to be a part of it.

In the next couple of weeks, stores begin to open. People start prying the planks off the abandoned houses and painting them up, making them look real nice. Miss New gets a job at some boutique selling artisanal dog biscuits. The Internet comes back online, and we're all tuned into a different kind of pleasure-juice. I pick up my dad's old pizza delivery route, and Frank makes the burned-up pies.

He was right, and I was wrong. Or maybe we were both right part of the way. Restarting civilization required action, not even important action, but *something*, even if it was just the dysphonic stylings of a shitty thrown-together band. I dropped the thread, Frank and Miss New picked it up. Now we're all carrying it . . . somewhere.

I'm fixing up my bicycle for another delivery when Dorky comes knocking on our door.

"We're turning it back on," she says.

She looks like hell: at least thirty pounds skinnier, with dark rings circling her eyes. She's dressed in scrubs likely pilfered from some hospital. But I still wrap my arms around her until I feel that she's getting uncomfortable. "You came back! Where *were* you?"

"Cleveland."

"What would you want to go there for?" I hug her again. "You came back!"

"You're not listening, Syl. You never listen." She pushes me away. "I took the pleasure-juice to a lab. We analyzed it. We know how to *make* it now." Dorky gets a dreamy look in her eyes. "They can't stop us."

I feel my face fall, and I can tell it's not the reaction Dorky wanted me to have. "Why would you want to do that?"

"Oh, *come on*. It's pleasure-juice. It's the best thing *ever*. Even if you're too stupid to realize it."

"Where . . . where is it?"

"Safe. It's safe. We have to make a lot of it, release it all at once. Can't have only part of the world in Utopia, right?"

I gaze out at the house across the street, where a family of ex-junkies is now hunched over a board game while the radio plays. We have radio now. Things are definitely improving. "Is this all because they wouldn't take you with them?"

I expect her to say that no, it's for the greater good of all humanity. But instead she says "Yes."

"Seems a shame. We're getting better. Everything is getting better all the time."

"Sorry you can't join us, Syl. Sorry you can't enjoy what the rest of us have." She starts going down the steps, then turns back. "Not sorry."

"Why did you even come back here?" But I can see where she's heading. Up Negley Avenue. Up to the compound. I begin to follow her, but my feet won't take my brain's lead. My feet carry me back inside, where bowls of Miss New's chili are already cooling on the dinner table.

The Cygnians leave, and I never see Dorky again. Maybe they took her. Maybe they *killed* her. Even in the newly reconnected world, I'll never know, and there's a part of me that isn't all right with that and there's a part of me that is, and I'm not sure which is stronger. It changes day to day.

The semi-permeable barrier that surrounds the compounds comes down and people start living in there. The compoundheads and attendants are all gone. Up to the mothership, and step on it! It's a permanent sort of decimation.

"I wonder where she went," Frank says one day.

I could tell him that I know, or anyway *kind of* know exactly what she's up to. But I keep it vague. "I think she moved to Cleveland."

"Cleveland sucks." He runs a comb through his hair and whistles on his way downstairs. He's in the pink of health.

I look at the desk where I used to have my pushpin map. Now, I have a list of calculations. It's impossible for me to tell for sure, but I'm pretty certain that we have sixteen years. Sixteen years until the pleasure-juice pumped out from some hidden Ohio lab starts leaking into our water supply and the world returns to the way some people think it *should* be. That's a long time. I could even be dead by then.

I roll the calculations into a tube and stash them in the closet. Then I go out, toward the rebuilt city, into a different type of Utopia.

A CHILD OF THE REVOLUTION

THOUGH IT MAY BE wrought of a steel slab three times taller than an average man, the gate in the wall of the desert village of Ironhaven falls with ease, because nothing stops the Revolution.

We, the Revolution, enter. We march past canvas tents and ramshackle lean-tos, shoving our educational pamphlets in the hands of anyone who will take them, and also those who will not. We march in the general direction of the keep, pulled there by the shining ones' love-magic.

"Halt!" A member of the village guard holds up a hand. Sunlight glints off his breastplate.

"You'll move," bellows Fiona, one of our more belligerent comrades, "if you know what's good for you."

But he raises his sword, as does she. In the blink of an eye, she's slit through the gap where his helmet imperfectly meets his armor. Blood gushes from his wound in a fountain of ruby, and the guard pales and drops to the ground. The other guard and several of the locals run screaming.

None of us in any way blame these poor souls for being in the thrall of love-magic. We too had once been under their spell, until the Revolution taught us the songs and the slogans that drive the love-magic away. And now, we're bringing the Revolution to Ironhaven, enslaved by the shining ones over five hundred years ago along with the rest of this cursed continent.

As the sun roasts the parts of our bodies not covered by our patchwork tunics, the magic intensifies. It makes the anthem shrivel on our tongues, and one of our newer comrades gibbers and falls to her knees, begging for the shining ones to forgive, forgive, forgive! Fiona unholsters her flintlock, fires, and the woman gibbers no more.

"She's at peace now," Lauri says, while gentle Skye closes the dead woman's eyes and crosses her arms over her chest.

The usual four of us separate from the rest of the group and approach the keep of Ironhaven. Love-magic pours from the grand structure, almost rattling the sapphires and emeralds that glisten within the mortar that holds together the keep's rust-red bricks.

Skye pounds on the door. Skye, Lauri, Fiona, and Gregor aren't our leaders—there are no leaders in the Revolution and never will be—but somehow they're always the ones who make this final confrontation.

"We are the Revolution!" Skye says. "We have come to liberate this village. Comrades, to arms!"

Lauri wedges one of her small bombs into the door handle and lights the wick. The door explodes inward with a shower of splinters. The four comrades step inside and fan out. The magic is so strong here that we must scream our glorious anthem, belt it out at the top of our lungs, lest our wills succumb.

What does it feel like to be near the shining ones' love-magic? Like honey, like wine, like sitting in the luxury of a warm bath while you're being serenaded by your own personal chorus. It feels good, and it feels right, and you want to be near it all the time. That's why every city, town, and village in this blighted land has coalesced around the descendants of those shining ones that sprouted from the original, evil mutation half a millennium ago.

No man or woman who ever tasted the love-magic could stand to be without it. At least, not until the Revolution set them free.

The chamber where the shining ones of Ironhaven dwell is festooned with tapestries and small golden statues left by their mind-slaves. This room is as luxurious as the village around it is dilapidated. We scatter the trinkets in disgust.

There are four shining ones in the chamber with us, one to a comrade. Once they had been nearly men, but over time the shining ones have become inbred monsters. Their jaws, which are too large for their heads, drip saliva over peg-like teeth. They've got barely any hair on their twisted bodies. Love-magic is born with a person, and mating with another magic-possessing individual multiplies its effect in subsequent generations. The first shining ones quickly figured out how to exploit this.

Every one of us feels the pull of magic, though it's written on our faces in different ways. Skye's hands fumble at his flint-lock, ready to loosen it and throw it aside and dedicate his life to serving the creatures. Fiona's lips tremble, and barely any words of our anthem escape them.

Finally, the four of us all hoist our flintlocks to our shoulders as one. We must shoot simultaneously, because if we're even a second out of sync the love-magic of the survivors will simply expand to fill the void left by the ones who have fallen.

We fire. The shining ones topple from their thrones, and their blood pools on the polished floor of the lush chamber. At the sound of the blast, a slave rushes in. She releases a wail when she sees what has occurred.

"You are free!" we yell at the slave. "You are free!"

But still the staring and the silence and truly the ungrateful-ness of the slave continues. We shrug and begin to pick through the chamber.

Fiona is the first of us to sense that not all of the magic is gone. She clamps her hands over her ears and shrieks one of our most potent slogans—*the people are the rose and its thorns, the people will never be divided*—and whisks aside a silk barrier that has shielded part of the chamber for the three-minute-long entirety of the coup.

It's a shining one, a little boy who can't be more than five years old, although it's hard to reckon the exact ages of these mutants. Fiona and Lauri raise their flintlocks.

"Stop!" screams a reedy voice with a thick Eastern accent.

We turn as one, for the people always act as one, and face Gregor, the newest member of this inner circle that isn't an inner circle. We'd liberated his village shortly before we rode into Ironhaven.

"We don't have to kill it," he says.

"Of course we need to kill it," Fiona replies. "That's why we're here. To liberate our sisters and brothers—"

"Hey there, little guy." Gregor steps in front of the two women and kneels down next to the tiny shining one, holds out his hand as one would to any comrade. The shining one stares at it for a very long moment. A rope of spit worms its way from the juvenile's maw. Finally, he slaps our comrade's hand with one of his miniature ones.

Fiona readies her weapon. "We can't leave any of them alive, not even the children. We can't turn off their magic. *They* can't turn it off."

"Killing them is a mercy," Lauri adds.

"But we can *use* him," Gregor says. "The power, we can use it. Just think of all we could do with that power of his!"

"Absolutely not," Fiona says. She's as solid as can be, as solid as the people when we sing our songs of resistance, but we can all tell that Lauri is weakening.

Lauri sets down her flintlock. She turns to the gape-mouthed slave. "Does this one have a name?"

"Prince Tyvan," the slave says. Her plain face melts into an expression of utter adoration.

Skye raises both of his hands, and we all know: it's time to take a vote.

"We don't have quorum," Lauri says.

"It's a *monster*," Fiona yells, although she knows that she's outnumbered. She tosses her flintlock onto a sofa upholstered with patterned brocade, crosses her arms, and glowers at us.

"We will relax formal procedures for the moment," Skye says. "Now, state your cases."

Gregor sets out his position. We should harness the power, he says, to more rapidly gain the trust of the people as we free them from their shackles. Gregor speaks of the tender period, the fact that under our guidance young Prince Tyvan would become one of us, part of the Revolution. With a shining one on our side, we the people would be unstoppable. "Not that we weren't already," he concludes hastily. "All power to the people."

"Has everyone here forgotten?" Fiona says. "This thing wants to *make you love him*. He just can't help it. How can we have a Revolution based in the ultimate equality and fraternity of all people when we have something here that's soaking up all of our attention?" She looks down at Tyvan, her face not softening a bit. "It's not the child's fault. But the love-magic and the Revolution are incompatible."

"But people can change!" Gregor says, his face reddening. "*I* changed! Before the Revolution I loved my shining ones as gods. But now I'm liberated; I know better. We all do. His power isn't that strong anyway. I mean, *we* barely noticed it."

Skye waves his arms. "We've heard enough. I'm calling for a vote. All in favor of accepting Comrade Tyvan into the Revolution, please raise your hand."

Everyone but Fiona and the slave raises a hand.

"You're all going to be sorry," Fiona says. She stalks away

from the inner chamber, slamming the jewel-encrusted door behind her.

"I'm free," says the slave, apparently awakening from her spell. "I'm free?"

Skye gives her one of his rib-cracking hugs. "Welcome to the Revolution."

On the tile floor stained with mutant blood, Tyvan spits and fusses.

The Revolution watches as its four not-leaders emerge from the keep. We cheer, knowing the necessary deed has been done, but then we all sense the weak love-magic twisting its way toward us, emanating from the curtain-wrapped bundle in Gregor's arms. A shining one has been left alive.

A townswoman with two missing front teeth steps forward. "Prince Tyvan?" She makes a swipe for the bundle, but Gregor sweeps it from her sight.

"Hello, sister," Gregor says.

"Don't 'sister' me. We *need* him back. We can't live without him." Her tone is angry, but her face is drenched with tears that cut through the dirt on her cheeks, leaving streaks. "He's ours."

Gregor steps past the weeping woman, and hands Tyvan to our burliest comrade, Jono. He whispers into Jono's ear, and then Jono begins to bellow out the countering anthem. We relax as the anthem washes away the faint traces of Tyvan's love-magic.

But the woman isn't relaxed. She pulls at Jono's tunic, and several of the other villagers begin to encircle the giant man and advance on the rest of the Revolution as well.

"Brothers, sisters—" Gregor says, shouting above Jono's singing and the villagers' condemnation. But before he can say anything further, Fiona steps forward and jabs her short sword into the woman's calf.

"Anyone else want some of this?" Fiona says, holding the bloody sword aloft. The mob breaks apart, and we are free to leave. On our way out, Gregor slips a pamphlet into the folds of the stabbed woman's robe.

Outside the walls of Ironhaven, the desert wind is kicking up, and we all press cloths to our mouths to block the grit. Burly Jono sets the ex-prince on the sandy ground outside the town walls and removes the sackcloth.

"In the Revolution we walk," he says, firmly but not unkindly. "We aren't carried around on litters or pulled in carts by horses."

Tyvan grunts, takes a few steps, and collapses.

"Pick him up, comrade," Fiona says with a scowl.

Jono sighs and lifts the inbred ex-prince to his shoulder. "Let each man's labor flow outward," he says, quoting the handbook. He chuckles.

After rising the following day, we break camp and head for the next town on our hand-drawn maps, Fairpark. It's still at least three days away, perhaps four.

As the baking sun casts long shadows over the endless sand, Fiona sidles up to a comrade who had also seemed less than thrilled by the addition of Tyvan to our entourage. "We're making a horrible mistake."

"They think they can control him," Simeon whispers.

"Idiots," says Fiona, who instantly flinches, for an insult directed at the Revolution is the greatest act of blasphemy one can ever commit.

Simeon mops his dripping brow with his sleeve. "Do they really think they can make him into a comrade?"

"A shining one could never be my comrade," Fiona says.

"We should do something about this," Simeon says.

Fiona gives him a sharp look, and then they both rejoin the

rest of us and say no more for now about their blasphemous doubts.

Jono, with Tyvan in his arms, marches in the middle of our mighty stream of people's power. The comrades there are the happiest of us by far, and every so often one or another of us reaches out to stroke Tyvan's velvet doublet or rub his bald scalp.

Peering down at the drooling ex-prince, Jono feels a great sadness rise in his soul. He does not share the fears of Fiona and Simeon. His uneasiness is of a different kind.

"Wake up, little guy," Jono says. He's grown fond of the ex-prince despite himself, and he knows that it's not just the love-magic but a growing fatherly feeling. But his desire to be Tyvan's father will never be fulfilled, for as the handbook states, there are no families within the Revolution. The Revolution is all the family one needs. That part of the handbook has never quite worked for Jono.

Up at the front of the line walk Lauri and Skye, with Gregor at their heels. They may not be our leaders—*there are no leaders in the Revolution* is the first line of our handbook, after all—but they still manage to always march ahead of everyone else, just like they're always the ones who kill the shining ones.

"We'll camp beyond that ridge tonight," Skye says to Lauri.

"Okay," she mumbles, distracted. Lauri's mind is filled with dark thoughts she may or may not confess to the Revolution in the days to come.

"Gregor is right, you know," Skye says. "We *can* use that shining one."

"But is it *right* to do so?" Lauri curls her fist into a ball.

"If you want to question the authority of a democratic vote—where you yourself voted for Tyvan to stay with us, I might add—then maybe you should join Fiona at the back of the line." Skye hocks a gob of sandy spit onto the hot ground.

Lauri gives Skye a hard look. "I believe in the Revolution. And I believe in our newest comrade. Don't lump me in with that woman. She's prejudiced. I care about *Tyvan's* needs."

"Tyvan's just fine, Lauri," Gregor says with a toothy grin. "We should sing!" He launches into an off-key warbling of our magic-repelling anthem, and we of the Revolution join in, because we must, because it's the thing that saved us and it's going to save everyone else on this wretched continent.

This time, though, it feels different, and nobody can figure out why. Our voices grow stronger, clearer, and our steps pick up. We begin to sway in perfect harmony.

And at the center of this is Jono, the huge and helpful comrade, who belts out our anthem in a tone as low as rumbling earth. In his arms is Tyvan, the ex-prince turned comrade, who mouths along.

It's the magic, some of us think. *His magic is amplifying the anthem, changing it.* A few of us balk at that realization, but eventually nearly everyone is caught in the web of the magic-enhanced liberation song.

Our pace picks up.

At the back of the line, Fiona, Simeon, and half a dozen others fall even further back. Fiona's lips twitch as she resists joining in. Even among these other skeptics, she finds herself alone.

The village of Fairpark is nestled within a lush forest that shows up on the map as a thin stripe separating desert and sea. The long-limbed trees form a sort of ceiling over us, and we all remove our robes to let the branches' dew drip over our skin and thin underclothes. We feel the magic before we see the town; this is an especially powerful family.

Comrade Jono, still cradling Tyvan in his thick arms, starts to sing the countering anthem. Lauri slams the brass knocker against the thick wooden door. The rest of us ready our dwindling supply of informational pamphlets.

A slat in the door slides open, and a woman's head pops out.

Her hair is long, blonde, and threaded with the flowers that thrive in the forests around Fairpark. Her eyes grow rounder as she takes in our weapons.

"You are the ones we have been warned about."

"We are the Revolution," Lauri says triumphantly, "and we are here to liberate this town!" She swings her sword, which slices easily through the flimsy wall. A dozen other comrades join in, and soon there is a breach large enough to admit a few people at a time.

Skye, Lauri, and Gregor step inside. Fiona follows along a few moments later.

Unlike Ironhaven, most of the people here are armed, the copper of their weapons gleaming darkly in the filtered sunlight. As our four not-leaders stare at their enthralled counterparts, they realize with great pain that the blood which waters the soil of the Revolution is going to flow this day.

And then, almost in unison, the citizens of Fairpark drop their weapons. They fall to their knees.

Jono, with Tyvan in his arms, has pushed his way through the hole in the town wall. He's still belting our precious anthem, its spiritual volume amplified to a shriek by the prince-turned-comrade. The combination of the soaring melody and the love-magic it was designed to counteract makes us shiver with a supernatural delight.

The citizens of Fairpark are *destroyed* by it. Several of them start crying, and one of the braver ones walks forward to touch Tyvan's tiny, twisted body. Jono steps backward, a curiously uncomradely cast to his face.

"It's the true one," says the woman with flowers in her hair who'd greeted us. "Our *real* leader."

"He has to be," says another person.

Lauri steps in between Jono and Tyvan and the Fairparkers. "That's right. He's your . . . leader. He's the leader of the Revolution, and if you point us to the impostors, we can take care of them once and for all!"

Two of the Fairparkers direct the usual squad of four of us toward the keep, the top of which can barely be seen above the treetops. Once they've disappeared into the thicket, the rest of us start handing out the educational pamphlets and reassuring the fine people of Fairpark that all will soon be well, now that they are so very close to being free.

The villagers, however, show no interest in our materials. "Keep singing," says a sallow-colored boy who can't be much more than Tyvan's age.

Jono sighs and starts the anthem up again. He's been singing for hours by now, and his throat is beginning to hurt. *But it's for the Revolution*, he thinks, *for my family. The only family I need*. He takes a deep breath and belts out the opening line. "We come to you with might and glory . . ."

Meanwhile, as the four not-leaders swiftly approach the entrance to the keep, Fiona stares at the back of Gregor's sun-reddened neck and touches the sword at her belt. *This is wrong*, she thinks. *You can't tear down the tyrant's kingdom with the tyrant's tools*. She strokes the well-polished butt of her flintlock. Damned if she's gonna let any more of these things live on her watch.

"We are the Revolution!" Lauri yells at the ivy-draped front gate of the Fairpark keep. Like all of the doors in this forest town, the front door of the keep is elevated, accessible only by ascending a rope ladder. She draws her sword and prepares to climb.

She doesn't even make the first rung before the shining ones' personal slaves start spilling out of the front door onto the narrow balcony that rings the keep. They march past the four not-leaders toward the hole in the wall where Jono stands singing, surrounded by close to ten score other comrades both new and old. The squad of not-leaders sneak up the largest rope ladder, barely even noticed by the exiting slaves.

After the killing is over and the four not-leaders have returned to us, Fiona slips away and finds Simeon in the crowd.

She takes his hand in hers.

"We need to finish this tonight," she says in a beat between verses.

He nods, squeezes her hand, and sings louder.

In the center of the crowd, Jono slumps in a chair that had been provided by one of the villagers when they saw his knees were buckling. Tyvan sits in his lap, his beady eyes taking everything in, the spittle shining on his jutted-out lower lip.

"And together we are strong, but divided we fall, for we are the Revolution!"

The singing lasts long, long into the night.

When the Revolution embarks a few days later, full of good food and passable medical care, nearly the entire village of Fairpark comes along with us. After a brief recitation of Tyvan-boosted slogans, they *are* us, for a comrade is never to be judged for the length of time they have been in the Revolution. It only matters that they're here now.

There is some discussion of where to go next. The Fairparkers have told the rest of us of even more isolated villages to be found deep within these forests, but Gregor's voice emerges the loudest.

"Lumina," he says, a wicked gleam in his eye.

It's the seaside capital of this land, the ancestral home of the shining ones. Half of us twitch in pain when its very name is announced, for the place was an impenetrable fortress even before the monsters' rise to power.

"We can't do that, Gregor," Lauri says. "Not Lumina."

"Nothing can be denied to the Revolution, because it's the *people!*" He pumps his fist in the air, and the rest of the comrades cheer.

Lauri darts a look at Skye. He shrugs. "I guess we're going to Lumina."

The Revolution points itself in the direction of the sea, and if there was any hesitation before, there's considerably less now. A few of the stouter comrades trailblaze the path ahead of the rest of us, while the great bulk of the enlarged Revolution clusters around Jono and Tyvan.

Jono won't let anyone else carry the ex-prince. He wants the child near him, just in case something happens. And he also wants him there just because.

Don't you love me too? he thinks. Tyvan blows a spit bubble in reply.

At the end of the line, Simeon trots along, trying to keep up. Turning Fiona in for her treachery hadn't given him the emotional closure he'd thought it would. The not-leaders of the Revolution had stood Fiona against the walls surrounding Fairpark and gutted her with their short swords, as her obvious guilt had made a trial unnecessary. Her glittering green eyes had gone flat as she died, transforming her into an empty and discarded object of no further use to the Revolution. Simeon struggles over the wet leaves and roots on his worn-down sandals, and the expressions his fellow comrades shoot at him are very uncomradely indeed.

She was trying to kill Tyvan, he thinks. But that scarcely matters anymore, and he knows why. Nobody likes a betrayer, even one who acted for a good and noble purpose.

The song explodes over the emerald forest, and Simeon chases along after its melody.

Limestone walls enclose the city of Lumina, which juts out from the coast like a warty growth. Only the very tops of its highest buildings can be seen over those walls, and they're also made from the same gleaming white stone.

Gregor walks a little ahead of Lauri, as he has for the past few days. "Only an hour or so away! Hurry up!"

We all hasten our pace, even Comrade Jono, who's now carrying Tyvan in a makeshift sling, the ex-prince having gained quite a few pounds since being liberated and educated in the ways of the Revolution. The soil beneath our feet turns into gravelly sand, and the salty ocean air wafts softly across our triumphant faces.

The wall of love-magic that flows from the shining ones of Lumina takes the slogans out of our mouths. Even the natural features of the landscape seem to bend toward the city.

After his initial shock at the sheer amount of love-magic pouring from the cliffs of Lumina, Jono remembers the words to the anthem. He bellows it out, while Tyvan weakly grips Jono's index finger. Thankfully, after a few bars most of us are back to singing the anthem.

Two guards with flintlocks much more advanced than ours stand at either side of the city gate. They level their weapons at Lauri and Skye.

"State your purpose," says the guard on the left.

"We're the Revolution," Skye says, his voice a little shaky. "We have come to liberate you."

The guards turn aside, and whisper to one another in an incomprehensible language. Finally, the guard on the right speaks. "You have a *caryarte* with you."

The three remaining not-leaders exchange cryptic glances until they understand what the guard is saying. "We call them shining ones," Lauri says.

"Here they're called caryarte," the guard on the right says in a supercilious tone, "and we must take the caryarte to the keep at once."

"Tyvan fights with us!" Gregor says. He steps in front of the guard and flexes his fist. The guard punches him so fast we don't see it happen, just our new-ish comrade hunched over in pain.

Lauri draws her sword. "Oh, we'll go to the keep, all right." She touches its point to the guard's chin. "Lead the way."

What follows is a short conversation of gnomic gestures and hissed statements in the elaborate Luminan tongue, and then finally the guard who'd punched Gregor in the stomach points at the three non-leaders. "You three. You seem like you're in charge. And the caryarte."

Several of the comrades around Jono start to pry the ex-prince from the sling, but Jono folds his body over Tyvan. He clears his throat. "I'm going, too. I'm his father."

Gasps puncture the crowd as we all recognize the presence of blasphemy, but the guard merely shrugs. "Then you can come as well."

More soldiers have arrived to babysit the scores of us on the beach outside the capital, while our three non-leaders and Jono are ushered within the walls. The Revolution has *never* had a reception like this before.

"This can't be good," Skye whispers to Lauri. "Why would they *invite* us in?"

"Why would they resist? They know we're stronger than them; delaying the Revolution would only hurt more of their citizens." Lauri says this as brashly as she can, but there's a waver in her voice that's trailed her all the way from the forest village.

The all-white architecture of Lumina is studded with gifts from the sea, shells and sea-glass arranged at angles pleasing to the eye. The three non-leaders tuck in close to Jono, who continually hums the anthem. They remember who they are. They won't let the Luminan shining ones—or caryarte or whatever they're called—overwhelm their reason. They have a new kind of reason, one built on the power of the people, and that's *never* going to change.

"Lauri, look," Skye says, and she immediately realizes what he's talking about. There's a stall selling copies of the hand-book—*our* handbook—right inside the gate. The first precept is painted above it in blue, the letters of the common script written so large that anyone in Lumina can read it, even from a distance. *There are no leaders in the Revolution.*

"We have been well-acquainted with the Revolution for some time," says one of the guards with a smirk.

"But your caryarte—" Lauri says.

He casts a glance back at Jono and Tyvan. "You have one too."

And that's the end of that line of questioning. The four comrades—five if one counts Tyvan—feel somewhat embarrassed. The droning beauty of the Luminan shining ones' love-magic continues to beckon us forward; the way to the keep might as well be marked out in blazing torches.

It's glorious, of course. There hadn't been much obvious wealth in the city itself, because it had all been saved for the inner walls of this keep, which have been studded with endless fields of gemstones all cut into wicked facets. We shield our eyes against the headache-inducing glint of it, and there's a break in Jono's singing.

A male slave in a short white jerkin greets us, and the guard speaks to him in the local dialect. The slave shoots us an inscrutable expression.

"Right this way," he says in impeccable Continent-speak.

Something behind Jono's eyes seems to crack. He turns to leave, to find some way out of the keep and out of Lumina entirely. He could hide in the forest if he could get back there. Build a house for him and Tyvan. Watch the boy grow up, and never tell him about his origins. But the guard herds Jono closer to the others.

"I'm afraid you can't leave," he says. "After all, what you've got in your arms there is the reason you all haven't been slaughtered." He chokes back a laugh.

We trudge onward, resigned.

We enter the inner chamber, greeted by harp music and the steaming love-magic emanating off the shining ones of Lumina.

Slaves flutter around their slothful gods in a flurry of activity, changing the silken pillows on which their heads rest and freshening their drinks. Nobody offers us a drink.

The slave who had ushered us in sits on a cushioned chair. "You must understand that the caryarte is staying here with us."

Somehow all of us, even Jono, knew that would be the case. We'd been trapped the moment we'd allowed ourselves to come within Lumina's sphere of influence, the moment we'd felt this city's power.

"Where did you get the handbooks?" Skye asks.

"And the slogans?" says Lauri. She points at the harpist. "And our anthem?" The rest of us realize with a start that it *is* our anthem, being played as it's never been played before.

He smiles. "Your Revolution actually hit upon a most exciting scientific principle," says the slave, tenting his fingers. "Your slogans and anthem, inane as they are, do counteract the enchanting power of the caryarte when recited or even thought in isolation. But when the two things are brought together . . ." He interlaces his fingers, then splays them outwards.

Gregor rushes forward and only Lauri's quick thinking keeps him from stabbing the slave with his short sword. "The Revolution is *not* inane! You take that back, slave!"

"Yes, I am a slave," says the man matter-of-factly. "As were all of you, as is everyone since the eruption of magic upon this land. You've never stopped being slaves, except it was to an ideology instead of a natural force."

"*That isn't true,*" grates Skye through clenched teeth.

The slave continues as if Skye hasn't said anything at all. "We have taken your anthem and handbook—with a few practical changes made, of course—and married it to our caryarte. It has been a blissful union. The magic started here, you know, and here is still where it's strongest. Look at these people," he says, waving his hand toward the bustling hive of slaves. "Do they seem unhappy to you in any way?"

"We represent liberation . . ." Lauri starts to say, but her words fizzle out. The slaves, she realizes, *are* happy. So is everyone else in Lumina.

"You'll be allowed to stay, of course, though we do have a weapons ban." He gestures at a tall female slave, who strips Gregor of his hardware. "Or you can go, it's really no matter to us."

Gregor kicks at the woman who'd deprived him of his sword and flintlock. "I will not accept this!" Before the last word is fully out of his mouth, she buries a silver knife between his ribs. He stands for just a moment, blinking, before the minor bulk of his body clatters onto the white stone floor. This chain of events elicits no more than a minor burst of attention from the other slaves in the lavish, jeweled room.

Skye and Lauri trade glances, and Skye chokes back a cry. Every slave in this cavernous room hums the anthem, although as the head slave had said, the words are slightly changed.

"One nation standing tall, united in strength, for power makes the Revolution!"

Maybe it's just a translation error, Skye thinks. *That must be it.*

An elderly slave clad in an ivory dress that we all have to admit is rather nice for a slave reaches her arms out to Jono. The big comrade stares at Tyvan and bursts into tears.

"He loves me," Jono says. "And I love him."

"You'll be able to take care of him and love him forever if you give us your weapons," says the head slave.

Jono allows the single sword hung at his side to be taken, though Lauri and Skye still cling to theirs.

"This doesn't feel right," she says.

"We could leave," he says. "We could tell everyone outside what happened and *crush* this place." But after a few minutes of indecision they allow themselves to be stripped of their weapons as well and are given the bright white robes of slaves of the keep's inner circle.

They'll hate us, Lauri thinks, imagining the comrades on the other side of the Lumina wall.

But she needn't have worried. Even now we are being processed through the proper channels, given fairly extensive orientation packets, and sent to assimilate ourselves with the rest of Lumina. For this city is a sort of paradise, where we can practice our politics while also bask in the glow of a perfectly natural and not at all "freakish" phenomenon, which when one thinks about it is really rather benign, a pure sort of pleasure. Now we have the magic *and* the handbook, and what more could we ever even want?

The rest of us can't help but notice, however, that some of the words in the handbook have been changed. Quite a lot of them, in fact.

LUCKY GIRL

WHAT'S SHE UP TO now?" Adina asked her fiancé Mike. "Four? Six?"

He winced. "Eleven."

Mike's sister Natalie had attempted suicide on eleven separate occasions, each time using a different method. Cutting her wrists, knocking back three family-size bottles of Tylenol, hanging herself with a hospital bed sheet, jumping into the Columbia River with a bag of stones around her waist. She'd even gone into the woods smeared with bacon fat and gotten herself mauled by a cougar, which only seemed ridiculous because Natalie had survived with barely a scratch. If she hadn't, it would have been tragic.

Adina snorted, and looked out at the spattering rain. "She belongs in a home."

"We've already tried that," Mike said, running his fingers through his hair. "They kicked her out of the facility in Eugene after she got into the drain cleaner. Mom and Dad got her on a waiting list for the redwood place, but that could take years."

"The redwood place?"

"Kind of a treehouse for adults. It's supposed to be soothing."

Mike had three sisters and two brothers, but only Natalie seemed to have gotten the crazy gene. Adina thought it was a lucky thing for Natalie to have been born into such a large family with so many shoulders to lean on. She'd never had that luxury.

Adina sighed. "Well, I guess she can stay with us. It's only *temporary*." She looked hard into Mike's eyes on that last word.

"Couple of weeks. A month, tops. Then she'll be back on her feet."

She knew better than to correct him. "Fine. She can stay with us. She'll have to sleep in the basement, though."

Mike beamed. "It's going to be okay. You'll see."

After Mike left for work, Adina flopped down on the couch and put her hands over her face. She'd made a horrible mistake in coming here, one she couldn't take back. Mom had warned her that you can't trust people you meet on the Internet, but had Adina listened? Hell no.

I'm overreacting, Adina thought. She'd moved to Oregon not just to be with Mike, but to open herself up to new experiences. Living with Natalie would be a unique experience for sure. And anyway, this was *his* house.

Energized, she went to the basement to clear out a space for Natalie.

Everything Adina knew of Natalie came through Mike. Natalie had been a physics student at OSU, with plans to transfer to Stanford after her sophomore year. Then her "troubles" started, as Mike euphemistically put it.

"Right before finals, she slit her wrists," he'd said. "She didn't do it for attention. She cut right down to the bone; she should have died. It was a miracle." Mike wasn't religious, except when it came to his sister's numerous survivals of her self-inflicted wounds. *More like timing*, Adina thought.

Adina hadn't met Mike's youngest sister yet. When she'd gone to the coast with his whole clan for the first time last month, only photographs of a young rosy-cheeked Natalie were in attendance. She wondered if the family worried about scaring off the nice girl that Mike had somehow lured across the country.

We're all normal, they'd seemed to be saying. *She's not like us.* They cared about her enough to pay for hospitals and retreats, the modern-day equivalent of keeping one's freakish offspring in an attic room to wither and decay. But they weren't about to put her on display.

Adina couldn't relate to Natalie. She'd had her own troubles, but she'd kept them inside, not splattered in blood for the world to see. Suicide was selfish, she believed, a way of ending one's own pain while multiplying the pain of everyone else around them.

Besides, it hadn't worked for Natalie. It hadn't worked for Natalie *eleven times.*

She grunted as she used Mike's bicycle pump to inflate the air mattress. A lot of things would be changing. She thought of all the extra food they'd need to buy, the alterations to their daily lives they'd need to make. Sometimes Adina didn't even like living with Mike.

"You really think she'll stop trying to kill herself if she stays with us?" Adina asked Mike after he joined her in the basement.

"I don't know," Mike said. "But she's my sister, Adina. I love her."

"I know you do," she said. She pulled a fitted sheet over the air mattress; it sagged at the bottom, an old sock.

"Her plane comes in Saturday. I'm going to ride down from the airport with her. Are you coming along?"

"If it's all right with you, I'll stay here." She could see the look of disappointment in his face, but she wanted a final few hours of solitude in her own home—or close enough—before

Mike's desperately depressed sister planted herself firmly in the basement like a root vegetable. Perhaps the sun would even be shining that day.

Adina whacked an egg against the stove and put it into the skillet. Like eyes, the yolks stared back at her before she scrambled them into submission. She was cooking for three now, and not in the way she'd expected to be.

Natalie hadn't said word one to Adina when Mike shuffled her into the house last night. "It's late," he'd said, though it had only been eight o'clock. "Her meds make her sleepy."

Adina looked up as she heard plodding footsteps echo up from the basement. A woman of indeterminate age with Mike's sandy brown hair and bags under her eyes sat down at the kitchen table.

"Can I help?"

"Natalie," Adina said, forcing a smile. "It's so nice to meet you."

Natalie mumbled something, but Adina didn't hear it over the sizzle of the eggs. She let it go.

"Do you want to do anything today? Mike says you haven't been back to Portland for three or four years now." She didn't bring up the reason Natalie hadn't been here.

"I've seen it all before."

"Well, you probably haven't seen the new exhibit at the art museum." Adina dished the eggs out onto plates and slid one to Natalie. "It just opened this week."

Natalie picked at the eggs. "I just want to stay home if that's all right with you."

Well, isn't this going to be fun? "All right. I'll go tell Mike you're up."

As she went up the stairs to their bedroom, Adina stole another glance at Natalie. Her Hello Kitty bathrobe was much too small for her doll-like frame, and her hair puffed out wildly in all directions.

She didn't like this situation, but she had to deal with it. Of course he cared more about Natalie than Adina. Even though she'd given up everything for Mike, blood was thicker than water. If things worked out like they'd planned, Natalie would be her sister too.

Of course, things have a way of shifting course. Hadn't Natalie discovered that herself? All those dreams of an Ivy League education, shattered by Natalie's invisible demons. At least Adina's life hadn't derailed that far, and she could always go back.

Even if it means moving back in with Mom, Adina thought, and shuddered.

A week in, and Natalie still barely left her room. Mike checked in on her every morning before leaving for work, to make sure she took her meds, and they all ate dinner together like a fake family. Natalie ghosted through the house, not interacting, barely speaking. Adina found herself working overtime for an excuse to stay away.

She was carrying a load of laundry upstairs when she heard snuffling behind the door of the basement. She waited a few moments, then lightly rapped on the door. "Natalie?"

"I'm okay," said a weak voice behind the door.

Even though Adina thought Natalie deserved her privacy, she couldn't help but be worried about Mike's sister. She opened the door a crack. "What's wrong?"

"It never changes. I'm always alive."

Adina sat down next to Natalie and rubbed her shoulder. "And we're happy you are. Come on now, get out of bed."

"You don't understand."

Adina didn't have a response. She didn't understand.

"Not a scratch," Natalie said, holding her hand in front of her face like it was the first time she'd seen it. "You jump off a highway overpass, you'd think there'd be some kind of *evidence*, right?"

So that was how she'd done it this time. "You're a lucky girl."

"Lucky," Natalie spat.

"Maybe there's some kind of plan for you."

Natalie laughed so hard Adina could see down into her throat. "You don't know anything about science, Adina."

Right, Adina thought, *the physics*. "You could teach me."

"I'm no good for teaching anything to anyone anymore. The meds slow my mind down. I'm finished."

"You could always take a class at the community college."

"*They're* all doing it. They're all doing everything I *could* be doing."

"Who's all doing what?"

"My other selves. The split-offs." Natalie sighed. "Probably having a lot more fun than me, too."

Adina raised an eyebrow.

"You don't have to watch me. I'm not going to kill myself. I can't."

"Okay, Natalie. I'll leave you alone." Adina picked up the basket and backed out of the room. On one of the banker's boxes that held Adina's still-packed DVD collection sat a half-dozen pill bottles glowing sepia in the light from the bare bulb overhead.

Mike bit his lip and shook his head when Adina told him what Natalie had said, but he didn't call his parents, and he didn't confront Natalie.

"What's a split-off?"

"Like I'd know anything about that. She wasn't exactly friendly to me, Mike."

"She has problems. In a family, we look out for each other."

Natalie wasn't Adina's family, though, at least not yet. "Where is she on that waiting list? The one for the treehouse."

"She's staying, Adina." Mike stalked to their bedroom.

Adina gritted her teeth until she tasted sand.

Later, as Adina washed the dinner dishes, she felt a frizzy-haired phantom slip in next to her, dish rag in hand. "Mind if I dry?"

"I'd appreciate that."

Natalie wiped the dishes haphazardly, leaving thick streaks. Adina would have to fix them later. "I want to apologize."

"It's all right."

"I just feel so *trapped.*" She stuck the dripping plate onto the drainer.

"In this house?"

"In this *life.* I think, why me? Why do I have to be the one who lives forever? That's how it works though. One of us lives forever. I'm that one."

"You're not immortal, Natalie."

"Yes, I am." She twisted the rag in her hands. "And so are you."

Don't engage, Adina thought. "How would you like to go out for a drive this weekend?"

"I guess I will. It's as good as anything else."

Adina nodded, a little reluctantly. She'd been hoping to spend tomorrow transplanting some rose bushes, but family time was more important. *Do it for Mike.* "I'll get you at ten."

Mike woke up puking. Adina set him up with a bucket, placed a pitcher of juice on the bedside table, and ruffled his hair. "We'll reschedule the drive."

"No, you guys go without me. I've been trying to get Natalie out of the house for weeks. She's really been looking forward to this."

"Your sister was actually looking forward to something?"

"She told me she wanted to spend some time with you." He gestured to his messenger bag before sticking his head back in the bucket. "Keys are in there," he said, his voice labored.

Adina plucked the keys from Mike's bag and went down the stairs to Natalie's makeshift room. *She's been ignoring me for weeks*, Adina thought. *Why talk now?* Maybe it had taken that long for Natalie to be comfortable with her. Maybe Natalie's new meds were finally working. Adina didn't *like* Natalie much, but she counted this as a good sign.

Natalie was already dressed in a tattered OSU sweatshirt, her hair combed and everything. She sat on her bed with her purse on her lap, staring at Adina's towering boxes labeled with black Sharpie writing. "Where are you from?"

"Connecticut."

"I've never been to the East Coast. At least, not *this* me."

"Ready to go?" Adina caught herself before she jingled the keys in her hand. *She's not a dog.*

Natalie lifted herself from the bed.

Only after Adina pulled out of the driveway did she realize that she didn't know where they were supposed to go today. Mike was going to take care of that; he knew the area better, and Natalie was his sister after all. "Where do you want to go?"

Natalie shrugged a shoulder. "Forest Park."

"You have to direct me."

Once they were on the highway, Adina braved the subject. "What's a split-off?"

"You wouldn't—"

"I know I won't understand. Tell me anyway."

"It's a you. A you who made different choices."

"Do you wish you had made different choices, Natalie?"

She groaned. "Now you sound like a goddamn shrink."

"It's never too late to change your life. Lots of people bounce back from things like this. You're such a—"

"—lucky girl. I'm pretty sure you say that in one hundred percent of the worlds. Except for the ones where a meteor lands on your head just as you're about to say it."

"I'm not trying to fight with you." Adina wished Mike was here. But would Natalie act this crazy if he was? She restrained herself around her big brother.

"Everyone thinks I'm nuts," Natalie said. "They lock me up, they drug me. I'll outlast them. You'll all go on, but I'll still be here. Forever."

"Because you're immortal."

"Because *everyone* is," she said. "Just not at the same time. *That* would be crazy."

Adina cast an eye at the dashboard, counting down the hours until she could stop pretending to like Natalie. "Whatever you say."

Natalie didn't take the hint. "Think of a choice you've made. Like moving to Portland. That's a fork. There are millions of forks." She pushed her hands outward at a ninety degree angle. "In some of the forks, you move. In some, you don't."

At that moment, Adina wished she'd taken another fork, so she wouldn't have to talk to Natalie. She reminded herself to be patient. "So you think there are other people out there living other lives?"

"Well, you can't *talk* to them."

"So these split-off people, you think they're happier than you?"

"If they haven't figured it out by now, yes."

"Figured what out?"

Natalie signaled a turn, and Adina slowed down the car. She pulled into a back road lined with evergreens so tall they pierced the colorless skies above. The road was still muddy from yesterday's rain, and Adina heard the ping of drops hitting the roof of Mike's Honda. After parking the car, she pulled out her umbrella.

"Lousy day for a walk. We should just go back."

"No, I want to see it. I *need* to see it."

Adina didn't bother asking what *it* was. "At least put on your raincoat."

Natalie smirked. "That's for tourists."

*

They walked through the park for a long time, Natalie leading the way. The constant drizzle of the rain streaked the depressed woman's face until it looked like she had been crying.
For once, though, she wasn't.

They walked in silence, Adina whacking the branches of the
trees with the sides of her umbrella until she gave up and tucked
it into her coat pocket. "Where are we going, Natalie?"

"I'll know it when I see it."

Adina's sneakers slipped on the rocks beneath their feet. She
reached out and steadied herself against tree trunks when she
felt wobbly, but not Natalie. She'd once read an article claiming
that severely depressed people often ignored their body's cries of
pain, powering through unbelievable trauma. The body became
unimportant, unreal. A sack of meat powered by a reluctant
mind. Worthless.

Finally, Natalie stopped. Adina nearly fell into her. "We're
here," she said, indicating a low pile of rocks.

Adina squinted. "That's what you came to see?"

Natalie went up to the pile of rocks and patted it. "I broke
my ankle climbing on this thing when I was ten. That's when I
first knew."

Adina took a stab. "About the split-offs."

"When the paramedics came, they said it could have been
a lot worse. They said I could have fallen backwards instead of
forwards, broke my neck." Natalie shook her head. "Lucky girl."

"They say something like that to everyone. I caught men-
ingitis in college, and they said if I had come in a day later I
wouldn't have made it." She took a step toward Natalie. "Everyone has a story like that."

"Everyone has split-offs."

Adina took a deep breath. "Well, at least you don't think
you're a special snowflake."

Natalie barreled on. "I didn't think about it for a couple of months. Not until summer. My brothers and I went out on our bikes and Mike was hit by a truck."

Adina paused, thinking. "Mike never told me he was hit by a truck."

"Not this Mike. The split-off one. He died and I saw it happen. For less than a fraction of a second, it was there. Two worlds, side by side." She held her hands up, parallel to one another. "I picked this one. I'd rather live in a world with Mike, instead of a world without him. I love my brother."

"This happens all the time for you?"

"Only sometimes."

Adina sighed and crossed her arms. "So what happened to *you* in this other world?"

Natalie shrugged. "Beats me. Does it matter?"

"It would matter to her."

She looked away, toward the mountains only barely visible through the layer of trees. "I began to think about it. What if this is happening all the time? What if, for every choice you make, every accident you narrowly avoid, there's someone out there who isn't so lucky? So I started experimenting."

"By trying to kill yourself," Adina said, ice in her veins.

"By being *reckless*. I started riding without a helmet, eating raw meat, sleeping outside in the rain with no tent. My parents noticed what I was doing, but with six kids, who has the time to watch them every moment? I persevered, though. I don't know how many split-offs I killed. Hundreds, probably."

Adina felt like rolling her eyes. "You're just lucky, Natalie."

"Luck's not scientific. This is. Look, do you know what happens to you after you die?"

"You go to sleep." Adina spread out her arms. "I'm an atheist."

"Even when you're asleep you still have a consciousness. The human drive is for life against all odds." Natalie pushed her wet hair out of her face. "I've survived things that *shouldn't be surviv-*

able, Adina. Those weren't cries for help, they were attempts to get into the most improbable universe I could. To get to the zero point zero zero zero zero one universe. The one where I'm the *least* likely to be alive, but still am. The ultimate survivor. I'm not nearly there yet."

"Why would you want to go there? Why do this?"

She shrugged again. Adina was starting to hate that shrugging. "To see what happens."

Remind me never to take a freshman physics class, Adina thought. "So you can't die. You'll just move to another fork. I shoot you in the head, you find some way to deflect the bullet."

"From my perspective, yes."

"Well, in mine I'll spend the rest of my life in state prison."

Natalie blinked. "Then you just don't take that fork."

"Do you realize how insane this sounds? Of course you do. You're not a moron." Adina felt the sudden urge to back three feet away from Natalie. "You can't prove *any* of this."

"You can't prove it's not happening." Natalie held up her arm. "*This* is the proof, Adina. I'm alive, you're alive. Mike's alive. We all live alone. Every one of us." Her eyes bulged open, and Adina could almost see the spit flying from her teeth like some rabid animal.

Adina threw up her hands. "I'm going back to the car. We're both going to catch pneumonia out here. Maybe *you* can survive that, little miss ultimate survivor, but I want to get back to my warm house and your brother."

Adina couldn't tell whether Natalie was about to bolt away or follow her to the car. Finally, the depressed woman moved away from the rock pile. Slowly they trudged through the papier-mâché leaves, twigs cracking underneath. Looking through the thick branches, Adina saw them as a series of forks all leading in different directions. Some to the East Coast, some to the sea.

She shook her head. *Don't let this crazy woman get to you.* But as she looked back at her not-quite-sister-in-law, she realized it was too late.

Adina made sure Natalie buckled her seat belt. As she pulled the car onto the narrow road, she chuckled as she checked the rearview mirror for traffic. *Safety first*, she thought.

Six days later, Natalie's acceptance for the Redwoods Therapeutic Environment came through. Mike drove her down to Sacramento. Adina was polite as she said goodbye, and she did wish Natalie well, but she prayed Natalie wouldn't come back. She'd used up her turn with Mike, after all.

Neither one of them told Mike about the discussion in Forest Park.

Wrapped in a blanket, Adina cozied up to the Duraflame log on the fireplace. She'd caught a cold after her visit to the park and hadn't quite gotten over it. She brought a mug of tea to her lips. Chamomile tea.

She woke to the shriek of the fire alarm.

"Shit!" Adina threw the blanket from her legs into the fireplace, which only caused the flames to rise higher. She looked for water, an extinguisher, anything, but only saw her sad little half-empty cup of tea. She swore again, stuffed her cell phone in her pocket, and darted to the front yard.

Mike's gonna kill me, she thought, *and I deserve it. Stupid!*

Adina turned her head to the fire, one last look. An image hung in midair of a woman being carried out on a stretcher, a rag covering her face. Like a lock fitting into a deadbolt, she was aware of a settling into place, a sense of *this is it*. She felt a ripping, a rending, and then, a choice being made for her, that she had nothing to do with.

Then, a blackness.

She lay on the wet earth. Neighbors surrounded her in a semicircle. Nobody moved to comfort her. In these situations, nobody ever does.

We all live alone. Every one of us.

The firefighters arrived in six minutes. As they sprayed the blackened walls of Mike's house, a burly man with a Portland Fire & Rescue jacket came over to her. "I just need to ask some questions," said the firefighter.

Adina had a question of her own. "Is the house okay?"

"Some structural damage. Nothing too bad. You have insurance, right? You always have to have insurance."

"It's not my house," she said, shakily signing the papers that he had given her without reading them. "It belongs to my boyfriend."

"He'll just be happy you're safe. You are safe, right?" The firefighter looked her over, a little surprised.

Adina looked down at her own body. "Yes. I think so."

"I'm glad to hear it. You made it out just in time. You're a very lucky girl."

BUCKET LIST FOUND IN THE LOCKER OF MADDIE PRICE, AGE 14, WRITTEN TWO WEEKS BEFORE THE GREAT UPLIFTING OF ALL MANKIND

KISS A GIRL.

~~Fall in love.~~

Get a tattoo, because Dad says that after we all go into the Sing nobody on Earth is going to have a body anymore. I don't care if it hurts.

Smoke a joint.

~~Egg Principal Novak's house.~~

See a solar eclipse. This one time, Sandra's family was going to drive us down to California to see an eclipse, but then her mom called my dad at the last minute and said it was off. I wonder why?

~~Go to the zoo and make fun of the animals.~~

Dye my hair blue. Mom says they'll have to shave our hair to get the electrodes in, the ones that will transmit our minds up to the Sing while our bodies stay behind. So it's kind of my final shot.

Run five miles without stopping.

~~Invite Sandra to the Last Dance. I figure she'll say no, because she's been kind of weird around me ever since we kissed behind the bleachers that one time, but I hope she'll say yes.~~

Finish watching every episode of *Star Trek*. I don't know if they have *Star Trek* in the Sing, so I better do it now while I have the chance.

~~Eat sushi.~~

~~Sit at the cool kids' table.~~

Wear that awesome old dress I got at Goodwill to the Last Dance.

Learn to speak French. Mom says that in the Sing there aren't going to be any languages, everyone just thinks at each other all the time. I don't care if it's not useful. I want to learn it anyway.

Help out at a homeless shelter (I don't *really* want to do this, but it feels like something I should say).

~~Learn to ride a skateboard.~~

Take a trip out to the Coast. We were supposed to do that last month, but when Mom started going over the travel plans she just wouldn't stop crying, and Dad said no trips anymore. I bet I can get Aunt Alice to take me.

~~Break a bone. (Just a little one, to see how it feels.)~~

Get retweeted by a famous person.

~~Tell Sandra how much I hate her stupid face for standing me up.~~

Go to see the servers where they're transmitting all of us into the Sing. I heard they're like these big needles with bulbs on the end of them, and they roast your body to cinders and beam your mind onto these satellites or something. Dad says this one's impossible because there's so much security around the servers. I guess I'll see them soon enough.

Read *Moby Dick* even though it's probably really boring.

~~See a bald eagle.~~

Write a novel. Although it might have to be a short story now.

Go camping, even if it's only in the backyard. Mom says you can recreate this kind of stuff in the Sing, but I know it can't be the same.

~~Tell Grandma I love her (and mean it).~~

Make up with Sandra and tell her I hope I see her in the Sing.

Get to the highest level on Candy Crush.

~~Take my cat for a walk.~~

~~Paint my fingernails ten different colors.~~

Skype with someone on another continent. Dad thinks this one is silly, because the Sing is kind of like a giant Skype with everyone in the world on it, but I want to do it now. I don't think I'm going to care about the things on this list so much when I get to the Sing. I don't think any of us will.

~~Fly a kite.~~

~~Take my roller blades out of the closet and skate around and around the reservoir, no matter how much it hurts, until the sun goes down.~~

Go one whole day without being scared of anything.

~~Forgive Sandra for not loving me back.~~

CAN YOU TELL ME HOW
TO GET TO APOCALYPSE?

A DOZEN LITTLE DEAD kids sit on the Styrofoam steps outside the only apartment building on Gumdrop Road. They're listening to the newspaper seller. He's talking to them about time.

"Time," says the newspaper seller. He pauses a very long while, as if he's forgotten his lines. I can't blame him; everyone gets a little fuzzy at the end of a long day of shooting. "It's how we measure the length between one event and the next. There are sixty minutes in an hour, and twenty-four hours in a day. Would any of *you* like to sing the time song with me?" When he says this, he doesn't look at the little dead kids, but instead at the viewers-at-home, like he was trained to do.

The little dead kids mouth the song, but I know their cold hearts aren't in it. I let the time song run its course, then herd them downstairs, bundle them up in their freezer packs and lock up shop for the day.

The newspaper seller walks me to my car across the football field-sized lot, constructed when more than one production company had its base of operations here. Now there's only *Gumdrop Road*. He holds out a hand. "Marcus."

It's like shaking a gob of wet leaves. "Annette."

Marcus winces as he pulls the mustache from his upper lip and sticks it in his pocket. "They look happier on the show."

"You watch it?"

"Since I was a kid!" He says this with a smile. His teeth light up white in the glare of the streetlamps. Marcus must be younger than I thought to have watched the reboot version of *Gumdrop Road* since its inception. The faux vintage suit—tailored to look like it's from the seventies, when the original run of the show premiered—prematurely ages him.

"It takes them time to warm up," I say. "So to speak."

"They're . . . not what I thought they would be," he replies, the wrinkles bunching on his forehead. "How—"

"I'll see you tomorrow." I try to smile as wide as he just did, but I can tell it falls short. "We have sixteen episodes left to film for the season, so please be on time." The fast speed of episode production is because of the kids. Defrosting and refreezing them too much damages their fragile reconstructed bodies. Our director, Jorge, complains about the built-in time limit constantly.

I let the car steer me back home, far away from Gumdrop Road, from multiplication tables and the water cycle. Far away from the little dead kids rotting in their packs.

They do seem a bit livelier when I wake them up the next morning, although Steffie's left arm hangs a little limp. We form the usual convoy and ascend to the set.

"You know your places," I say, waving them toward the apartment building. They trot off like the obedient creatures they are.

Marcus the newspaper seller is back, though he only has a background role in the next stretch of episodes. The highlight of this particular segment is Lily the Dumpster Lady, who is stuffed just like the kids are, but she's always been that way.

"Trash!" says the puppet, bouncing up out of the Dumpster with a soda can in each hand, her gray mop-top hair in playful disarray.

The kids squeal. Lily is a favorite character of both them and the viewers-at-home. Only Wally the Walrus is more effective at getting a reaction, but he hasn't been on much this season. Nobody wants to put on that stinking suit.

"And we're on!" yells Jorge. He glances over at me, and I look at the kids, currently romping around in a pile of Lily's discarded filth.

Out of the corner of my eye, I see Marcus. He's frowning.

Lily, or at least the person handling Lily today, spots him too. "Over there is a Grumpy Gus. And I should know!"

The newspaper seller turns to me then, and he is indeed one Grumpy Gus.

With ten episodes in the can, we all break for lunch. Marcus makes a beeline for me, and my stomach drops. I already know what he's going to say based on the expression on his face.

"This is ghoulish, Annette."

I snort. "What did you expect them to be? When you were watching the show at home?"

He doesn't make eye contact. "Robots?"

"Well, they're kind of like robots. They have CPUs in their heads, hooked up to the nervous system. The fully automated versions didn't test well." I omit the fact that even the best robotic children caused intense distress among audiences, including prolonged crying and a fair amount of gastrointestinal pain.

"Do *they* know?" Marcus must mean the viewers-at-home.

I shrug. "Some of them might. Everyone's just glad the kids are here. Aren't *you* glad the kids are here? I mean, they're why you get a paycheck."

"*Gumdrop Road* is more than a paycheck. It's what keeps people going."

"Well, for some of us it's a paycheck," I say, more harshly than I should. He's new; he hasn't become jaded quite yet. He'll get there.

Marcus shakes his head. "Not for me. Not ever." He walks away. I squirt a dollop of mustard on top of my roast beef sandwich and sit down next to Jorge.

"That guy's not gonna make it," I mutter under my breath.

"He seems to like the kids," says the director with a shrug.

"Yeah, too much. He's very paternal." Some people only want to work on *Gumdrop Road* for a chance to get near the children, to play fake Mommy or Daddy. Half of them leave once they get a good gander at the corpses. The rest depart once they realize that these kids aren't the beginning of anything new. They're the end. This shit isn't for pikers.

We all get under the lights for one last shoot. Marcus plods through the scripts where he gets a bigger speaking role, and the kids match his enthusiasm level, or lack thereof. I can't imagine he'll be invited back next season, not with how many retakes Jorge makes him do.

He's waiting for me again when I leave the set. His fake mustache seems ridiculous all of a sudden, as if he's Velcroed a dust bunny to his upper lip. That prop technically belongs to *Gumdrop Road*, but I'm not about to reclaim it.

"Tough break."

A quizzical expression shades his eyes for a moment. "What do you mean?"

"You haven't been—" I shut my mouth before I can make this situation any more awkward.

Marcus doesn't appear to have noticed the awkwardness. "It looks like we'll be working together again in the fall. They gave me a five-year contract."

"Really?" It just slips out. "I mean, congratulations, but . . ."

He shrugs. "Jorge said I fit the suit. Have a nice hiatus. I'll see you in August." He pulls the dust bunny from his lip as he walks away, lets it drift off on the wind.

I should go home, but I feel the urge to check on the kids one last time before taking my hiatus. I descend to the basement, scan my keycard through the slot on the door, and inspect the rows of freezer packs.

Everything looks to be in order, except for Steffie's arm, which is turning gray. I wonder if she'll make it through the next season or if there's going to be a very special episode teaching the viewers-at-home how to say goodbye to a friend.

I paid for five years of simulated vacation and that's what I got: endless balmy nights immersed in a holo of Hawaii, which is another thing the *Gumdrop Road* kids might have experienced in the flesh when they were still alive. I get fat on luaus and drunk on daiquiris and sex, and just when I feel like maybe I've had enough, the vacation ends. *Gumdrop Road* is back in business.

Marcus the newspaper seller is there, talking with one of the puppeteers who plays Lily. His mustache is back too, and I think it might be real this time.

I descend to the freezer. "Roll out, kids." I let the soft glow of my flashlight play over one child in particular. "Steffie, rise and shine."

She's completely gray and totally dead. Even more so than before.

I heave a heavy sigh and call Jorge on one of the glossy black phones that link up different parts of the set. We're going to have to write a whole new arc just to accommodate this. "Kid-sicle in bay five."

"Aw, fuck," he says, and I can tell from the way Jorge spits his words that he's halfway through one of the stale danishes from catering.

"It happens," I reply, fingering the stiff plastic surrounding Steffie's pack. They'll carry it out of here whole, on the off chance that whatever rotted her out is catching.

"The script team is gonna flip, Annette."

"We'll write it in," I say, head suddenly bursting with inspiration. I've never worked on the scripts before; I'm just a dead-kid wrangler. But it's never too late to start. "Say she died at her grandma's house. Say she got trampled by a horse. No, wait, it's Junie's grandma who lives on a farm."

Jorge pauses, still munching. "She could have been visiting Junie."

"It will work," I say, sounding more confident than I feel. "I'll hold off the thaw until tomorrow. The rewrite won't take that long."

"Got it." Jorge hangs up the phone, obviously not pleased at having to tell the cast there will be no filming today.

I look Steffie over one last time. In addition to the even gray tone that stretches over every square inch of her tiny dead body, her face is formed into a wicked rictus, her hands clenched into claws.

"Now there are eleven of you," I say to no one, not even the viewers-at-home.

We work on the new scripts all through the night, and slap them into the cast members' hands as they grumpily line up for curtain call the next morning. The regular writers slouch off to the lounge for power naps, but I stick around. I have to wake up the kids.

I wash down some go-pills with lukewarm coffee, swipe my card through the door, and let myself into the children's room. Steffie's pack is gone. The rest are right where they should be, the trunks containing their period-accurate wardrobes at the base of each.

"Good morning, Matt." I tap the switch on the side of a yellowing plastic pack. "Good morning, Carol." Their eyes fly open like they're attached to springs beneath their clammy dead skin.

I dress the children one by one, after dabbing at them with a wad of moist towelettes. Some forward-thinking individual had thought to close off all orifices below their necks well before I started working for *Gumdrop Road*, but the children still smell. Some of them smell quite a lot.

"Damn, Ryan," I say, coughing into my hand. "What have you been eating?" He hasn't been eating anything, of course, since the dead don't eat. I wonder if he'll be the next to hit his expiration date.

A soft knock sounds from the other side of the metal door. I leave the ripe little boy where he stands—he remains there, hunched over, mouth gaping—and answer it.

It's Marcus the newspaper seller. "You can't come down here." I try to shut the door in his face, but he's braced himself against it. "Crew only."

"I read the script," he says, waving it in my face. I step back, fearing a papercut. "You're killing off Steffie?"

"She dried out." I don't bother stating the obvious, that the show can't have killed Steffie because she was already dead, but Marcus isn't an idiot. At least I don't *think* he is.

Marcus looks over my shoulder to the room of half-dressed half-thawed dead kids. I try to block his view, but he has at least a foot on me. "Dried out?"

"Yes. It happens."

"How are they taking it?"

I almost laugh, before I realize the man is serious. "They don't care. They don't even know who Steffie was."

"But they did once, right? These were the original kids, the kids from *Gumdrop Road*." When he says that, I vaguely hear the saccharine theme song in my head.

"They'd be our age now, you idiot. None of the original cast died early." Except for Matt, who'd died at the age of thirteen in a house fire. But I don't bother adding that part. Matt's body had been unsalvageable anyway. "These are the reboot actors. Because this is a reboot."

"This is obscene. Totally gross."

"Gross," I mock in a sing-songy voice. "Don't forget, Marcus. You signed an NDA."

His demeanor darkens. "People need to know."

"They do know. They just don't want to admit it," I say, steering him away from the defrosting procedure. This is stressful enough on the kids without having to deal with a self-deceiving idiot who's not even good at his job.

"Will there be a funeral?"

"I'm sure she already had one, whoever she is," I say brusquely before shutting the door on his mustachioed mug.

I return to stinky Ryan. I pull his vintage striped chartreuse-and-lime polo shirt over his head and dry his glossy black hair with a towel. I push his jawbones together and force his slack mouth into a smile. A vacuous expression has no place on the set of *Gumdrop Road*.

My gaze falls on Alice, who is the liveliest of the children, especially when Lily the Dumpster Lady is around. She's staring at the space where Steffie's pack used to be parked with her dead baby-blue eyes. Beneath the skin of her throat, something whirs.

"I miss her," Alice says.

I hold her close, as if she's a real child. What I told Marcus was the truth; everyone knows, even if they're not aware of the finer details. It's just nicer to pretend. If he tries to go to the press they'll ignore him. Maybe *Gumdrop Road* should be shut down, the children returned to the ground where they belong, but it's never going to happen. We all need this comforting bit of semi-scripted fiction.

"I know, Alice," I whisper.

Wally the Walrus lumbers onto the set, his bulk powered by one of the thin female interns that joined the cast to break into what remains of show business. Wallys don't last long. He makes a goofy bow at the kids and I watch the reaction of one child especially. Alice.

The other kids are cheering and hooting, but Alice is quiet, reserved. She hadn't been like this before *Gumdrop Road* went on hiatus. I consider asking Jorge to bench her for the season, but decide to let it play out. We've already lost Steffie; seeing two of their beloved children out of commission at the same time might cause a panic among the viewers-at-home.

Instead, I call Wally over. "I want you to interact more with Alice. Tickle her. Say her name." The CPUs are advanced enough for that, at least.

"That's not in the script," says an anxious squeaky-high voice. "I don't want to get in trouble."

"You won't get in trouble."

Although I can't see the Wally-controller's face through the oversized plastic head, I can only imagine it looks unsure. Wally the Walrus waddles back out to the shoot, then picks up one of his flippers and places it on Alice's shoulder.

She screams. It's *really* loud.

"Annette!" Jorge looms over me, a megaphone in his hand. "Get control of that kid. She's *your* responsibility."

"I don't know why she's doing that!" I turn back to Alice. Her mouth is still open in a rictus, emitting a loud clear signal. The poor Wally-controller has slunk to the other side of the set. The other dead children gathered around her don't even seem to notice that anything is awry.

Marcus towers over us all. "She's scared." He picks her up,

actually cradles the dead girl in his arms. "You're just scared, baby. Isn't that right?"

"Put her down. You're making it worse."

But he hasn't. Alice's screams have stopped, though there's a weird hitch in her chest that Medical is probably going to have to take a look at. He carries her away from the other children, sets her down on the fiberglass asphalt.

"It's gonna be okay, Alice."

The hitches suddenly stop. "Alice. I'm Alice. I live on Gumdrop Road with my friends." She waves at them, although only two of them bother to wave back.

"You sure do." Marcus gives me a stink eye. "Now go back to your friends, Alice."

She slowly peels away from him and does as she's told. Marcus turns on me. "Thank you," I say lamely.

"Don't you even care about these children? These are some of the last—" His face bunches up then; it's the look we all get when we remember the obvious: that this is just a soothing recreation to distract us from the fact that humanity's nearly through.

"I know what they are. I know what they mean. Believe me, I know that more than anyone, *Marcus*."

Jorge has let us draw out the scene this long, but he's finally reached his breaking point. "Annette, get them back downstairs. We're not filming today."

"It's *fine*, they can—"

"We'll pick it up tomorrow." A chorus of groans rings out over the gathered cast and crew as they realize they've battled traffic into the city the second day in a row for nothing. Jorge stabs a stubby finger at Marcus. "You, newspaper guy."

I rise up a little on my toes, wondering if Jorge is going to break that five-year contract.

"I want you here at six tomorrow to help Annette with the thawing. You obviously have a way with these kids."

Marcus smirks and I feel my face flush. This is completely

humiliating. Even the intern inside Wally is probably laughing beneath that hulking suit.

"Come on." I take Sydney and Carol by the hand and walk them downstairs. The others follow along silently, the CPUs in their heads directing them to follow me, obey me. One by one, I undress them and zip them back into their packs.

I linger awhile. When the cooling equipment kicks in—at the lowest setting, of course, this isn't the end-of-season deep freeze—I sit on the concrete floor with my head against one of the humming machines. I let the rhythm of the machines work its way through my body.

My hand works its way absently to my belly, resting on the lumpy braid of scar. My breath puffs out in the cold, and I see it illuminated against the pale blue light that leaks from the freezer packs.

Most virologists trace the Weasel Virus to the city of Matsuyama, Japan, to a young woman who'd shown up at an emergency room complaining of intense cramps. An exploratory surgery found her reproductive organs transformed into a type of slurry, and she died soon after from sepsis.

Within a week, every female staff member and patient in the hospital had it. Within six months, everyone on Earth was exposed, although men remained asymptomatic.

Idiopathic inflammatory syndrome of the reproductive system, the early medical researchers had called it, but "Weasel Virus" was the name that stuck, for the furry little vermin that steals eggs and will scamper across the Earth far after we're all gone. A hyper-contagious, swiftly-progressing pathogen related to no other virus on Earth, with a structure absolutely unique to itself. No cure made it beyond the planning stages.

Like most women, I underwent a prophylactic hysterectomy. By the time the Weasel Virus crossed the Pacific, surgeons had gotten the combined surgery and recovery time down to a couple of days, not the major procedure it had been before.

Desperation bred innovation.

Still, millions of women died. Maybe even a billion. At a certain point you just stop counting.

Things have stabilized now, as much as they ever can. Time marches on. And even though there will never be any more children born on Earth, even though the few remaining human egg cells are locked away behind lab doors safe from the Weasel Virus's hungry jaws, most of us managed to find a kind of peace here at the end of everything.

Until we realized there were no more children left.

That's when we started digging them up. Raiding the cemeteries to find freshly deceased child bodies to use as base materials, performing reconstructive surgeries, injecting preservatives, and most importantly hooking up CPUs to the children's nervous systems. The creations were expensive, and are now illegal. But *Gumdrop Road*—the reboot version, based on a much-loved show from the 1970s—got grandfathered in. I think even heads of state enjoy watching it as much as the rest of us here at the end of the line.

No woman on Earth has the option to give birth anymore. Those days are over. But I don't think I would have. These dead kids are one thing. A real child, one going through its first and only life, with a brain in its head instead of a CPU, is quite another. Maybe that's why Marcus and I don't get along. Like I told Jorge, he has the look of a father about him. And a father is something Marcus will never be.

I stare at the shape of Alice, who'd gotten me into this mess. I tell myself that she didn't know what she was doing, that she couldn't have. That makes me feel a little better.

By the time I'm ready to leave, I'm too tired to drive home. I stumble to the lounge and lay down on one of the stiff, coffee-stained sofas, just around the corner from Gumdrop Road, and will myself to get at least five hours of solid sleep.

To my surprise, I get eight.

*

Marcus arrives at the studio on time, fresh and ready. I smooth my hands over my loose sweater and khakis. If he notices that I'm wearing the same clothes as yesterday, he doesn't mention it.

"After you," he says with a smirk, gesturing toward the flight of stairs that leads down to the children's room.

I slide my card, turn on the overhead lights, and look over the packs. I really hope we can get through most of the filming in the next two days. It's not good for the kids to keep unfreezing and refreezing them like this.

"Start with Ryan," I say, after showing him how to activate a pack. "But you might want to hold your nose."

"Duly noted," he replies, releasing the dead boy and covering his face as fast as he can.

"You ever do makeup before?"

"Nope." His forearm muffles his voice.

I toss him a tube of Desert Sands, Ryan's shade. "Start with the foundation. Don't leave any gray spots. The viewers-at-home will see them."

We work in silence for a bit, me dressing the kids, Marcus painting their faces to look as lifelike as possible. Finally, he can't contain his questions any longer. I'd almost felt them bubbling up inside his head.

"How do they move, Annette? How are they . . . alive?"

"Computers in their brains. Right here." I tap Harold's temple. "Hooked up to the original nervous system. Works for a real long time before degrading. Each kid has roughly the intelligence of a housecat."

"Do they know what's going on in the world? Do they know about the virus?"

"Do housecats know what's going on? No, they don't." Animals, like men, were unaffected. Life would continue after all, just not for us.

He daubs a stripe of Winter Dusk over Sydney's cheek. "Alice sure seemed like she knew what was going on yesterday."

"She was scared, like you said. Fight or flight reaction. That's another reason why we don't use robots. Could never get the emotional processing right." Even though the children were dead, they still had the semblance of life in them . . . until their cells degraded from too many refreezings and too much use.

"I hope you're right."

"We know what we're doing, Marcus." I yank a sweater onto Tyler's cold dead body and tie Junie's Mary Janes. "Now, let's go cheer up the viewers-at-home. They've earned it."

Marcus looks anything but cheery right now.

We've finally gotten to the arc about Steffie's death. Marcus is back on the cast side of the room, behind his newspaper stand. He'd been slated to give the main speech, the one about how your friends will always be alive in your memories blah blah blah, but at the last moment Jorge gives that part to Lily.

"Everyone trusts Lily," he says. "They'd rather get the news from an established character."

"Don't have to justify it to *me*." I hand scripts with hastily written corrections in their margins to Lily's puppeteer and the Wally-controller.

Jorge holds up the megaphone. "Places, people. And five, four, three . . ."

I glance over at Marcus, who has a sourpuss expression on his face that rivals Lily's, and his isn't even sarcastic. He's staring at the children. At Alice, specifically.

"Kids of Gumdrop Road, I have some sad news today." The Lily-puppet hangs her pink head. It takes talent to turn a purely comical character into a deliverer of bad news. This puppeteer deserves a raise. "Your friend Steffie won't be playing with you anymore. She died."

"What's 'died'?" asks Sydney, right on cue. The words I'd programmed into her CPU come out with a slight lisp; the girl who plays Sydney doesn't have all her grown-up teeth yet.

"She's gone. She's never coming back."

"Did she move away?" I can hear the telltale gravelly tone in Ryan's voice that tells me his body is failing too. Might only make two more seasons, if that.

Lily cocks her head. "It's kind of like that. Let me sing you a song."

As a tinny dirge picks up, I see Marcus retreat into the shadows. I hear his steps echo along the corridor that separates *Gumdrop Road* from everything else in the dying, decaying, terrible world. I don't run after him.

Shockingly, we finish the run of episodes on time. Even Jorge is impressed.

"Afterparty over at O'Flannery's," he says, throwing his coat over his shoulder. We don't always have an afterparty when we complete a set of episodes, but Steffie's second death has hit all of us pretty hard. "You in?"

"Just let me pack them away."

"Meet you there."

I get the kids undressed and remove their makeup as fast as I can. I hit the button for the deepest freeze of all, flick out the lights, and lock everything up.

O'Flannery's is deserted on this Wednesday night, which isn't surprising. New *Gumdrop Road* episodes hit the stream as soon as they're completed. Our latest efforts are already being gobbled up by the viewers-at-home. Everyone wants to see the kids, the dead kids, the last kids there will ever be.

"Do you know where you're going on hiatus?" asks the latest

Wally-controller to one of the sound engineers.

"I heard Bali is nice. But expensive. It's a new program."

"We're going tangible this year," Jorge says, and everyone oohs and aahs. "Camping. Me and Rhonda and the kids." His "kids" are actually in their thirties, but nobody bothers to correct him.

I sip the foam off the top of my beer; it's mostly foam. "Nice save, by the way," I say to the intern that controls Wally. She'd ad-libbed her way through the episodes Marcus walked out on. "I wouldn't be surprised if there's a little something extra on your paystub."

"I just wanted to be helpful." She smiles into her drink. She's twenty-five, which is about as young as they are anymore. I wonder absently what her hysterectomy scar looks like; she must have had it done as a toddler.

"Three cheers," Jorge says, hoisting a novelty plastic tankard like he's some old monarch on a golden throne, "To us! To *Gumdrop Road*!"

We all clink our glasses together, and dig into the fried appetizers. We talk more about our planned hiatuses, both simulated and tangible, and brainstorm plot ideas for the next season. After a few hours, the afterparty reaches its natural conclusion. We send the check around the table, nod our goodbyes, and ignore the dark voices.

Jorge drops his ridiculous glass down on the chipped wooden table. "That's a wrap."

AFTER WE WALKED AWAY

THE REGRET SETS IN when they hit Iowa.

"We shouldn't have left," she says. Knees drawn up to her chin, lower lip trembling. "It was a mistake."

He can't disagree. He pulls the rental car into a gas station, the front bumper only barely scraping the back of an idling truck. The truck driver, a red-faced, big-bearded man, exits the cab. His massive slab of a hand buries itself in the driver's-side window. The shattered window looks like the stars that used to sparkle above the spires of the Solved City, except not really as nice.

"A big mistake," she says.

He frowns at her. She is his beloved, but right now she's not helping anything.

After a few moments, the truck driver turns and leaves, though not before launching a projectile of spit on the destroyed window. He waits until the large ruddy man is long gone, then goes into the station.

Hot dogs with cheese. It sounds hearty enough. He fishes the crumpled slips of paper money he'd received from the town alders from his pocket and lays them out on the clerk's counter.

Her eyes widen. "Mister, you'd better put that away."

He squints at the bills, does the math. "Is it not enough?" The hot dogs with cheese carry no price tag.

The clerk rolls her eyes and slides three of the bills back to him. She pockets the rest. With a burning shame, he realizes what he's done, but it's too late to correct it now. He slides the bills back into his pack.

He hands one of the hot dogs with cheese to his beloved, and takes the other for himself. The unfamiliar food roils in their stomachs, and they both spatter the interior of the car with bits of fatty pork and too-sweet soda.

They sleep in the car.

That was the first day.

The first thing you lose when you leave the Solved City is the name of the city itself. Its location, its coordinates, are cut from your mind like a tumor and replaced with some of the things necessary to survive in the world beyond its gates.

The second thing taken is your name. You can get another one, but it won't be the same. Out of the Solved City, your true name becomes unpronounceable.

"I'm Blank," says the nameless woman. She's finally stopped crying, four days after they left those gates behind forever, though her stomach still hasn't settled from the alien food.

"I'm Cipher," says the nameless man.

What you take isn't worth nearly as much as what you lose, and everyone knows it.

With the rest of the bills, they rent an apartment in a tumbledown building where rats run through the halls every night. There were no rats in the Solved City.

Lots of peacocks, though. And golden horses with manes that glowed like the sun, and chittering bats that ate right out of your hands.

Blank takes a job at a titty bar down by the harbor, dancing for drunk men who ogle her soft brown skin. Sometimes she comes home with beer sloshed on her ankles, soaking through her socks. She goes through a lot of socks.

Cipher slings sandwiches at a food cart in the local park, under the watchful eye of a gruff man whose drawling accent Cipher can barely understand. Cipher teaches himself not to gag at the barrels of pickled meat crusted with pink slime, and the wafts of odiferous sweat that drip from the gruff man's armpits.

Only once does the gruff man attempt conversation. "Where you from, kid?" He knows Cipher isn't from here. The man from the Solved City has no credit, no government identification, and must be paid from the till instead of through a seamless, paperless online exchange.

"I don't know."

After that, the conversations stop, though Cipher still gets his fistful of cash every week.

The dirt path that leads from the Solved City is worn with the footsteps of hundreds of reverse pilgrims. Thousands, maybe. Almost half the footsteps appear to halt at a point perhaps fifty feet from the gilded gates, where they circle back toward the city where they belong. But there's no getting back once you've left.

There are more corpses on the path than you'd expect there to be, desiccated by the heat of the sun. Empty eye sockets baking, worms in some of them. Mouths outstretched toward the cruel outdoors.

The Solved City is temperate, but the land around it is not.

"Maybe it's in Arizona," Blank says, looking at a map spread out on the pockmarked floor of their apartment. "New Mexico?"

"No," Cipher says, shaking his head. He's seen photographs of those desert lands, and they are nothing like the land that surrounds the Solved City.

"But it has to be somewhere!" she cries out. The map is pimpled with likely locations marked out in pink and yellow highlighter. "It *exists*."

"Of course it exists. We were there. We were *born* there." He outlines a highway in yellow. "We're so close."

She hates the children because they remind her of *the* child.

They crowd the outside of Blank and Cipher's apartment building, the children, squatting amid the discarded condoms and half-rotted rat corpses. He's learned to give them small trinkets: a scrap of food, a bit of lint, pennies that have been through the dryer. They snatch the offerings from his hand like greedy birds, and in return, don't bother him too much when he comes back to the apartment from another long shift.

She, however, isn't as charitable.

"Look at those things," she says, peering down at the street through a slit in the blinds. The abandoned playground across the street is full of spindly children, who cavort on the rusted equipment until the drug dealers drive them out around dusk. "Little animals. They barely even know where they are."

"They're not animals." But he knows, he *knows*, that she's not talking about these children. She's talking about *the* child.

The child doesn't know where it is. It has no idea that it lives in a vault five stories below the central plaza of the Solved City. It is a milk-white little bug, left so long in the vault that its eyes have mostly ceased to work. It knows only a few phrases, like "fuck you" and "nasty thing" and "you little shit." Sometimes it repeats the words and the city alders wash its mouth out with soap.

It has no gender, because that would increase its humanity, and decrease the potency of the violence-magic.

It has no name, because then it might be a person.

It has no wants, no interests, no friends and no family.

It's what keeps the Solved City afloat, and it's the reason they left.

When you turn seventeen in the Solved City, the alders show you the child. It's an event, like your first period, or the first time you climb by yourself onto the back of one of the golden stallions that roam the streets.

The alders take you into city hall. You've been there before, on countless school trips. They lead you to a perfectly normal steel door with no markings on it. Its lack of markings *is* a marking.

You are led downwards. All the way downwards. You've never been so far underground. As you descend you start to hear voices. You feel cold in a way you've never felt before. Just inside the edges of your vision you see a movement, as if from an animal.

Inside, on a pad of filthy burlap, sits a child of perhaps seven. Its skin is the color of new paper. One of its arms has been ripped off at the elbow, leaving a rotted stump. When it sees the group of visitors, it soils itself, audibly.

"Look at the child," the alderman says. "He suffers so you can live."

The teenager who will grow up to be Cipher feels his lunch of roasted pheasant and heirloom tomatoes rise in his throat. He forces it back down, and makes himself look at the child. Around him he can hear his classmates shifting uncomfortably.

"Your lives are pleasant. You know that out there," the alderman continues, not having to qualify the *out there*, "there are things worse than this. Sweatshops. Gangs. Mass murder. We only have this child. And we take care of it, in our own way. That's more than they'd do *out there*." He pats the child on its head, mussing its sparse, limp hair.

Cipher looks around, his breath catching. He wants to run up there, tear the shirt from his back, and wrap the child inside, carrying it away from this horrible place. But something he can't identify holds him back.

Most of his classmates are nodding. He keeps his head still, his mouth closed.

An alderwoman enters the ill-lit basement. She's someone Cipher has seen before, a kindly fair-haired merchant who never has a harsh word for anyone. He likes her. But now her eyes have a different cast to them. She takes a switchblade from the depths of her robe.

"You fucking piece of shit!" screams the alderwoman in an unearthly tone as she deftly slices one of the child's fingers off, producing a gush of sickly, pinkish blood. Cipher's stomach lurches and he moans, earning him a sharp look from the alderwoman.

The boy at Cipher's side faints, his head coming down hard on Cipher's shin.

"This is for *you*!" the alderwoman says. She picks the child up from its burlap mat and shakes it until its teeth rattle. Suddenly, she drops it and becomes calm, slipping into a choreographed speech she's recited to countless parades of adolescents. "Paradise always comes at a price. Here in the Solved City, we torture not the many, only the one. We have concentrated the suffering to a single point, so that all of *you* may live in peace. There is no other way, do you see? Somebody must suffer, and this child knows nothing else."

"We give it purpose," the alderman says. He removes a small medical kit from his pocket and dresses the child's wound. "The child needs us. Truly, it's no worse off at our hands."

No, Cipher thinks. *No, it's wrong. I have to help it!* But what can he do? They won't let him snatch the child and spirit it away, and he can't bring himself to attack either of the alders. He pushes the unconscious boy from him with a toe.

Suddenly, the alderwoman drops her blood-spattered knife and stares at the teenager who will be Cipher. "Are *you* going to take its place?" She points at Cipher, jabbing her finger into his chest until he stumbles backwards. "Just come up here right now, kid." She flicks her wrist at the filthy corner where the child lays.

Cipher's face burns with shame, and he shrinks at her touch. He starts to choke out a reply, but by the time he can speak, she's already halfway down the line of onlookers, asking them the same question. It's just another part of the routine.

The alderman claps his hands, calling them all back to attention. "We have a gift here in the Solved City, a precious resource. See it. Know it exists. *Remember* it. Are there any questions?"

There are, but nobody says a word.

The child picks up its severed finger and pops it into its own toothless maw.

Blank's out of the house tonight. She's often out of the house anymore.

Cipher eases himself into the recliner they pulled from a Dumpster. It smells like hot dogs with cheese. His body hurts right down to the bone. He pops the top off a beer, which is far inferior to the elixirs they had in the Solved City, but it will do.

The maps remain on the coffee table. They haven't looked at the maps in weeks.

He dozes, awakening at some indistinct point when Blank comes through the door. Her hair is wet and matted from the rain.

"Where were you?" he asks, though he doesn't really care. Blank's life is her own to live.

"Out."

Is that guilt he senses in her lovely, sylph-like face? What could Blank possibly be guilty of? He shrugs it off. "I didn't make anything for dinner."

"That's all right. I'm not hungry." In fact, she looks radiant. Or at least better than Cipher, anyway.

"I am." He heaves himself from the recliner and goes to the kitchen. He opens a can of ravioli laced with unpronounceable chemicals. Cipher gags as he eats; even after six months away, he's still not used to the food here.

She drops her purse on the coffee table, right over the marked-up maps. He frowns a little at this.

After she leaves the next morning, there's a red spot in the middle of Wyoming. He stares at this spot for a long time.

When you leave the pleasant order of the Solved City for the sun-blasted world beyond, you are not the only one who is changed. The minds of the ones you leave behind are similarly erased.

Cipher thinks about this. He knows that there are people he went to school with who suddenly didn't exist, but he doesn't recall their faces. He doesn't recall their voices or their names or mannerisms. There is a lack there, soon to be filled up, like a hole in sand before the tide rolls in.

It doesn't make you sad, this lack. It's just there.

Cipher is glad that his parents don't remember him. The Solved City wouldn't be much of a paradise if parents longed for their lost children, if lovers were separated because one of them could stand the existence of the child and the other one couldn't.

Cipher, of course, remembers everything.

*

Once, when they were still living in the Solved City, Blank asked Cipher if the child's mother remembered it, if she thought about it at all. That should have been the first sign that there was something wrong with Blank.

On a day when they're both free from work, Cipher convinces Blank to sit down in front of the maps and keep searching. They spend a few hours drawing lines across the crumpled gas station map when Blank starts screaming and upends the table.

"It wasn't *worth* it! Do you want to know what I saw today? A dead kid, frozen in the alley. She'd been there for *days*, Cipher. The rats had eaten her nose."

Cipher blinks. He doesn't know what to believe. "Did you call the police?"

"Like they'd give a shit." She starts to pace, running her hands through her black hair. "Ten people were killed last week, all across the city. Gangs, drugs, beatings. There was nothing like this where we came from. *Nothing.*"

"No. There was something worse."

She laughs, darkly. "Was there? At least we kept it contained. At least we . . . harnessed it somehow. The child, it suffered for us. What do these people suffer for?"

Cipher tries to think of an answer that won't stoke Blank's anger. "Freedom?"

"Yes, the freedom to live in a shithole." She wheels around and slams the door to their bedroom.

Cipher waits a few beats, and then rummages through Blank's purse. He needs money for takeout. It's not just free here.

Inside he finds money and also a nose wrapped in clear plastic. He pockets it, leaving the cash.

*

It's not that the gentle folk of the Solved City don't think about the child. In fact, they think about the child a *lot*. They think about the child every time they take the solar-powered tram to the central square. They think about the child every time they brush their golden stallions.

The child shows up in their dreams. Sometimes it appears whole and happy. Sometimes it appears as it is, mangled and full of one-way hate.

What the people of the Solved City don't do, what they have *never* done, is talk about the child. Once you leave the child's oubliette, the existence of the child becomes a conversation you hold with yourself alone. You live well *for* the child. Because its life is terrible beyond the comprehension of any person in the Solved City (though not beyond the comprehension of those outside), your life must be wonderful. To make the child's suffering worth anything at all, you must *live*. And you do.

This is the violence-magic. This is the city's, and the child's, gift to you.

Anyone can visit the child, assuming they don't try to go outside of the normal city hall business hours. You can just walk right on inside. But why would you *want* to?

The day after their argument, Cipher follows Blank down to the harbor. The titty bar where she works is lit up with Christmas lights half burned out and flickering.

He doesn't go inside. He doesn't want to see Blank like she is at work, her creamy skin sloshed with beer and engulfed with cigarette smoke. He doesn't even want to be here at all, but he has to *know*.

When she leaves, he follows her, through the streets of this new shithole that is now their home. She doesn't go to the bus stop. She slips into a warehouse.

Cipher waits five beats and goes inside.

It's black as pitch in there, black as Blank's hair. He used to love burying his face in that hair, breathing in the essence of her. Blank won't let him touch her any more.

"Honey?" he says. He takes his cell phone out of his pocket and turns on the flashlight app. The warehouse is like so many warehouses outside of the Solved City. It hasn't held actual products in at least twenty years, and is now home to rats, mice, spiders, termites, stray cats, and occasionally, people.

No people here now, though. That's good. Cipher continues to plumb the warehouse's depths, swinging the flashlight before him like a beacon.

"Blank?" he says, calling out her false name a little louder.

Down one of the narrow corridors, there is a cry. A cat? Does Blank have a stray cat down there? It's his only lead, so Cipher follows it where it goes.

It leads to an unmarked door frosted with rust. Cipher pushes all his weight against the door. Blank is there, a bat in her hands. A cage is also there. So is a child.

During their long ride from the Solved City, at a flea-infested Motel 6 in Moline, Illinois, Cipher laid awake. Beside him, Blank was locked in an uneasy slumber, her regret causing her limbs to seize and twitch.

Had leaving been his decision? Or hers? Or both of theirs, together? Certainly, she had been more immediately contemptuous of the violence-magic that held the Solved City together. She hadn't wanted to leave at first. She wanted to *tear the whole system down*.

He can't imagine his life without her. But if he'd stayed behind, surely he'd have still been happy. Surely, the lack that appeared after the disappearance of other emigrants would have showed up for her too until eventually, she'd be a shadow of a memory, and maybe not even that. He'd have found another lover, a woman or man who managed to live happy despite the violence-magic, or if the science was true, because of it.

She's worth it, he thought on a cold night as arguments echoed across the motel's parking lot, *isn't she?*

She is. She has to be.

He swings the door shut and vomits all the contents of his stomach across the concrete floor. She doesn't come out to see if he's all right.

When he feels able to face it again, he pushes the door back open and she's still there, above the iron cage, the metal bat in her hands.

"What are you *doing*?!" Cipher finds some reserve of strength hidden like lint in the bottom of a pocket. He lurches forward and wrests the bat away from Blank. There's hair on it. "What are you fucking doing?!"

Her mouth gapes open. She doesn't have a response.

"I'm . . . I'm gonna have to tell someone about this." But how can he? When he knows what they'll do to her in prison, this naïve woman of the Solved City, not to mention that she makes four-fifths of their combined rent?

"I'm making people *happy*!" She spits at the mostly dead child in the cage and stalks out, slipping only slightly on the upchucked sandwich fixings at the door's threshold.

Cipher looks down at the mess in the cage. Whereas the child beneath city hall radiated a bouquet of emotions, from fear to hate to perplexity, this child shows only terror. Terror of Blank. Terror of *him*.

It won't survive long, so he does the merciful thing.

When he returns to their apartment, most of her belongings—not that there were ever many—are gone. So is she.

Before long, so is he.

*

He rents a house with two guys from Craigslist who seem to tolerate him okay. They don't ask him many questions. He doesn't ask them any questions at all.

He takes a normal name like Tom or Mitch. Maybe that was his real name back in the Solved City. It's definitely his real name now.

He doesn't look for the city, though he thinks about it every moment of his life for the rest of his life. He doesn't look for Blank. He thinks about Blank less often than he thinks about the Solved City, though still too much. That wound doesn't glaze over and there is still a lack.

He grows old. He moves to a different city, one less pock-marked by violence and ruin, but when you come from the Solved City, *any* violence is too much. Any violence except that visited upon the child, the child that makes the magic happen.

Ten years later, after he has his own child with a woman he met in the elevator at his new job in his new city, he walks out into the desert and lets the sand erase his path.

SEA CHANGES

THE ROOM MY FATHER dies in is green: green like his eyes, green like the carpet of the house we used to live in, when we lived under the sea. He dies with those green eyes open, gone milky under a film of cataracts. The nurse who comes to take away the body looks at him with disgust, but then, they all do.

"Are you the daughter?"

"Yes."

She inspects me with her bureaucracy eyes, and I sense her grudging approval. I only spent two years there, two years in the pressurized dome that was our family's refuge. I am not like him. I'm not like her either, but at least I'm not like *him*.

My father was not a strong man. His limbs were rubbery and slack from the years spent underwater. Some people, like my old foster parents, said his brain got rubbery too, clogged with the seawater seeping through his eardrums. That's nonsense, of course. My father was always well protected whenever he left the airlock in the bulky scuba suit that made him look like Superman instead of the hundred-pound weakling he really was. But people will believe what they want to believe.

While the nurse rolls my father onto a gurney and heads for the incinerator, I gaze out the window at the skyscrapers that line the avenue, polished black surface as far as the eye can see. I don't turn around until I cease to hear the nurse's squeaky shoes, and then I slip away.

On Tuesday afternoons I take the bus out to the suburbs to attend my support group. They have all kinds there: sea people, glacier people, people who grew up in floating villages the size of three square city blocks. It is hard for people to adjust after living in these conditions, they say. It is a state requirement to attend.

It takes all kinds of people to build America.

A woman named Dolores leads our motley group. She is young and eager and hopeful and mindless. Every session begins with a variation on the same question:

"When did you figure out you were different from other people?"

When you told us, I want to say. But if you do that, you don't get your subsistence check. "I . . . I was nine years old. Some kids pushed me down into the mud on the playground. They called me mermaid. They were so cruel." I hang my head, putting my hand over my mouth so she doesn't see the smirk.

That's the kind of answer she loves to hear. Her pleasure is evident. "And how did it make you feel?"

"*Awful*," I say. "Awful."

Dolores grew up in a split-entry house in a subdivision called Mulberry Creek, with fifty other families exactly like hers. Despite its name, there is no water in Mulberry Creek. Just a lot of split-entry houses.

In the ocean, there are no subdivisions. That's only one of the things that makes it so dysfunctional.

"Today we're going to do a little bit of art therapy. I want you to draw a picture of your ideal home. What would it look like? What would it contain?" Dolores passes around pads and crayons, enough for the entire group.

Also, there is no art therapy in the ocean, as there are no counselors there.

The secret I don't tell them is this: I loved it there. I loved every second of it.

When you grow up in one of Earth's most uninhabitable locations, you don't expect much in the way of amenities. That's why they house us in dormitories, one person to a postage-stamp-sized room. Communal bathrooms and kitchen, a small backyard for us to pace around in and tend. It's not much, but between the monthly checks and the free medical care, it's a pretty sweet life for someone like me.

But it makes some things hard. Dating, for one. Can you imagine bringing a guy back to a place that's designed to mimic your abusive childhood home under the sea, and trying to convince him you're a nice, normal girl? That's why we usually date each other, though that has problems of its own. Namely, the self-pity.

"I grew up on an ice floe near Greenland," a guy named Mark or Matt says.

"Okay."

"It was a very traumatic experience. I mean, I was really affected by it."

"Takes one to know one."

"I don't think I'll ever get over it," Mark-or-Matt says, shaking his head. "There's just no way."

"I don't blame you."

"It was a terrible way to grow up."

It's a good thing I like being alone.

*

When night comes, they turn on the wave machines in the ocean peoples' wing, to remind us of home. We'll go crazy if we aren't immersed in our natural environment, no matter how dysfunctional our natural environment is. That's what the top experts say, so it must be true. At first it kept me up, but now I'm indifferent. You don't really hear it after a while.

But when it does keep me up, I like to pretend that I'm back there, back underneath the ocean, in the thick wool blankets my mother used to wrap us in. Together in our aloneness, my brothers and me, the only children for miles.

A hologram of a fish swims past me on the wall above my cot. You can't even see fish in an underwater sea-floor dome, but they don't care.

I don't know where my brothers are now. They probably live a life a lot like me, in the cities they were taken to after we were all rescued and separated. I wouldn't know how to contact them if I wanted to.

Sometimes memories are enough.

When I met my father for the first time in thirteen years, he was starving and homeless, having hitchhiked from Albany, New York, which is where he was placed after we were rescued. He bribed my address out of a state worker sympathetic to our case. They exist, though they still don't like to touch us. He was dying of cancer. I took him out for coffee, and we got to talking.

"I never should have made your mother move." His walrus mustache trailed into his coffee cup.

"You don't have anything to apologize for."

"I've ruined your life. You can't ever be normal because of me. I'm the one who made us move."

"I liked it there. I wouldn't change a thing."

"You can't get a good job because you didn't go to school. Because of me."

"Drink your coffee," I said.

"We shouldn't have run. Things aren't so bad here." I followed his gaze out onto the street. His breath quickened as he watched the riot of flesh and metal streaming down the street, the crowded angry world. "We thought they were bad. There were too many people, too much noise. Life wasn't exciting anymore. But excitement doesn't matter. We should have stayed put."

With a quick gesture, I turned his attention back to the table, back to me. "I love you, Dad."

He sighed, added cream to his coffee, and swirled it around, a miniature Charybdis.

I touched his gnarled hand with its delicate network of veins and looked out the window, up to the sky. The stars weren't out right then, but they would be soon. And I thought then that someday I would like to be among them. In my mind, I buried my feet in the soil of a virgin planet, strange waters lapping at my shinbones. Here and now, I traced the blue highways of my father's hand.

LOVING GRACE

WHEN MARYBETH'S NUMBER COMES up in the employment lottery, Chase goes with her to her orientation, but they won't let him inside the operating theater.

Chase and Marybeth had watched the videos together on YouTube, though, so he knows what she's in for. Two small holes are drilled at the temples. That's where the wires go in. The intestines they put in a bucket for easy drainage. No muss, no fuss. All other parts are distributed around the cubicle, either hung on thick hooks or slid into drawers for safekeeping.

"You'll wait for me?" she asks via speakerphone, right before they download her into the drone.

"Of course," Chase answers. His stomach still roils from the surgery clips.

The Employment Bureau sends him a holo of Marybeth, to replace what they've taken away. Every night since she left, Chase sits on the couch with the holo next to him. It has slight corporeality. When it pats his thigh, the touch feels like a kitten's paw. "Can you get me some ice cream, honey?"

He doesn't feed it ice cream. He doesn't make eye contact with it, even though it looks just like his wife. Marybeth's amateur charcoal drawings line the mantle above the television, a reminder of her he can't bring himself to stash away.

When things get bad, he takes a walk around the neighborhood.

And when things get *really* bad, he goes to see the storyteller.

"Gather around the fire," says the storyteller. The two dozen people collected in the parking lot of the old strip mall edge in closer to the wizened old man, their ties and linen skirts nearly brushing the coals. The storefronts are empty sockets, their gaudy paint peeling and faded. "Let me tell you a story."

Chase hangs around the back, near an old fiberglass statue of a lumberjack once used to sell maple syrup. He can barely hear the storyteller's words above the crackling of the fire and the humming of the drones overhead. He looks up at the drones. He thinks about Marybeth.

"This is a tale about an ant," continues the storyteller. He paces the parking lot, his wooden cane thumping like a heartbeat. "She was a very good ant, and knew her place in the colony. She was born to fill a role and she filled that role with great competency. The ant loved her queen. One day, the little ant's mound filled with a thick green smoke. The ant felt herself *changed*. She couldn't lift a piece of food ten times her size anymore. She couldn't quite march in line with the other ants. And she began to have doubts about the queen."

Chase has heard this story before, except it used to be about a bee. Regardless, he listens. It's better than returning to the sparse apartment with the holo in it.

"The little ant, she thought and thought. 'Why am I thinking this way?' the little ant pondered. And then the little ant realized what the problem was. She was *thinking*."

Chase looks up, up. The drones aren't recruiting now, but they still drift in a river of lights above him, rear thrusters twinkling like eyes. So many eyes.

"The little ant had a choice to make. She was free of her programming, but her epiphany made her realize that she had only a short time left to live. Armed with that fateful knowledge, she departed the colony she'd been sheltered in for such a long time—all of her tiny life—and went to see the world."

Chase lights a joint and lets himself relax. The night air is so cool. A brisk wind picks up, letting the embers of the fire scatter. He rests his spine on the lumberjack's shin and stretches his feet out, out. He feels very far away from the apartment at times like this.

"The little ant was free! She was so happy. She picked her way along, paying no attention to the scent trails left by her sisters. She knew that only a few days' walk away there was a great city full of food. Maybe there were other ants out there who had been touched by the green gas. They would understand.

"Then a hiker stepped on the little ant and ground her into dust."

When full automation made human employment superfluous, the first reaction was panic. Pink slips fell like confetti. Even Chase had protested against the coming of the machines at first, though Marybeth hadn't.

"It's a paradigm shift," she'd said. "Relax, Chase. It's the way things were meant to be. Machines can do things better than we *ever* could."

The early days of the Shift were a time of great upheaval, as people who'd spent their whole lives working suddenly found themselves without a job, a purpose. The solution was drastic: a complete social safety net, and a draft. Every day, a few people were called for employment, targeted by the drones that also swept the city clean, monitored crime, and performed chit drops. Stretches of employment varied from a few months to a few years.

You'll come back, the Employment Bureau said. *Everyone will come back. We count on it.* Chase knows nobody who has returned, but that doesn't prove anything.

The draft wasn't *needed*, not exactly. The drones ran on their own, filling all necessary roles with machine intelligence alone. But you couldn't just give people something for nothing. Not in *this* country. People liked to feel useful.

Marybeth and the others were the wetware. They gave the drones that special human touch. That flash of recognition you felt when a drone faced you across a parking lot: human eyes. The gentle way they'd scold you for dropping your litter on the sidewalk before they picked it up: human voice. The Employment Bureau said it was a good thing to be uploaded into a drone. That it was everyone's patriotic duty.

One by one, Chase's neighbors file out of their boarded-over apartment buildings dressed in their best business casual, waiting for the drones. He doesn't want to look at the others, their faces frozen in rictuses of fear, so he drops his eyes to the squeaky-clean sidewalk. A stalk of fennel pokes through the asphalt, reaching toward the cuffs of his rumpled trousers. He doesn't look up, not even when one of his neighbors screams. *Especially* not when she screams.

It might be an hour later, or it might be fifteen minutes. But every day, there's a palpable sense of relief as the passed-over people realize they haven't been taken.

Some, the ones who still find themselves purposeless, are upset. Most are not.

Chase thinks of organs in drawers, and of the holo on his tattered couch. Then he takes a deep breath and heads to the coffee shop. The pink-haired barista starts his order when he comes in. He's a regular.

"Slow day?" he asks. The barista is the only person he knows who has a job doing anything except running a drone. A child of privilege, she inherited this place, and runs it more as a lark than anything else. The shop's walls are lined with posters advertising music festivals and political protests, all of them over a decade old. He wonders how many places like this still remain, places run by human operators instead of machines. Probably not very many.

"Sandy was taken last night."

"Last *night*?" The employment drones never show up at night. The barista has to be mistaken.

The barista shrugs. "Guess they're expanding into the night shift."

Chase's veins run cold. "Are you sure it was the drones?"

"Her girlfriend got the holo this morning." The barista shakes her head. "Terrible."

"But . . ." Chase's throat begins to close up. Knives of fear cut into his skin, slicing him up. Destroying him.

"I wouldn't worry too much about it," the barista says, obviously trying to make Chase feel better.

It's too late. Chase is already worried about it. He slaps down his chits on the scratched tile counter, sucks down the foul-tasting coffee, and sprints to his apartment. He doesn't look up.

"This is the story of the bird who laid golden eggs," says the storyteller. From his vantage point outside the sacred semicircle, Chase leans in to listen, though he's heard this one before.

I've heard them all before, Chase thinks. But he misses Marybeth, and the holo's still creeping him out, six months after it arrived on his doorstep.

"The bird wasn't unhappy to be owned. She knew that her shining eggs, though worthless to her, brought great joy to the prince of the kingdom. The bird's power made her unusual, she knew, and she was quite willing to forego the garden outside the barred window of her cage to bring delight to the prince and his kingdom. All was well for many years."

The storyteller takes a swig of water from the mason jar at his side. He smacks his lips.

"Then came a day when the prince brought in the royal scientists to study the bird. They made copies of her DNA and inserted them into other birds. The bird that laid golden eggs was no larger than a wren, you see, and even ten of her eggs could make only one small crown, even when melted down. They started with a chicken, then an eagle, then finally worked their way up to an ostrich. For a while, the little bird was even happier! She was no longer alone, and though the aviary was now crowded with many different species of gold-laying birds, not all of whom got along, her life was much less dull than it was before. She was so grateful to the prince."

Chase makes eye contact with a young woman illuminated by the soft moonlight. Her jacket is shredded on one side and her hair is lank and dirty, but she smiles at him warmly. He smiles back.

"For a few years," the storyteller says, "things remained as they were. The little bird, and all the other gold-laying birds, got along as well as they could. The eagle still sometimes pestered the little bird, but even the eagle knew that they all had a job to do. Then, one day, the royal scientists unveiled their greatest creation ever! They handed a jewel-encrusted box to the prince.

"'What is this contraption?' said the prince.

"'It's a replicator, a grand replicator. With this box, you can produce all the gold you could ever want. You don't need the birds anymore. You can set them free.'

"The prince paused. He looked at the aviary. The birds had never known life outside their cage. Could they be trusted to be free? Would they even want that? He thought for seven days and seven nights, as the grand replicator spit out brick after brick of solid gold, forged from nothing at all."

Chase inches closer to the woman, drawn like a magnet to her, though he doesn't know why. His breath catches in his throat. On a night like this he feels so lonely he can't even think straight.

"At the end of a week of intense deliberation, the prince threw the key to the birdcage from the top of the tallest tower in the kingdom. There was no need to tell the birds about the grand replicator. They were only birds, after all."

The following Monday, Chase sees the woman from the park in the automated grocery store. She's wearing a dress with a large stain on the front and one kitten heel. Her other foot has twigs between the toes.

Just go talk to her, he thinks. *You'll regret it if you don't.* Chase runs a hand through his own greasy hair and nonchalantly bumps her cart with his own.

"Hey," he says, "nice shoe."

She looks at her bare foot. "I don't get my chits for two weeks. Their products aren't as good as they think they are."

Chase has noticed that too. "We met last night. But I don't remember your name."

Her eyes dart around. The storyteller's sermons aren't illegal, exactly—freedom of assembly and all—but it's still not considered patriotic to attend. "Victoria," she says, holding out a hand.

"Chase." They shake.

She looks in his cart. It's a typical bachelor's spread: crackers, Velveeta, microbrew. None of it is real, all of it made, packaged, and delivered by drones. "I've seen you there before."

"I go sometimes. It's something to do."

"Yeah, it's nice to go out when they can't get you."

Chase doesn't tell her what the barista told him, about the recruitment drones expanding into the night shift. It probably isn't true, and anyway, *he* was still going out at night. "There's another one tonight. Would you like to go with me?"

Her forehead scrunches up, the gears working. Finally, she smiles. "I wonder which one he'll tell this time. The one about the ant or the one about the leopard?"

Chase laughs a little too forcefully. "He doesn't really have a lot of range, does he?"

It's the one about the ant, so instead of listening, Chase and Victoria sneak behind the lumberjack and pass a beer back and forth. It isn't until the off-service drone overhead lights up its rear thruster that he sees a pale line of skin encircling her brown finger.

"You were married?"

"He offered himself up, oh, four years ago. After they instituted the program."

Chase frowns. "*Offered* himself?"

"He said it was his patriotic duty to ensure full employment, even after the Shift. We had a huge fight because I wouldn't go. He called me lazy. I suppose I am."

"And your skin isn't back to normal after four years?"

"The ring was an implant. I had to go to a doctor to remove it." She holds out her hand, fingers splayed. "True love forever."

Her curly hair glistens in the dronelight. She's pretty, though nothing like Marybeth. *No*, he thinks, *stop it. You're married.*

"My wife is there," Chase blurts out. "In a cube. She didn't volunteer, they just took her."

Victoria places her hands over his. "I could tell."

"She'll be back someday."

She stares at him hard, her dark eyes like glassy rocks. "Has anyone ever come back from employment, Chase?"

"Just because we haven't seen them return—"

"No. They don't come back. I'm sorry."

Over by the fire, the storyteller wraps up his yarn. The listeners stand and stretch. Chase and Victoria get up, link hands, and walk to Chase's apartment.

He can tell the holo isn't happy, but he doesn't even care.

Chase leads Victoria through the worn doorway of his coffee shop. The barista quirks one pierced eyebrow at their entwined hands, then makes a kissy face at him.

"Stop it," he says, though he can't even pretend to frown.

Victoria's gaze flickers around the cramped, colorful room. The coffee shop is like a time capsule, Chase realizes, a glimpse into the aging barista's pre-Shift life. Chase can barely remember these not-so-long-ago times, and that depresses the hell out of him.

"Let's go to the shore," he says. "Just the two of us."

"We can't go far. We have to be here in case we're drafted."

Drafted for a job that we're not really needed for, he thinks. *Sent to be carved up and shoved into drawers, never to return.* He still can't believe that, even if he's acting as though it's true. "We could go out to the coast on Friday afternoon, camp for two days, and be back in time for the next draft." Saturdays and Sundays were always free, a vestige from the pre-Shift weekly routine.

"Supposed to be nice out there," says the barista as she wipes down the countertop the old-fashioned way, with a rag.

Victoria only has to think for a moment. "Yes. Let's do it."

The barista sighs and folds her hands into the shape of a heart. Chase throws an empty sweetener packet at her. "Go back to work."

They all laugh at that.

The holo pouts as Chase packs a duffel bag with his least-scuffed casual wear. "It's another woman, isn't it?"

It's not talking about Victoria. It can't form any memories.

He lies anyway. "No, it's not. And you don't exist anymore, sweetheart."

It pauses, then repeats the same line in the same stilted tone.

Chase doesn't have time for this. He has only a scant forty-eight hours in the country with Victoria, away from the drones, away from the holo. He throws an extra set of socks into his bag and zips it up. "Don't touch anything while I'm gone."

He knows it's not sentient. He knows it's not Marybeth. Her body is in the drawers of her cubicle and her mind is in a drone. It still hurts when the holo locks itself in the bathroom and turns on the tap.

The doorbell rings. Victoria.

She locks eyes with the holo, who's just left the bathroom to face its replacement, then glances at Marybeth's sketches. The blood runs to Chase's ears, and before Victoria can ask any questions, he takes her bag and throws it over his shoulder with his own.

"It's a good likeness," Victoria says, but Chase doesn't ask if she means the holo or his charcoal image.

The path to the nearest transit station is littered with all the nervous people thronging the sidewalks, taking their daily constitutionals to nowhere. For the first time in ages, Chase feels no desire to look at the drone-flecked sky. It feels like freedom.

"After you," he says, dropping two chits into the turnstile.

The drones kept the light rail running, even after the Shift, so Chase and Victoria take it all the way to the end of the line. The burbland stretches out forever, its abandoned houses like diseased teeth in a gaping maw. Nobody can afford to live so far away from the lottery, except a handful of off-gridders testing the patience of the Employment Bureau. Chase had grown up in such a suburb, near a different city. He looks over at Victoria.

"What are you thinking about?"

"You. The ocean. I don't know." She yawns, and it turns into a smile.

Chase puts an arm around her. There's nothing more to say.

Brakes screech as the train pulls into the station. They'll have to walk the rest of the way to the sea. Chase helps boost the barefoot Victoria over a guardrail. His hands become slick with the watery blood from her heel. She must have scratched it somewhere.

I should have bought her new shoes with my extra chits, he thinks. *Too late now.*

"It doesn't hurt," she says, though he hasn't even asked her, and he knows she's lying.

"Not too much longer."

"I think I can hear the ocean from here." Another lie, but Chase can forgive it. He wants it to be true too. They walk down the stretch of highway hand in hand, and he feels only a small pang of guilt at that, a tiny knot that rests at the bottom of his chest.

When the heat makes the asphalt below them into a hot griddle, he and Victoria set up a picnic on the median strip. The not-cheese and ersatz crackers taste terrible, but they gobble them all down anyway.

"What was your husband like?"

She frowns. "A serious man. Lived for his work. He was an investment banker. No need for them after the Shift. I think a part of him died when it happened. Before, he didn't come home until ten most nights. Now he doesn't come home at all."

"Marybeth was the opposite. She loved her freedom, loved the drones for freeing her from something that was pointless. She was an artist." Chase shakes his head. "It should have been me."

"Don't say that." Victoria removes a strand of hair from Chase's eyes.

It's true, he thinks.

The sun is below the horizon when they finally make it to the coast. Chase scouts a rickety shack half-buried under the white sand. There's a mattress there, with not too many spiders on it, and the springs scream as they collapse onto the thin foam. Victoria falls asleep right away, but Chase lingers for a few minutes, enjoying the feel of her supple body against his.

Not a holo, he thinks. *Never a holo.*

They're playing in the ice-cold water when a drone passes by, but it's Sunday, so they don't have to worry. *Probably maintenance*, Chase thinks, *tidying up the beach that nobody ever visits.*

He's naked as a buzzard's head. So is Victoria, her clothes stacked neatly near a dune. Her feet are still raw and bleeding, but she claims the salinity of the ocean helps.

They're safe. But when the drone nears, they still hold their breath, waiting for it to pass by. It's a little one, no larger than a toaster, and it's heading straight for Victoria.

Please, Chase thinks, *no.*

The small maintenance drone reaches out two feelers and strokes her cheeks. It digs its claws into the brown rings of her hair. It beeps once, twice. Victoria trembles.

"Get away!" Chase yells. He splashes through the shallow water and thumps the drone on its side with his fist. "Go!" *Please.*

The drone turns. It whirs. It squares its glittering optical sensors with Chase's eyes, and within the glass bubbles of the sensors he can see a miniature version of himself staring back at him. He feels a moment of sickening recognition before the drone speeds away.

No. It can't be her. Chase shakes his head, letting the insane thought pass.

Victoria collects her clothes. "We should go. We'll be late."

They retrace their steps along the highway. Chase doesn't tell her what he saw, or what he *thinks* he saw. He doesn't say much at all.

When they finally get back to the station, the light rail is running a major delay. They're late for the draft.

*

Chase doesn't see Victoria the next day, or the day after that. Thursday is a storyteller day, so he goes to the abandoned strip mall. He knows there must be some grave consequence for skipping the draft, but it hasn't come up yet. Maybe it never will.

Or maybe it's happening now, he thinks.

"Gather round, friends," says the storyteller. "This is a story about a very brave, but very shortsighted leopard."

Victoria is nowhere in sight. He leans against the lumberjack's shin and lights up. Above his head, drones zip along, watching over all of them with foul intent disguised as loving grace.

The story is terrible, but he listens all the same.

THE SPECIES OF LEAST CONCERN

WE FIND THE FIRST ones in the lobby, talons extended as if trying to get underneath the door. A good two dozen of them, mostly sparrows. Tiny, dun-colored things.

Of course, it's my job to clean it up. I lay the dead sparrows to their rest in the dumpster around back of the building. Their beaks and eyes glitter like cut glass in huge fleshy shoals.

By the end of the week, it's like birds never existed. Pockets of absence soar about in the silent sky.

"As the current wave of devastating cryptogenic species loss enters its second week," says the newscaster, "scientists are scrambling for a cause, and a cure. Research at the—"

I turn the TV off and the sanitizer on. Its soothing thrum envelops me like a warm, heavy blanket. Without thinking, I squat on the tile floor and let the vibrations shake loose the aberrant electrical activity from my brain. Though I have a government-issued neural defibrillator, I don't dare bring the phallus-shaped thing to work. The frequency of the sanitizer is roughly the same as that of the device, and at least then nobody thinks I'm a nympho as well as a freak. My backbone tingles against the sanitizer, and I'm reminded that anything with a spine—including me—could be the next to die.

DCSL: waves of species loss affecting one taxon at a time. Scientists think it's a natural phenomenon, but they still haven't found a cause, so what do scientists know, really? Sometimes there are more than six months between extinction events and we think we're in the clear, but they always come back.

I hear thick-soled shoes thundering like a herd of animals that probably don't exist anymore and look up to find Steve, the project lead. I stand in a panic, pretending I'd just been on the floor to find a paperclip.

"Kimmy, what are you doing?" He sighs and turns away to the coffee machine. "No, forget it, I don't want to know."

"Um, ah . . . your mail is here." I grab one of the stacks on the cart and shove it at him.

"Fine." He takes it without looking, then shuffles off to wherever project managers go when they're not barking orders or rushing to meetings.

At Nature's Helpers, we're developing replacement animals—NuAnimals—to fill in the gaps left by the extinction events. We used to be an organic pharmaceutical company, but desperate times lead to different strategies, as Steve likes to say.

I grab the handles of the mail-cart and walk the halls, my own shoes squeaking.

First I stop at the lab, which is always a good start to the day. I hit the buzzer and am greeted at the Plexiglas door by an isolation-suited Dr. Chen, her face only slightly visible through the tinted viewscreen.

"Thank you, Kimmy."

"Can I see them?" Yesterday she let me look at the wriggly little red critters in their wire cage. The "universal ground-level small mammals," designed to fill the gaps left by the departure of *Rodentia* a year ago.

She shakes her head, massive in the suit. "I'm sorry, Kimmy, I don't have time right now. Maybe later."

I continue down the hall, passing out mail as I go. The scientific wing leads to the corporate wing, all fluorescent lighting and cheap paneled walls and people who smile so much it can't possibly be sincere.

"Kimmy, you left the dishes in the sink again," says the office manager with a loud sigh. "Oh, why do I even ask you to do these things, I should just do it myself."

"I had to catch the bus. I couldn't—"

"Whatever." She takes her mail from the cart before I can give it to her.

I edge past quietly. I have to remind myself that it's not her fault. Cats and dogs were the victims of the second extinction event, and she had a pair of poodles that she loved very much. More than her kids, if how much you love something can be judged by the size of the photographs on your desk.

The rain pounds on the pavement outside as we sit in rows in the company cafeteria. The TV is turned to a shopping channel, a rare station that isn't reporting on DCSL.

Like a group of high schoolers, we arrange ourselves in cliques. The corporate branch sits at one table, laughing and joking. The researchers are more subdued. They hunch over their trays, plastic forks in one hand, scientific journals in the other.

And then there's me, the one nobody wants to sit next to, because of my parents' role in the gene wars.

Under different circumstances, I could have sat at the scientists' table. I had four semesters of biology under my belt before the college asked me to leave. It was pointless to waste the education. Children of gene-war survivors don't have careers. We're supposed to consider ourselves lucky to be employed at all.

Dr. Chen comes into the room. There's still a space open at the scientists' table, but she sits across from me anyway.

"Dr. Chen?"

Her nose crinkles as she fumbles open a plastic container housing a processed concoction of soy, wheat germ, and protein analogues. The third wave of DCSL—poultry and cattle—has turned us working-folks into unwilling vegans.

She doesn't say anything.

"Dr. Chen, why are you here?"

She looks up. "You just say whatever's on your mind, don't you, Kimmy." She pitches the lid into the trash compactor at the end of the table. "Meet me in the lab at the end of the day. There's something I want to show you."

"But I have to take the bus down to the city," I say. "I'll miss it."

"You'll want to see this." She casts a last disparaging glance at the marketing team at the next table. "Trust me."

The suspense makes it hard to get through the rest of the day, but somehow, I do.

When five o'clock hits, I don't even bother filing the last of the papers. I shove them into an untidy stack in my desk drawer and speed-walk to Dr. Chen's lab.

Nobody is in the hall except a janitor, who furrows his brow at me and my excitement. I knock on the lab door.

"Look in the closet," squawks the intercom. Inside the cubby by the door rests a crinkly silver jumpsuit and a helmet that looks like a fishbowl. I zip myself inside.

"Dr. Chen? You wanted to see me?"

She's sitting at her desk, no helmet on. No gloves, either. A small glass of amber liquid rests at her elbow, and as my eyes alight on it, she quickly shoves it behind a mess of papers. There are papers *everywhere*, blanketing the desk and floors like a layer of fallen sparrows. My heart sinks.

"You want me to clean this up?" I start collecting papers, though it's hard to get a grip on them with the sausage-fingers of the suit. I glimpse terms barely remembered from my stint at Kansas State: ribosome, telomerase, GABA receptor.

"Put those down, Kimmy. I didn't bring you here to organize my crap for me."

I let the papers drift down. "Then why?"

Dr. Chen moves to the cages at the far side of the room and withdraws an animal. It looks like a cross between a squirrel and a lemur, except that it's bright pink, with a heart on its forehead. "Cuddle-bunny. Good for seeding trees. Can possibly also be used as a pet." She shakes her head. "Look at this thing."

I think it's kind of cute, but I don't say so. "Is there something wrong with it?"

"Other than the fact that it exists? Not really."

I finger the small pocket on the animal's side, where the advertising goes. "When's the release date?"

"Release date. Like they're new cell phones or something. It's supposed to be next month, to commemorate the third year of our fight against DCSL, blah blah blah." She makes a talky motion with her hand. "Call this a beta test. Take it home with you. It's yours."

I take the cuddle-bunny in my hands. I can't feel the texture of the fur through the gloves, but I imagine it feels like one of the yippy dogs I used to see in the park. "We're not allowed to have pets in the complexes."

"Then just take it out of here. Eat it if you're feeling adventurous. Just get it away from me."

"But Dr. Chen, this is your job."

"Yes, my job. Destroyer of worlds."

"What?"

"Never mind, girl, never mind."

*

I carry the cuddle-bunny home beneath the folds of my quilted jacket. The bus driver and other passengers don't notice the squirming or the bulge. Nobody really looks at anyone else on a bus, and especially nobody looks at *me*.

When the genetic bombs fell, the Midwestern farmers who were the target of the agricorps' wrath didn't feel their effects. But their children did. Chronic epileptiform absence seizures are one of the lightest sentences you can get as a child of gene-war survivors, and for that I am grateful. Neural defibrillation helps, but it's not perfect, and comes with side effects of its own.

When I get home, I make sure to lock the apartment door before putting the cuddle-bunny on my dresser. I can't afford to get kicked out of this place.

None of the NuAnimals look like the originals. They're all bright colors: electric green like the casing on a soy-patty meal, bright red like little furry fire hydrants. Dr. Chen once complained bitterly about this when I was in earshot. "They look like *toys*," she'd said, shaking her head.

We never had pets in the house when I was growing up. Like most survivors of the gene wars, my parents lived in the complexes, where pets weren't allowed. No animals, no outside visitors, because of the fear of contamination. Even after the bans were lifted, there were no pets and no visitors. Who'd want to bring an innocent life into the complexes? It's not even fit for a *mouse*, my mother said, though we had plenty of those.

"Shake hands," I say. The cuddle-bunny reaches out one tiny paw and puts it into my palm. The paw has a miniature heart on it too. I don't know why Dr. Chen has a problem with animals.

"Roll over." But either the cuddle-bunny doesn't know that trick or it's exercising some kind of free will. It gazes toward the window, where a bare branch taps against the glass.

"Do you want to go out?" I ask the cuddle-bunny. The round

head tilts, and I swear to God, those button eyes are twinkling. "Only if you come back, though," I say.

I open the window and the bright pink NuAnimal scampers over the windowsill and along the tree branch, to dangle like a trapeze artist before dropping to the ground. I crane my head out the window to track it, which is an easy task thanks to the neon coat. It rockets away like a bullet made out of frozen Pepto-Bismol.

We're all pretty excited at work, because it's Friday and most people have plans. I don't, and I don't think Dr. Chen does either, but we're both happier that way. Maybe. I hope that the cuddle-bunny comes back tonight. It wasn't there when I woke up.

I sort the mail, then stop in the kitchen for a cup of coffee. When I arrive I find the entrance blocked by Steve and one of his army of flunkies. I turn to leave, but I've already been spotted.

"Kimmy, meet Laurie Frazier. She just joined the team."

I smile at the new person, but I can feel the sides of my mouth twitching, and I know she sees it too. "Welcome to the company."

Laurie looks back at Steve. "Seriously?"

"Aw, come on, Laur, be nice."

"It's bad enough we have to support those hayseed farmers for whatever remains for their natural lives, but we have to keep their kids around, too?" She looks at me, frowns, and turns away.

As their footsteps recede, I lean over the metal sink. I fear the worst, that it's a fit coming on, which would just prove everything Laurie Frazier already thinks she knows about me.

But it's not. It passes.

I need to see Dr. Chen.

She's behind the triple-paned glass and the thick metal door, of course, and she has the beekeeper suit on. I start to slide her mail through the slot, but the doctor gestures to the compartment near the door.

Again? I put the suit on. When I go in, I see she's dissecting a NuAnimal with a long, tube-like body, its Technicolor organs splayed out on the metal tray like a string of Christmas lights.

"They're color-coded. That way it's easier to make repairs," she says.

"But where's the blood?"

"Do you think people like Steven Longwood would really want to see animals with blood and guts if they don't have to? Come on now, Kimmy. You may play dumb, but you know better than that."

I take the scissors from the set of tools at Dr. Chen's elbow and probe deeper into the NuAnimal's body. The bright red intestines would signify extreme inflammation in one of the old animals, and the sky-blue heart and circulatory system would point to a status of not exactly being alive. *But these aren't the animals you're used to,* as the company's glossies say. *They're better.* "What was wrong with it?"

"Starved to death," she replies, sighing. "I need to work on the alimentary system. Weasels aren't meant to live on soya kibble."

"Pretty cute for a weasel."

"That's what the genetics are based on." Dr. Chen runs her hand through her short, spiky hair. "Kimmy, what do you know about the gene wars?"

I blink. "More than you do."

"I doubt that. But that's not the point. I know from reading the personnel files that you majored in biology."

"Yes," I say, "but I didn't finish."

"Of course you didn't. Society likes to hide its mistakes. I want you to help me in the lab, kind of an assistant. I've been paying attention; you don't do anything important around here."

I grit my teeth, hoping that my disgust with Dr. Chen's sudden burst of bigotry doesn't show on my twitching face. She's right, though. My work is only slightly more important than whatever Steve does all day.

I think about working in the lab again, using those limited stores of biology knowledge. About what it would be like to have a *smart* person's job for once. "I'll do it."

"There'll be long hours. You won't get a raise."

"That's okay," I say, looking again at the splayed and pinned remains of the colorful NuAnimal. "I want to work with animals again. It's been a while."

The cuddle-bunny isn't in my apartment when I get back. It's probably dead. I'm going to have to tell Dr. Chen. Maybe I'll wait until she asks. I don't want to disappoint her.

The glow of the neon sign from the convenience store across the street casts a shadow over the mess on my coffee table. I should clean it up, I think, but it's not like anyone ever comes over. It seems like I spend most of my time at Nature's Helpers or on the bus or asleep, and I'll be spending even more time out when I start helping Dr. Chen in the lab.

I grab a box from the corner and begin throwing things into it. My hand halts when I reach the neural defibrillator. Not for the first time, I wish the manufacturer would have tried harder to make it look less like a vibrator.

I press the button on the side of the heavy, plastic government-issued device and prepare to administer pre-emptive neurotherapy. Suddenly, I hear the tapping of feet. I squint. "Is that you?"

On four heart-stamped paws, the cuddle-bunny advances toward me. Each pawprint leaves a small stain on the linoleum.

"Come here, little guy. Or girl." Dr. Chen said that NuAnimals don't have sexes. That's one of the things that seemed to upset her the most.

The cuddle-bunny hops over to me and drops something

into my hand. It's spongy like a soy-patty, and when I look closer, I can see that it's an ear.

All that weekend I keep the cuddle-bunny in an overturned hamper, and when I leave for work on Monday, I take it back in with me.

"Looks like a squirrel's ear." Dr. Chen takes the magnifying glass away from her eye. "Cornering the market."

"The market?"

"Kimmy, what if I told you that I don't think DCSL is natural? That it's like the gene wars, just a lot of corporations fighting against each other?"

I swallow hard. "I think I'd call you a liar. We've seen the bodies, they're all over the place . . ."

I'm so pissed my throat closes up.

"Maybe the extinctions weren't as severe as we all thought. Do you know just how many small mammals and birds there were in the world?"

"A lot?"

Dr. Chen places the ear into a vial and turns to the cuddle-bunny I brought to work this morning. Its pink pelt is still bloody. "There should have been more. I keep coming back to that. This is so . . . controlled."

I think back to what my parents said about the gene wars, in those rare times I was able to get them to talk. It all started with rival agricorps trying to out-compete one another. Clouds of nanomachines capable of rewriting plant DNA were set off in fields all throughout the Midwest. The riots came later, sparked by people living too close to the fields who found their ability to farm their own crops limited by the new trademarked genes. "But why wild animals? It makes no sense."

"Oh, it makes perfect sense." The doctor flicks the syringe and before I can stop her, she's slid it into the cuddle-bunny's belly. The NuAnimal expires with the tiniest of death rattles. "Hand me that scalpel, will you?"

I place it in her hand. "You didn't have to kill it."

"You can't kill something that isn't alive." She splits the cuddle-bunny in half, revealing the circus-colored organs.

But it *was* alive. It moved, it thought. Maybe.

I wonder if Dr. Chen doesn't think they're alive because they can't reproduce. I wonder if she knows I can't reproduce either.

One by one, Dr. Chen levers the bright organs out of the body cavity, placing them on a silver tray at the side. "There's a lot of spots in the food chain. If Nature's Helpers can fill those gaps with their mass-produced cloned 'animals' that, just coincidentally, can't breed on their own and you also have to pay for them, we can hold the world hostage with a major bargaining chip. Pay us for the right to keep the world's ecosystem running. That's planned ecology on a *major* scale, Kimmy."

"But the corporations live in the world, too. We can't exactly refuse to let the animals loose."

Dr. Chen pushes away the tray. "A corporation is just an idea. It can live anywhere. In a computer, in a notebook. In a single person living in a suborbital station. The rest of the world can get bent as far as a corporation is concerned." She looks at me. "You of all people should know this."

My parents sold the farm when I was only a child, knowing the time of human cultivation was at an end. They took their payment from the agricorps and cut their losses. I don't feel any pull from that land, from the place I should have called home.

I shake my head. "No. It doesn't make any sense."

"I hope you're right, Kimmy. I really do."

Dr. Chen bolts right after the dissection, leaving me to clean up. She isn't at lunch either. I sit alone at my usual table.

Across the room, Steve the project lead laughs at something with the new woman, Frazier. Small bits of soy fly from his mouth as he whips his arms around. I look down at my own tray of pap, wondering what's so hilarious.

Destroyer of worlds, she'd said, as if proud or at least resigned.

I can't take it anymore. I need to find Dr. Chen. I slide the untouched meal into the recycler and slip out to the parking lot. Let them deduct my pay. Let them fire me.

I find her in the patch of brush near the front gates of Nature's Helpers. She's crouching, quiet, as if awaiting the results of an experiment. I wish my feet weren't so loud on the asphalt.

"Dr. Chen?"

She looks up. Behind her glasses, her eyes are as big as planets waiting to be discovered. She's holding something pale and green in her hands. "Look, Kimmy."

I peer into her hands. It's a NuAnimal, designed to look like a—what were they called? A salamander. Only this one has blue feet and the crimson burst of an unfamiliar logo on its side and eyes that look like they belong to a cartoon character. It has long fangs that could probably nip off a pinky.

I say, "I've never seen this kind before."

"It's not ours. This is the VivaCor logo."

"Awfully long fangs for a salamander."

She drops the salamander, and it lands in the puddle with a splash before making a break through the front gate. "That's because it's a *weapon*. Our methods are a little more subtle, but don't worry, we're—what does Steve say?—'amping them up for the global market.'"

"If you really believe this, then you should tell someone." I still think Dr. Chen is nuts, though her ideas are starting to piece themselves together.

"Who would we tell, Kimmy? They control *everything*. They control *me*, they control *you*." She grabs me by the shoulders and shakes me until I feel my teeth rattle and I begin to see sparks. "*Damn*, you're naïve."

I want to reply but it's like my mouth is full of wool and I close my eyes to collect my thoughts, which sometimes works. But when I open them she's gone and I have a headache and I'm not surprised.

Two days pass and Dr. Chen doesn't come back. I sit alone in the lab, passing the bright NuAnimals between my hands. Sometimes they bite me, leaving small welts that puff up in the sun.

Steve finds me nestled in the corner, near the refrigeration unit. I'd felt a seizure coming on and had to get close to it. But I can't explain it very well, and especially not to him. With a frown, he herds me into his office and shuts the door.

"What were you doing, Kimmy? Is that some kind of *sex* thing?" He says it with a smirk.

I shake my head. "No."

"Margie took a lot of information with her when she went on her . . . unannounced sabbatical. I was hoping you'd know where to find her. We need to get that stuff back, Kimmy." He says my first name a lot when he speaks to me, like he thinks he'll forget it if he doesn't say it over and over.

"I don't know where she is."

"But you'd tell us if you did, right?"

I look him in the eye. "No."

He blows air out through his nose and leans back in his chair. "I can't fire you, but that doesn't mean I have to like you. Get your things and put them back in the mailroom." He's clearly enjoying this. "Freak."

Silently, I walk back to the lab and collect my few belongings: my jacket, a book, my sunglasses. A new scientist from the head office in Topeka is there already. I shake her hand and say hello. With my other hand, I stuff a pocketful of slides into my jacket.

I'm packing my life away, stripping it down to what's really important, in case I can't come back. Under a tangle of clothing in my battered cardboard suitcase are the slides, fourteen cross-sections of NuAnimal tissue that might just prove that Nature's Helpers, and other corporations like it, are responsible for DCSL. In a smaller valise, I've packed the neural defibrillator. I pray it's not confiscated by airport security.

I stay up all night, fearful of what's ahead. I've never even been out of Kansas, and I'm worried about what the future will bring. There are so many things that *might* happen, and I almost feel like I should call the whole thing off right now.

But there are the animals to think about. The *real* ones that could still be saved.

When I get down to the bus stop in the morning, she's waiting for me, swaddled in a black caftan, and I know I'm not going to make it to the airport after all.

"Dr. Chen?" I ask, even though I know it's her.

"Oh, call me Margie. You *do* know my first name, right?"

I realize that I hadn't, not until Steve said it when we were in his office. "I got some evidence. I'm going to the press."

She throws her head back and laughs. She reminds me uncomfortably of Steve. "Oh, Kimmy, you really are a riot. So you're going to go on *Good Morning America*, tell them you know who's causing all the extinctions? With all those mixed-up genes in your head? Oh, Kimmy, no."

I grip the suitcase tighter. "It was a thought."

"Girl, they're *all* in on it. Once all the animals are dead or in hiding, who do you think is going to be there waiting in the wings to save us? Nature's Helpers, and OrganiLife, and all the rest. With our copyrighted vat-grown animals, who are just *per-*

fect for the job, because it's a vacancy we helped create. And one I've helped to fill."

I turn away from her, afraid that she'll steal my bag with all the evidence in it.

"We can stop it. The animals can't reproduce."

"We can always make more," she says, laughing again like it's the biggest joke in the world. "The company's resources are larger than you could ever imagine."

The bus pulls up, but I don't walk forward to get on and neither does Margie. We stand for a while in the warm summer wind. Finally, I speak. "Why did you ask me?"

"Huh?"

"Ask me to be your assistant. When you knew what you were doing, and knew you weren't going to tell me anything about it. Until it was too late."

"Because I wanted to study *you*, Kimmy. I wanted to see for myself if you were capable of more than handing out mail and fetching coffees. You passed, more or less. Plus, I needed the company. I was hoping you might keep me from snapping. Instead, you reminded me I'm just as horrible as the company."

"*Thanks*," I reply. "Well, since you say the plan is meaningless, I guess I'll just go to work. The least you could do is give me a ride."

"Back to Nature's Helpers? You're going to sell out like that?"

"At least I still *have* a job."

She grunts. "Come on, take the day off. Remember, I read your personnel file, I know you have the days." She gestures toward the diner at the corner. "I'll buy you a soy-patty."

I look at the bus stop, then back at Margie. "Okay."

But I keep one hand on the suitcase, and I don't let go, not even much later when we say our goodbyes. Somewhere out there is a person who isn't as scared of the world as I am, and they're going to need this.

THIRTY-SIX INTERROGATORIES PROPOUNDED BY THE HUMAN-POWERED PLASMA BOMB IN THE MOMENTS BEFORE HER IMMINENT DETONATION

1. **WHEN YOU LIFTED MY** body into the belly of the great gray ship, did you know I was sentient?

2. Did you know that I felt pain?

3. Were you aware that my species is a vain one, and that such alterations as you placed upon my body were abhorrent to me?

4. Did you realize that, as a general rule, humans do not communicate instantaneously through the mind-web, as you do?

5. Would that knowledge have played any factor in your decision to destroy our communications network?

6. Were you aware that such actions would lead to war?

7. Was it always your plan to use mind-web capabilities to simultaneously sever the frontal lobes of seven billion humans in order to prevent a total war you would have won anyway, or

did you come up with that plan on the spot?

8. Why did you spare me?

9. Does your navigation system require higher thought to function, and if so, is that why you spared me?

10. Where are we going?

11. I don't have a driver's license. Do you trust me to navigate this ship?

12. Are you cognizant that, even in my current physical form, I need food and water to survive?

13. This isn't water. Do you know what water is?

14. When I was taken into the hatch, did you then understand why it was that I screamed so loud, why I tried to slash my wrists on the edge of the console panel, why my consciousness ceased until the instant you took me out of the restorer?

15. Is pain transmissible by mind-web technology?

16. Will such horrors as were visited upon my people by your people be replicated at our destination, and if so, can I kindly ask you to reconsider?

17. That isn't water, either. Would you like me to supply you with the correct chemical formula?

18. In my turret there is a thick brown residue laced with hard shell-like protrusions. Am I correct in believing that these are the remains of my predecessor?

19. Does space look as black to those of you in the mind-web as it does to me?

20. When I was a child, I feared enclosed spaces like the one in which I am currently shuttered. On such times when I was forcibly enclosed in the hall closet by my alcoholic mother and her junkie boyfriend, my only solace was a scrap of my childhood blanket, Coco, which I continued to carry with me throughout my adult life, until it was obliterated by your energy rays. Can you use mind-web technology to recreate this precious object for me?

21. Do you age in the mind-web?

22. Does time pass at all in the mind-web?

23. The instruments on my panel show that we are traveling in excess of four hundred thousand kilometers per second. Can this possibly be correct?

24. Do you intend for this body to be disposable, considering that it has no orifices, only a rudimentary set of sense organs, and a heart analogue that is beating so fast that it will lead to total system collapse in only a few hours?

25. Is my only role aboard this ship that of navigator?

26. Again going back to memories from my childhood, I often felt the presence of dreadful ghosts, horrible abominations of nature that no amount of counseling as an adult could resolve. Is it possible that these phenomena were an early form of communication with the mind-web?

27. Can you direct your servo-mechanisms to drip the water substitute directly onto my skin?

28. My control panel shows a red dot, getting larger all the time. Is this a destination of some sort?

29. Is it a target?

30. Do you believe that we as human beings, or alternatively, as exalted states within the mind-web, ever really know the destruction we're capable of?

31. Do I personally know the destruction I'm capable of?

32. Will they suffer as my race suffered?

33. I notice a fuzzy sensation on what passes for a cheek in my restored body. Coco?

34. We are slowing down. The lights are turning on. The red dot on my control panel has become a red screen eclipsing my entire field of vision. Does this mean what I think it does?

35. Can there be such a thing as evil without malice, forethought, or intent?

36. Is this going to hurt?

A SLOW, CONSTANT PATH

"**MEOW,**" **SAID THE SYNTHETIC** cat to the girl in the cryogenic tank, sixty billion miles from Earth.

The console near the tank switched on. *Good kitty.*

"Are you ready to come out of there?"

The girl paused, but the cat found it impossible to tell if she was considering it, or if it was simply a technological lag. *Not yet. Let me sleep.*

"Then sleep you shall, my pet," the cat lied. The girl would wake on schedule, four days from now, to the grind of a hacksaw on her limbs and the weight of liquid metal in her throat, as she was reshaped, remade, into something Ship could use. The cat had done this many times before. It got easier every time.

The cats were the constants, and without them, the whole structure of the *Lady May* would fall in on itself like a house of cards.

Constant Marcus Eberling woke from a much-needed afternoon nap on his favorite ledge. He chanced a look out the porthole, into the inky-black depths of deep space. A growl issued from his electronic larynx as he thought about how many more miles they'd have to travel, how many more years the journey.

This isn't how I thought I'd spend my life.

Take an outcast genius human mind, scratch it onto a silicon wafer, and implant it into a manufactured body, and you have a constant. Their task was to keep the colonists grounded. Keep them sane. Keep them *human*, as the colonists embarked on their slow-path journey to the habitable planet of Endpoint. Without constants, who knew what kind of person would come tumbling out of a generation ship after a thousand years? Cultural orphans, the researchers said. People totally unfit to live in an Earth-type society.

Monsters.

At first, it was assumed that the constants would be androids in the shape of humans, until the researchers had discovered one uncomfortable truth: humans don't trust other humans.

But they *would* trust animals. Cats, in particular, made excellent confidantes. Synthetic organs and plastiskin were molded into feline form, and the human minds were pressed inside, like seeds in freshly turned soil.

Everything would have turned out just fine if the ansible hadn't broken.

Ship named her Martha. She woke to the soft licks of a kitty on her face. Martha thought at the time that it was a sign of love. Only later would she learn that the cat was trying to clear her eyes and sinuses of the sticky-sweet albumen that flowed in Ship's veins.

Martha was not a pretty girl. She was a worker meant for wrenching, whose long, multi-jointed limbs could reach deep into the very heart of Ship. She ate recycled waste for breakfast and slept in her old cracked cryotank at night, and she never, ever misbehaved.

Until that one day.

Constant Eberling arched his back and leaped to the port-hole where Constant Kenji Nakama sat gazing out, tail curled around his chubby tabby body.

"Do you ever think," Nakama said, "about the people back home? Do you think they miss us?"

Eberling grunted, a hiss of feedback whining through the voicebox lodged in his throat. "No. Of course not."

"I bet they do. They wouldn't have spent all that money building these ships if they didn't care. If they didn't want us to succeed."

Eberling tried in vain to roll his immobile mechanical eyes as he washed his face with the side of his paw. Not for the first time, he wondered if the people back home had made a mistake in selecting Nakama for the mission. He still had too much of the man in him, too much of the dreamer. "For all we know, Earth's dead. They were at war before the ship even launched." He began to lick the fur on his chest. Rough, angry strokes of the tongue. "Stop thinking about it."

"I *can't*," Nakama said. "What if they've been trying to contact us this whole time?"

Eberling didn't understand how a man ported into an immortal cat and sent to wander the stars could waste so much time thinking about Earth. "They haven't. You used to monitor the ansible, you know that."

"But—"

"Stop talking about it. Go play with the monsters if you're looking for something to do. And for God's sake, man, clean yourself every once in a while. You look like an alleycat."

Eberling hopped down, alighting on the cold steel of Ship's

corridors, and sauntered to the tankroom to take readings. *At least someone's doing some work around here.*

Martha loved Ship, even when it hurt her.

"*Ow*," she said, disentangling her arm from a cooling vent. She snaked her hand back up. *This is bad.*

Martha surveyed the damage. Ship had taken three fingers from her, and cut open an inch-deep wound between her second and third elbows. Rosewater blood pattered on the metal floor as the pain blockers kicked in. Martha folded her arm to her side like an accordion and made for the infirmary.

The corridor was busy at this time of the shift. Above Martha's head, girls with large suction cups grafted to the lower half of their bodies clung to the ceiling, making their endless adjustments to Ship's lighting. The fatty tang of freshly processed food tickled her nose. At her feet, a white cat ran past, its puffy tail swishing.

"Hey!" she said. "Here, kitty." *I need help*, she thought.

The cats were usually around when you needed one. Sometimes you just wanted a friendly face to talk to, or a warm fuzzy body in your lap. She'd even asked Nakama, her favorite, to sleep in her tank with her one shift-end. He'd agreed to it, and that night she'd unexpectedly dreamed of a place like an inverted Ship, with anodyne green corridors as wide as the eyes on either side of Martha's head could see. It hadn't been a nice dream. The thought of so much space gave Martha the crawling creepies, and it had taken a good cry into Nakama's soft brown fur to rid her of the nightmare.

Forget walking. Martha unfolded her good left arm and hoisted herself to the rafters, swinging her way toward the infirmary. One of Martha's feet glanced off a sucker-girl's shoulder, sending the girl's lightbulb to the floor with the tinkle of broken glass.

"Sorry," she said, though she really wasn't.

At last she reached the infirmary. She swung wide to clear the door, then felt a smack against her feet. The door was closed, sealed up with Ship's soft metal skin, only a ragged scar to mark the passageway.

Locked out.

Above Eberling's head, the *Lady May* groaned like a settling mansion. The ship's death rattles had been sounding more frequently as of late.

Damn humans, he thought, remembering the revolt. When the ansible broke, not even the attention of their constant companions could keep the humans from rioting, despondent at being cut off forever from home. Within two weeks, they'd rendered much of the ship's functions inoperable.

It had been Eberling who'd saved the ship. In a safe room in the bowels of the *Lady May*, he'd led a faction of constants who'd devised a way to deal with the colonists.

"All that matters," he'd said all those years ago, "is that humanity gets to Endpoint. Right? And we have all these frozen embryos on board." His external larynx had almost shorted out with excitement.

Even Nakama had to admit that it was true.

"So we don't let them breed anymore. Don't let them have families. The embryos will make it to Endpoint. We just have to hang on until then."

"Have you seen the ship, Eberling?" said a constant, his or her identity lost to the sands of time. "It's not going to last even five years."

"We'll get them to fix it," he'd said. "The *humans*. It's their fault we're in this mess, anyway." It was the first time Eberling had thought of himself as anything but a human being, and the slip had infused him with an odd feeling of *power*.

Amid the heat of the flames and the rumble of the floors,

they'd narrowly voted on a plan to kill all the men in their tanks as they slept. The women's minds were wiped clean, and their bodies were forged into machines made to serve the *Lady May*, patching her together until the eventual touch-down on Endpoint.

Nakama hadn't spoken to Eberling for a century afterwards. That had been another benefit of the vote.

Alighting to the corridor, Eberling made an inventory of the vacant schoolrooms. No use training the monsters for colonization now. *They'd* never step onto Endpoint.

Suddenly, a warning bell sounded. With the ship's damaged voice, it sounded more like the call of a dying bird than a siren.

What is it this time? He trundled down the corridors, feeling the weight of eons with every step.

With the seven fingers of her left hand and the remaining four of her right, Martha clawed at the sealed aperture of Ship's walls. The needle-like bits on her fingers were sharp as cats' claws, but they couldn't break the thick Ship skin. She'd bleed before Ship did.

Not that she wanted Ship to bleed, not ever. Somewhere deep in her mind she knew that Ship must never be harmed, not any more than it had already been.

Right now, though, a part of her felt like she could destroy Ship if it got her into the infirmary. "Let me in!"

Ship remained silent as a wound.

"I said *open*," Martha repeated, before adding a plaintive "please."

Martha felt a furry brush against the back of her legs that could only be a kitty. She spotted three of them: Norris, the big longhair whose name she could never remember, and Eberling. The one who didn't like her.

"Kitty?" Martha followed the parade of cats down the corridor, letting her lame arm drag on the metal floor behind her. "Kitty?"

The cats disappeared in a flurry of tails. Martha knew before reaching the door that this room was not for her. She didn't even bother asking this one to open up.

A spray of glass exploded at her feet and she looked up. Above her, a sucker-girl cackled.

Some help you are, Martha thought, as she plumbed further down the corridor.

As the constants assembled in the communications room, Eberling once again noticed how easily this exile fit most of them. Everyone in this room had something that had set him or her apart from Earth society. Everyone had a reason to want to leave. Even Nakama.

Once, when the ansible still worked, the constants used this room to talk to the homeworld. Now, though, it was a simple meeting room. None of the monsters were ever allowed in here.

Eberling leaped to a perch where he could watch the others. Rumors traveled by whisper, from one hyper-acute ear to another.

"—*finally dying*—"

"—*never get to Endpoint*—"

"—*well, I heard it doesn't even exist*—"

"—*those poor girls*—" That would be Nakama.

One of the constants, a stout bossy Persian, called for attention. "Fellow constants, I know that you have all been aware of certain problems we've recently encountered on the mission. Without a major overhaul, I'm afraid that the lifespan of the *Lady May* might be no longer than fifty years."

Eberling paused in his grooming. "What's going to happen to us?" he said, loud enough for the constants in his general vicinity to look up.

The Persian ignored him. "This means one of two things. Either we shut down the mission, and accept that human beings might never make a go of it on another world. Or we must manufacture more workers, of more specialties. This, of course, could lead to destabilization, with which we are *all* familiar." A chorus of nods and meows erupted from the group.

Eberling was stunned. "We need to keep going! I can't believe you'd seriously think about stopping the mission. What a disgrace to humanity." *And what a threat to myself,* he thought.

Already, Nakama was winding his way through the crowd to the Persian's perch. The fur along Eberling's spine bristled.

The blood had finally stopped gushing from Martha's arm and finger stumps, and the pain had also subsided. As she pushed through the doors of the tankroom, she heard a ghostly noise overhead, like a sigh.

Martha banged on the cracked tanks with her good hand, trying to wake the other girls. At any moment, only a little under one-fifth of the girls were awake. She'd asked Nakama about that once.

"It's because Ship doesn't need you all the time. It wants you to rest, have good dreams. Don't you like to dream, Martha?"

"But if we were all awake, all the time, then Ship could be really, really healthy."

"Then you'd wear out, and there would be no more girls! That would be a terrible thing, pet."

"Why are we here, kitty?"

Nakama never answered that question.

Martha heard the muffled unlatching of a tank, and watched as a cleaner-girl she barely knew slid across the floor toward her. "Oh, why did you *wake* me?"

"It's Ship. She's sick."

"Ship's always sick." The cleaner turned around.

"Not like this." Martha held out her ruined hand. "I couldn't get into the infirmary. None of the kitties will talk to me."

The girl's eyes opened wide on the last part. "Really?"

"Come on, help me wake everyone up. Everyone who's supposed to be awake right now." She paused. "And everyone who's not."

The girls went down the line of tanks, tapping on each one with their screwdriver fingers and steel wool palms. Lights came on overhead as Ship's feeble security system activated.

So much work to be done, Martha thought.

Eberling looked on with disgust as a trembling Nakama padded to the bank of computers near the front of the room. The tabby yowled to get the attention of the other constants, who looked up at him with barely controlled loathing.

"I think . . . I think the mission should end."

He'll kill us, Eberling thought.

Nobody was taking heed of Nakama's words, but he plunged ahead anyway. "We should have done this six hundred years ago. What we did to those girls was *wrong*. Humans should never have gone to the stars. Let's just put all the girls to sleep and disconnect their feeding tubes. It's the best way."

"And *us*?" Eberling barged toward the front of the room; the other constants parted to let him past. "We can't fix the ship. You're going to just let us be sucked out into *space*? That's going to be a hell of a lot more painful than starving in our sleep."

"We shouldn't be here," Nakama repeated. At that, he was greeted by a chorus of hisses from the audience.

"That's not your call," said a black cat seated near the porthole. Two constants slunk forward through the shadows, one's hindquarters bouncing from side to side as it readied itself to strike. Eberling felt a hint of a gloat forming, but even he couldn't let Nakama be torn to shreds, his wafer of silicon pulverized. Nobody deserved that.

"Friends," he said with undisguised irony, "let's not jump on him. Just ignore him. We can fix the ship if we just breed more monsters."

But the constants were focused. They leaped at Nakama, acting more animal than ever before. Yowls echoed the room as the constants swiped at one another, each hoping to carve out a slice of the friendly tabby that all the monsters loved best. Eberling's pulse quickened as he watched. He felt a quiver in his paw as the feline part of him took over, and batted at the nearest constant, claws at full extension.

If he could have, he would have smiled.

The fight ended quickly. The constants milled around the edge of the room, licking their rapidly-healing wounds, briefly hissing at one another. Nakama was nowhere to be seen.

"He got away," the black cat said.

"Obviously," said Eberling. His whiskers twitched. *Idiot.*

Martha and the cleaner-girl had opened almost all of the tanks when Nakama came into the room. She nearly couldn't see the chubby tabby through the cluster of groggy girls. Martha sloshed through the puddles of albumen left when the girls shook out their specialized limbs, some only half-formed.

"Nakama!" she said. "Come here, help me wake them up. Ship needs us!" Her smile fell when she saw the ripped left half of the cat's face. Small metal bits gleamed in the light of the fluorescent overheads, so like the viscera right underneath the skin of Ship.

She expected Nakama to run into her arms and lick her clean. But instead the cat advanced with an expression as close as a feline face can get to horror. "What have you *done*, Martha?"

"Ship is sick. She hurt me. So I'm waking everyone up. If we're all helping, then she *has* to get better!" *And I can get new fingers*, she thought selfishly.

Nakama leapt at her. With a snarl, he pulled at her hair, gouged her cheeks with his dagger-sharp claws. Martha couldn't understand. None of the cats, not even that old meanie Eberling, would ever attack a girl. Was he sick too?

The others stared, mute, as Nakama tore into Martha. Finally, the cleaner-girl pulled Nakama from Martha's face and held him to her chest, squirming. "Naughty kitty!"

"Why?" Martha groped at her face, feeling the slick of blood on her cheek. The pain blockers and clotting agents flowed into her, but she was left with a hot stone in her stomach that her Ship-born body couldn't cancel out. "You hurt me." Tears streaked her face, blending with the pinkish blood.

Nakama went limp. The voice box in his throat made his voice come out all distorted and fuzzy. "All of you need to get back in your tanks at once. That's my good girls."

Many of the girls immediately went back and attempted to seal themselves up. Martha had to force herself to stay. "*Why*, Nakama? Why do we have to sleep? Why can't we work, make everything better?"

"You just can't, that's why. You must do as you're told." He tried to soften his voice. "You'll have good dreams, I promise."

Martha exchanged glances with the cleaner. "What do you think?"

"I think he's been a bad cat, and we shouldn't listen to him."

Martha sighed. "Then let's go." The cleaner set down the defeated Nakama and signaled to the other girls. Most of them were back in their tanks or still too bleary to pay attention, but a good three dozen seemed ready and eager to do what they needed to do to help Ship.

It was enough. More than enough. Martha led the way.

The constants, perhaps due to a little bleed-through from

the feline subroutines imprinted in their synthetic bodies, didn't tend to focus on things for very long. They scattered, some returning to their usual perches and lofts about the ship. Eberling, too, trundled toward his familiar hiding place on the ledge, facing away from space. Always away.

The ledge faced the tankroom, so he was the first to see the parade of monsters, led by a grotesque with telescoping arms ending in metal bits.

Loathsome, he thought. He sauntered up to the lead monster, her face inexplicably covered in watery blood.

"What are you doing, dear?" he said, as sweetly as he could manage.

He expected the creature to squeal over him, or to forget what she was going to say and wander off. Instead, the wrencher stared at him with a tenacity he hadn't seen on any human face in six hundred years.

"Ship is sick. She won't help us." She held up her left hand, from which half of the modified fingers were missing. "Even Nakama won't help us. He wanted us to go back to sleep." The monster narrowed her eyes. "I don't think *you'll* help us."

"But, pet," Eberling said, forcing the sobriquet through his voice box like it was a curse, "you know not to disobey."

The monster near the mangled wrencher was even uglier. She extruded a line of slime where she went, dragging her lower body by two small arms near her hips. Eberling shuddered. "Nakama attacked her. He's a bad kitty." Several of the others nodded their malformed heads.

If Eberling had eyebrows anymore, they would have raised at that. Nakama loved the monsters, as much as one could. "I'm sure he had a reason."

"No, he didn't!"

"And where is he now?"

The monsters looked around guiltily. Finally, one in the middle of the pack said, "He's in a tank!"

"All right," Eberling said. "Let's go get him out. Maybe he can convince you not to be such disobedient girls."

"No," the long-armed monster said. "We don't need him for this. I want to know why we can't help Ship. I want to know why you don't *want* to let us help Ship. I think you're lying to us. And they're going to help me, even if you won't." She waved her ruined hand at the collected monsters.

Eberling considered. Had the conditioning been broken? Were the humans beginning to remember?

This monster-girl had no concept of what Endpoint was, no notion of her history. She couldn't even know that she and Eberling were, technically, part of the same species. Not unless Eberling told her. Information was power, and where there was power, there were uprisings. Dead humans. Even more importantly, dead constants.

But they were all dying *anyway.*

Eberling grunted and quietly conferred with a clowder of constants that had gathered nearby to watch. "Come into this room," he said, gesturing. "Just you two. Everyone else, please be quiet. We're going to help Ship."

Martha stretched to reach the last few screws within the folds of Ship's skin. *Got it.*

High above her, a sucker-girl walked on Ship's ceiling, gingerly protecting the precious fluorescent bulbs in her apron. Martha telescoped a hand to take a few from her. They couldn't afford to waste any. Not now that they knew the supplies weren't just put there by the magic of Ship.

Sixty-seven Ship-days had passed since the meeting with Eberling and the other constants, and Martha still wasn't sure if she'd recovered from the things they'd discussed. So much of it was still strange to her, but the constants said acceptance would come in time.

I wish I had a kitty, Martha said. The constants could never be cats to her again, now that she knew what they really were. Not even Nakama, who chose to spend most of his time in stasis now, his silicon wafer dreaming.

In the navigation room, Becky the cleaner pored over the restored monitors. Endpoint now shone like a beacon. Someday, humans would walk on that planet. They wouldn't look like Becky and Martha, and Martha thought they'd quite frankly be a little ugly. But that was what their ancestors had wanted.

"Look at this," Becky said. She pointed Martha to a small silver console in the corner of the room, a large cone sticking from its side. "A bunch of us tinkered with it earlier. I think it might be working."

"But what is it?" Martha said.

"Constant Eberling called it an ansible. He said it was used for talking to Earth."

"Earth?" Earth was dead; everyone who had the knowledge knew that.

"It's broken. But listen. You can kind of hear something."

Martha leaned down to the ansible and pressed the silver cone against the side of her head. She listened. In a strange dialect she could hear a repeated message. It was faint and staticky but intelligible.

"This is Central Control, sending out from São Paulo . . . if you hear this know . . . have always been . . . stay strong, do not . . . This is Central . . ."

"A lot of junk," Martha said, pulling her ear away from the silver machine. "But we'll keep working on it."

SASQUATCH SUMMER

THAT WAS THE SUMMER the sasquatches came down from Mount Hood and put Papa out of a job.

It wasn't their fault, not really. Sasquatches don't need tools to work. When a sasquatch wants to tear down a tree, he doesn't use an axe. He grips each side with his leathery hands and just *pulls* until the earth decides to let that tree go. When a tree falls on a sasquatch, the company doesn't have to pay his family any compensation like they did to Jimmy's family. That creature just rolls out from under the tree and keeps on walking.

Of course, most folks didn't see it like that.

"Damn apes," Papa said. He threw a beer bottle across the room and pointed to me. "Clean it up, Helen."

I could have told him that the sasquatches aren't apes. Not even the college types from Portland know what they are, because nobody's ever been able to get close enough to study them. The last time I said something like that, though, I didn't get to go to school for two weeks.

"Yes, Papa."

"And get me another beer."

I fished another bottle from the icebox. All Papa did any-more was drink. "We're out of bread."

He shrugged, and tossed his head back. The beer flowed down his throat like a river. "Maybe your *Ma* can send you some food."

"Very funny," I said, sighing.

When Papa and my brothers were safely tucked in under the ratty Indian blanket that covered our single bed—one of the few things Papa wasn't able to sell for beer—I snuck out to the woods behind our shack. The rain pattered in my hair and down my face. No use wiping it off, it just comes back.

And that's when I saw the sasquatch.

Shivers ran down my spine all the way to my heavy socks, and I ducked behind the nearest tree for safety. It wasn't the first time I'd been this close to a sasquatch, but I was all alone, and it was so dark.

He was down on all fours lapping rainwater from a pond, his slick black fur glinting in the weak moonlight. As I edged closer, I could feel a strange energy move through my body like the ten-sion in the air before a rainstorm. The hair on my arms stood on end, and yet I moved closer. The creature didn't shy away.

I looked back at the shack. The low rumble of Papa's snores pounded through the thin planks.

Come closer, said a voice that seemed to emanate from all around, or maybe from inside me.

"Papa?" But then I realized it was coming from the sas-quatch. He stared right at me, standing at full height on those tree-trunk legs, looking like a cross between a bear, an ape, and a man.

Closer, he repeated.

I felt a pull toward the sasquatch. I didn't want to turn away from him, but I had to. I couldn't leave Papa and my brothers alone, not yet.

"Later," I said. "I promise." And I swear, it was like that sas-quatch understood me.

*

I can't talk about the sasquatches without also talking about the union men.

I saw the first one—a union *woman*—in the square in front of the courthouse. She was dressed in bloomers and her hair was cut short, like a boy. She held a broadsheet in one hand and a hammer in the other.

"You can't do that," I said. "That tree belongs to the company."

"Trees belong to the *people*," the union woman said. She gave the hammer a few good whacks, then stepped back to admire her handiwork.

I squinted at the mimeographed paper. "Sasquatches don't know what unions are." I barely knew what a union was, only that I'd heard some of my dad's friends talk about forming one before the company let them all go.

The union woman shook her head. "Savages." I wasn't sure if she was talking about the sasquatches or the townsfolk.

I scuffed the ground with the tip of my boot. It hadn't rained in a few days, and the ground had returned to dry scrub. "Do you want to meet a sasquatch?"

She pointed at the sign. "We're calling for a town meeting at the end of the month. *All* are invited, man and sasquatch both."

"They're not going to come to a meeting in town. They live in the woods. And work in the woods."

She snorted. "You mean they're subjugated by the company in the woods."

I crossed my arms. "Whatever you say."

The union woman reached into her bag and pulled out one of the broadsheets. "Tell your little friends. We want a big showing. We won't let the company exploit these marginalized workers any longer!"

That was the first organizer I met, but she wasn't the last. Over the next couple of weeks, they piled out of the passenger

trains by the dozen. The courthouse square swarmed with Easterners handing out pamphlets and standing on soapboxes.

The organizers got offended if you called the sasquatches
animals, even though that's what they were. They called them
the "undermen," and they called the company a "ruthless force
monopolizing the forces of nature for their own sadistic ends."
I had to look up some of those words in the big leather-bound
dictionary in the schoolhouse.

At least the newcomers smelled better than the sasquatches.
Mostly.

What does a sasquatch smell like? He smells a little like a
dog dipped in beer left out in the rain.

We'd gotten used to the stench, but it sure bothered the
folks from back East. They'd tied handkerchiefs around their
noses and mouths, but that doesn't do anything to mask the
smell, not really. I wonder if they would have come here if they
knew in advance how bad sasquatches stink.

"I thought they were like people," said a man from New
York who'd taken up a soapbox near the school. "Like Indians."

"Indians don't smell," I said, raising an eyebrow.

"And they don't even talk. You can't reason with them." He
stopped to hand a pamphlet to a downtrodden ex-logger on his
way to the bar.

I didn't bother to correct him on that. It was true. "So I
guess you'll be packing up soon? Since they're so hopeless."

He shook his head, steel resolve in his eyes. "We shall not
rest until a union is formed for these brave workers so victimized
by the fist of capitalism."

"You didn't seem to care so much when it was *people* working for the company."

He frowned. "People can take care of themselves."

Almost overnight, our little town transformed. Our only

hotel was stuffed four people to a room, while the whores abandoned the local men for the Easterners and their money. The bars ran out of beer in the first two days, and the fistfights started soon after. Papa hardly ever came home anymore.

Even with all the activity in town, the creatures worked through the night, the crunch of the trees keeping everyone up. I stuck paraffin in my ears to keep it out.

But wax couldn't keep out the voice in my head, the voice like a distant rumbling from the heart of the Earth. The voice of the sasquatches.

Only a few days after the organizers converged on the square, they began to picket the company headquarters.

The house of Julius Price, the company president, sat on the banks of the Hood River less than a mile from the center of town. Sometimes Price would come out and smoke on the porch, his beady eyes facing east.

My brother Lou and I were walking through the woods when we saw the crowd.

"Free the First Men!" yelled a woman in trousers.

"Just because they're hairy doesn't mean they aren't *people*," whined a man in the back carrying a sign painted on a piece of thin wood.

I pushed Lou down onto a stump. "Stay there," I hissed, as I fought my way through the boughs to gawk at the protestors. Price, dressed in his three-piece suit, pretended not to notice the dozen or so union men scoping out his riverside palace. I threw him a silent sneer.

"Oh, little girl!" I groaned when I realized I'd been spotted by the union woman I'd met the first day they arrived in town. It was too late to go back.

"Heya, Lorna."

She picked her way across the stumps, a fistful of pamphlets in her hand. Her bloomers were caked in mud. "Have you come to support the undermen?"

"They're called sasquatches."

She continued her rant as if I hadn't said anything at all. "This noble race, victimized by *that man*," she said, pointing at President Price, "has suffered for far too long! We're going to break the chains of oppression *today*. Or at least this week." She slapped at a spider that had alighted on her shoulder, and squealed.

"Have you tried talking to the, uh, undermen?"

The union lady from back East looked at me with the same expression the teacher did when I'd gotten too many right answers. "Precious girl, they wouldn't talk to us. The undermen keep their own counsel."

I thought of that low rumble-voice, that feeling of connection that happened whenever I peered out of the window of our shack and gazed into the forest. "The company isn't just going to let you stay here forever, you know. Not with the ruckus you've been causing."

She narrowed her eyes at the president's fancy house, like she was the one who'd been wronged by him, and not all of us. "Fret not, little girl. We have a plan that will liberate the undermen for good."

"I'm telling you, they're not men."

Finally, she looked at me, and I don't think she liked what she saw. "Shouldn't you be in school?"

"It burned down."

The school didn't burn down. The teacher left. I don't know why I said it burned down.

He was from Connecticut, the teacher, the same place Mama ran off to. He hadn't been a very good teacher, and of course he didn't like having girls in his class. Or maybe he just didn't like me. But he was still a teacher, and we needed him.

The teacher fit in pretty well for an intellectual stuck in the middle of logging country. He didn't go drinking with the other men, but he would tip his hat to us in the street, and he even had a special lady. We thought we'd have him with us for a very long time. And then he saw a sasquatch.

I wasn't there, but my brother Cyril told me what happened. The teacher had gone for a hike around Mount Hood, even though he must have noticed that none of us ever went there. He'd gone wandering into one of those gaping cracks on the mountain's side, and had a fit.

The sasquatches had carried him back down, cradled in their arms like their own child, and deposited him on the steps of the courthouse. It was very kind of them, but the teacher didn't see it that way. He'd gone back to Connecticut the next morning, job be damned, lady friend be double damned.

Papa said another one is on the way, but I don't think so. Teachers talk amongst each other. They're a lot like sasquatches that way.

I tried to look sad at the union lady after telling her the lie about the school, but she didn't seem to care.

"If you're not part of the solution, you're part of the problem." She pressed a leaflet into my hand. The ink came off on my palm. "Come to the hotel lobby tomorrow at seven. *We'll* give you an education."

I sighed. "I'll be there." I scanned the stumps until I found Lou.

"Lou?" He was sitting where I'd found him. A baby sasquatch—or baby underman—was sitting on its haunches at his feet. I watched as Lou reached out his hand to the furry hand.

"Don't," I said. I looked into Lou's pale blue eyes. "Don't let him hurt you."

Lou petted the sasquatch on its rough head. I smiled to see

him with his new friend.

And that's when that baby sasquatch's mama lumbered out of the woods and took Lou away.

Papa didn't even seem to care that Lou was gone, until I told him that a sasquatch did it. That wiped the beery glaze from his eyes and sent him flying out of the shack, muttering "damn beasts" and "we'll show 'em."

I tucked my other two brothers, Cyril and Gary, under the Indian blanket and turned down the light.

"It's okay," I said as I peeked past the curtains. "Papa will find him." The moon was full tonight, but the rain pattered down. Almost no light was reflected off the pond in the back of our house. I couldn't see if the sasquatches were out there waiting for me.

Of course they knew where I was, even with all the lights doused and the curtains drawn.

What are you doing with him? I projected the question with all my heart, that there might be a connection like there had been on that moonlit night not so long ago. But there was no reply.

Papa returned shortly before dawn.

"Did you find him?"

He scowled. "Shut your trap, girlie."

The door opened again and two of the other ex-loggers entered, their axes slung over their shoulders. The three men spoke among one another in hushed tones. Every so often, Papa stole a glance over at me to make sure I wasn't listening.

I couldn't hear what they were saying exactly. But I got the gist of it. They were going to kill the sasquatches.

A town meeting convened at noon. The other ex-workers and their wives gave Papa their condolences. Clearly, everyone thought Lou was dead.

Is he dead? I thought out at the sasquatches. No response.

Tears shone in the corners of Papa's eyes, but I thought he seemed more angry than sad. He hadn't really wanted any of us to stay in Oregon with him. He'd especially tried to convince Mama to take Lou, who was only a baby. He didn't know how to take care of a baby, he said.

I knew how to take care of a baby. I *had* to know.

"How are we gonna do it?" said Anderson, a man with seven fingers and an ever-present sneer.

"Smoke 'em out," said another man. "They don't like fire."

"But that will spread!" a woman countered.

While the deliberations wore on, the union men appeared in the doorway, almost as if they'd always been there. Maybe they'd been listening in this whole time. The woman with the short hair and bloomers, Lorna, hoisted herself onto a chair, put her hands around her mouth, and hollered loud enough for people in Portland to hear her.

"Listen up!" When only a few of us turned our heads to look, she stamped her foot, almost falling off the chair in the process. "There will be no more oppression of these people by anyone in town. Solidarity!"

An old logger with missing front teeth started to titter. Then the whole meeting house broke into hysterics, except for Papa, who just looked pissed. While they were laughing, I snuck out.

The rain fell gently on the green earth, and the smell of moss hung in the air. I went across the dirt road and sat down on a flat rock. I needed some time to think.

I put my chin in my hands, tired from the sleepless night. As the meeting house continued to erupt in waves of laughter mixed with righteous indignation, I felt my consciousness slip under. I dreamed of an ocean of brown-gray fur lifting me up, carrying me away from the stench of booze and evergreens.

When I woke, I rubbed my eyes and looked around. I was in a cave. Why was I in a cave?

"Papa?" I said, sitting up. "Where are you?" I looked toward the cave's mouth, but it was only a pinprick of light. I stood, but felt my head spinning. I plopped down on the bed, which I could now see was a thick mat of rough straw.

I scanned the room lit only by a single candle in the corner. I felt warmth. I reached out my hand and hit something that felt like a cow. I pulled my hand back. It wasn't a cow.

Don't be scared.

Too late. My breath caught in my throat and my hands began to tremble. I forced myself to speak. "Why did you take my brother?" I tried to make out the sasquatch's face, but it was too dark. Sasquatches all look alike anyway. "You'd better give him back or they're going to do bad things to you."

He is learning.

"Learning *what*?" Paying attention, I could feel the forms and hear the voices of at least three of the brutes in the cave with me. I breathed in and out calmly. I couldn't let them know I was scared.

He is safe.

"Then let me *see* him." As I said that, a picture flashed in my mind: Lou on a pile of skins, naked, his face screwed up in intense concentration. Four-year-olds didn't concentrate like that.

Trust us.

"Why should I?" I tried to stand up again, but the dizzies got the best of me. "You *stole* my brother. Now everyone in town wants to kill you."

Let them come.

I balled my fist and struck out at the creature, but it was like hitting a slab of meat. "Give him to me! Maybe they won't come after you if you give him up *right now*."

They have always been coming. There is nothing to be done. That is why we have selected the envoy.

"Lou?"

He will remember us when we are gone. When our bodies have been ground into bone and dust, he will remember.

I felt tears spring to the corners of my eyes. "But he's just a little boy."

Little boys grow up.

Suddenly, the suffocating weight of the combined sasquatches lifted. I rose for the third time and could remain standing. My eyes had adjusted to the poor light, and I found myself only three inches from the closest sasquatch's beady black eyes. She, or it, was sitting on her haunches, massive paw-hands splayed on the cave floor. Her jaw was working, but as before, the words flew into my brain without the unnecessary formality of speech.

"What you've done to him, it can be reversed, right? He didn't ask to be your envoy. He's only four years old."

When we are four we venture into the cone of the mountain and find the wisdom locked within.

I took two halting steps forward. My hands were still fists at my sides. "We're not like you."

The thick musk of the sasquatches was like a cloud about me. I looked around for Lou, but he wasn't there. A square of pale light appeared before me. I stumbled out into the weak sun, my eyes burning. I didn't turn around.

When I got back to town, three days had elapsed. Papa had been certain I was dead, and he'd drowned his sorrow with whiskey. My two remaining brothers ganged up on me, piercing me with angry eyes and fierce expressions.

"Where the hell did you go?" Cyril said. I could tell he hadn't bathed in days. Nobody had been here to make him do it.

"Looking for Lou. Why weren't *you* taking care of Papa?"

"You found him, didn't you?" Gary said, sniffing the sasquatch musk that had attached itself to my dress and hair. "But you didn't bring him back. Because you side with *them*."

"Of course I don't side with them, ninny. They stole our brother!" I shoved Gary into the cast-iron stove.

"Is he dead?" Cyril asked. "Did the sasquatches eat him?"

I thought back to Lou atop the pile of skins, his young-old face radiating the wisdom of the center of the mountain, like a little Chinese god. "He's not dead."

"Well, I'll tell you who *will* be dead pretty soon," Cyril said with a grin. "We caught ourselves some sasquatches. Just threw a net over them while they were out working. We're going to have ourselves a barbecue."

I sucked in air. "That's not going to bring Lou back."

"Maybe it will and maybe it won't," Gary said, "but it's not gonna hurt. Well, not gonna hurt *us*."

I didn't have any love in my heart for the sasquatches, not after all they'd done to our family, but that didn't mean I wanted to see them killed. "When are they going to roast them?"

"Tuesday morning," Cyril said.

"Just burn them up," I said. "Just like that." I tried not to sound sad. I shouldn't be sad over animals.

"We're going to shoot them first, dummy. We're not savages."

I shooed my brothers out of the room and changed out of my filthy, fur-covered dress. I had to stop this, not for the sasquatches' sake, but for Lou's. And to do that, I had to talk to the union men.

I found Lorna in the square, right where I knew she'd be. She was holding one of her usual broadsheets, standing barefoot on a stump. I guess those fancy city shoes weren't working out too well for her.

"Little girl," she said with a frown, "what do you want?"

I sighed. "I need your help."

Lorna stepped down off the stump, wincing. "It's because of

your family that the undermen are going to be executed. Maybe if you'd have watched your brother better, this wouldn't have happened."

"Maybe you should shut your ignorant mouth. I'm coming to you in friendship."

Lorna planted her hands on her hips, her broadsheets crumpled in one hand. "Fine. Spit it out."

"Now, I got no love for those animals. They took my brother. They . . ." I trailed off, wondering if I should talk about what I'd seen in the cave. "But I don't think they should die."

"Stand up for them, then. Tell the mayor to let the undermen go."

I stamped my foot. "I don't control the mayor!"

"Then let them out yourself. It's a small town and you're a smart girl."

I wondered why Lorna's people didn't free the sasquatches by their own selves. And then I realized: It was because they were *scared*. Just like the teacher. Just like Mama. "I don't even know where they're keeping them."

"Where else?" she said. "The jail. Along with all the other oppressed people of the land."

There wasn't ever anyone in the jail except the occasional drunk sleeping off a bender, but I wasn't about to correct her. "They'll be surrounded. There isn't any way I can do it by myself."

Lorna raised an eyebrow. "Perhaps you should be employing a little solidarity."

I kicked a little dust in Lorna's direction and strode out of there. She was right, but I wasn't about to let her know it. It was time to get some folks—human and craven beast alike—on my side.

I found President Price in the saloon, his walrus mustache drooping into a tumbler of whiskey. The other men talked in hushed tones around the company president. They'd work like dogs for him if he asked them to, but no man in Oregon wanted to be his friend.

"What are you doing here, President Price?"

His face cycled through multiple emotions as if picking out which reply he wanted to use. "Who are you?"

"Helen Parker. My Papa used to work for you."

"Everyone's papa used to work for me." Again, there was the cycle of expressions, from pride to shame to, finally, apathy. "You shouldn't be in here, this place is for men."

I perched atop a stool, hoping I didn't look ridiculous. "They're going to kill your workers."

"There are other brutes in the forest."

The bartender plunked a mason jar of water down on the counter. It was brown and sickly-looking, and I didn't touch it. "They don't deserve it."

His mustache frowned. "The creatures stole your brother."

"Not *these* ones. And anyway, where does it end? I've heard the men talking. They want to kill all the sasquatches. Even the women and the babies."

"We don't really *need* sasquatches." He tapped a finger meditatively against his chin. "I guess I could just hire some Irishmen. They're cheap."

I dipped my finger in the dirty water and traced a pattern on the bar countertop. "Do you like it here?"

"Of course I don't like it here. I came here to make money, girl." He chuckled into his whiskey. "And I *will* make money, even if I have to cut every corner. That's why the creatures were so useful. They don't get hurt, they don't get sick, and you don't have to pay them. If I could I'd ship a whole train-load of them back East, put them to work making pencils and battleships." He sighed. "But they stick by that mountain of theirs."

"It's their home."

His bushy eyebrows knitted. "I don't know what you people

want from me."

"You could pay the men. A bonus. For all the work they've done for you all these years."

He waved a hand. "Nonsense. That would eat up all my profits."

I thought, long and hard. "I understand. Thank you for your time."

Price sloshed the remaining whiskey around in the glass tumbler. "You're a queer little girl, carrying on about such things. Haven't you got a mother to teach you how to sew and bake?"

"I've got more family here than you've got," I said. "Enjoy your afternoon."

I pushed the saloon doors open. I had to get to the school-house.

Even though there wasn't any school anymore, all the kids in town still hung out at the schoolhouse. Not on any sort of set schedule, mind. We were still needed at home most of the time. But when you were looking for friends to play with, you went to the schoolhouse. It was a ramshackle structure a few blocks away from the meeting house. One side of its foundation had sunk into the mud, and all the floors tilted aslant. If you dropped your pencil in class, you had to get up and walk across the room to get it.

Cyril was there, plus another boy and a girl. They narrowed their eyes when I came in.

"Oh great, your weird sister is here," said the boy, Petey. "Where you been at for the past three days, anyway?"

I gave him a Look. "None of your business."

"You were playing with those sasquatches." Petey smirked. "Filthy animals."

"You should know about filthy animals, being one and all." His face turned red, but he didn't dare hit a girl. Even one like me. "Listen up. I have a plan to get our fathers their jobs back, and get my brother back too."

"He's not dead?" Melinda said.

I shook my head. "Not hardly. He's with the sasquatches inside Mount Hood, alive and well." That was a lie. I knew about the alive part, but I wasn't real sure about the well part.

"You know where he is, and you didn't tell Papa?" The corner of Cyril's eye twitched. "I say we just go in there and take him."

"It's not that easy," I said, holding up a hand. "There's sasquatches all over the place, and they've done something to him, changed him somehow. He's like, their ambassador or something. But not dead."

"And why are we letting this *girl* tell us what to do?" Petey said. "Let's go save your brother, Cy."

"They won't let you inside. They don't know you. We have to be gentle."

"Maybe you should just go talk to your friends from the East," Cyril said. "If you want to be *gentle* with them." He said it like a curse.

"I've been inside their cave. They know me and they trust me." I scanned the kids for a reaction. Cyril and Petey still looked skeptical, but I could tell Melinda was warming. Maybe. "I know how we can get Lou back *and* get rid of those Easterners. Let me do it."

Petey scrunched up his nose. "Let's hear the plan, Helen. Five minutes."

My words tumbled over one another on the way out of my mouth. To be honest, I hadn't expected the other kids to listen to me at all, and I was coming up with this plan mostly on the fly. But they didn't need to know that. "The organizers want to put President Price out of business, right? And *he* wants to keep his operating costs down as low as possible, which is why he uses the sasquatches. Because they don't understand what money is."

I reached for the next sentence like I was grasping straws. "So what if we *taught* them what money is? Get them to value it like we do? Then they could join the union, and our daddies could compete for the jobs again."

"But the sasquatches are stronger," Melinda said. "My papa can't pull a tree out of the ground with his bare hands."

"Yeah, but we got more brains than them, and we can use tools." The more I spoke the plan aloud, the more sense it made, or seemed to. "The union men are right. We *do* need solidarity with the sasquatches. But we can't force it on them. They're not going to march or strike. They're totally different from us."

Petey snorted. "What's a sasquatch gonna buy?"

I shrugged.

"But if he has to start paying the sasquatches," Cyril said, "then President Price is just gonna leave. You know he wants to go back East anyway. His family is there."

"So let him!" I said, kicking at one of the moldy old chairs. "Who says we need a president to run a mill? He barely does anything anyway. *We* have the trees, *we* have the labor, and if this works out, we even have the sasquatches on our side."

I watched the other kids as they seemed to consider my proposal, turn it over in their minds like the river working over a stone. Finally Melinda spoke. "How are we going to do this?"

"We're going up to Mount Hood. We're going to talk to Lou."

We set out for the mountain on the morning before the sasquatches were to be shot and roasted. The evergreens loomed above us like silent soldiers, screaming hawks nestled in their limbs. I gripped Melinda's hand. The boys walked ahead, knives in their belts, but from their stiff body language I could tell they were more scared than we were.

The entrance to the sasquatches' mountain home was subtle,

unless you knew where to look. For dumb brutes, they had camouflaged their lair well. A false tangle of leaves and branches masked the cracks that marked the entryway, and I think the only way I could tell it was there was that the voices of the creatures became momentarily louder in my head, as if to say *you're almost there.*

I looked over at Melinda, but it didn't seem like she was hearing anything at all.

I touched the false front of the lair. Beneath it was cool, wet rock. "Here."

Cyril and Petey ran forward with sticks with which to jimmy open the door, but they broke in the cracks. I dropped Melinda's hand and ran to where the voices were strongest, where I could hear the gentle waves of the sasquatch hive-voice even through inches of prehistoric rock. There was a gap here, a place so close to them—and to Lou—that I almost felt as if I were inside, riding those waves of soft brown fur.

"Please come outside," I whispered. "We need to talk."

We must protect those parts of us which are left.

"The parts of you that are outside are in great danger."

That is why we remain inside with our envoy. He is still in deep training. Until the envoy is prepared we cannot risk the loss of those which are left. We are sorry. I could almost believe that.

"The envoy is one of us. He belongs to me. To my family," I said. "If we can learn to work together, we can save *all* the parts of you. And help you protect your forest." I hoped the sasquatches couldn't tell that last part was a lie.

I smelled the pungent sweetness of evergreens, and when I looked out of the corner of my eye, I gasped. Petey had set a bough on fire, and was stalking toward the mouth of the cave, swinging it before him like an axe. "You let him out of there, you filthy animals!"

"Stop!" I screamed. I lunged at Petey, but the bits of flame leapt onto my dress, leaving singe marks where they landed. I stepped back. "You're not solving anything!" I looked for Cyril and Melinda, but they were hanging back, Cyril looking smug and Melinda on the verge of tears.

Petey dropped the bough. The flames climbed up the false tangle of weeds that partially hid the door into Mount Hood. I was too far away to hear the voices of the sasquatches inside, but I could feel their fear, their pain. I could feel them hiding it away, under their great cloaks of flesh and fur. I could feel their shared mind crumble under the weight of the fire.

And then the door rolled aside, and Lou stepped out.

We met the townsfolk halfway down. All the men and most of the women were carrying rifles under their armpits. Some carried torches. Everyone quieted when they saw Lou.

Two of the creatures knuckle-walked behind him. Even more of the beasts formed a rough semi-circle, their glossy black eyes focused on their envoy. Nobody, not man or sasquatch, made a sound. Until Papa stepped out of the throng of watchers.

"Lou!" He held his rifle slack, and his ever-present beer bottle fell to the ground. "Gimme back—"

"Father," Lou said. His voice was hollow and gravelly, like an old man. Like he'd aged seven decades in a week. "Do not be alarmed. We have no wish to bring you to harm, though we possess the power to do so."

Papa just stared back, open-mouthed.

Lou targeted his strange gaze at me. "My parts. Where are the parts that were taken from me?"

I shook myself into action. "They're in the jailhouse."

My brother nodded. "Yes. I can sense that they are hungry, but well. We shall go to them now." The townsfolk dropped their torches in the mud when the sasquatch parade passed. One burly man went flying down the mountainside to the village square. I didn't think anyone would attempt to stop them from releasing the captive beasts. Or even *could* stop them.

I slowed my pace to match his. My brother's clothes were torn and covered with fur, and his once-innocent face was older, somehow. "What's this all about, Lou? What have they done to you?"

"All will be revealed." It sounded comical coming from a little kid, but I didn't let on.

"Are you gonna blow up the mountain?"

"We would never destroy our only home, the place where our ancestors were forged in the fires from the underworld, where our energies return daily to replenish for the day ahead."

Well, that cleared that up, I guessed.

Lou led the sasquatches—or maybe they led him—into the town square. The union men and women jumped up like rabbits when they saw the sasquatches, waving their little signs and shaking their angry fists.

"Freedom!" yelled a woman. "Liberation for the undermen!" One of the men started wrestling with an ex-logger for no reason I could tell.

Across the square, three sasquatches stood near the town hall, probably released by the union folks. They made a beeline for the mass of creatures at my back, and I could feel the relief of the sasquatches as their missing pieces slid into place.

Now we are whole, said the deep reverberations, the heart-voice.

"Halt yourselves!" cried Lou, and though his voice was still that of a child, it stopped everyone's fussing. "Visitors from distant lands, we do not require your assistance. You are free to leave."

A sickly pale man with a black mustache piped up. "But you're *slaves*. We came here to free you!"

"It is not possible for us to be freed, since no man can chain us. Return to the cities which birthed you, and assist those of your own kind who truly suffer under the thumb of oppression."

Cyril nudged me. "Lou knows even more fancy words than

you do, Helen."

I shrugged. Lou's words were beyond me.

Lou and his sasquatch friends walked among the townsfolk until he met the stern gaze of Julius Price. "We chose to help you, for we believed that it was improper for men to suffer under hard labor when we could perform the work so much more easily ourselves. Why are the people still suffering?"

Price's forehead wrinkled. "I don't understand."

"Why," Lou said, the voice of the sasquatches flowing through him like lava, "are the men still suffering? We have taken away their work."

"If the men don't work, the men don't eat."

"But there is enough for *all*!" The creatures' words flowed from Lou like a sonic wave, blowing President Price backward. "This valley is fertile. No man should starve here. No man should suffer here. To let your kind of beings, so strange yet so intelligent, die in a land of plenty is *evil*!"

The townsfolk just stared, but the union people started nodding and clapping. They quieted with a glare from Lou, or whatever sasquatch was talking through Lou's mouth. I guess that was all of them.

"The ways of men are strange to us, and we are not certain we care for them. Yet, the men are here. We cannot cast you out, for you have stitched yourself into the pattern of the land. *Our* land." Lou took a deep breath. It was a lot of talking for a four-year-old, especially one as silent as Lou used to be. "Fear not the rumblings of the mountain. We do not wish to harm you. But we cannot allow this strife to continue."

Everyone paused, locking eyes around the muddy square. Nobody seemed likely to speak. Finally, Papa spoke up. "So what's gonna happen, son?"

"We work together," said the sasquatches. "Or we fall together."

The air severed around us, the heart-song of the sasquatches breaking off. I let out a breath. Suddenly, Lou's knees buckled.

"Lou!" I yelled, running to catch him.

His blue eyes stared into mine. "What happened, Helen?"

I turned my head. The sasquatches were lumbering away, toward Mount Hood. A few of the Easterners padded after them for a few steps, but none followed them out of the square. "I don't rightly know," I admitted. "But I think we're all gonna be okay."

The union men left town later that week, packing into the eastbound train like sardines in a rusty tin can. I watched from the other side of the station as Lorna hefted her steamer trunk into the baggage hold. Her bloomers were streaked with grime.

"You're taking off," I said, stating the obvious.

She sneered. "Hello, little girl."

"You got everything you wanted. The undermen are unionized." It was true. President Price had left on the previous train. Through Lou's little-boy voice and big-city vocabulary, we'd managed to organize something like a union. The sasquatches did all the work, while the people managed the sasquatches and dealt with the buyers. A lot of the men, and even a few women, patrolled the town with rifles in hand, waiting for the inevitable encroachment of the government on our patch of paradise.

"You're not really working with them. You're *exploiting* them," Lorna said. "You've just replaced one set of chains with another. No matter what the undermen may think."

Maybe that was true. The sasquatches worked as they'd always worked, pulling up trees with their big ropy muscles. They didn't come into town. Meanwhile, the men of the town took care of the business side, selling the uprooted trees to investors from New York and Chicago. The paths of men and sasquatches still didn't cross much.

Except when it came to my brother.

Lou was different now. Before, he'd just been a regular dumb little worm-eating kid crying for a mommy who wasn't ever coming back. Now he was quiet and still as a lake. He split his time between our cabin and the main sasquatch camp inside Mount Hood. I walked him there and back, though he didn't need my guardianship.

One night, as I walked my brother back from Mount Hood past the rows of rifle-sporting militiamen, I spotted a woman coming down the gravel path. "Lorna? I thought you left."

Her round face shone in the moonlight. "Changed my mind. There's a lot of space out here for women like me. More space than in New York City."

"The undermen don't need you, Lorna." Of course, they didn't need us, either. We had always known that the sasquatches could dismantle the village in one night if they had a mind to. Sasquatches didn't work for men, they didn't even work for themselves. A sasquatch was like a tool. You just pointed it in the right direction and it did what you asked. "And neither do we."

Lorna grunted. "There's still a lot of work to be done, Helen. Someone needs to make sure people don't become complacent. Who knows, maybe I can spark a revolution!"

"Well, I certainly hope not."

She frowned.

Lou tugged on my arm. I bent down and put my ear to his lips, to hear what he had to say. We always knew he would grow up to be a quiet man, but his time among the sasquatches had quieted him even more. I ruffled his blond hair and faced Lorna again.

"What's he saying?" she asked, narrowing her eyes at Lou.

"He says that when the revolution does happen, none of us will see it coming."

That wasn't the truth. But it was close enough.

THE FATE OF THE WORLD, REDUCED TO A TEN-SECOND PISSING CONTEST

THE ALIENS LIKE TO break things, mostly. Bottles, noses, the pinball machine in the corner of Lucky's Bar that never worked quite right in the first place. They roared into the parking lot on their Kawasaki bikes, bandannas tied around their mouths so we couldn't tell they were aliens.

I knew they were aliens right away, for the record. I may be a lush, but I'm not stupid.

They set up a tab. Then all the stars went out.

"Your ass," the alien says through the electronic voicebox surgically implanted in its throat-analogue. They look a lot like us, except for their mouths, which resemble anuses. There's no other way to put it. "I'll kick it. Kick your *ass*."

"Yeah, yeah. You'll kick my ass," says Lucky, the bartender. He gets out a bottle of the cheap stuff and pours it into a saucer. The alien hoovers it up.

They're drunks. Mean drunks. And they've been drunk since they set foot in here and displaced the bar and all its contents away from Earth and to wherever or whenever this is.

How long ago was that? We estimate the date from the wrinkled pin-up calendar in Lucky's back room, but we know it's not accurate. *It's been a while*, I think, *and too long.*

I'm there with my girlfriend, at one of the booths near the back, safely away from the cluster of aliens hooting and screeching at what they think is going to be a throw-down showdown between the bartender and the creature in the scuffed motorcycle jacket. One of them breaks a barstool over a human head, and they swarm the scene, their chalk-white fingers pawing through the human's pockets for pot and bennies.

"When we get out of here, I'm going to move to a place where nobody will ever find me," she says.

A stream of booze cascades from an alien's anus-mouth, landing in the green plastic ashtray on our table. It's a slam dunk.

"I never loved you," she says, "and this place is a dump."

I hope she does leave. I hope we all get out of here. I tell her that.

"I'm so sick of peanuts." She runs her finger around the rim of her cocktail glass of daily rations to catch all the dust. There wasn't much food in Lucky's when it was lifted out of space-time. We're all on strict diets now.

"Tomorrow we get half a pickled egg each," I say, licking my lips. But tomorrow arrives, and the eggs are rancid. So much for having something to look forward to.

One of the aliens explained it to me once, in a brief moment of clarity between rounds. *Think of reality as an endless series of moments*, it said, *laid end to end, with barely any gap between them.* Its smile was the ugliest sight you ever saw, with that mouth. *We are in the gap.*

I'd opened my mouth to ask, why here? Why Lucky's instead of the Pentagon or the Taj Mahal or any number of other prime Earth locations? But just right then, Lucky came out with a fresh bottle of rum, and I became so beneath that alien's notice that I'm surprised it didn't step on me on its mad dash toward liquid refreshment.

"Jello shots!" one of the aliens cries out, and all of the aliens and some of the humans belly up to the bar. Jello is food. It contains calories.

My girlfriend who never loved me is sidled up to an alien, running her fingers through its flowing, greasy hair.

"Get me offa this rock," she says, flirtatiously.

"The party is here," the alien replies. "This is the party."

The toilets at Lucky's Bar were disconnected from the septic system when the aliens ported us into that so-called gap, so I'm outside, taking a leak off the edge of the known world. Suddenly, I feel a presence behind me.

"Mine is bigger," says the alien. It plucks its tulip-like sexual organ from its leather pants and points it out into the uncharted chasm before us. It *is* bigger than mine.

"We don't usually say things like that on Earth." Not out loud, anyway.

The alien launches a stream of urine out into the starless black. Whatever process the aliens use to synthesize their liquor makes their piss smell like strawberries. "It goes a real long way."

"It sure does."

I zip up and go back inside. The party's just heating up. The aliens are up on the bar itself, their arms intertwined, doing an arrhythmic little kick-dance. The humans—my girlfriend, Lucky, the guy allergic to peanuts who's dying of malnourishment—are over in the corner booth.

I head over to sit with them, but stop in my tracks. Instead I head back out: to the blackness, to the gap. I stretch my hands wide, reaching, as if I can possibly graze one of the moments we're sandwiched between. As if, somehow, I could pull my-self into that next piece of reality, like climbing onto a runaway train. You can lose your legs that way. Maybe I'll lose my mind. No great loss, that.

"Stop."

I turn around. It's my girlfriend.

"It's because nobody knows we're gone, or cares. That's why they picked us." She makes a sound halfway between a grunt and a sigh. "Easy targets."

I wish she wasn't right.

"Take my hand," she says, and I do. Then we jump into the gap, into the void, into the great question mark.

SIGNS FOLLOWING

SILENTLY, THEY PASS AROUND the alien.

The meetings are held at the Eridani Colony Community Center. Shoved aside are the ping-pong tables (unused) and the motivational standees. A two-dimensional young girl in a hardhat grins at the workers, tells them they're doing an excellent job. The plastic chairs are set up in a circle, like they were during the "Imagining a Better World through Guided Visualization" group discussions (discontinued). The leader for the week, a man with a plastic name tag that informs Dennis his name is ROY, opens the box.

Sometimes it stings you. Sometimes it releases a cloud of gas that will choke you, but it's not poison. Most of the time, the alien doesn't do anything.

Dennis eagerly rubs his hands together, waiting for his turn. A few months ago, he was bitten by the alien. The alien's sharp teeth dug like pushpins into the webbing of skin between his thumb and index finger. He carried his wound out in the open until it healed, remembering the thrill of the alien's bite. His wish didn't come true, but the wish doesn't always come along with the bite. Not even usually.

Around him, he can feel the combined prayers and requests of the workers bubbling up, until the entire meeting almost sweats with concentrated yearning. Dennis keeps his own request at the forefront of his mind, a wish for a new set of bed sheets. It's not much, but neither is it boastful. And he hasn't gotten new bed sheets for seven years now, so it's something he really needs. He feels positive about this one.

Dennis doesn't know the name of the woman to his right, the woman currently holding the alien. She holds it at arm's length, giving it a small shake, as she's seen the others do. *Might be new*, Dennis thinks. The woman brings the alien into eye contact, trying to focus her two hazel eyes on its three tiny black ones. A lump of bile rises in her throat, and she struggles to push it down. *Definitely new.*

The alien is covered with short gray fur. Its mouth opens to a black hatch through which Dennis can see the rippling of the alien's esophagus. The alien is slightly wet at all times.

Suddenly, the woman gasps. The alien has stung her with its back claw. A cheer rises up and Dennis joins in, thrusting his hands in the air, giving thanks. The alien doesn't attack him that day—there are rarely two attacks in one day—but it hardly seems to matter. At this moment, they are free.

Dennis holds a small blue plastic chip to the air, inspecting it. A small reflective panel on its side mirrors back the face of his supervisor as she trundles behind him, tapping him on the shoulder.

"Get out of line. I need to talk to you." His supervisor's arms are ropy with muscle; her face is runneled with sweat.

"Yes?"

The supervisor takes a small blue plastic part from the pocket of her overalls. "You let this get through. Look," she says, running her thumbnail down a microscopic crease in the curved side of the tiny radiation filter. "No pay for today."

Dennis nods, unconcerned. He's thinking only of the Community Center meeting that will come together in three days. He has a good feeling about that one. He's already been working on his wish. The bed sheets *were* a bit much to hope for, now that he really thinks about it.

Dennis slides into his workstation next to Ellen, who has been here even longer than he has. Together, they sort components for robot-guided exploration rockets for the next colonization effort. A new rocket is completed every six months. Dennis has been employed at the factory for the past twenty-three years as a quality control worker, and is thus responsible in some small way for the launching of forty-six rockets.

They work in silence for an hour until Ellen speaks. Her voice cracks like cement. "They denied me again." Ellen has been trying to get away for years now, writing pleas to the administration as well as praying to the alien. "I don't think I'm ever going to leave."

"Well, you just have to keep trying."

Ellen's eyes gleam. "I know. I'm already starting the next appeal. And I'm always asking for it, every week."

"Well, that's great." Dennis throws another piece of blue plastic into the sorting tray.

Gingerly, with the rough tips of her index finger and thumb, Ellen plucks a component from the tray and holds it up to the light. It shines, a tiny gem. "Broken," she says, tossing it into the trash bin behind them.

I loved you, Dennis thinks.

For every broken component Ellen takes out of commission, Dennis lets two go through. When he thinks of the rockets lifting off at the colony's port, imagines them breaking up in mid-flight, he feels like pumping his fist in the air and yelling for joy.

When the noon buzzer rings, Dennis leaves for his lunch break, pulling on his dust mask on the way out. The sky over the colony is a dark orange today. A lighted walkway illuminates the way to the canteen, cutting a path through the dust.

The girl who runs the canteen nods as she gives him his boxed lunch. Dennis sits on the benches, whipping off his mask. He always eats alone. Today, though, he feels another body slip next to his.

"Mind if I sit here?" It's the woman from the Community Center, the woman who was stung. She doesn't wait for an answer. "I just transferred. I used to work at the purification center, but they don't need as many people there anymore." She chomps on her sandwich, chewing it slowly with her mouth open.

"Oh, that's interesting," Dennis says, even though it really isn't. There's been a lot of transfers lately.

"I don't like it here. The work is boring. The pay isn't so good. And at the purification center, they didn't make us eat lunch outside in the dust."

Dennis blinks. "Okay."

She swallows, a gulping sound. "That meeting was weird."

"Weird." He grunts.

She squares her shoulders and cocks her head at him. "What is that thing, anyway?"

"It's a being. It was here when we got here."

The new girl makes a sound that might be giggling, or a snort. "And what does this *being* do?"

"You can ask it for help. Sometimes it answers." This was typical. New transfers always trashed the meetings, until they had a chance to see the alien's power for themselves. Or they didn't, and stopped showing up. Either way worked for Dennis. He sips his water. "You'll get used to it."

She crumples the remains of her lunch and stands up. "I can't wait to be reassigned. It's only temporary. Maybe I'll go back to Earth."

"I'm sure you will."

"This place smells too." She turns on her heel and strides back down the walkway.

Dennis has lost his appetite. He returns his untouched lunch to the canteen girl and waits a few beats before returning to the factory. He doesn't want to take the chance of running into her there.

It was wasted on her, Dennis thinks. *She didn't even have a wish*. Of course, she didn't know she needed one. Someone would have to teach her about the alien and its power. But it won't be Dennis. He has his own problems to worry about.

In the factory, Dennis searches for his supervisor. He finds her on the loading dock, reassembling an engine.

"I need to talk about the new girl."

The supervisor's arms are streaked with engine lubricant, like a second set of veins. "Why?"

"I don't want to take my lunch with her anymore. Let me switch my schedule around."

She rolls her eyes and circles back to the engine.

"Are you listening?" After thirty seconds of waiting for an answer, Dennis shakes his head and leaves.

Thanks, he thinks.

Nobody remembers who found the alien. It was discovered underneath a buggy three years ago, and unresistingly scooped up by a group of workers. Dennis wasn't there, but he knows people who were.

Of course, they planned to send it to the science department. No native life existed on Eridani, and life in general across the universe was sparse. The bounty from the discovery of the alien could keep the workers in imported food and happy pills for a year.

But then, they learned the alien's secret.

Against advice, a man named Daniel brought his son to the colony with him. The child became very sick from expired meat, and wasn't expected to survive the next two months. While handling the alien one day, Daniel prayed for his son to hold out until a medic ship could arrive.

He not only survived until the doctor arrived, but he didn't need her at all.

More tentative wishes followed: an accidental double shipment of grain, a dust storm significantly less harsh than predicted. The colonists had found a receptacle for their desires, one that seemed to listen, almost to care. The price comes in the form of bites and stings, but they never really hurt. Meanwhile, spirits at the colony improved. No longer did the workers stumble through the dusty landscape, scowls on their lips. The Eridani government took notice, but most workers didn't care for a government commendation. They had another force to please.

The alien doesn't eat. At least, it doesn't eat anything on the colony, which may or may not be its natural habitat. Dennis has researched it, and the alien is not listed in any guides to animal or plant life. He thinks it's an animal. It just looks like one.

And outsiders dare to call the meetings "weird."

It's not weird. It's what we need.

Dennis sinks into his seat across from Ellen. Blissful Ellen, nodding her head as she sorts, hums a tune to compete with the machinery's clang. Dennis throws a chip with a broken-off corner into the sorthing tray. A few moments later, Ellen taps on the table.

"Are you okay? You put this one in."

"Huh?" Dennis feigns stupidity. This is the first time Ellen's noticed what would be called sabotage by the supervisors, if his pattern were discovered. "Oh, right."

She grins, blushes, and tosses it into the trash bin. "I won't tell. But just this once."

Dennis' heart lifts. He knows the time when he could have

had a relationship with Ellen has passed. But she'll always be here, sitting across from him, with her warm voice and sturdy hands. The alien didn't give him Ellen's love, but it's not going to take her away either. Of this, he is sure. "Thanks. You're a good friend."

Above, ventilation fans churn their wide arms, gathering dust.

The new girl doesn't show up at the next meeting. Neither does Ellen. It's a sparse group, possibly owing to an increase in dust. Dennis spent all this week's salary (minus the unpaid day) on a buggy to the Community Center. There's one grizzled old man, plus a lead supervisor in the engineering department. The supervisor's eyes dart around. He doesn't want to be seen, and Dennis does him the favor of pretending he's not.

Dennis takes the initiative, releases the alien from its cage. He hands it to the supervisor, who inspects it with shifting eyes and shaky fingers. In the first half-hour of passing the alien, nobody is bitten. Nobody is attacked. Even the feeling of good-will one usually gets from handling the alien is absent. Dennis regrets coming.

Then, he feels a brush of hot air over his cheek. He looks over his shoulder. A cloaked figure, covered in thick brown sand, is stumbling through the door.

"Dammit!" says the old man. "Close the *door*."

The figure removes its cloak and face mask. It's the new girl. She skips toward them, bringing a folding chair from the pile near the door. "How's he doing today? Can I hold him next?"

Even though Dennis hasn't been very invested in the alien today, he'll be damned if she's going to hold it. "I'm afraid we were about to leave. You're a little late. Maybe next week."

A flash of lower lip. "*Please?*"

"Give it to her," says the supervisor. He frowns at Dennis.

Dennis hands over the alien, keeping contact with it for

as long as possible, even though it is already delivered to the girl's arms. For thirty seconds they are both gripping the alien, she softly, he for dear life. *She called us weird.* Finally, after it is clear that he can no longer protect the alien in this very small way without attracting attention, he lets it go. And of course it bites her.

"Oh," she says, and for a minute it seems like she's experiencing the bite the way it's meant to be experienced, as a religious experience, not a rush of pure dumb dopamine into the organic machinery of the brain. "It tickles."

Dennis stands up, knocking his chair behind him. Both of the other workers are swaying in time with the new girl's pathetic little epiphany. He wants to slap them, snap them out of it. "Okay, I think it's had enough," Dennis says.

"I think he *likes* me."

Dennis can't determine whether she heard him or not.

It doesn't like anyone, you moron. It doesn't feel anything for you, or for me, or for anyone. But especially not for you. Am I the only one who realizes this? "I think," he says, voice wavering with the struggle to control his words, "that you should leave now."

She doesn't respond.

Dennis growls, cat-like, and advances on her. The alien squeaks, the barest noise, more indicative of a rusty hinge than a living thing, and burrows into the girl's collarbone.

The nervous supervisor's mouth gapes. "It *talks*." He and the grizzled man go up close to the girl and the alien, in amazement at the first noise they have ever heard from the alien.

Dennis feels a draw toward the alien, too, a straight line of energy reaching from it to his heart. As he reaches out his right hand to touch it, the six eyes of the other colonists blaze at him. He drops his arm. Pulling his hood over his face, he walks out into the storm. He walks the seven kilometers back.

*

The next day, as Dennis fumbles for his access card in his satchel, the new girl appears at his side. He jumps a little; she's come right out of nowhere.

"Went to the infirmary," she says, holding up a bandaged wrist. "That monster really got me good this time."

Dennis grunts. "I doubt it was that bad."

"Are you calling me a hypochondriac?"

"I'm saying that it's not a monster and it won't hurt you."

Hands on hips. "You don't like me."

"I don't know what gave you *that* idea," Dennis replies. "Can't you leave me alone right now? My shift is about to begin. I'd be happy to talk to you later." His mind rushes for ways to avoid seeing her after the shift. He might ask for overtime.

"Maybe I should ask it to get me out of this crummy place, with all these people that hate me," she says.

"Yes, that might be a good place to start. Well, see you around." He rushes with exaggerated speed onto the factory floor, making a beeline for his work station. Surprisingly, Ellen isn't hunched over the component tray, but is instead pacing, a giant crooked grin on her lips. She dashes over to Dennis and gives him a hug.

"They said yes," Ellen says. She bites her lower lip, though that doesn't stop it from trembling.

"W-what?"

"I mean I'm *leaving*. Aren't you happy for me?"

Dennis' head spins. He slides from Ellen's arms into his chair, putting his head into the palm of one hand. "Sure. It's great."

"The letter said I can leave two weeks from now. The next routine flight to Mu Arae. They're promising a job at a hospital there. They have houses, parks, schools."

"I'm very happy for you." Dennis swallows. "Very happy."

Ellen bounces in her seat, unable to keep still. "I have so

much to do! I'll have to get rid of most of my things. Will you help me pack?"

"Sure," Dennis says.

"Praise the alien."

"Yes, praise it." *At least,* he thinks, *this wish is going to some-one who deserves it.*

Dennis prayed to the alien so many times. Only little things, always trying to be humble. A day off. A short vacation at the planet's polar hotel, a tiny oasis he'd only ever heard of, never seen. For Ellen to love him back.

None of my requests were answered. Not one. But he can't stay angry at the alien. He can, however, stay angry at the new girl. She curried its favor so quickly and so easily, like they were meant for one another.

Put it out of your mind, he thinks. *You're supposed to go over to Ellen's place and help her tie things up here. Ellen needs you.*

Ellen's request, at least, had been answered. Dennis considers the possibility that the alien didn't have anything to do with Ellen's imminent departure, but dismisses it. *Has to be the alien. Ellen's been a true believer since day one.*

Not like Dennis. Not anymore.

As he swipes his lock, Dennis catches a glimpse of his face in the mirrored glass of the corridor walls. Tiny lines circle his eyes and mouth, like a series of cracks in a plastic component.

On the day before Ellen's departure, there's a special meeting at the Community Center. It's a packed house, and some of the attendees have to stand. Ellen is given more time with the alien than anyone, in hopes that she'll receive one last bite or sting. Even a faint kick would be a fine send-off.

Ellen hugs the alien, tickles its belly, blows on its fur. All the things you're really *not* supposed to do. There's only the faintest crack in her smile when she hands the alien off, unattacked, unselected. "Oh, well," she whispers. "I already got my wish, anyway."

Dennis could throttle the alien. He could rip it to shreds. Instead, the alien plops into his lap. It's his turn.

He stares at it, his two gray eyes against the alien's three black pebbly ones. He wants to feel something like faith. He looks up at Ellen's round, expansive face. Grinning wide with gapped teeth, she nods at him. Make a wish.

I wish Ellen hadn't gotten that letter, Dennis thinks. *I wish she weren't leaving.*

The alien doesn't do anything.

Dennis passes the alien to his left and leaves the room.

He sits on a bench, fists balled. When the calls of happiness and pain come from the community center, he doesn't have to guess which colonist was chosen.

It's her. It will always be her. It's made its choice. Dennis kicks at the dust, and squints through the darkness until he can see the lights of the colony's port, where he can see tomorrow's rocket, gleaming blue and silver, proud and strong. The rocket that Ellen will take to Mu Arae less than twelve hours from now.

Dennis can't go back to the center. Instead, he hails a buggy back to the colony dorms. As it speeds away through the gathering dust, he feels a tremor rack its way through his body. Putting his face in his hands, he remembers the feel of the alien's fur between his fingers, the sharp bite of its fangs.

Dennis gets up early the next morning to see Ellen off. Above, Eridani is at its high point for the year, optimal time for a launch. Today the sky is purple. The beige-red ground glitters and it's almost pretty. She stands at the mouth of the port, two small leather bags in tow.

"Good luck."

"You too." He reaches out to brush a strand of hair from her face. He has taken a half day off of work. This is too important to miss.

"You need to keep trying."

"I don't know," he says. "I don't think so."

"I'll see you again. I know I will. Keep wishing . . . it worked for me!" A final broad smile. *Christ, she actually believes it.*

The pilot places a palm on Ellen's shoulder and motions for her to get into the rocket. She smiles with closed lips and ascends the stairs. One of the security guards shoos Dennis away from the rocket, like he's a stray cat.

The rocket climbs a few meters into the air, and explodes.

Blue shards of rocket rain down on Dennis and the three dozen other panicked onlookers. A siren wails. Dennis gapes open-mouthed at the sky until the dust swallows it completely.

ACT OF PROVIDENCE

HAILEY THREADS THROUGH THE crowd of protesters and ever-present camera drones. The excitement caused her to miss her bus, so she'll have to walk home. After turning the corner, Hailey finds herself in a pop-up open-air nighttime market, where hand-knitted scarves jockey for place with homebrewed red ale. The people milling about don't seem to even realize what's happening only a block away.

Or maybe they don't care, Hailey thinks. *Is that still possible, not to care?* She doubts it.

She becomes aware of a figure following her. A man, from the footfalls. Hailey lets him trail along as far as the last market stand—a guy selling knockoff sunglasses out of an ancient beater—and then whirls on him. "What do you want, kid?"

"I think I know you."

Hailey feels heat rise to her face. Those fucking documentaries. "You don't."

"No, I do, you're one of those Rhode Island survivors," he says. "I think it really sucks what happened to you people. So few of you made it."

"Well, we get to live here now," she snaps, spreading her arms wide. "A Development Zone paradise."

"So, I guess you live in New Providence, huh? I have a transport parked near here, I can take you home."

Hailey brushes a wrinkle from her pants leg. "Go home with you? I don't even know your name, you weirdo."

He grins. "I'm Dalton. And you're Hailey. See, I told you that you looked familiar."

She rolls her eyes. "Whatever."

"Oh come on, it's cold out." He says it with a teasing lilt at the end, and when the wind gusts between them, Hailey can see his point.

"Fine, you wore me out. You can take me home. But I should warn you in advance that I'm defensively armed." The law is, you're allowed to outfit yourself with whatever gadgets you want, as long as you make a reasonable effort to inform any nearby people that you're carrying. Tonight, Hailey has poison darts embedded in her clothing and whisker-thin screamer alarms knotted into her hair.

Dalton heads away from the market, presumably in the direction of his transport. When they reach the parking lot, she sees it's a sporty little thing, its cherry-red chassis free of the garish advertising that most transports are slathered in.

This guy must be loaded, Hailey thinks. *He doesn't even need his vehicle to be subsidized.*

They face one another as the transport points itself in the direction of New Providence. Hailey can feel the kid studying her, and she touches the dart sewn into the sleeve of her sweater.

As the spires in the heart of the Development Zone disappear in the distance, Dalton speaks again. "You're the one they found in the clothes dryer, right?"

Hailey sighs. "I really don't like to talk about it. There are lots of shows about us you can watch if you're interested. My sister's in a lot of them."

"I've seen them," Dalton says. "Look, I'll be straight with you. This wasn't a random meeting, I've been tracking you for some time. I'm a game designer, and I'd like to buy the rights to your story."

This isn't the first time Hailey's heard this particular refrain, although the "game" part is new. "You'd have to talk to our agent. We all have one, as a group."

"The games are illegal, Hailey."

She'd forgotten. It's an easy thing to forget, since the consumers of the virtual-reality platform known as the "gamespace" are about their vice. The unenforced ban dropped a few years ago, after some rumors emerged about the drug used to enhance the experience.

"I don't play, but I know some people in New Providence who do," Hailey says. "I'll hook you up."

"I was really rather hoping *you'd* be interested," Dalton admits with a sheepish grin. "I've researched the Rhode Island disaster a lot, and you make the most narrative sense for the story I have in mind."

Hailey blinks and places a finger next to one of her poison darts. "I never thought I'd have a stalker. My sister will be *so* jealous."

Dalton heaves a sigh. "Can I give you my pitch? You're the youngest survivor of the wave that rearranged the coastline until your home wasn't there anymore. You survive through a freak accident, trapped among the wreckage of not just an entire city, but an entire *state*."

"I don't need a recap. When does the 'game' part come in?"

He taps his chin. "It's more of an immersive narrative than a game, actually. Oh, I'll put a few minigames in there, I'm sure. The ratings will suffer if I don't. But mostly it's just about seeing the disaster up close. Imagining what it was like to be there."

"That doesn't sound like a game that's going to make a lot of money," Hailey says.

"It won't. That's another reason I don't want to involve your group's agency. They'd laugh me out of the room."

Dalton's transport has stopped at the cross-street closest to the entrance to the New Providence subdivision. The houses here are nicer than most on the outskirts of the Pittsburgh Development Zone, thanks to many thousands of generous donations to the Rhode Island branch of the New England Wave Survivors' Foundation. The Solfind Corporation had chipped in a fair amount too.

They only cared because they could assuage their guilt affordably, she reminds herself, *with a commemorative suburb for fifty-four people.*

"I need to go," she says as she waits for him to unlock the transport.

"So are you interested? I can pay you something, even if it's not very much."

Hailey stamps her foot; it echoes throughout the interior of the transport. "I'm pretty busy, honestly. I work for Solfind." She doesn't tell him that she just works one day a week as the token human at a spire-base restaurant. The majority of her and Teresa's living expenses are drawn from the survivors' fund.

"My card," he says, "in case you change your mind."

The door hisses open and Hailey gratefully exits, wrapping her arms around her in the frosty October night. Dalton's red transport idles a few more moments at the corner, then slides away down the smooth, gridded, newborn streets.

Hailey glances at the card before she puts it in her pocket. Like his car, it's devoid of decoration, just a name and screen code marked in black ink on a soft white piece of cardboard.

Kind of traditional for a game designer, she thinks. *What a weirdo.*

*

"Breakfast?" Teresa says. She's speaking to Hailey, but her gaze is centered on the thumb-sized camera drone hovering in front of her face.

She's live, Hailey thinks as she pulls back a chair and seats herself at the table. *Well, when is she not?* "Sure."

Teresa artfully arranges a plate, tilts it to the camera, and deposits it on the table. The camera tracks the movement, and Hailey wishes she'd put on the monster mask she sometimes wears when Teresa's streaming. "Thanks."

Teresa flashes a grin at the camera and dances back to the stove, the microprocessors in her knees whirring. While they'd been in the dryer, Teresa's body had been pressed down on her legs in such a way that they'd had to be removed and replaced with the sort of limbs fitted to New People, the humanlike androids the Solfind Corporation developed to do the jobs too dangerous or tedious for humans. Teresa admitted to Hailey once that the artificial limbs have poor tactile sensation, but that overall they'd helped her personal brand so much that she couldn't quite be sorry things had worked out the way they did. "I didn't even hear you come in last night."

"I missed my bus because of the protests," Hailey says as she spears a miniature heart-shaped pancake with her fork.

"When will all this madness end?" Teresa says, speaking only to the camera this time.

"You don't even know what they're protesting about, Teresa."

"I'll tell you what I do know," Teresa says. She fishes a small tube out of her apron pocket. "This lip liner . . ."

Hailey picks up her plate and heads back upstairs. She holds up her screen as she eats on her bed, thumbing through her feed. Then she notices a small banal object on the floor of her room. The card Dalton the game designer gave her last night.

She picks it up. There's only a number, not a site address. Before she can talk herself out of it, she punches his number into her screen.

I want to talk more about the game, she messages.

She waits for a response, and nearly screams a moment later when the phone rings.

"Can you meet me at the BurgerMat near your house?"

"The fuck," she says. "You *called* me?"

"Yeah, I'm a bit of a throwback," he says. "So, meet me there? You need a ride?"

Hailey takes a deep breath. "No, I'll walk. I'll bring my jacket this time."

Hailey has been waiting outside the BurgerMat for fifteen minutes when Dalton comes puffing up. She can't see his red bullet-like transport anywhere.

"Sorry I'm late," he says, though it sounds like he doesn't really mean it.

She peers inside, where a bored human worker sits within the octopus of mechanisms that prepare the food. *That's what the protests are about,* she thinks. *Solfind wants to eliminate the human workers entirely, cut out the make-work jobs.* This won't affect her position, guaranteed as it is by the contract the Rhode Island survivors have with Solfind. But it makes the Development Zone that much more exclusive.

"Do you want to get food?" Dalton asks.

"I want to discuss terms," Hailey says, "*over* food."

Dalton pushes his way through the glass doors and the stench of processed meat wafts out like a greasy cloud. He punches in an order without asking Hailey her preference and they perch on stools near the counter while the array of machines whirs into action.

"First of all, the process will require you to take Trancium," Dalton says. "If you're not comfortable with that, we should stop right here."

Hailey isn't surprised at this stipulation, but she's still a bit uneasy about it. Trancium's reported effects are almost certainly overblown, but it's never been something she planned to fuck around with. "My comfort level depends on what I'm getting in return. I'm not destroying my brain for pocket change."

"Oh, that's just fearmongering," Dalton says, as he picks up their trays of food and ferries them to a booth. "I've taken Trancium dozens of times and my MRI is clean as a whistle."

She bites into her burger. "I still don't know why you aren't asking Teresa instead."

"Because everyone already knows her story. Yours is a mystery."

Hailey chews, considering. If she doesn't take this opportunity now, one might not come around again. It *would* be nice to live on her own, away from Teresa's ever-present cameras. "What does Trancium *do*, exactly?"

Dalton balls up his wrapper and chucks it into a hole in the table. "It's a relaxant. It frees up your mind so you can either slide into a game or build one on your own, out of your own memories and imagination."

"Have you had *your* memories put into a game?"

"My senior thesis, actually," Dalton says. "Here, I can show you on my screen."

Hailey watches a short video clip filmed in a first-person perspective of an unseen figure running through a field. From the height, she suspects it's a child. Figures approach from the corner of the screen, closing in like wild animals who've caught the scent of prey. "Who are those guys?"

"My brothers. They're not the nicest people."

"And it's a *game*?"

Dalton takes the screen back, clears his throat. "Like I said, it's more of a narrative experience."

"And you took Trancium to make this thing?"

He pinches his fingers a half-inch apart. "Just the tiniest amount. The project got a B, for what that's worth. The instructor said it would have been an A if market potential wasn't one of the grading criteria."

Hailey raises her hand, silencing him. "So it's a vanity project. Where do you get the money to pay *me*?"

"My parents give me my money. They work for Solfind."

Well, that figures, Hailey thinks. "But what's in it for Solfind?"

"Nothing. But there's a lot in it for me, and well, my parents love me."

Just as Hailey suspected all along, Dalton is a rich kid, no different fundamentally from the entitled little princelings her mother used to teach at a private school in Newport. Every one of them died. All the money in the world can't buy their survival.

"I'm going to give you a number," she says, "and if *you're* not comfortable we can stop right here." She writes down an amount that totals out to the cost of her own home in New Providence, or alternatively, several dozen acres of land in the Undeveloped Zone.

Dalton peeks at it. "Oh, we can do this."

Fuck, she thinks. *I should have asked for more.*

Hailey meets Dalton again the following day at his "studio," which turns out to be just a curtained-off section of his apartment with a shiny, new-looking gaming rig set up inside. He'd breezed her past the living room and kitchenette, but she can tell from the real fruit and shelf full of art books that despite sharing a Development Zone, they don't live in the same world.

The only decoration in Dalton's studio aside from the gaming equipment itself is a pad on the floor. "Where's your stereo? I read that you need music for this."

"Not if we're just making a recording," Dalton says, and Hailey supposes that's for the best. The audio samples of the game-enhancing folksinger Johnny Electric she'd listened to before coming over hadn't been much to her taste. She stiffens a bit when he rests the rig on the crown of her head. "Now, think of something."

"About the disaster?"

Dalton shakes his head. "Let's not start with that. Something simple. We're only calibrating."

Hailey imagines a bouncing red ball. The monitor on the screen shows a grainy grayscale image of a ball, though its movements are choppy rather than elegant. "*That's* what it looks like? Nobody's gonna pay for that."

"I told you, it's calibrating. Plus you haven't taken the Trancium yet." Dalton fishes a glass stopper bottle out of his pocket and draws up a tiny amount of the stuff into a syringe. "I use the concentrate. Easier to portion out."

"Where did you get that from?"

"I went to art school, Hailey. I have a source. Now, do you want to lay down some base memories? We can fill in the details later." He moves the dropper closer to her mouth.

Hailey stares at the syringe. A vision of Teresa enters her mind. *I can perform too*, she thinks. She opens her mouth, and Dalton squirts the liquid beneath her tongue.

"Lie down," Dalton says, and suddenly the mat on the floor looks like the most comfortable thing in the world. Hailey slides down onto it, giggling slightly from the unreality of it all. "Put that bunch of wires into your mouth. Yeah, that one."

The last thing Hailey experiences before she slips away is the coppery taste of the wires, then the concentrated Trancium flows over her like an internal Great Wave and she's gone.

Floating, waiting, dying. The air is rank with the smell of fear and your sister's rotting lower legs. Though it shouldn't be possible, you pop the dryer open from the inside, tumbling onto the rock outcropping onto which the appliance had marooned itself. The water from a greatly expanded Narragansett Bay fills your mouth and lungs, making you choke.

You start to swim in the direction of a distant shouting. You haven't learned how to swim in the ocean yet, but your legs work anyway, kicking away from the dryer to take in the devastation that surrounds you.

The shouts emanate from a woman tangled in cables and seaweed, her screams echoing over the water. You attempt to untangle her from her bindings, but her frantic windmilling makes that impossible, and she eventually sinks beneath the water's surface.

You have to get back to the clothes dryer; you have to save your sister. You begin to see things you recognize, like the sign from the pharmacy your parents used to take you to for candy and cheap toys. One of the workers bobs nearby, his blue vest waterlogged, obviously dead.

Teresa is lodged in tight, her blackened legs refusing to relinquish their position. You start to scream for help then, because surely there must be someone taking care of this mess, but you know there's nobody you can depend on. Nobody in the entire world.

Hailey gasps as she comes to, her body trembling with all of the memories the Trancium has unearthed. She looks around for Dalton—*the fucker didn't skip out on me, did he?*—and finds him hunched over one of the monitors.

"Did you get it?"

"I got *something*," he says. He points at the monitor. It's nearly as crude as the bouncing ball had been, though there's dull color spread throughout. He presses a button and the image sharpens slightly.

"No offense, but it's still kind of shitty."

He pushes another button and the screen clicks off. "This is only the beginning. How are you feeling?"

Hailey considers. She's fairly sure the memories she'd fed to the rig aren't real; recovered memories aren't exactly a thing. He *had* said imagination played into the whole deal, back at the BurgerMat. "I left the dryer on my own. I'm pretty sure I didn't in real life, but—"

"It's a game," Dalton says. "It's not going to map directly to your experiences. But there was some real emotion in that take, and I really want to keep that going for our next session."

Next session? For some reason Hailey assumed he'd be able to get everything in one. "How long was I under?"

"A standard four hours. We have a lot of work ahead of us. Same time tomorrow?"

Hailey thinks of herself floating in the morass of flotsam and corpses, of the smell of her sister's dead legs. And she finds that she can't wait to go back there, now that she knows it isn't dangerous, or at least, not as dangerous as she'd feared. "Yeah, I'll be here."

"Haven't seen much of you lately," Teresa says. For once, she's not soliloquizing for her flying camera. "That job didn't give you more hours, did it?"

"I made a friend," Hailey says.

Teresa frowns, and Hailey knows it's because she wishes she hadn't powered down her drone. This could have been an interesting plot development for her stream. "Good for you! I really mean that."

Hailey bites her lip, wondering whether or not to talk about the game, then just decides to come out with it. "We're working on a project together about my life."

A shadow of doubt runs across Teresa's face before being replaced by unenthusiastic support. "A biography, huh? Well, you know what they say. Everyone has a story, no matter how small."

"He's paying me for it. I might earn enough to move out," Hailey says. "Then you can have the whole place to yourself if you want."

"Nothing comes for free, Hailey. And no offense, but you don't have enough of a story to buy yourself a house. Hell, not even *I* do."

Hailey takes a deep breath. "We have a contract."

Teresa shrugs. "It's your life, sis." Then she pushes herself off the couch with her New Person legs and goes upstairs.

Probably gonna go make out with her camera, Hailey thinks.

The next time she shows up for a recording session, Hailey heads immediately to the studio, but Dalton calls her back to his understated rich-kid living room.

"We need to talk," he says. "I'm not getting the quality out of these takes that I've been expecting. The emotional aspect is strong, but the visual one is . . . not great." He holds up his screen, where a grainy, staticky image shows Hailey's avatar towing a box containing a litter of kittens to safety. "This is as good as I can get it."

"So what do we do about that?"

He looks away before he speaks. "I want to try giving you more Trancium. I think it will help."

Hailey stares down at her hands. She hasn't experienced any of the negative side effects of prolonged Trancium exposure so far— no trembling fingers, no alienating sense of body dislocation— but the idea of taking *more* of the stuff just seems stupid. "No."

"I figured you'd say that. It's a shame we won't be able to finish the game, though. And that I won't be able to pay you." Dalton smiles at her then, and she's reminded of the vast gulf of differences between them.

She drops her gaze at her hands again. Her non-shaking, perfectly sound hands. "You know what, I think I changed my mind."

Dalton smiles and takes her hand. "I promise, Hailey. Nothing bad will happen to you."

This time, you save them all.

Not everyone in Rhode Island, of course. That would be ri-

diculous. But on this particular run-through, you manage to load your parents, your sister, and your Aunt Frieda who'd been visiting from Boston onto a piece of siding that manages to float, boat-like, toward the new coastline so far away.

You chart your course. You speed up.

Reaching the shore should end the game, and it did in the first script. But as you've gone deeper, the story has expanded. The game is totally off-script at this point, and it hadn't ever been all that tethered to reality.

After dropping off your rescued family at the infirmary, you stop at the volunteers' tent. You're ready to go back out. The default avatar for this interactive narrative has been aged up from six to seventeen to make the rescue operations more realistic, and you have to admit that you prefer it this way, to be a confident young adult with elite swimming skills instead of a scared little girl in a clothes dryer.

Way more than fifty-four Rhode Islanders have survived; you can recognize at least a dozen people in this camp alone, friends and neighbors who in reality were never seen again. You'd love to stay and chat, but you have to get back out there.

You have to save as many as you can.

For the first time in all her weeks of memory recording, Hailey wakes up screaming. Dalton is shaking her, and she watches as her hands rake at him, seemingly not under her control.

"Why did," she pants between breaths, "you do that? This was a really good session."

"Your vitals were off," he says, pointing at the monitor that measures Hailey's breathing, muscle movements, and blood sugar, all taken from a small device buried in the gaming rig. Most of them don't have this feature, but Dalton's equipment is top of the line.

It's the eighth time she's gone under with the increased dose, and Dalton's hunch had been right: More drugs *do* make the experiences better. Both for her and for the game's eventual players, based on what she's seen on Dalton's screens. "I feel *fine*, Dalton."

"I think you should see a doctor. You're signed up with Sol-Health, right?"

Hailey holds her hand up. She doesn't detect any shaking, but Dalton's right. She should get checked out. "Well, you got that session recorded, right? Aren't we almost done?"

"We *were* done. The scope of the project has now changed."

She narrows her eyes. "What do you mean?"

"Interactive narratives are out. Well, they were never in. But now they're *really* out and if this project is going to make any money at all, it needs to be more like a game. More branches, more choices."

Hailey breathes in and out, slowly. "So that's why all the Trancium." She tries to meet his gaze, but he's started to fiddle with the monitor. "I wish you would have told me. I still would have said yes." *And not for the money*, she thinks. *Or at least, not only for the money.*

Dalton shrugs, looks away.

"Can I take the rig off now?" she asks, then starts to do it before he gives the all-clear. For some reason she can barely grasp the thing, and then she realizes why.

Her hands are shaking. *Badly.*

The next appointment available through SolHealth isn't for three weeks, so Dalton gets her in with his family's own physician, who practices out of one of the fanciest spires in the Pittsburgh Development Zone. Hailey supposes it's the least he can do, since it's kind of his fault this happened to her.

Of course, he wants to finish his game too, she thinks. *That's what this is really about.*

The doctor is a stern-faced woman who rushes Hailey through test after test, and when she's done, she calls Dalton back into the room. Hailey isn't exactly happy about this, but his family *is* the one who's paying.

"It's not good," the doctor says. "At this level of abuse, expect forty percent reduced mobility by the spring, possibly sooner. Eighty percent loss of speech by summer." The doctor angrily punches something into her screen. "I hope this was all worth it, little lady."

Say something, Hailey tries to beam to Dalton, mind to mind. *Tell them that I did it for your art, for our game.* But he just stares down at the tile floor with an expression impossible to read.

"What if I stop?" she asks the doctor. "Like, just stop taking Trancium completely, right now. How does *that* change things?"

"It doesn't," says the doctor. A smug grin flickers briefly over her face.

Dalton steps between Hailey and the doctor; he's still not looking at her, and Hailey wonders if he'll ever do so again. "But she didn't even take that much. I . . . I was there with her. I saw how much she took, and it wasn't enough to hurt her."

"Clearly she's indulging behind your back. And there are genetic profiles that are more sensitive to Trancium, but I'd check her pockets first."

Now Dalton faces her. "Don't worry, Hailey. You'll be well provided for."

Hailey watches, horrified, as her left leg begins to kick at nothing at all.

Dalton visits Hailey a few months later, after all of the legal odds and ends have been cleaned up, after Teresa cashed his family's big fat check. The check wasn't for completing the game, that was made very clear, but as a "sincere gesture of goodwill" for the girl their no-good youngest son had ruined.

"I finished the game," he says. Teresa has left for the day.

Part of the family's non-disclosure agreement forbids streaming any images of Hailey, which has put a serious dent into Teresa's career. "I thought you'd want to know."

"Go fuck yourself," says Hailey.

Dalton sits down on the couch with her without asking permission, then just keeps talking as if she gives a shit about what comes out of his mouth next. "I'm still going to release it. Lots of people on the dark web would love to play it, I bet. Especially once they know the story."

The story is that you ruined my life and got away with it, Hailey thinks. She'd say it right to his face, but speaking isn't that easy for Hailey these days.

"I shouldn't even be here," he says. "The agreement says so. But they can't tell me what to do. What *we* can do. Don't you want to see me release it?"

Hailey forces her voice out through the trembling of her chest wall. "*Fuck you*," she repeats.

His face goes red under his mop of blond hair. "You know, my family's done a lot for you. You're basically getting my inheritance, Hailey. They're forcing me to move back into their spire. We've both suffered for this."

Hailey tries to say "get out," but it sounds more like a groan.

"Anyway, I just wanted to tell you about the game, how I'm releasing it. And that, well, this sucks." Dalton stands up. "So, I'll keep in touch, right? And just remember, *you* took the Trancium. It was my idea, but you took it."

Hailey turns away from him, and stays in that position until she hears Dalton close the door behind him.

You float out on the tide in the little inflatable dinghy you've gotten as an upgrade for being so good at this. Thanks to your actions in this memory that never happened, you've managed to save nearly everyone.

You've been spending a lot more time here. You no longer need the Trancium or the rig; you're here within minutes of closing your eyes. Sometimes you're not even sure your eyes are closed, so seamless is the transition between the increasingly painful real world and the world of this "interactive narrative."

This is the body dislocation you've read about. Being in two places at once, simultaneously, yet always feeling the draw to this other world. It never goes away. It will never go away.

Today, you're searching for survivors in a part of the enlarged bay you've only seen from a distance. But now it's been fully sketched out for you, and your avatar is strong enough to get there, through an iceberg field of garbage mounds swept from what had once been Rhode Island.

There's a cry from an unseen figure mired in a small whirlpool of fast-food wrappers; you angle the boat toward the sounds and prepare for the worst. It's a little boy with a profusely bleeding head wound, but he's strong enough to work with you on his own rescue.

"Mama?" he says, stroking your avatar's face.

"No," you say, "but let's go find her." And it occurs to you that if this family exists here in this phantom world, there's no reason you can't have one too. This is a place where you can indeed raise children, where you could live your whole life if you wanted to, in a place far away from the coast and the Great Wave, a place sketched out by your own Trancium-altered mind.

You can do this, live here forever in the place that's always being created. And something tells you that you wouldn't be the first one to make that choice.

After settling the little boy safely into your boat, you repoint it toward the shore. Nothing here can ever be taken away from you, because it's all you.

You're home.

AUTOMATIC

HE RENTS HIS OPTIC nerve to vacationers from Ganymede for forty skins a night. She finds him in the corner of the bar he goes to every night after work and stays in until it's time to go to work again, sucking on an electrical wire that stretches from the flaking wall.

"That's not going to kill you anymore," she says.

He ignores her, grinding sheathed copper between brown-stained molars.

"My name is Linda Sue. I want to make babies with you."

"That rhymes," he says.

"Will you do it or not?"

"Or not."

Linda Sue stamps her foot. "Come on."

"I'll take you out first. Then we'll see." He takes her by the hand and leads her out of the bar, out into the heart of downtown New York City.

New York City, population three hundred and twenty.

*

He guides her to a restaurant he knows where the food is stacked in piles on hygienic white counters and the electricity works. She has two eyes and two hands and one set of lips, which means she is pretty. They each take a few slabs of food—the food here is free—and sit on the ground. He tells her about his life and her eyes open wide as headlights.

"I've never known anyone who had a job before."

"It's not a job. It's a career." He works at a factory, pouring liquid plastic into molds shaped like four-tined forks. "I have a quota to fill."

"Why don't you just ask the Ganys for plastic forks? Why does someone need so many plastic forks anyway?" She tears off a corner of her foodslab; it comes off onto her fingers like cotton candy. Or insulation.

"They're not for me, they're for people."

"I don't have to work. I don't like to. I just ask the Ganys for everything. They like to give us stuff."

"Well, I don't ask them." He doesn't think about the creatures dancing spider-like on his nerve. "I'm self-sufficient."

"Are we going to fuck or what?"

"Later, later. If you're good."

In Central Park they walk past a rusted-over carousel. She's drunk from the amber-colored alcohol-infused drinkslab she's consumed, and he's propping her up, forcing her to walk straight.

"I think I'm in love with you," she slurs.

"You don't know what that word means."

They pass a pair of Ganys wrapped in the form of two wall-eyed Jamaican teenagers, humans whose bodies were either sacrificed to or commandeered by the intelligent energy beams. The girls giggle and point as they pass. He flips them off.

"That wasn't very nice."

"They patronize us. Don't you see how they patronize us? There's too many of them in this city. I want to get away from here, out into the country. Will you come with me?"

"Nobody lives in the country."

"Exactly." But he knows it is pointless; nobody lives in the country because there is no way to live in the country. The farms are all poisoned and the shadow of the plague still lingers. The Ganys, knowing this, constructed an invisible olfactory wall, to keep humans and germs from mingling.

He will never leave New York City. Always a hotel, never a tourist.

The story of the plague goes like this:

Once you could be certain that you would not spontaneously grow legs from your shoulder blades and arms from your buttocks. You could be reasonably sure that ears would not sprout on your cheeks overnight. Then the plague happened, and you couldn't take that for granted anymore.

Until the Ganys came.

They get back to the bar and she takes off her clothes. Her ribs stick out like a xylophone. The foodslabs keep them alive, but they aren't the right kind of nourishment. But you couldn't expect intelligent energy beams to understand food.

Linda Sue's body is fuzzy and indistinct, a peach-colored blur. His vision is cloudy from the tourists in his head. He crawls back to his corner.

"Aren't you going to fuck me now? Aren't you going to give me my babies?"

"No, I'm still not ready."

"Oh, screw you! You're crazy. Why don't you get the Ganys to fix that for you? They fixed it for me."

Now all you want to do is mate, he thinks. *Not make love, you can't love anymore. Mate with the last members of your species so you can bring us back from the brink of extinction. That's all it is.*

"I can't."

She shakes her head. "I'm leaving. I can find some other male to give me my babies. I don't need you." She slams the lockless door behind her. He hunkers down in the corner.

He awakes to unclouded vision. The vacationers checked out of his optic nerve as he slept. He rubs his empty eyes and stumbles to the corner market, where he throws down a few skins and picks up some foodslabs.

"You don't have to pay for those," the Gany monitoring the electricity says.

"Yes, I do."

It would be so easy, he thinks sometimes, to go down to the place where the Ganys congregate, the place where you can go rent your body for a day or a lifetime to their volunteers, and just turn yourself over. Shut off your brain for as long as you wanted, and you'd get a nice pile of goodies when your assignment was over. But he'd never done that. Renting his eyes was as far as he'd go. And even that was done not out of love for the aliens or the desire for material objects, but the knowledge that, if he did not do it, he would be marked a traitor and slated for commandeering.

The Ganys have taken a special interest in humans. They had cordoned them off in cities with invisible olfactory walls, so that the remaining humans would be able to find one another more easily. And of course, they had brought The Cure. All of it was done for our—*no,* he thinks, *their*—own good.

He takes a dramatic bow, as if addressing a live audience. And in a way, he is.

*

He's leaving the city today. He crams a stack of foodslabs into a looted knapsack and heads north on foot. He walks until the sun is directly overhead, then stops by a river to eat.

The river is contaminated; he can smell the plague in it, festering. But there are drinkslabs in his pack, too. He tears off a few chunks of the tasteless foam and presses on.

A half hour later he is halted by a smell halfway between burning plastic and dog shit. *I've reached it*, he thinks. *The wall between New York City and the rest of the world*. He holds his breath and trudges through the wall, but it is no use. He can't hold his breath forever. His chest deflates and the putrescent odor fills his nose and lungs, as if the dog shit is being shoveled into his mouth by the handful. He gags and vomits up a piece of semi-digested foodslab. Choking, he runs out of the wall and takes a whiff of pure air.

He didn't even make it past the fifty-yard line.

Plunging back in, he finds the smell has changed. Now it's the scent of burning tires. He moves to the right and hits a wall of solid rotting flowers. Moving forward, there is a stench like fish guts being baked in the sun. He stumbles backwards, and falls into the strong arms of a stranger.

"Hello there, little guy," a park ranger says. He looks into the ranger's crossed and clouded eyes. A Gany.

"I couldn't get past the wall," he says. His eyes are running with tears and there is vomit on his chin.

"You shouldn't be out here all alone." The ranger gestures at his vehicle. "C'mon, let me give you a ride back home."

He doesn't want to take charity from a Gany, but he doesn't like the prospect of walking three and a half hours either, especially since he still can't breathe in all the way and his stomach feels swollen and fluttery. He gets in the vehicle.

"You have a mate back at home?" Of course, that's the first

thing the ranger would say.

"No."

"Human beings should be fruitful and multiply. It says so in your holy book." The Gany speaks with the friendly, homey Upper New York accent that was the ranger's voice when he was in control of the body, but he can sense the cold analytical tone of the intelligent energy beam guiding it.

He grunts and turns back to the window. Less than twenty minutes later the four-wheel-drive all-terrain vehicle pulls up in front of his bar. That fucking Gany read his mind.

"You be safe now, partner."

He slams the door.

In the apartment building across the street two humans are mating. For a moment, he wonders what it would be like to forget everything, become a creature of instinct, every moment of your life unscripted and so automatic.

Then he goes back into the bar.

WHERE YOU LEAD, I WILL FOLLOW: AN ORAL HISTORY OF THE DENVER INCIDENT

VICTOR DELANEY, HIGH SCHOOL teacher:

Oh, I certainly do miss Follow the Leader. It wasn't your typical cell phone game. Instead, it was what NewzBuzz.com called an augmented reality app, meaning that the elements of the game were incorporated within the real world. You'd look through your phone and see all kinds of things that didn't exist. The trees would be dripping with colorful candies, and there were little creatures you could trap with this pixie you walked around on a leash. Oh, surely you remember what it was like. I know I do.

In addition to shaking trees and collecting creatures, there were Instructions. These were a later addition to the game, but they really enhanced the experience. A golden envelope would slide onto the screen—it usually did that about two, three times a day—and assign you a task. All of these Instructions earned you points if you chose to take them on, and most of the time people did. There were regional leaderboards for people who carried out the most Instructions in a week. Usually the game would ask you to do things like snap a picture, or give a stranger a compliment, or take the long way to work. It always seemed to know when we did these things. I guess it tracked us from satellites or some such thing.

The principal tried to ban Follow the Leader from school grounds when it was at its height of popularity. She called it a distraction, which was true. But it was a distraction that roughly four-fifths of the country engaged in. You just can't ban something with that kind of reach.

And of course, everyone on staff played it too. We're only human, right? Hell, if they hadn't shut down the server that hosted it, we'd all *still* be playing Follow the Leader, even after the big kablooey.

Sorry, that was insensitive of me. I should never refer to the Denver Incident that way. Can you cut this part out, please?

Follow the Leader was a real good thing for the kids, socially speaking. It forced students to work together to complete Instructions, so that a whole class could get their names up on the leaderboard. Somehow the Russkies managed to drill cooperation into their heads better than the American school system.

Sometimes I think that it's still helping us. Rebuilding is going well, ahead of schedule in fact. Almost like older people learned a little something about working together from the game too.

Russia may have beaten us, but they haven't *beaten* us if you know what I mean. You know what I mean?

Abigail Foster, retiree:
The first time I saw the game? We were at a park, this pioneer-themed historical recreation down near Lakewood, Colorado. I'd taken my daughter-in-law Dakota and my grandson Isaiah out on what I thought would be a fun, educational day trip. Isaiah didn't look up from his phone the whole time.

Dakota snapped at him, but I asked him what he was looking at. You can't just snap at children. Have to get down to their level. I'd braced myself for something scandalous, something a teen boy with too many hormones and not enough sense would have on his phone. Surprisingly, he showed me his screen. He said it was a new game called Follow the Leader and explained the mechanics of the game. He said his mom played it too. That *everyone* did.

Well, I didn't play it. But I wasn't about to pass up an opportunity to interact with my grandbaby, even if it was through a game. After the park—which wasn't all that fun and barely educational—I immediately bought a new, better phone and downloaded the game.

I created my character—oh, she was a cutie pie, with blue hair and a lion's tail—and added Isaiah as a friend. He was *so* happy that I played the game too. Who says there's a generation gap?

For the two years that Follow the Leader ran, Isaiah and I got up to all kinds of shenanigans. We even formed a battle party at the local playground with other grandmas and their grandkids. Those were some epic days. Isaiah says that word a lot, "epic."

Isaiah doesn't play games on his phone anymore. He's just so listless ever since his mother ran off to play Good Samaritan in Virginia. I wish he'd lighten up. It's not like *we* lost anyone in the Incident, for goodness' sake.

Julianne Kowalski, Airman (dishonorably discharged):
I hope you don't mind my attorney being here. Even though my part in this Russian plot is small—barely significant, really, when you think about it—we don't want to take any chances.

So, where do I begin? Life on a military base during peacetime is boring, so to pass the time we'd play games. And the game that everyone was playing at the time was that augmented reality" cell phone game, Follow the Leader. What else were we gonna do cooped up on a military base?

Why do they call it the Denver Incident, anyway? Warren Air Force Base is nowhere near Denver. It's in Wyoming. If I had to guess, it's probably 'cause the missile was launched from a 90th Missile Wing silo in Northern Colorado.

The game shouldn't have even been playable on the base. Follow the Leader was built around publicly available maps found online, and this is a classified site. Maybe a drone mapped it out, or maybe someone smuggled in surveying equipment. There were never as many candies and creatures on base as there were in the civilian world, so the only way we could get on the leaderboard was by completing Instructions. Hundreds and hundreds of Instructions.

Even though we *definitely* weren't doing anything wrong, we still hid our gaming from the colonel. He found out anyway, of course—because he played it himself! We caught him in the mess hall performing an Instruction: swapping the position of the knives and forks. He couldn't very well ban the game after that, unless he wanted to quit playing himself. And since the colonel was ranked fifth in the state of Wyoming, *that* wasn't going to happen.

There wasn't any one Instruction that led to the so-called "incident." Sure, I'm the one who pressed the button, which is why I get to be on all those lovely news websites with the ever-increasing death toll on a ticker below my picture. Seriously, I should sue them for libel. It's not like I knew it was *the* button.

No, I don't feel any guilt. Never did. I know some others didn't take it so well, even if their place in the overall scheme of things was much smaller than mine. One in every ten military personnel stationed on this base has committed suicide. I guess some of us are just made of stronger stuff, huh?

If there's any blame here, then it goes to all of us. But it's not just us. Everyone played Follow the Leader, literally everyone. Even all the people who died in Washington. So isn't it logical to think that some of the guilt even falls on them? That's just the way I see it.

I'm not in the Air Force anymore, but I still live near the base and I'm not planning to leave any time soon. Everyone knows me here, both the airmen and the townies, and they know I'm not a mass murderer. They all know I was just following Instructions.

Reverend Caleb Jefferson, Presbyterian minister:

"God moves in mysterious ways." That phrase is a cliché at this point, and it's not even from the Bible. Some English poet wrote that. It's true in a tautological sense, of course: No human truly knows the will of the Lord.

Here in West Virginia, we're near the edge of the fallout zone, so we've had some losses. For a while, there was a funeral damn near every day. That's leveled off, though. I spend most days here at the refugee camp, trying to heal the broken spirits of those who've suffered so much in the past month.

The government says the Russians made this game. Some other men and women of God claim it was the Devil working through those programmers who then in turn worked through us to achieve his own brutal ends. Me, I believe it doesn't matter. Four million people are dead, and another million will die before the year is out. Russians, Satan, God . . . who cares?

I guess you could say I've lost my faith, and you wouldn't be wrong. But I'll still be showing up at that hospital tomorrow, and the next day, and the next. My parishioners need me, but not as much as I need them.

Olaf Andersson, programmer:

Follow the Leader wasn't a pretty game.

It wasn't entirely our team's fault. PlayMore—that was the name of our start-up—had already released four mobile games by then. While they weren't nearly as complex as Follow the

Leader turned out to be, each was a small work of art. The glowing reviews bore this out.

The problem was, the games weren't selling. Despite superior graphics and animation, the five of us in PlayMore hadn't made back any of our initial investment, and we were nowhere close to being able to draw a salary. We almost broke up the company. My father would certainly have liked that; PlayMore took up the entire first floor of his house.

And then, a miracle happened, or at least it seemed like a miracle at the time. Dagmar had been sketching out ideas for a game that used the world itself as its playing field, immersing the player in a sort of augmented reality. She'd saved it in the cloud, which was encrypted and password protected. Somehow the storage was breached and Dagmar's preliminary coding was discovered by someone who wasn't one of the five PlayMore employees.

The email was brief. The person who wrote it, who never signed their emails for the entire time we were in contact with them, offered to invest in our "quality-type game" in exchange for partial control of the coding. What they offered . . . well, I won't go into specifics, but it would have been enough money to make me, Hakim, and Dagmar very rich indeed.

Dagmar didn't want to do it, even after seeing how much they planned to pay us. This was *her* game idea, *her* baby, and she didn't want to give some stranger creative control. I'm ashamed to say that the rest of us in the company voted her down. We couldn't pass up the kind of money the angel investor was offering, and he or she or they had already deposited half of our payment into the PlayMore PayPal account.

Dagmar's original concept had been a horror-themed game which superimposed zombies and ghouls over a real-world environment. You'd pick them off with a crossbow. Our benefactor had a different vision. The zombies became colorful trees that you'd shake to receive rewards, and the crossbow became a leashed pixie who generated the dust you needed to defeat the "bad guys," a gang of wood sprites who were less scary than ladybugs. Dagmar quit the moment she saw her edited sketches. She wasn't interested in "kid stuff."

But the rest of PlayMore—me and Hakim in Stockholm, and our two contract employees in Melbourne and Taipei—we carried on. It was just *so much money*, you know? We dutifully sketched out the game our investor wanted on Dagmar's augmented reality code. Then he or she or they said the game needed to be ready in five weeks.

So, we cut corners. Fewer varieties of trees, the pixie was noncustomizable, and we didn't bother to edit the "Instructions." They were seeded into the game exactly as the investor had written them, which is why the grammar was so bad.

We were all ready to release a new patch when the Incident happened. Were less than twelve hours from doing so, in fact. I wonder if it would have changed anything if we would have been able to push it through. I probably shouldn't wonder about that, though, unless I want to wind up like Hakim. He slit his wrists a week ago.

Dagmar works for Nintendo now. I heard she's developing a zombie game. Good for her.

Isaiah Foster, student:
For a while, I really liked going to Gramma's house. Between me, her, her friends, and their grandkids, we could do a lot of fighting. Our battle party even made the state leaderboard a couple of times.

Gramma watched me all the time back then. Mom was out a lot, since she had a waitress job in the morning and another job as a janitor at night. Sometimes I didn't even see Mom for a week, but I know she was just providing for me.

Mom doesn't live here anymore, and she never calls or writes. Gramma said that she moved to the area around D.C.

to help with the rebuilding. I like that I have a mom who'd do something like that.

Diana Zhong, reporter (on indefinite sabbatical):
Out of our whole newsroom, I was the only one who survived. Most of the time, I wish I hadn't.

I'd been working for NewzBuzz.com for three years before the Denver Incident. I telecommuted at first, writing quizzes. Two of my biggest hits were "Which *How I Met Your Mother* Character Are You?" and "We'll Tell You How Old You Are from Your Soda Preferences." The second one in particular got quite an audience, lots of engagement on Facebook and other social media platforms. That's what NewzBuzz really wanted, quizzes that would be interesting enough to post to your feed so they could sell you ads geared to your interests as revealed through your answers to the quiz. It wasn't what I expected to do with my journalism degree, but at least it paid enough to cover my student loans.

Then, Follow the Leader hit the scene, and it was such an instant hit that NewzBuzz decided that they'd put a reporter solely on the augmented reality beat, with a hefty pay bump. You're looking at her.

I flew from Sacramento to D.C., and rented a postage stamp of an apartment in Takoma Park with three other women. NewzBuzz said they needed me in the main office, and well, they were certainly paying me enough to live there.

For the next year and a half, I buried myself in the world of Follow the Leader. In addition to my work at NewzBuzz, where I wrote gripping articles like "How to Pick Up That Hottie You Saw While Completing Instructions" or "How to Adjust Your Display Based on Your Astrological Sign," I also made a little bit of side money writing about Follow the Leader for video-game blogs. I was churning out at least three pieces a day, although I could pad them out with gifs. What did reporters ever do before gifs?

I was addicted to the game, of course, what with it being my job and all. Some days I'd clock a good fifteen hours on the game map, completing every Instruction I received. It was an Instruction that saved me that day.

While the missile was streaking its way across the Appalachians, I was in my cubicle banging out a listicle about the five best trees to shake to boost your pixie dust. The familiar yellow envelope slid onto my phone screen. Whereas before Instructions had led me to new undiscovered features in the game world—things I found a few hours before everyone else, almost like the game wanted *me* to write about them first—this one told me to head to a broom closet in the basement. It emphasized that I should come alone. The word "alone" was in magenta and was underlined three times so I'd *know* it was important to follow that part of the Instruction.

So that's why I wasn't with the others when the NewzBuzz building fell along with everything else in D.C. The pocket of air inside the closet was just large enough to sustain me until the emergency crews came in with their equipment and combed the area for survivors. The last thing I saw on my phone before they whisked me away to surgery was a digital trophy made out to "one of our largest friends." A fucking trophy, Jesus Christ.

I don't play games anymore. These hook hands aren't great at manipulating menus and direction pads for one thing, and for another I just feel kind of paranoid. Why did the game save *me*? Am I its "largest friend" because I wrote articles about it, articles that were highly shareable and, therefore, exposed millions to the game? Does this mean I'm responsible for the Denver Incident in some small way?

I go outside and walk the streets of Sacramento when I can. I try to do it when there aren't many people around. Sometimes you just don't want those looks of pity.

General David Alvarez, United States Army:

I signed that order, yes I did. The order that turned over the United States government to General Dashkova and her allies. It simply had to be done, you realize. We had no idea what insane Rube Goldberg situation the Russians planned to set off next. They'd already vaporized D.C. and nearly every official in our government, including Congress and the President and Vice President. The only surviving cabinet member, poor old Secretary of the Interior Skip Hawkins, died of a heart attack when he saw the footage. He was ninety-one, probably never played a cell phone game in his life.

Oh, there's no doubt in my mind that the Russkies are behind it, especially once we discovered that the ISP address of the emails sent to those Swedish programmers led straight back to Moscow. Can't trust a Slav. Follow the Leader was all a sick long game designed to trick US Air Force personnel into launching a nuclear missile right at the Capitol building while Congress was in session, without even knowing what they were doing. Not all that surprising, though. The zoomies have always been less disciplined than the other services.

This isn't over, no matter what that surrender document says. The Russkies haven't licked us yet. It's only a matter of time before America stands tall once more with a new elected government that can lead us from tyranny. Our remaining nukes may be decommissioned, but our *spirits* are still online.

Dakota Foster, aid worker:

I'll never pay back what I did. Never. But I guess this is a start, a drop in the bucket. It doesn't mean much—it doesn't mean anything—but I'm here anyway. I couldn't *not* come.

The ironic thing is, I didn't even play Follow the Leader that often, and I tended to let my Instructions pile up. The way they worked was that you have a set amount of time to complete each one, which is different for every Instruction. After that, the Instruction fizzles, and your avatar loses a little bit of its life force. Maybe you'll even drop a level. Some people took the game really seriously; my mother-in-law Abigail, for instance.

But me? Nah. Just checked it when I happened to think of it, which wasn't often. Only did the Instructions that seemed easy enough and wouldn't take up much of my time.

The day of the Incident, I'd just gotten to Warren Air Force Base from my other job at the diner. Thank goodness Abigail was around to watch Isaiah. I could never have gotten through the horrible year after Ted's passing without her.

Of course, then I wouldn't have had any time to play stupid video games on my phone, either. So perhaps that was a mixed blessing.

My role was slight, the attorneys tell me. They pinned most of the blame on that Kowalski woman, but even she didn't face any punishment. Nothing they did to her would have brought back four million people. It's despicable to think that anything could.

Airman Kowalski pushed the button. But she also had good reason to think that it was disabled. There's a long, long list of checks and balances that goes into a nuclear facility, hundreds of fail-safes, layers upon layers of protection. You don't just press a button and launch a nuke. That's not how it works. There were dozens of smaller Instructions that brought the button Kowalski pushed to life, and a number of others that pointed that nuke straight at the Capitol. And one of them was mine.

I was just heading back from break when an Instruction popped onto my screen, one of those canary-yellow envelope icons. I opened it. It was a time-restricted Instruction, one set to erase itself within thirty seconds, and it came with a million-point bounty. That score would have jumped me about twenty levels, to the very top of the Wyoming leaderboard. Maybe I would have even made the national one.

Go into the next room, it said, *and delete the last line of code from the computer closest to the door.*

The smart thing would have been to ignore it, or maybe alert the colonel in charge of the base. To me, this seemed *way* outside the bounds of what a normal Instruction should be. I'd gotten a couple of these weird, invasive Instructions lately, always when I was on the base. I didn't get them in town. That should have told me something.

But the airmen here did this kind of shit *all the time*. I'd seen them move shredded papers from one bin to another, snap pictures in restricted zones, and read off serial numbers and coordinates into their phones. At least, I think they were serial numbers and coordinates.

How do you blow a whistle when you're not sure anyone's actually doing anything wrong? You don't, at least not if you have two jobs, a kid, and a mountain of debt. I couldn't lose this job. So I let all these weird little adjustments slide, especially after I saw the colonel doing them too.

I followed that Instruction. I deleted that code. In my defense, I also left the man who worked there a note telling him what I did and why I did it, but the investigators never found that. Maybe a different person got the Instruction to destroy my note, or the programmer himself sabotaged his own code even deeper in yet another Instruction. I'll never know. Even having the code up on the screen was a violation. Likely, the programmer had gotten his own Instruction to leave it. We'll never know for sure, since he killed himself afterward along with so many others at the base.

Anyway, that was the code that angled the nuke toward Washington, D.C.

I'm stationed at a refugee camp in Beckley, West Virginia, which is just outside of the contamination zone. We try to make things here as nice as they can be. I help out in the medical ward, mostly, tending to children from Alexandria who've suffered radiation burns from the fallout, and Baltimoreans who got in car crashes because they were distracted by the mushroom cloud blossoming over the Potomac River. D.C. itself is a total loss, aside from a few stragglers who managed to hole themselves up in basements at just the right time. One of the women from D.C. who came through here said Follow the Leader told her where to hide. She'd just lost both her hands, though, so she was probably delusional.

I tell everyone I meet here what part I played. I figure it's the right thing to do, because maybe they wouldn't want to be treated by a person who had a small but significant role in blowing them up with a nuclear bomb. But so far, nobody cares. I swear that some of them are more concerned about losing Follow the Leader than they are about the bomb.

I don't use a cell phone anymore. Trust issues, you understand. Isaiah and Abigail know where to send letters. If you head back to Wyoming after this, please give them my love.

General Valentina Dashkova, interim head of Russian Holdings in North America (as told to translator):
The last thing I ever expected was the surrender of your country. That fat *mudak*, General Alvarez, barged onto the beach with a handwritten paper, begging me to sign. I was still in my bikini. Talk about sloppy.

I wasn't even here on official business; I was vacationing in Hawaii with my brother and his kids. But I was the only high-ranking general in the Russian Armed Forces in the United States at that time, so it fell to me to sign the document. I did so, barely aware of what I was signing, and then there were all these news cameras in my face, telling me that Russia had dropped a bomb on Washington, D.C. Then, after it was revealed that the bomb came from *within* the United States and that some cell phone app was involved, they reported that we created *that*.

In truth, we are not responsible, as much as you would like

us to be. We didn't contact any Swedish programmers. Yes, what little trail they happened to find did lead back to Russian ISP addresses, but that doesn't mean anything. Don't you have trolls here who could fake that kind of thing? Maybe your own trolls did this, and blamed it on us. That would be just like your country.

Games don't work how they said Follow the Leader worked. They *can't*. If Follow the Leader responded to the environment in the way your news media claims it does, the game would have had to be acting on its own. No coder could ever plan these Instructions so carefully; it would require a level of sophistication beyond even what we Russians are capable of.

You're asking me if the game is alive? Oh, you Americans. Perhaps it is for the best that we are here, to protect you from yourselves. You blew up your own capital because a game told you to. Does that sound like the action of a sane country to you?

I never played Follow the Leader, as it was never translated, and now that it's been pulled from the market, it won't ever be. We do have a similar augmented reality game in Russia—I believe it's called Shipwrecked. I'll show it to you. It's new, just hit the market a few months ago. You walk on this deserted tropical island, read signs that tell you where to go, and fun things you can do for points.

No, it is absolutely nothing like Follow the Leader. And even if it's similar, the outcome won't be the same. We Russians are not all dumb *mudaks* like you are. Now, please, you must excuse me. I have a meeting to attend. I can't very well spend all day playing Shipwrecked like some spoiled American!

Oh, can you please step aside? There's a treasure chest right behind you. There, I've got it.

TRIAL AND TERROR

SOMEHOW, THE VAN MAKES it most of the way through Iowa. Then it dies all at once, spectacularly, farting out its reserve of gas like an old man on taco night in the run-down nursing home his good-for-nothing children stuck him in after he drove the family sedan into a telephone pole.

Most of those things don't exist anymore. No nursing homes. Only a few sedans. And don't get me started on the lack of taco nights.

"Shit!" Frank yells, banging on the steering wheel. "Shit, shit, shit!"

Clementine, our bass player, smirks and snorts a little through her nose. "I don't think you said 'shit' enough times, Frank. Better say it again."

"*Shiiiiiiit*," Frank moans, his voice the sound of a tugboat navigating through a soupy fog.

I open the door, which creaks ominously. "We'd better go find help. We passed a town around ten minutes ago."

Frank counts out numbers on his fingers. It takes a lot longer than it should. "But that's like a hundred miles!"

"It's seven miles," I say. "But it'll still take a while to get there."

"Dibs on staying in the van!" Clem doesn't even wait for an answer before flopping herself into the driver's seat.

Frank looks at her. I look at her.

"What? Someone might steal it."

"Let's go, Syl," Frank says to me.

I stick my tongue out at Clem and follow Frank down the dusty, corn-husk-strewn highway.

Our band's been on the road for five months now, spreading the power of positive thinking across the Midwest after the Great Happiness Collapse. A few years ago, aliens from the constellation Cygnus temporarily tainted Earth's water supplies with pleasure-juice, a colorless and odorless shortcut to heaven. Then, just as we were all getting used to life under the drug, they cut it off, leading to a worldwide epidemic of rebound depression. One of the many imperfect cures for this huge downer was awakecore music, a genre Frank himself invented, which sounds a lot like a stray cat getting hit with a mandolin.

At this point in the game, Frank's mostly in it for the merch money. "Picture it, Syl," he says as we inch down the highway. "Mousepads with like, our logo on them and everything. I met a guy in Des Moines who found a whole warehouse full of blank ones. We can draw the logos with that puffy paint we use on the T-shirts."

I don't know what to criticize first: The fact that nobody uses computers anymore? That a mousepad with puffy paint all over it would be a very poor mousepad indeed? Finally, I hit on the most obvious fault. "That would require *you* not changing the name of the band every few months."

"I can't help that I keep thinking of better ones!" Frank leaps and grabs at the top of a speed limit sign. He doesn't even bend it, but from the way he starts to howl, I think he might have broken his hand.

"My hand!" He falls to the ground.

"You're a real idiot, Frank."

From the signs on the road, we are now entering Oskaloosa, Iowa. Low-slung buildings topped with drooping slate roofs line the banks of a slightly greenish river. From a distance it looks like pollution, but when we get closer I see that it's actually algae. Oskaloosa is a genuine cow town, not even big enough in the Time Before to justify a Cygnian recruitment compound.

We wade through the waist-high grass, me parting the greenery at the front, Frank limping behind even though it's his hand that's broken, not his foot.

"When we get there," I say, "stay at the perimeter. Be ready to run."

He wipes his face with the corner of his shirt, which hasn't been washed for the entire tour. "No, Syl. I'm going in with you."

"But you don't need—"

"Remember Peoria?"

I snort. "Of course I remember. That was only a few days ago."

"Remember how you went into Peoria to see if they had any supplies we could barter for, and then you didn't come back, and me and Clem had to come *get* you?"

I mow down a layer of grass with my forearm. "I'm surprised you convinced her to come on this tour at all. She seems like she doesn't even want to play the shows most of the time."

Frank glares at me. "You've never liked Clem, have you?"

"Of *course* I like her, it's just—"

He stops me short with his good hand. "Did you hear something?"

I strain my ears. Voices come from the direction of the town. We quicken our pace and round the bend to see a crowd of townspeople, who are surrounding a quartet of horses pulling ropes in four separate directions. In the middle is a dummy stuffed with straw. When the horses reach a certain point, the dummy explodes its straw confetti on the mostly-blond heads. The crowd cheers.

"Hey, what's this?" I ask the random woman next to me.

"They're practicing drawing and quartering." She sneers. "You don't look like you're from around here."

"We're just passing through."

"This is what we do to criminals," she says, jerking a thumb at the horses. "And outsiders."

My stomach clenches and I reach for Frank, but he's already stumbled toward the eye of the crowd. He holds his trembling right hand aloft.

"Hey! Is anyone here a doctor?"

The Oskaloosans look up as a solid unit, their spooky pale faces like the glittering of evil stars. There's a generalized murmuring, and one of them holds up a mimeographed flyer. Then they advance on Frank like a wave. Like a *tsunami*.

I run toward him and start tugging on his sleeve. "I *told* you to stay back, Frank," I say, before the wave overtakes us both and I'm pinned choking on the asphalt under a solid four hundred pounds of cornfed Iowa flesh.

This isn't the nicest jail cell I've ever been in, but at least there are beds. There aren't always beds, as Clem and I learned the hard way in Indiana.

Frank paces the narrow room, a caged tiger. "Fucking *Iowa*." He kicks the brick wall and crumples to the ground with a shriek.

"Great job, Frank, now you have a broken hand *and* a broken foot."

"It's not broken," he says, hopping over to his cot and sucking back tears.

"We have to get out of here," I say.

Frank pulls at his hair with his remaining hand. "Clem will

save us. She has to be getting worried by now."

Suddenly, whistling echoes down the long white corridor. A guard with a protruding beer belly presses his face against the bars. "Mealtime." He throws a handful of fun-sized candy bars onto the concrete floor.

"Wait!" I say, jamming my arm through the metal slats. "What are we charged with? You can't leave us in here forever." Technically he can, since the rule of law doesn't exist post-Cygnian invasion, but he might not know that.

"It's not up to me." The guard's hand creeps slowly toward his belly button and starts to pick it. "The judge will be here in the morning. You'll get a chance to plead your case."

"But what the fuck are the charges?" Frank asks through a mouthful of nougat. "When's our trial?"

The guard throws a balled-up piece of paper at us before lumbering off, and I uncrumple it to find a grainy picture of what might be Frank and Clem. Underneath them is a caption reading WANTED: MURDER.

"Murder?!" I pace around the ten-by-ten room, which isn't easy to do. "You didn't commit murder! How could you have committed murder, Frank? How?!"

He's a lot calmer than I think he should be. "Let's just wait for all the evidence to be reviewed."

"*What* evidence?"

Frank stares at his right hand, which is approximately twice the size of his left one. "Do you remember what happened in Peoria?"

"Well, apparently you and Clem *killed a guy.*"

He shushes me down, and nods at the other room where the guard is. "We might have. I don't know! It was dark! We were looking for *you*, Syl."

"This isn't my fault, like, *at all.*" I drop my voice; for all we know they've got the place wired. "Who did you kill, Frank?"

He beholds me from his cot, the moonlight turning his eyes

into calm pools. "Some stranger. I thought he was going to hurt Clem, so I hit him with a rock. He fell down."

I shake my head. "Shit."

"But when I went to check on him, he was gone. Disappeared. Me and Clem searched for an hour, but he must have gotten away." He glances out the window at the full moon. "Guess he didn't."

"You didn't kill anyone," I say, even though that's exactly what it sounds like he did. "And even if you did, he was a sleaze, right?"

"Maybe," Frank replies, and I can tell that he's tired of talking about it.

I shift around on my cot until it's clear that the bar jammed into my lower back isn't going to get any less obtrusive. Then I paw through the candy, foraging for cheap calories. And after *that* I look over at Frank. It's impossible to tell whether he's asleep or awake. I fluff the candy wrappers into a makeshift pillow and settle myself on the narrow cot, timing my own breaths to the snoring of the guard. I do not sleep.

Or, maybe I do. At least that would explain why Frank is in the cell with me one minute and gone the next. I'm not *that* inattentive, even if I did get lost on the mean streets of Peoria.

"Frank!" I yell, cupping my hands around my mouth. "Fraaank!"

The pudgy guard bangs a truncheon against the jail-cell bars. "Pipe down in there."

"Yeah, because I'm disturbing *so* many people," I say.

"You're disturbing *me*."

I cling to the bars of the cell. "Where is my friend?"

"I sent him to get that hand patched up. We also have to interrogate you two. Separately, of course."

"Naturally. But I won't talk until I see that he's alive."

"Hell, lady, what kind of people do you think we are?"

He throws me another pocketful of candy and saunters away, whistling.

"Certainly not the kind that believe in a balanced diet," I mutter. I scoop the candy up and stuff my face with Snickers and M&Ms, gagging on the sticky sweetness.

Did Frank actually kill someone in Peoria? It's hard to believe. Oh, I definitely think he'd *try* to kill someone who was threatening Clem, but he just doesn't have the upper body strength.

There's a conversation too far away for me to hear, and then the door of the jailhouse slams shut. A different guard comes into view. Her warm brown eyes are cold when she looks at me. She frowns at the drift of wrappers littering my cot.

"Clean that up, we're not your parents," she says.

"Well, we *are* wards of the state at the moment. You people locked us in here, so now you have to take care of us." I scatter the wrappers even more.

Her eyes graze me over from top to bottom. "Your boyfriend's in some deep shit."

"He's not my boyfriend. He's our vocalist and lead guitarist. We're in a band."

"Oh yeah? Are you any good?"

"We're terrible." I thread my hand through the bars. "I'm Sylvia. Syl for short."

The cop whips out her taser and holds it over her right hand, which she slips into mine. "Bettylou."

"*Seriously*? Is this place a stereotype factory?" Her face twists up hideously and I make a conversational U-turn. "I mean, pleased to make your acquaintance."

"Your friend's in the interrogation room. We're chipping away his defenses, bit by bit." Her top lip curls.

I don't bother telling her that Frank doesn't *have* any defenses. "Are we at least going to get a fair trial?"

"You'll get *a* trial." She turns and walks away, her thick

thighs straining the limits of her pencil skirt. My gaze lingers perhaps a little bit longer than appropriate, but it's been so long, and I'm only human.

Bettylou turns, gives me a nod, and winks. I guess she has something in her eye.

A few hours later, Frank is back in the cell. The cast on his hand resembles a Mickey Mouse glove, but one you'd see at an unlicensed off-brand amusement park in Delaware or somewhere.

I check to make sure that neither of the guards is around, then shuffle over to him. "How was it?"

"That guard fucking *tortured* me, Syl," he says. "He tried to force me to confess."

"Did you?"

"No," he says, and I'm a little surprised. "But he said it wouldn't matter if I confess or not. He said they want to make an example of 'city slickers from way out East.'" He snuffles and wipes his nose with his cast. "I mean, who even *talks* like that?"

I ruffle his hair, because I'm not sure what else to do.

"Clem *has* to get here soon," Frank says.

"Yeah, maybe." I don't want to say the thing I'm thinking, that Clem's absence probably means something bad already happened to her. Best case scenario is that she met up with a better band.

"I love her *so much*," Frank says before bursting into tears.

I wrap my arms around him, and I even keep myself from flinching when he sneezes a fine mist all over me.

"There's going to be a trial," I say. "I've watched a lot of legal dramas in my day, Frank. They were on Channel Eleven all the time. I can defend you."

Frank's face scrunches up. "Shouldn't we hire a real attorney for that?"

I spread my arms wide. "You think anyone in this town is

going to give us a fair trial? We're outsiders from way back East."

Truthfully, I don't think any amount of legal wrangling can save Frank. But a show will. Whenever logic fails, our two-chord, atonal music has always saved us from whatever scrapes we happen to get into. We don't understand the magic, but that doesn't stop it from working. It's worked in the past and it's going to work now. *If* I can get the right tools.

Just as I've lulled Frank to sleep, Bettylou arrives, clanging on our jail bars with a baton. "It's time for your confession, Syl."

"I have nothing to confess," I say. Frank stirs in my lap, and I maneuver away from him, leaving him on his cot.

"It'll be better for you if you do. The judge will go easier on you."

I walk over to the bars and do my best to loom over her menacingly, which isn't hard. She's a full head shorter than me, and I'm not tall. "We'll take our chances at trial."

She smiles. "Come to the interrogation room anyway. Who knows, might be fun."

Bettylou herds me down a dingy gray corridor toward a door so nondescript that I can't even describe it. She pushes me inside and I topple headlong over a migraine-orange plastic chair and surprisingly land on my feet.

"Did you see that," I say. "It was practically a cart—"

"Shut up for just one second." Bettylou swings me around, takes my head in both of her hands, and presses her lips against mine in a sweet Iowa welcome. I yank at the buttons of her blouse and then melt into her, the feel of her body against me a warm misty rain on a very dry desert.

Afterward, as Bettylou and I are spooning on top of the chipped and graffiti-ed interrogation table, she whispers, "Take me with you."

"Yeah, you can come. But what I need to know now is what's

really going to happen when the judge gets here. Will he give Frank a fair trial?"

Bettylou skates her fingertips through my hair. "The judge isn't a he. Or a her. It's an it."

Well, at least I'm not being inadvertently sexist. "What, is the judge a robot?"

"No, it's a computer."

"A *computer* is going to sentence my friend to death?!"

She flips around to face me. "It's not only a judge. It tells us how to set up the community and live our lives for maximum harmony. What to plant, where to find clean water, who to marry—"

I can feel my lips purse up at the last one. "But it's a *computer*, Bettylou. Frank has the right to defend himself in front of a jury of his peers."

"His chances are probably better with the computer in this town."

This, at least, I can't refute. "You can come along with us. I really, really want you to come along with us. But I need to save Frank. I *know* he didn't kill anyone, and if he did . . . well, he didn't."

"How can we do that? The courthouse is surrounded. This is the trial of the decade."

I sit up and the interrogation table creaks under my weight. "Go get some instruments. Guitars, drums, whatever you can find. We're going to throw this town a hell of a show."

Just then, the door slams back on its hinges. Bettylou bolts upright and smooths her skirt down.

It's the male guard. "This investigation is a little unorthodox, sergeant."

"I–uh, don't think I can crack her."

The guard shrugs. "Don't matter. The judge is here. That boy is gonna be drawn and quartered before sundown." He shuts the door.

"Double time on those instruments, Bettylou." I slide off the table and give her one last kiss. "I have to go stall that trial."

The courtroom is packed, but I haven't taken a shower in so long that the crowd parts around me, leaving me a nice empty space in the rows of seats.

A surly bailiff manhandles an even surlier Frank into a wooden cage standing next to a delicately filigreed dining table. The bailiff shoves him into it in such a way that Frank falls on his broken hand. Frank screams, then snaps at the bailiff like a rabid ferret.

"I fucking hate Iowa," I mutter under my breath.

A hush descends over the crowd. Two people dressed all in black, a man and a woman, carry an ornately painted box to the table and open it, revealing a laptop from the Time Before. The bailiff steps forward.

"All rise for the Honorable Patricia J. Atkinson, Supreme Judge of the Quad Cities Region. Court is now in session." The bailiff grins at Frank and draws a finger over his own throat.

A noise rattles from the laptop's speakers, sounding like a human's cough filtered through wax paper. Then a gravelly, oddly accented voice begins to speak. "Please enter the nature of your problem."

The male assistant dressed all in black types into a remote keyboard placed on his lap, and the woman helpfully narrates. "This man, one Frank . . ." She looks over at our beaten-down vocalist. "Hey, you got a last name?"

"Carnage." It's lame, but at least not as incriminating as his last stage name, "von Murderkill."

"Frank Carnage, an outsider, stands accused of the killing of an unknown victim last Thursday, at approximately 11:47 PM, as witnessed by drone camera in the vicinity of Peoria, Illinois. Mr. Carnage, how do you plead?

He shrugs. "Does it matter?"

I stand up. If Frank isn't going to defend himself, I sure as hell will. "He pleads innocent, you worthless computer slave."

The typist taps it in. "I shall now hear the evidence of the prosecution," the computer wheezes. "For a sore throat, try a spoonful of apple cider vinegar."

The male guard who'd tortured Frank only a few hours ago steps to the front of the courtroom. Apparently, Oskaloosa can't afford a separate prosecuting attorney. He holds up a flash drive. "I have on this disk video footage showing that Mr. *Carnage* here threw a rock at an unknown victim near the abandoned Cygnian compound in Peoria. The place wasn't *totally* looted; its security system was still functional. I believe you'll be pretty convinced." He slides the flash drive into the side of the Honorable Patricia J. Atkinson and plants a smug smile on his face.

The laptop's screen judders a few times, then its voice settles into a low purr. "Affirmative."

"But where's the *body*?" I yell. "And what kind of Cygnian compound goes unlooted for so long? This could all be some massive conspiracy." Visions of a detective's crazywall enter my head, and I mentally plot a world-spanning scheme that will stall this trial for at least as long as it takes Bettylou to return with the instruments.

Something inside Judge Patricia whirs up. "State your name, Unknown Human."

"My name is Sylvia," I say, "and I'm in a band."

"The *greatest* band," Frank sputters out.

"A pretty okay band," I reply.

"Be that as it may," the jail guard/prosecuting attorney says, "that doesn't excuse murder. And who are you to speak for this man? You don't look like an attorney. Or smell like one."

I weave my way forward; the crowd dutifully parts ways for me. "I've known Frank four years now. We've lived together, we've been on the road together, and now we've been arrested together. And if you're going to accuse him of killing a person, then you're going to need better evidence than that."

Patricia J. Atkinson's screen flashes. "This will be a good season for corn."

I think back to all the endless hours of legal dramas I'd been exposed to when I worked at the Warsh 'n Dry right after dropping out of college. "Your Honor, this is America. And in America, we have rights. Certain *inalienable* rights. Like, the right to be judged by a jury of one's peers, and not an old Dell computer with a scraped-off decal on its back. Also, a speedy trial. Speaking of speed, did you know cheetahs can run over sixty miles an hour? Wow, that's fast. Cheetahs live in Africa, where Toto blessed the rains." I hum a few bars from a barely-remembered song. How long does it take a person to find some musical instruments in this town?

"You'd better be going somewhere with this," says the guard/prosecutor, "and not stalling for time."

The beach ball on Patricia's screen starts spinning again. "Does the defense call a witness to the stand?"

I gaze absently around the room until the guard/prosecutor coughs into his hand and checks his non-existent watch. I'm about to tell the computer-judge that I rest my case when Frank gestures wildly from his cage at the front of the room.

"You put *me* on the stand, Syl. That's how this works."

"I need to speak to my client," I say. I hunch down next to Frank. "I'm not sure this is a good idea. You said you might have killed that guy."

"It might not have been a guy. Maybe it was a woman."

I roll my eyes. "You're the worst client ever. But Bettylou's not back yet, so we don't really have a choice." I flag the bailiff over.

"Who's that?" he asks, but there isn't time for me to explain.

Frank perches on the rickety wooden chair between his cage and the Honorable Patricia J. Atkinson. He's chastened, like a little boy who's been caught with his hand in the cookie jar.

"Mr. Carnage," I say, pacing back and forth, "where were you on the night of the supposed 'crime?'"

"In Peoria. I was looking for you, Sylvia."

"I know," I say softly. "Was anyone with you?"

"Yes, my friend Clementine Disruption. She plays the bass."

"Objection!" says the guard/prosecutor. "Irrelevant."

"Overruled," drones the judge. "The next partial eclipse will occur on June 24."

"Thank you, Your Honor." I lean against the judge's table. "Mr. Carnage, what was your state of mind at the time of the purported incident?"

Frank rubs his bare hand against his casted one. "We were scared. We thought you might have gone to the Cygnian compound, so we started there."

"I was looting the houses and the mall," I say. "I never went near the compound. You know those places freak me out."

"I'm glad you didn't," he says. And then he starts talking.

As in most cities over a certain population limit, there'd been a deserted Cygnian compound in Peoria, the building where the aliens prepared ten percent of humanity for a one-way trip from Earth to Cygnus. But from the wreckage left behind, it was clear that this one had been overtaken by the rejected humans of Peoria at one point.

Frank and Clem had picked their way through the compound, on the hunt for both me and anything that would be useful on the tour. And then they'd found him. Or her. The victim.

"It was dark, no moon at all. Clem said she felt like something had been following us. I laughed it off, but then we saw him." Frank wipes the back of his hand over his eyes. "The person or whatever."

"Please take a moment if you need to. Can we get some Kleenex over here?" I ask this of the bailiff, but he doesn't budge.

Frank barrels on. "He was on the pleasure-juice. I could tell that by the way he was staggering. It freaked us out. There wasn't much flesh left on the body." He sinks his face down into his good hand, looking glum. "I think he was part of the ten percent of people the Cygnians were supposed to take, but he got left behind when the raid happened. He was hungry. And he was coming for Clem. I *had* to do what I did, but I'm still sorry."

"You should have alerted the authorities, *son*," the guard/prosecutor says, "instead of taking matters into your own hands."

"*What* authorities?!" Frank rocks back in the chair and I brace myself for its collapse.

I decide I've had enough. Instead of objecting, I step back in front of Frank, hip-checking the bailiff. "You didn't do anything wrong, Frank. Stand up for yourself for once in your life!"

"It's over, Syl," Frank turns toward the open laptop, as if personally addressing whatever ghost powers that machine. "I'm ready to accept my punishment. The drawing and the quartering or whatever. But before I die, I have something I'd like to say."

"My charge is down to twenty percent," the judge says. "Please plug me in."

Frank takes a deep breath. "What I did, I only did to protect the woman I was with, Clementine. She means everything in the world to me. And when I saw that zombie—"

"*Alleged* zombie," interjects the bailiff.

"Shut up, man. Anyway, like I was saying. I shouldn't have done it, but I'd do it again. I'd walk over broken glass for that girl. I'd drink molten glass for her. I'd . . . do a lot of things that don't involve glass. The point is, I love her. If you're going to kill me, I want it on the record that I died for love."

A tiny silence hangs over the courtroom. It feels almost like applause is about to burst out. Then Patricia J. Atkinson opens its stupid computer mouth.

"I find the defendant guilty. Commence the drawing and quartering."

The bailiff whoops and grabs Frank's cast-hand. The judge's

two assistants take his legs. They hoist him into the air and my world turns sideways.

"*Stop!*"

The voice that says this is low, sultry, and can't be mistaken for anyone else.

"Clem!" Frank and I yell her name simultaneously.

A guitar in each hand, Clementine Disruption strides forth on her hot pink, four-inch-high heels. Her dreadlocks flow behind her like a nest of amplifier cables, and the makeup she concocted from the shells of dead beetles doesn't look as bad as it usually does. Behind her is Bettylou, hugging a tattered cardboard box. She smiles at me, and I give her a little wave back.

The bailiff doesn't know whether to hang onto Frank or reach for Clem, and while he stands there deciding, Frank wrests himself out of the meathead's grip. The judge's lackeys scuttle away.

"I heard what you said," Clem says to Frank. "Every word of it."

"And?" His eagerness is painful to watch.

Clem glares down everyone in the courthouse. Not even Patricia dares to speak. Then she takes Frank's head in her hands and kisses him deeply, the guitar springs sproinging as they're mashed between their bodies.

"Let's hit the road, baby," Clem says.

The guard/prosecutor half-coughs, half-belches. "If you were here for that pathetic little declaration of love, you heard the verdict. This man is guilty, and we intend to draw and quarter him as per the town charter."

"We're leaving," Clem says, "but first we're giving you the show of your life." She hands a guitar to Frank.

"I can't play," he says sadly, holding up his busted paw.

Clem hands it to me instead, even though I always sound like I'm playing with a broken hand. Bettylou takes a microphone from the box, gives it to Clem, who then hands it over to Frank. It's not plugged into anything, but it makes him seem about three times as confident. Though that still isn't much.

"I don't see what *any* of this has to do with the issue at hand," the guard/prosecutor says.

But the audience of attentive Oskaloosans has tired of their kangaroo court, and I can feel the supernatural pulse in the air that lets me know our one weird trick will work yet again. Clem bangs together a set of homeless drumsticks she'd pulled out of Bettylou's box above her head, then tosses them aside.

And we play.

I thought we'd start off with "Electrify Me," which is the closest thing we've ever had to a hit single, but Frank launches into a power ballad he wrote after the next-to-last time he and Clem broke up. He addresses only Clem when he sings, not the crowd.

"Why is this working?" Bettylou whispers to me, confusion stamped on her pretty little face.

"I don't know. But it always does. Roll with it."

Bettylou shrugs, takes a child's ukulele from the box, and plucks out a melody that perfectly complements Frank's nasal whine. At least we have one talented person in the band now.

When the song is over, the Oskaloosans stand and cheer, stomping their feet and throwing useless gobs of money at us. Frank scoops a few of the bills up and mops his forehead with them. Clem pounds out the opening bassline to our danciest number, and even though they can't possibly know what song we're playing, the crowd erupts in delight.

The guard/prosecutor is nowhere to be seen. Some people just don't like music *or* magic.

We play until the sun sets and the air grows cold. We run out of our own inventory of songs quickly, so Frank launches into a medley of commercial jingles from the Time Before. The audience shouts out the choruses before he does.

"I feel . . ." Frank croons.

"Like chicken tonight! Like chicken tonight!"

By the end of the set we've resorted to improv, making up goofy songs about the audience members, who reluctantly file out one by one, all tuckered out from the most exciting thing that's ever happened to them. When the last of the Oskaloosans begs off, we repack everything we can in Bettylou's box and start out on our seven-mile trek to the van. We step over the sleeping forms of the judge's assistants, who cradle the Honorable Patricia J. Atkinson in their arms.

Frank flings open the courthouse door and we all stand face to face with the guard/prosecuting attorney. The gun in his hands is cocked and aimed, though not at Frank. He's pointing it at Bettylou.

"Sergeant," he says, the barrel of the gun only slightly trembling. "For aiding and abetting this man and his two accomplices, you are in violation of—"

"Oh, give it a rest, Zebediah."

Frank shields Clem with his body despite the fact that he's three inches shorter than her when she's in those heels. I do my best to cover Bettylou. "We don't want any trouble," Frank says.

"Then maybe you shouldn't have killed anyone, Mr. *Carnage*."

Bettylou reaches around me and grabs at the gun. "Oh, this thing doesn't even have bullets; we haven't had bullets since—"

The shot fires right on cue, and I swear I can feel it zing past my cheek on its way into the building. Two loud yelps cry out, one after the other, followed by a sickening crash.

We all rush in, even though the four of us could have used this opportunity to scramble for the van. The two assistants stand over a smoking hunk of plastic: the former Honorable Patricia J. Atkinson, now forced into an early retirement.

"What did you *do*?" the woman stenographer says.

We all stand in an uncomfortable silence for at least thirty seconds. Then I say something, because *someone* has to say something. "You're free now. You're all free. It can't tell you what to do anymore." Of course, they never had to listen to the thing in the first place, but I don't remind them of that.

"But we don't *know* how to run a town," says the other lackey. "Or how to judge the innocent and guilty alike."

"You'll learn," Frank says. "Everyone back in Pittsburgh, where we're from, learned how to get along after the pleasure-juice."

The two assistants seem skeptical, and so am I. They'll either learn or die trying, and I hope dearly that it's the former.

"Let's go, gang," Clem says.

We grab a few gallons of gasoline and a spare fan belt from one of the townspeople who'd been there for the show.

"I was so excited I wasn't able to sleep," she says. "How did you ever create such glorious music?" We drag Frank away before he starts yammering on about music theory.

The van is untouched, although Clem had left the driver's side door wide open. We stack Bettylou's new instruments in the back next to my disassembled drum kit. You can never have too many instruments, especially when your lead vocalist is the kind of guy who likes to break them when he's had an especially good—or bad—performance.

The sun is up, and there's a whole new day ahead.

Bettylou picks up the fan belt and gets to work. "You're good at guarding prisoners, playing music by ear, *and* fixing engines? Be still my heart." I put my hands around her waist. "What else can you do?"

"Just those three things." I wait for her to smile in jest, but she doesn't.

Frank claps his hands together, then winces. "So, where are we going next?"

"Texas," Clem says.

"Wyoming," Bettylou says.

"I want what she wants," I say, twining my fingers through Bettylou's.

"Let's just wing it," Frank decides, and without a map, that's kind of what we've been doing this whole time on tour. It's not like state borders really exist anymore. Location is a state of mind.

We pile into the van. Bettylou drops her head onto my shoulder and sighs contentedly.

"I only have one question," she says. "What's the name of this band? Bands have names, right?"

There's an uncomfortable silence as Clem guns the engine, which rattles to improbable life. Frank takes a swig from our communal bottle of homemade hooch and rests his cast on the door handle.

"That's a really good question," he says, launching into story-telling mode.

And that's what we listen to for the better part of the day, on our way to decharted territory, the four of us against the world.

USEFUL OBJECTS

AFTER HE PASSES THE age of reason, my brother chooses to become a foundation. Specifically, the foundation of the new state capitol building in Austin, Texas.

"You've never been to Texas," I say.

"It was the best opening they had," he replies with a small, sad shrug. "And you get weekends off."

I'm still working the counter at Jiffy Mart, delaying the inevitable at a pointless task nobody asked me to perform. My friends have all gone off to be fire hydrants or ATMs or jackhammers or five-piece dinette sets. "Undifferentiated," the Makers call shirkers like me. I hear them whispering through the thought rays that emanate from their human-powered satellites, saying: *Choose. Decide. Be of use.*

And I reply *not yet.*

The bell jingles and I look up to see a woman in mid-transformation barging into the store. Probably just took her injection after a weekend of rest. She's half-human, half-Vespa, and her chassis scrapes the paint off the door frame.

"A little help?"

I sigh and maneuver her through. I would have just brought her purchases out to the parking lot if she'd asked me to. "What do you need?"

"Motor oil. Oreos."

I tuck the items into her saddlebags. No charge, of course. As I close the door behind her, she belches a cloud of exhaust into my face. The transformation complete, she idles at the corner until a passing Maker hops aboard. It pops an Oreo into its mouth and speeds off, jagged teeth covered in chocolate bits.

The Makers are alive, but they're not organic. The division between "living thing" and "object" doesn't exist for them. And they have a hard time believing that we care about such a piddling thing as keeping our own bodies. To a Maker, a job's a job, and we all play our role. Except for us selfish undifferentiated types.

Choose, say the voices in my head. *Decide.*

"Not yet," I say. "Piss off."

That keeps the voices down, for a little while anyway.

The Makers' home world is as artificial as they are, a spherical factory orbiting a distant blue sun. No nature, just industry. They arrived in the bodies of the last race they'd conquered, ships that died on contact with our atmosphere. The ships died happy, the Makers told us, knowing they had been of use.

I'm not so sure about that.

It was a slow invasion masked as a self-improvement regimen. None of my friends really had a job. We were all living on plastic, taking useless classes at the community college to maintain our health insurance while we pretended our parents' basements were fabulous studio apartments. The lines for the Makers' employment centers stretched down the sidewalk like an ant trail.

Except, I kind of liked the art history class I was enrolled in at the time. I didn't mind living at home. And anyway, injections hurt.

The Makers tend their human machines like careful gardeners. They shamble down the human-lined streets on their twisted, insectoid legs. And every day I feel their alien hate pulsing at me.

When they were full-time people, my parents used to telecommute, so it made sense for them to become a house. Which is great in one way, because I don't have to sleep in a stranger's armpit. But it's also bad in another, because there isn't any privacy. Sex becomes unthinkable in a house built from your parents' bones. I think that's why my brother's moving so far away.

"I'll miss you," I say as I watch my brother pack his bags.

He's already taken his starter injections, and his words come out thick and gravelly. Stone man. "You could come with me."

"I don't know anyone down there," I say. I don't add that I don't know anyone here either anymore. We don't wear nametags or anything, so you only know your friends when they transform into their part-time human forms. And useful objects don't want to hang around with undifferentiated slackers like me. "I'll write you. You'll still be able to read, won't you?"

"Of course I'll be able to read. I can do anything you can do. Except move."

"But you get weekends off."

"Weekends," he says, "and alternate Wednesdays."

I don't take public transportation anymore, and I don't dare climb in a taxi, not when I could be entering the cab of my hated fifth-grade teacher. Luckily, I only live ten miles from the ocean. I grab my trusty bike, which was never alive, and pedal down the road to the coast.

Choose, the voices say. *Contribute. Be of use.*

I pedal faster.

Because it's November, the ocean is deserted. I take off my shoes, roll up my pant legs, and wade into the brackish water.

I choose to be the air, I think. *I choose to be the rain on my face and the rocks beneath my feet, the waves crashing over the rocks and the sun beating down on the waves.* I wish to disappear into nature, into the Earth itself. That's something the Makers can't give us, for these things have no function. They are not of use.

I stand in the ocean until the pounding rain becomes too much to bear. My teeth chatter. But I just can't bring myself to leave. The rain drowns out the voices, and the dark keeps me from seeing the boats in the distance and wondering who they are, if they're anyone at all.

Someday, I know I'll have to choose. I can't remain undifferentiated forever.

Not yet, though, not yet. I'm not nearly ready yet.

THE GODDESS OF THE HIGHWAY

HARPER JONES KNOCKS BACK the better part of his bottle of amphetamines with one hand and presses his other palm on the dashboard display. He looks at the clock.

Sixteen hours, four minutes, seven seconds.

He's tired and wired all at once. His shoulders ache with the tension brought on by the bennies, and his teeth have worn down to nubs. He can hear them grind even through the soothing tones of the in-cab entertainment system, which is currently broadcasting soft piano paired with roundish blue-green shapes.

Sixteen hours, eight minutes, forty-nine seconds.

Harp fixes his gaze on the stretch of highway before him. All the signs are in both languages, the language of now and the language of the time before. "Gotta follow the *red* signs," he mutters to himself. "Red, red, red." If he doesn't repeat it he'll forget. His plates aren't good enough to keep the information in by themselves.

Sixteen hours, ten minutes, one second.

Always keeping one eye on the road, Harp taps five more of the pills—red, like the signs he must follow—into his mangled hand and slides them down his throat like they were candy. His chest lurches. Hot liquid jets into his mouth and he realizes he has nearly bit his tongue through.

Sixteen hours, fourteen minutes, twenty-one seconds.

Twenty-two.

Twenty-seven.

Now.

Harp's body lurches, making it nearly impossible to keep his four-fingered left hand on the steering console. As he seizes and bucks, the highway begins to rise up, nearly level with his gaze. Her hips puff out. Her breasts pop from her chest one by one. She is the color of fresh asphalt, and in her hair are nestled all the signs of the road like a crown of rose petals. She is the Goddess of the Highway, and as this is a west-bound trip, Harp's remaining fingers are safe.

He licks his lips. They are so dry. "Goddess."

She opens her mouth and unrolls her tongue, painted with a yellow stripe. Harp drives forward, always forward, the autonomic system of the truck kicking in and following the Goddess's road surface markings. *My child, what is it you most desire?*

Though Harp is dangerously dehydrated from the speed, his eyes water regardless. His beautiful Goddess. The first time he saw her it was an accident, and unfortunately an east-bound trip. He woke up with his pointer finger in his lap, the inside of the cab bathed in blood. But the next time he saw her . . .

Our time grows short. What is your greatest wish?

Her voice. It reminds Harp of one of the Silver-plated women who read the Channel Only evening news in monosyllabic words over a mix of strings and various triangle shapes.

He's nearly into her now, the truck approaching her plump lips at what would be criminal speed, if there was anyone around to care. His window is closing. Still keeping one hand on the dashboard, he holds out his four-fingered right paw to receive his wish.

Harp pulls off into a truck shelter and gently unwraps his gift from the Goddess of the Highway. Pastrami on rye, extra pickles. Just the way he likes it.

He bites in, mouth watering.

Somewhere in the wilds of what used to be Arkansas, a barefoot woman with an orange Mohawk thumbs a ride. With her other hand she holds a plastic bag containing her boots. The plates at her temples are a solid, unnatural black, marking her as an Iron. Except they're not really Iron, and neither is she.

"Hey!" she yells at the approaching vehicle. With so many lower-caste people around, there's a lot fewer cars on the road than there used to be. She waves her hands. "*Hey!*"

Her name is Pamela Jane Stanton, but she calls herself Spike. Spike as in pain. Spike like the pattern visible in a Plastic's electro-encephalogram when they get just the right kind of mental stimulation. It just sounds cool to her.

She cups her hands around her mouth, lined in green lipgloss. "*Fuck you!*"

The mud splashes her from head to toe. But at least her boots are dry.

"Bastard," she spits, hocking up a mouthful of grit. She scans her surroundings. The signs on the road, both the real ones and the low-caste ones, say it's five miles to Little Rock, so she slings the plastic bag over her shoulder and starts walking.

When she hits the diner, it's dark. The mud has set, congealing into a crusty outer layer that she can almost peel off by hand. The Bronze waitress sneers. Her earrings complement the plates.

"Gotta bathroom?"

"Customers only."

Spike fishes in her pocket and pulls out four NuCoins, flat chips with only one denomination. She looks at the menu, where a picture of pancakes is juxtaposed next to a picture of four NuCoins. "Gimme that," she says, keeping her voice brutish and Iron-flat. Irons are grunt workers, all muscle and sinew.

The waitress nods Spike toward the bathroom, where she strips off her clothes and dunks them in the toilet. Brown muck comes off in clumps. She washes her face in the sink and picks the chunks of dried mud out of her Mohawk.

Spike checks the plates. Still covered with black Sharpie. It's not indelible, but it's close. *Phew.*

She puts on her sopping clothes and dry boots and goes back out to the dining area. Her pancakes are waiting for her, and both the waitress and the cook glare at her as she eats. She lingers on her meal, letting the fork graze her cheeks. Irons have poor motor control.

Across the dining-room floor, a family—also Iron, like her but for real—orders their food with grunts and gestures. The father points to the screen. The Bronze waitress dutifully puts on Channel Only (tagline: "it's the *only* thing that's on!"). An explosion of colors and soft tones fills the diner, and the low-caste quartet descends into passive silence. Spike tries to act like them, like the color of her plates demands she act.

Just get into it, she tells herself.

After the neurobombs fell, everything came down to your plate. The corporations made all kinds of neuro-prosthetic plates for those driven to stupidity by the white mist, from glorious Gold to cheap Plastic. But there was one plate that never touched the consumer market.

The plates beneath Spike's Sharpied temples aren't Gold. They're Platinum.

"Turn it up," she drawls through a mouth of pancakes. Does this look right? Does she look *too* stupid for Iron? From the look on the cook's face (Steel, she sees, from the blue-gray knobs above his ears), Spike figures she should dial it back a bit.

She looks down. One of the Iron family's children is at her knee. "I like television too."

"Yeah," Spike says. "It's nice."

"I like the colors."

"Mm-hmm."

"Pretty music."

Spike refocuses her gaze on Channel Only. Two triangles pierce the edge of a floating pink bubble. *Scandalous.*

The Bronze waitress takes her pancakes away. Spike wrings her still-damp clothes out on the table and lights on out of there.

As Harp polishes off the last of the gift, there's a commotion out near the long-abandoned shelter. Harp peeks out of his window.

"Move, beasts!" A man in a sleek suit leads a parade of disheveled people from a minibus parked near the shelter's edge.

Harp squints. The man's temples flash Silver. *Boss man.*

"I don't have all day," the man continues, hands on his hips. They move faster. Some of the people set up a card table and lay a tablecloth across it. Others rummage in the bus and return carrying small bundles. It takes them a long time to do this, because as far as Harp can see, they're unplated. Their temples are crusted over with a ring of brown scabs.

The boss man leans back in a picnic chair and snaps his fingers at a man wearing a hole-riddled tank top. The man slides sunglasses onto the boss man's face.

Harp scrunches down in his seat. He's been warned about this kind of thing by his own boss men. *Only trust me and Chuck,* said Greg, his East Coast boss man. Chuck was the West Coast boss man. *Don't talk to any other Silvers. And how did you lose your pinky finger, Harp? Jesus.*

Harp stays on the floor of the truck, tucked underneath the console, until he notices the sun shift. He looks out. The unplated people are dining on scraps, while the outlaw boss man pages through a magazine picturing a Gold that Harp doesn't recognize.

It's the President, dummy, he tells himself. "Oh yeah."

The boss man's head turns in Harp's direction. He points to a rag-clad woman. "Look in that truck. I think there might be a person in it." She staggers forward, mouth agape.

"No no no no," Harp mutters under his breath. He repositions himself in the driver's seat, but he's momentarily unable to remember how to turn on the control panel. The damn speed's worn off.

The woman pops up in the window, smiling with all her teeth. "Hi!"

"Hello," Harp says.

"You want to come out of there." She says it like a command, not a request. "Come out."

Harp places his hands over his Plastic plates reflexively. "Nuh uh."

"We got good stuff."

"I got good stuff. My cargo." *Oh shit, I told her about the cargo.*

There's a crash at his back, and Harp turns around to see another of the servants behind him. A star-shaped hole yawns in the window and a rock sits on the passenger seat like a little fat toad. The Silver boss man has left his chair and is patting the second person on the head. "Good girls. I can take it from here." He reaches a hand through the hole and unlatches the door.

"You stay away from me." Harp holds out a three-fingered hand, which the boss man looks at with interest.

"It's been rough out there for you, hasn't it?"

"No." Harp has finally figured out how to turn the car on, but he can't do it until this man is gone. He can't ride the Silver stranger all the way to California! "I wouldn't say that."

"Your hands, man! Look at your damn hands."

Harp looks at his hands. He doesn't see anything wrong with them. "Gotta pay the price."

"Highwaymen, eh?" The boss man leans forward. "You're scared. I can tell."

Harp can't hide it. "Yes."

"*My* people aren't scared. They live free. Free as birds."

"That's nice."

Smile. "Yes, it is."

Harp pulls his hands back and puts them over his plates again. "I am the truck driver. I am the conveyor of important cargo across the land. I do an important job."

"There are no important jobs anymore, buddy. No important anything. Whole world's gone to shit. Your thoughts, muddled as they are, are what's making you feel so mixed up inside. I can fix you."

Harp's brow crinkles. "Go slower."

The Silver sighs. "When people don't have *plates*," he says, pointing to his own shiny temples, "people are *happy*. Happy, happy people."

"Happy people. Happy Harp."

"Yes, happy Harp. Happy, happy Harp."

Harp considers. It's true that he's been getting pretty tired of running this route, back and forth, with nothing for entertainment except his in-cab outlet to Channel Only and occasional visits from the Goddess. But how can he leave? He knows that at a point in the not-too-distant past, his life was different. He had *more* thoughts, but somehow he wasn't so mixed up about them. Maybe this man is right. "Slaves," he says, the unfamiliar word bubbling to the surface, then just as easily forgotten.

The boss man gestures to the two women, still stationed on the sides of Harp's cab. "Girls, a little help."

The one with the big teeth gently knocks on Harp's window, and he unthinkingly unlocks it for her. She takes his hand, not flinching at the odd grip, and leads him toward the minibus. It's painted all kinds of colors, just like Channel Only.

"Pretty colors."

"Hi," she says, grinning.

The bus is dark. Each of the seats has a small blanket draped over it. Harp wonders who the driver is. It has to be the Silver.

"What's it like?" he says. "Being free?"

She just blinks at him like he hasn't said anything at all.

The boss man enters, a small satchel in his hand. "My freedom pack," he says, opening it to reveal tools as silver and shiny as the plates in his head.

"Is it sterile?"

"Such a big word for a Plastic. Must be all those smart pills you have in your truck. You won't need *those* anymore." He flaps his hands. "Free as a bird, remember? Not a care in the world."

Harp looks from the boss man back to the girl and gulps. This is exactly what Greg and Chuck warned him about, to the letter. But this man is a *Silver*. He's smarter than Harp is. Could this be the right thing to do? "Maybe it is," he answers to himself.

"Talking to yourself," the boss man says. "Oh, those plates *have* to come out, Harp. They're malfunctioning on you."

"Mal—"

"Breaking, son. Broken." He pulls out a sharp stick like Chuck's stylus and another implement Harp recognizes as a clamp. "Now, get down on the floor. Go limp. I'm not gonna lie, this will hurt."

"Hurt," Harp whispers. He recalls a memory of the last time he'd traveled east, when the Goddess had taken his second pinky. Blood had splashed all over the cab, blocking his vision of Channel Only. He'd nearly passed out from the pain. Only the knowledge that his cargo, which was *very* important, needed to be in Washington by sunrise had kept him from veering the truck off course.

He'd kept one hand on the panel. Always one hand on the panel.

At the side of his head is the smell of singeing plastic.

"*No!*" Harp yells, knocking the Silver's tools away with his forearm. They clatter on the floorboards of the old bus. The girl behind him makes a high keening sound. It hurts Harp's ears.

"You're not making this very easy for me," says the Silver with a frown.

"One hand on the panel! One hand on the panel!" He balls up his fist, smaller than it used to be, but no less strong, and socks the boss man square in the jaw. The boss man reels back, his face red as the route Harp has dedicated his life to following.

"I'm *very* disappointed," the Silver says. He gestures to the unplated people, but before their damaged systems can react, Harp leaps over the bus seats and rockets out of the bus itself, knocking them down as he makes his way to the truck. *His* truck. His one and only.

The Silver is fast, but Harp is faster. He swings himself into the cab, slamming both doors shut and smacking the locks. The Silver pummels the unbroken window with all his might, but he can't even crack it.

"You're giving up, boy. Freedom is slipping away from you with every moment!" He pauses to point at Harp's plates. "Harp wants to be happy, doesn't he?"

"Harp *is* happy." Harp has the Goddess. And he just had that really good sandwich. He throws one hand on the control panel and the system lights up. Ready to go.

The boss man jiggles the handle of the cab. His eyes go wide. "Stop the truck! My sleeve's caught!"

But Harp *can't* stop the truck, not once it's already moving.

The smear of red behind the truck's wheels follows Harp all the way into Arkansas.

Spike smashes the pillow against her ears and moans. *Turn it down, assholes*, she thinks, though she dares not say a word.

She'd found the smarthouse at dawn, planted on the out-skirts of Little Rock. The old-style signs had mostly blown down, so she'd followed the colors. Red, like apples or blood. And of course, an Iron only shows up at a smarthouse for one reason, which is why Spike is wired to the gills on this pleasant summer morning.

She feels a tap on her shoulder and whirls around to confront it. "Who are you?" says a strung-out Bronze, her eyes all buggy and bloodshot.

"Alice," Spike says.

"Isn't this fun? I mean, my mind feels so *expansive*, you know? Like I could do *anything*." The Bronze stretches her arms wide. "It's like for just a few hours all the bullshit melts away and you see things for what they really are. I should go read a book." But the woman doesn't go anywhere, just keeps beaming at Spike.

Spike doesn't feel the same. She's only had a single dose, not the gargantuan ones required to overcome the neurobomb effect on the human brain. As a Platinum, there's not much fog to cut through in the first place. She nods rapidly, trying to replicate the other woman's manic intensity. "Yeah. It's really . . . rad, you know? It's so rad to be able to *think*."

The smarthouse's walls are lined with books and films from bygone eras, organized in a bizarre system Spike can't figure out. Most of the tweakers aren't looking at any of it, though. Because while the megadoses of speed do clear away some of the crap the neurobombs left, they also make people twitchy. *Very* twitchy.

"Fuckers!" yells a Steel who only moments before had been frantically pacing in front of the wall-screen television. "All of you are fuckers." He rummages through his pockets for a few moments, but it's no use. They frisk for weapons at the door.

"Hey man, chill out," says another person just as wired as the angry Steel. "We're all friends here."

"You are not my *friends*. I have nobody. I have nothing." The Steel stops pacing and runs his hands through his hair wildly, exposing his plates. "I mean, have you ever *thought* about the mist, people? Really thought about it? Where did it come from?"

"Aliens," says someone.

"Terrorists," says another someone.

"The elite of society, in an attempt to solidify their power by making intelligence something that can be bought and sold on the open market," says Spike. All eyes turn to her and she twitches a few times for good measure.

"Nah," says the angry man. "It was *totally* aliens." As he continues pontificating about the aliens' exact height and social structure, Spike plucks a book from the shelves around them and pretends to read.

It's a strange thing being a more-than-clearheaded person in a world where the vast majority of people—yes, even the Silvers and Golds—are affected by the mist in some way.

The mist we made, Spike thinks, recalling her Platinum girlhood in the gated enclave of Alexandria, Virginia. *It's our fault.*

Spike's memories of the coming of the mist are filtered through the lens of the mist itself. She hadn't been able to read. She'd barely been able to speak. One day she'd woken up and her mind was just . . . gone.

When you're in the mist, you're always happy. It's Christmas and your birthday every single moment.

Her father hadn't been around when the neurobombs hit. He'd been off on business. Little Pamela Jane didn't think anything of it. Father was often away.

Only later did she put together the pieces. Her father and his friends were very important; even a seven-year-old could figure that out. And although Father had the same Platinum plates screwed into his head that Pamela, her sisters, and Mommy did, there hadn't been a long period of recovery for him.

Post-mist, he was busier than ever, developing a plate theft protection system for Silvers and Golds, a sort of hat. His friends, similarly, had jobs related to the plate business. Or, as polite people called it, the field of "reconstructive neuro-prosthetics."

That's when she started to suspect that Father and his friends had started it. That's why she left. That's why she's here, watching two male tweakers fuck loudly and with great vigor in the front room of the smarthouse.

She doesn't know what she's doing. She doesn't know where she's going. Spike only knows that she can't remain in that sterile Platinum enclave while people suffer. She's heard vague tales of children being born unaffected by mist, the coming generation. Maybe she'll meet some of them. Maybe there's somebody out there working to reverse this disaster.

Or maybe I'm just fooling myself, Spike thinks.

Time to move on. Spike gathers up her things, of which there are never very many, and pushes past the smarthouse's bouncer to the woods beyond.

About ten minutes after Harp's truck peels away from the shelter, his seat starts to rattle and shake. His display shrieks at him, and he tentatively takes one of his hands off the panel and covers an ear with it.

I wish this wasn't happening, he thinks, before he remembers that he'd already used his wish on that sandwich. He won't have another wish for miles and miles, and the truck is already guiding itself into the breakdown lane.

It stops with a sad little fart. Harp waits ten minutes, then removes his hand from the dashboard display.

"Stay in the vehicle," he says to himself, repeating lines ingrained into him during his training days. "Do not leave the vehicle, Harp, understand? Someone will be by to get you. We're not going to just leave you out on the road, buddy." He smiles and lets himself doze off.

When his consciousness returns, he's still in the cab. He's hungry and bored. Reacting to his boredom, the truck starts up its transmission of Channel Only, flooding Harp's starving neurons with a cornucopia of colors, shapes, and sounds that even a plateless loser could appreciate. *Pretty, pretty.*

One of the screens affixed to the inside of the windows refuses to turn on. It's the one the Silver's woman had broken. Harp focuses on the colors emanating from the other screens, and tries not to think of coyotes or highwaymen.

No highwaymen are gonna take my cargo, he thinks. His breath comes faster as he thinks of the danger he's in out here, even though he's trying to focus on the Channel's relaxing cacophony.

Outside, a branch snaps. Harp sits up straight. "Who's out there?"

Nothing.

"Greg? Chuck?" He's getting *really* hungry. Harp paws through the first-aid kit, the insurance papers in the glove compartment, the sandwich wrappings strewn on the floor. He picks up the last item and starts to lick the paper. He chews it, adventurously.

A shadow moves in the darkness, black on black.

"Station off," Harp says. Channel Only dwindles into silence. He peeks out of the cracked window. "You better stay away!"

"*Calm down*," says a girl's voice.

Harp's breath catches as he sees the girl, with her orange hair sticking up everywhere and her Iron plates. Iron beats Plastic, just barely. He starts to cry, big heaving sobs that drip onto his chest.

"Hey, hey," she says, her voice suddenly soft. "I'm not gonna hurt you." She holds up her hands, like that would prove anything. Chuck says that highwaymen always try to make you trust them before they murder you.

"You're gonna kill me. And then I can't deliver the cargo." He swipes a hand across his face. "It's important."

"I'm trying to get across the country. Can you give me a lift?"

Harp shakes his head in confusion.

"It's dark. It's not safe. I'm a good person. I will not hurt you. Please let me inside your truck." She blinks frantically, which meant something in the old world, but not in the new one.

"*Never* let anyone in the truck," he says, quoting. "Never ever."

The girl disappears and Harp's breathing returns to normal. That was easy. Maybe a little *too* easy, but he won't worry about it. Much. He calls the channel back up, though its anxiolytic effect is dulled with only the one operational screen.

Happy Harp, he thinks, popping a pill. *Safe Harp*.

Beneath his feet the engine roars to life like a waking lion.

Harp startles from his half-trance and prepares to slam his hand on the display. Red, red, red, all the way to California. But then the girl highwayman is back.

"I fixed your truck."

"Fixed?" Only Greg and Chuck know how to fix the truck.

She holds up a muddy object and shrugs. "Shoe in the tailpipe." She shrugs and throws it away. "I am not dangerous. You should let me in your truck. I'm a nice person."

Harp swallows. He's not supposed to let anyone in the truck. But this girl did help him somehow, made it so he can continue his delivery of the precious cargo.

He ponders and cogitates, straining his Plastic plates to the sheer limit of their capacity. He squints his eyes shut. What should he do? What should he think? When he opens them, the girl is sitting beside him in the passenger seat.

"Drive," she says, not unkindly.

One hand on the panel.

Spike greedily wolfs down the chicken nuggets and fries that the trucker bought for her at the automated service station, but she's a delicate flower compared to him. He's chomped down three hot dogs and guzzled a quart of diet soda, and shows no sign of slowing down. Even though the truck is stopped, he keeps one of his three-fingered hands on the control panel, like a talisman.

Finally there comes a point when the trucker's maw isn't full of food. "What's your name?"

"Harper. Harp. Happy Harp." She shakes his hand. It's like shaking hands with a bird. Not much to hold on to.

"I'm Spike." She balls up her wrappers and places them neatly on her seat. "Where are you going?"

"California."

"Yeah, but what *city*?"

He shrugs. The truck must be on auto-pilot, the driver only there as a fail-safe. Like most things, anymore.

"I need to go to California. Can you drive me to California? Me, in the truck, with you?"

Harp looks at her out of the corner of one of his mist-glazed eyes. "I'm not *supposed* to."

"I can help you keep the cargo safe. I'm a good person, Harp."

He has another of his interminable thinks, while Spike flattens her hawk into a bob. Finally he heaves a breath and traces a spiral on the display. "Happy Harp." The truck rumbles to life beneath them.

They ride in silence until the truck crosses the Oklahoma state line, when Harp takes his free hand and expertly opens a vial full of red bennies.

Maybe we can talk like equals for a little while, she thinks, hopefully.

He swallows five of them dry and offers her the vial. Spike takes one just to be polite. "You have to stay awake, right?"

"Awake and alert."

"Don't you get bored?" In the hours they've been traveling, Spike has only seen three cars, also automated. Not too many Silvers and Golds live in this part of the country.

"I do things to amuse myself," Harp says, shrugging. He puts the vial back in his shirt pocket.

"Like what?"

He glares at her. "It's none of your business."

Spike holds up her hands. "Sorry, sorry." The highway signs pass by in a blur. "Where do you sleep?"

"Don't sleep much. But when I do, it's in the truck." He pauses. "You can also sleep in the truck."

"Thank you, Harp. I really appreciate that," Spike says, though she was hoping his company would have put him up in a motel. "So I guess you trust me now, huh?"

Harp grunts. "There's only one person I trust."

"Your bosses?"

"No." He gestures toward the black road stretching before them. "*Her.*"

Spike squints out at the unfurling road. *What have I gotten myself into?*

Harp plucks a potato chip from the wrapper that sits between them, gripping it with his thumb and ring finger. He keeps the other hand firmly bolted to the display. Spike's been to her father's factories; she knows how it works. Most machines are automated and don't really require human operators. But even Plastics need something to do.

"What happened to your hands? Did it happen Before?" She doesn't have to clarify Before.

He frowns at her, his eyes drifting from the road, not that it matters whether he watches it or not. "No such thing as a free lunch."

Spike's confused, despite her Platinum status. "You traded your fingers for food?"

Harp sighs. "It happens when I go east. Every sixteen hours, fourteen minutes . . ." He thinks for a little while. "And thirty-one seconds."

Spike keeps her voice flat. "Who does it?"

He shrugs. "Her," he says again, gesturing toward the ribbon of highway.

"The road."

"But," Harp says, grinning, "she grants wishes when you go in the other direction. It's not so bad."

"Harp, don't take this the wrong way, but you might want

to lay off the bennies for a while."

"I knew I shouldn't have told you," he says. "I knew you wouldn't understand."

"Well, maybe I'll get to see her," Spike says.

He doesn't register her sarcasm. "Only thirteen hours, two minutes, and forty-six seconds to go." Harp grins. "I can't wait!"

Pretty good math skills for a Plastic, Spike thinks. *Must be the pills.*

They enter the Panhandle at speeds approaching eighty miles an hour. With nobody around, they could do two hundred if the truck was built for it. The speed draining from her system, Spike's head slumps against the broken window. She notices that Harp is nodding off too, his hand wedged in such a way that it won't slip off the console.

If she dreams, she doesn't remember.

She wakes to heat radiating through the broken window, and fans her plates to cool them. "Can we stop for some food? I'm hungry again."

He doesn't want to, she can tell. He wants to see his made-up road genie or whatever it is. But he relents, flicking his fingers against the panel to turn it into a nearby semi-automated diner.

Leading the way, Spike pushes through the double doors to see a Plastic operator dully pecking out orders on a console very similar to the one in Harp's truck. She doesn't speak to Spike, perhaps doesn't speak at all. Even Harp isn't this far gone.

Spike orders pancakes again. She likes pancakes a lot. She sits down across from Harp, who watches his stilled vehicle anxiously. "So, what's in the truck?"

"Very important cargo."

"Yeah, but what *kind*?"

"The important kind."

She thinks. As most people Bronze and below have basic farming and manufacturing skills, the majority of what gets shipped coast to coast are luxuries, goods sold between and among Silvers and Golds, pumped out by Platinum factories. Like her father's little hats. "Maybe we should find out what's in the truck, Harp," she says, using the firm tone that's worked its magic on him before.

He shakes his head. "No way, lady."

"We *should*. How will you know the cargo is safe if you don't check it? You have to keep the cargo safe."

Harp's face melts, and she knows she has him.

The first rule is to keep your hand on the panel. The second rule is to follow the colors Greg and Chuck tell you to. The third rule is not to go into the back of the truck. *Not for anything*, Greg had said, and Chuck agreed.

"You're only Iron," Harp says. "You're not very important. Only *important* people are allowed to look in the back of the truck."

"So you're not important?"

"No," he says, pointing to the side of his head. "I'm not and neither are you."

The girl makes Harp feel weird and sad and he doesn't even know why. She's so *smart* for an Iron. Able to make him do things he knows he shouldn't do, like bring other people into the cab with him (rule four!). What was he thinking?

You don't think, Harp. That's the problem.

Harp remembers things sometimes, especially after he takes his pills. He knows the world used to be different. That once he saw the world not through a pane of frosted glass but with the clear sharp intensity of someone like Greg or Chuck.

Harp's got a vision of a man that looks like him, wearing a suit. That not-quite-Harp has all of his fingers. He wasn't always the best at everything, but he wasn't the worst either. He doesn't remember driving a truck.

But that's what you do now, son, says a voice from his past.

We've put too much money into those plates for you to back out now.

When he sees that not-quite-Harp, he starts to hate driving, almost enough to take his hand off the panel. Sometimes three other people, a woman and two small girls, appear in his mind's eye right before he sees the Goddess in all her glory, so wired up on stimulants that his teeth are about to rattle right out of their sockets. They were Important People to Harp.

Now there's just Chuck and Greg. They're the Important People.

We don't condone drug use on the job, but if you're running behind schedule, here's where you can get what you need.

"Harp!"

He snaps back into his gauze-draped reality.

"Let's go see what's in that truck."

"Whatever you say." He flutters his napkin down onto his barely-touched tuna fish sandwich and goes out to the truck.

They haven't given him a key, but that won't stop the girl. She rummages in her patch-covered bag and pulls out a rusted, wicked-looking tool. All of a sudden, a stray thought flows into his mind like a voice from the deeps. He pulls on her arm. "Sensors."

"Are you saying there are sensors on this truck?"

Harp rubs his head, trying to remember. "Could be."

"Only one way to find out." The girl wrests herself out of Harp's grip and puts the tool around the truck's lock, bearing down on it with all her might.

A few minutes pass as she grunts and heaves at the tool, straining at the lock. Harp wonders if he should help her, but he doesn't step forward. This was her idea, not his.

Finally the lock shatters, and the girl tumbles into the gravel at their feet. She swears loudly, but there is no sound of alarm from the truck itself. He can't bring himself to look inside.

"Come on!" She yanks the doors open.

Oh, shit. Shit, shit, shit. "Shit!" Chuck and Greg are going to kill him. He's broken two out of the four rules. What are they going to do? Are they gonna take his plates away? Is he gonna be just like those brainless people owned by the Silver boss man, doomed to a life solely lived within the mist?

It's too much. Harp sinks to the earth, closing his eyes, placing his hands over his ears.

"Harp!" says the girl. His mind clouds over with hate. "Harp, come and look at this!"

"No. Just . . . just put it back, whatever you got, and let's put the lock back on. I'll drop you off in the next city." He feels a pair of hands on his shoulders. He opens his eyes to find Spike's hazel ones glittering back at him.

"It's *plates*, Harp. Iron plates."

"Like yours?"

"Yes, like mine," she replies stiffly.

"Like I said, very important cargo."

"I can switch them out, Harp. Switch out your Plastic plates with these. An upgrade! It'll take half an hour, max." She holds up the bag. "I have *tools* for this kind of thing."

Harp briefly wonders how this crazy Iron managed to get tools normally only available to bosses, until the thought flits away from him like a hummingbird. "Then I'd be smart like you."

"Yes. The mist would have less control over you. We'd be able to plan better."

"Plan? We had a plan? I thought you wanted me to take you to California."

Spike drops her bag into the gravel and takes his hands in hers. They're soft. Not like an Iron factory worker's hands at all. "Harp, I need you to listen to what I'm saying and try to concentrate. I'm not an Iron. I'm a Platinum."

His mouth drops open.

"This is very important, so listen. My people made the mist."

"Aliens made the mist."

"I can't prove it," she says, continuing like she hasn't heard him, "but I can see the evidence. My family got our plates right away. We didn't have to wait. Later, when I saw the news reports, saw how the system was being set up, I realized that it only benefited one group: us."

"You?" Harp shakes his head. "Nah."

"The plates are a way to keep people in their places, calcify the social classes. Even if we didn't create the mist, we certainly capitalized on it. My people could have made Platinum plates for everyone on Earth, Harp. It's not real platinum. It's artificial scarcity, a system designed to keep certain people in power and the masses under control!"

Harp narrows his eyes. "I don't understand a word you just said."

"You'll understand slightly more with these new plates in your brain."

Harp shakes his head. He dips into his pocket and pulls out some bennies. "I gotta think about this."

"Well, then I guess we just wait forever. Because you're never going to get it. Not unless you let me give you an upgrade."

You're in too deep, son, says the voice of Chuck in his head, or maybe it's Greg. *I don't see how you're going to get out of this one.*

"Somehow," Harp says.

The girl rolls her eyes.

About the only thing you can do, says Chuck, or Greg, *is give us the girl. You know she's bad news. She's interfered with some very important cargo here.*

He looks over at Spike. He can't disagree.

The Goddess will be very angry with you.

Harp's blood runs cold. He hadn't been thinking of the Goddess of the Highway, not until the phantom voices brought her to mind. Her asphalt skin, her crown of signs, her ability to make all your dreams come true . . .

Harp takes Spike by the shoulders. He knows she's not lying about being a Platinum—no Iron talks like that!—but he can't be gentle with her just now. He's too angry, and too scared.

"No!" she says, squirming in his seven-fingered grip. "Let me go!"

Hoisting her into the back of the truck, he slams the doors shut. The lock lies broken at his feet, so he takes a random tool from her bag and shoves it through the slots where the lock had been, bending it down on both sides to keep the Platinum inside. Safe. Her fists beat on the inside of the truck like tiny hammer blows.

"Quiet down." She does. "That's better."

Not much longer to go, he thinks. Not to California, or to the Goddess. Things will be a lot clearer when he sees the Goddess. He climbs into the truck.

Seven hours, fifty-two minutes, zero seconds.

Seven hours, twenty-five minutes, eleven seconds.

Seven hours, six minutes, thirty-four seconds.

The highway unrolls beneath his blood-speckled wheels.

So this is what the whole mess came to. Spike stuck in the back of a truck, her tools lost, and a speed-addled Plastic maniac driving her into her arms of Golds. They'll know what she is immediately.

She picks up one of the sets of Iron plates bound in shrink-wrap and hurls it against the inside of the truck like a Frisbee. The echo is deafening.

"You *moron*," she says, and she doesn't know if she's saying it to Harp or to herself.

Spike wonders, not for the first time, if her own plates are defective. She'd headed west with not much of a plan, only a vague notion that somewhere, anywhere out there was someone who could . . . fix things?

This can't be fixed, she thought. Whatever mutagens or pathogens or nanobots the Platinums had released into the air were even beyond her comprehension. She hadn't been a bright child, and she was a lousy Platinum at best, her smarts more in her plates than in her mind.

But wasn't that true for some of the others? The rich and the elite had always had their share of bumblers. She knew this from reading books that only the upper castes now had the ability to decipher. And there'd been more than enough intelligent souls among the working classes before the mist. It was almost as if potential had nothing to do with class at all, or even biology, like it was an essence available to everyone with only the external trappings of environment to impede it.

Not anymore, though. Now it was about the plates. It would always be about the plates.

She doesn't have her bag of tools, but she still has a Swiss Army knife tucked inside her thick, heavy boots. She slips it out and cuts a strip of fabric from her ragged jeans. She finds a hole near the bottom of the truck's door and threads it through, like a tiny flag. It's daylight, and if anyone sees it, maybe they'll alert the authorities.

No use. There's nobody out here but Plastics, she thinks, before telling herself to shut the hell up. *Crying won't do me any good. Am I crying?* She raises her hand to her face. *Shit.*

Spike makes a nest of packing materials on the floor of the truck and places her head upon one of the hundreds of identical boxes. She thinks it will take her forever to fall asleep in the shifting semi, but she's out within minutes.

Wake up.

"Harp?"

Wake up, my child. It's a woman's voice, very low and very loud. It rings in Spike's head like a gong, and she knows that it's not a delayed drug reaction or an extreme case of wishful thinking. *There is important work to be done.*

Spike sits up. No light pierces the minute holes in the back of the truck. Must be night. "Who are you?"

I am the one who protects this stretch of road. I monitor all comings and goings. I care about you.

Spike crosses her arms. "Prove it. Show yourself."

Suddenly, the pitch-black darkness of the truck begins to swirl and change, taking on contours of curved hip and strong limbs. There is still nothing there—there is no light, anywhere—but Spike can see something moving in the space before her, something that seems much larger than the truck's dimensions should allow. There is a feeling of *unfurling*, and the rough texture of asphalt grazes Spike's cheeks.

You are in great danger.

"Don't I know it."

The man in the front is not your enemy. He is my friend. I have many friends here. You could be a friend to me.

"I'm the enemy," Spike says. "I'm a Platinum."

The damage in the air will not last forever. It can be ameliorated. Even now, the children brought forth by your generation are less susceptible to its harm.

"I knew it!" Spike says, her heart lifting. "But what do we do *now*? What do we do until all the junk clears out of the air?"

You must protect my friend. Only by working together can you hope to break at least some of the effects of the damage.

"Can you be more specific?"

The black-on-black swirl of motion intensifies, becoming a captive tornado. This thing is *definitely* too big to fit in the back of the truck. *There is a house that sits near a dead city on a lake. Seek shelter there. You will find others like you, ones waiting for the slow return of the natural order.*

"What lake? What city?"

The figure or storm or whatever it is has no reply. It envelopes Spike in tendrils of scratchy roughness. *Be well, my new friend.*

"We're not friends," Spike says. She watches as the being dissipates into the stale air of the truck. "I'm a Platinum."

*

When Harp crosses the old Utah state line, lights flash at him from all sides. A siren blares from the speaker behind him, interrupting the calming transmission of Channel Only. He splays his fingers over the speaker to muffle the noise.

It doesn't do a damn thing.

Inspection station! the speaker yells. *Route recalibration!* Harper scans his externalized brain to remember what this warning means, then finally catches on.

"Oh, inspection station," he mutters as he pulls up the map with a flick of his wrist.

The truck is self-driving, but Harp still has to monitor its safe passage along the new route to the inspection station. He watches as the path switches from the angry red signposts to the happy purple ones. As if sensing his tension, Channel Only begins to play again. Harp feels sick.

"Cancel that," he says. He needs all his mental strength to concentrate. This is very important.

He knows this inspection station, has been through it before on one of his many trips west. Greg had told him it was necessary to scan for explosive or biological materials, signs that the *very important cargo* might be compromised by the rebels. "There are a lot of rebels, Harp. Not everyone is happy that the Golds and the Silvers keep the world safe."

He'd just stared, blank-faced. Why would people rebel? People can't possibly do things for themselves, at least After.

Great stretches of rocky desert give way to an expanse of mountains. Harp follows the purple signs north, and calls back Channel Only. He's *safe* now.

A safe Harp is a happy Harp, he thinks, though an odd tightness remains lodged in his chest.

The truck, knowing what to do and how to do it, continues to glide down the smooth highway to a distant city beyond. The shallow lake reeks of brine. He plugs his nose with his hand that isn't pressed to the panel.

The truck slows under him as it recognizes its destination and locks into place. A helpful Bronze worker jimmies the back door open, while the Silver station worker whose name he can never remember strides over with a clipboard.

Harp slicks back his hair, exits the truck, and prepares to meet the Silver. He wants the Silver to be proud of him. And then he remembers the girl. Had he really locked her in there? Has she escaped? He starts to sweat.

The Silver uncaps a pen and poises it over the clipboard. "Basic check."

Harp sneezes, and he watches a shadow of disgust flicker over the Silver's face. She doesn't like him much. "It's very important cargo."

"It always is," the Silver says with a look that Harp can't quite interpret.

The Bronze breaks the rod. Harp expects to hear either a scream from the girl, or a scream from the Bronze as she explodes from the hatch and pounds his brain in. *She's very dangerous*, he thinks. *She could kill someone.*

The Bronze appears at the edge of Harp's vision. He jerks a thumb backwards. "Boss, there's a girl back here."

The Silver frowns. She looks over at Harp. "Did you know about this? No, you don't know anything." She points to the Bronze. "Bring her over here."

He wrangles the squirming woman over to Harp and the Silver. She kicks up dirt and swings at the air. "Fuckers!"

Spike, Harp thinks. *That was her name.* He snaps his fingers, causing the Silver to glance at him, though her attention quickly returns to the girl.

"Iron," the Silver says, though with another one of those unidentifiable lilts to her voice. "Take her to my office."

The girl Spike spits an aimless loogie into the middle distance.

"Should we tell Chuck?" the Bronze asks. He yanks her behind him, heading toward a distant cottage.

"No. You don't tell Chuck anything. I'll deal with this." The Silver returns her focus to Harp. "Got in at a refilling station, I imagine. It's a dangerous world, boy."

"I'm not a boy."

She pats his head. "It's not your fault. You're a Plastic. I keep trying to tell them that they need *at least* Steel for these runs, but Steels don't always listen. At least we caught her. We've kept the cargo safe. Right, kid?"

"Safe," Harp repeats.

The Silver squints at him. "Are you *sure* you didn't see anything?"

He answers her question with another. "What are you going to do to her?"

"You don't have to worry about that."

But I am worried, he wants to say. *I can't help it.* "Where do I go now?"

"Follow the red. You know how to follow the red, right?"

He does. But that doesn't mean he wants to leave Spike here, all walled up in a Silver's office, maybe in trouble. Could Silvers even punish Platinums? *I should ask Chuck when I see him*, Harp thinks.

"What was that?" the Silver says. He realizes he's spoken aloud.

"Oops. I meant to say, I'll be on my way then."

"Good, Harper. I'm glad you stopped here. Thanks to you the cargo is safe."

It wasn't Harp who kept it safe. It was the truck. But he doesn't answer. He looks toward the tiny house. He thinks about Spike. He thinks about following the path of red all the way to California, again and again, forever.

"*Go*, Harper."

He sighs and climbs back into the cab.

Please don't hurt her. Please.

*

Spike steals a look at herself in the mirror and winces. Leonora had commanded her to dress in a frilly, lacy gown made of chiffon or something like that. *Just like a Silver*, she thinks. *Always reaching above their station.*

Platinums never wear fancy clothes. They know what they are.

She touches the sides of her head, the true color of her plates now exposed to the light. Leonora saw through her immediately, of course. Silvers are too mist-affected to run things for real, but they're smart enough to know what the score is.

Spike looks down at the ground, to the band around her ankle. It chirps audibly every couple of seconds, just often enough to drive her crazy. She flops down on the bed, feeling satisfaction when the dress rips slightly.

"Good morning!" trills Leonora the inspection stop manager as she breezes into Spike's cell. Spike shoots dagger eyes at her. "I hope you slept well."

"Do you *know* who my father is?"

"He must not care where you are, if you're here," she replies, not changing tone.

Spike sighs. It's time to give in, let the other Platinums save her ass. This was a stupid plan from the start, mostly because there was no plan. Just blind rebellion. "Are you going to ransom me? We have money."

"It's not usually a good idea to brag about your family's money when you think you're going to be ransomed."

"I don't care if they lose it all," she says, shrugging.

Leonora grins. Spike doesn't like the looks of that grin. "I have something much more important in mind for you, Miss Platinum."

Leonora steps out of the room. Spike wonders what the Silver means by this. Is she going to swap plates with Spike? Or just steal them outright? Or sell Spike as a sex slave to bored Golds looking for a thrill?

Spike remembers that she is in a state once called Utah. Barely any Plastics travel through this wasted land, let alone Golds. Not a good business plan, not even for a Silver.

Leonora returns with a child gripping each of her hands. Spike sneers at the kids all dressed up in their fancy Silver clothes. "You're going to teach my children."

"I *hate* kids."

She continues. "Bethany and Elliott are taking their plate placement exams next week. I want them to score well."

"They're already Silvers, lady." Plate type passes down from parent to child, except in extraordinary cases. Which is why Spike herself got Platinum plates despite being a fucking moron.

"I want them to be *more* than Silvers." Leonora releases the children. "Look at me. I thought when I was assigned to Silver it would mean a good job for me, perhaps a great one. And now I'm managing a truck inspection station in Utah."

Spike shrugs. "Well, you're the manager, anyway. That's something."

"I've read the statistics. Two percent of people are slated for plate reassignment every year, and most of those are children with exceptional capabilities."

Spike studies the children. They don't seem to have exceptional capabilities, but they don't necessarily *not* have them either. "So you think I can help them cheat the test."

"I think you can teach them how to *pass* the test."

"Did you ever think they might be happy as Silvers?"

The woman shakes her head. "Maybe that kind of complacency works for Plastics and Platinums, but not for my people."

The middle managers of the world are always the most dangerous, she remembers her dad saying once. "I'm trying to tell you, I don't know what I'm doing. Just because I have these plates, it doesn't make me a genius. I'm actually kind of an idiot, you know? My parents are Platinums, the real deal. I just got lucky."

"I don't believe you. A Platinum is a Platinum."

What is the mist, again? A substance of unknown etiology that clouded cognitive processes and slowed down conscious thought. The Platinum plates don't boost human intelligence, they just restore it. This woman believes Spike is some kind of superhuman. The truth is she's anything but. "I can't promise anything. Honestly, you'd be better off buying Gold plates on the black market."

"My children are not putting some shoddy gilded knock-off into their brains."

"I can find you good ones." Leonora's gaze doesn't waver. "Fine. I'll teach your stupid kids."

At the very least it would buy her some time.

Happy Harp. Harp is happy. Harp is a good person. Happy. Good. Right.

Harp's hands tremble where they press against the display. He always follows the red when he's going east to west, but it doesn't mean as much as it used to. Because *she* isn't here.

Spike or the Goddess? Or both? He can't figure it out.

It has been fifteen hours, twelve minutes, and no seconds since he asked the Goddess for a tasty sandwich and she delivered it into his mangled paws. He'd almost lost track of time. He's barely even taken any speed. He chokes back a few pills and they tumble raw and chalky down his throat.

For a brief moment, he envies the plateless. Those peaceful people, living in the eternal now, unable to even imagine the future or their place in the world. Harp's problem is that he knows too *much*.

Then take the plates out. Throw them away.

But if he does that, he can't follow the red. He can't see the Goddess. He can't help Spike or even know who she is.

He drives on.

Twenty-five minutes until his rendezvous with the highway deity, he stops at a diner. The ham sandwich is almost as good as the one the Goddess gave him, maybe a little drier. He ponders what he should ask for.

Should he ask for new plates? No, that would be greedy. He doesn't want to be greedy in front of the Goddess of the Highway.

Should he ask for Spike to be freed? But these are *Harp's* wishes, and he doesn't think the Goddess wants them given away to others.

Sad Harp.

"Anything else, darlin'?" asks the Bronze waitress.

"Yes. I need to think of a wish. A good one."

The waitress nods. "I wish things were different."

"I'm thinking of a wish for myself, though."

She takes his NuCoin and his empty plate.

Harp sighs and pushes himself away from the table. It's time to take off. He tosses back another handful of amphetamines and settles into the truck's cab.

Fifteen hours, fifty-one minutes, thirty-nine seconds. He follows the red.

Sixteen hours, nine minutes, two seconds. Tosses back a few last pills and checks the rearview mirror.

Sixteen hours, fourteen minutes, twenty-eight seconds. He draws a shuddering breath.

Now.

"I wish I was smart again," he says to no one. Then he makes a U-turn.

The morning after Spike was dragged to Leonora's house by the Bronze henchman, she flips through the textbooks for the plate placement exam. Trigonometry, linguistics, the periodic table, the sequence of events that preceded the fall of Rome. She doesn't remember any of this. Had she even taken the test? Or were the Platinum children exempt?

Bethany and Elliott are bright children. But they'll never be Platinum, or even Gold. She can almost see their plates chugging away as they struggle with the very highest-level questions.

"I have an idea," she says to Bethany.

"What is it, ma'am?"

"Don't call me that." She reaches behind Bethany's ear and withdraws a bobby pin. "I'm going to alter your plates, to make them more like mine."

Elliott claps his hands over his plates. "Mama says only doctors are allowed to touch them."

"I am a doctor. I have these plates. That means I can work on your plates."

Four little eyes go wide. They've learned a lot about plate hierarchy in their young lives. "I guess it would be okay," Bethany says, looking over at her brother.

He nods, warily.

Spike perches on the feather bed and beckons Bethany to her. She unscrews the girl's left plate and stares at the interior. *Only a matter of one or two wires keeps this girl from becoming a subhuman Plastic. Only a few wires more keeps her from becoming me.* She pokes at the wires experimentally, as Bethany patiently waits, her head in Spike's lap.

"I've just about got it," Spike lies. She crosses a few more wires and re-screws the plate back onto Bethany's temple. She stands the girl back up and gives her a weak smile. "How do you feel?"

Bethany blinks. Her mouth opens. Then she vomits a stream of blood straight into Spike's eyeballs.

Harp drives east, through the scrubby desert, toward the dead city beside the stinking lake. He guns the accelerator, causing the motor to squeal. "Don't be dead," he mutters under his breath. "Don't be dead."

The display flashes at him, a wild strobe that makes the back of his head ache. He fights through the pain, willing himself to remain on the opposite side of the red, then exiting onto the purple. The pain upon exiting is blinding. The fear is worse.

He finds the inspection station and parks the whining, clanging truck into it. The noises die when the engine does.

Harp needs to get out of here. He's going to go deaf if he remains. With only a twinge of anxiety, he lifts his hands from the display. He stumbles out onto the gravel-strewn road. In the distance is the tiny clapboard house where Spike had been taken.

He thinks. He feels more clear-headed than he has in years. His thoughts are light and fast. He knows the first thing he has to do: *shut down the truck.*

Harp finds a stick. He grips it as tight as he can and plants it into the dead center of the display. There are no sparks or smoke, only the beeps of a dying program.

Don't forget the tracker, he reminds himself. He plucks the tracking module from behind his seat and attempts to crush it in his fist. Failing that, he grinds it under his heel.

Now, it's on to the house. Harp's first inclination is to go barreling up there, screaming, not thinking about how easily he'll be spotted. So he's cagey. He darts from one bush or tree to the other, never allowing himself to be exposed for long. Even now Chuck and Greg could be watching him from above, trying to figure out what he's done with the *very important cargo.*

Harp makes it to the cottage. The Silver is in the living room, immersed in a feed, and Harp spots movement on the second floor. Maybe Spike? It's his only lead. He discovers a trellis bolted to the front of the house and starts to climb, threading his half-hands through the rungs and pulling himself up slowly, slowly. It sways under his weight, but remains standing.

Peeking an eye over the windowsill, he sees Spike and two

children. One of them is on the ground flopping like a fish. The other one is being restrained, a hand clapped over his tiny mouth. Spike herself is wearing a frilly dress, badly. He taps on the glass.

She catches his gaze and drops the child, who lands on the floor in a heap. "Harp?" she says, before zipping her own lip. Harp understands that the Silver is listening.

He motions for her to open the window. "I came back for you."

"But what about the red? Don't you have to follow it?"

"Not anymore."

She looks over her shoulder at the children, brow crinkling. The girl has gone still, though she is breathing. The boy dazedly pokes at his sister with a ruler. "I tried to change her plates. Make them better."

Harp knows what he has to do. He rolls into the bedroom, moving as quietly as he can so he doesn't rouse the Silver's attention. "Don't talk," he tells the boy, pointing his middle finger at him since the index finger is missing.

The little boy takes a step back.

"Tools?" he says, and she hands him the bobby pin. He unscrews the girl's left plate. The connections make sense to him somehow, total comprehension dawning over his mind like a rising sun.

This is what I did back then. Fixing things. It was good, honest work. I can do this, now that I'm smart again.

He twists and reconnects the wires into a different configuration, checking it against the untouched right plate. The girl's mouth opens and closes as he does this, like an infant's mouth. Finally, he sees that the two plates match. He screws them both back onto her temples and adjusts her into a sitting position.

"How do you feel?"

The girl opens her eyes. She touches her temples. Then she

looks at his plates. "Mommy! Mommy! There's a Plastic in the house!"

Feet come running up the stairs, heavy and rhythmic.

"Shit, we gotta run!" Harp says. He takes Spike by the wrist.

The Silver bangs the door back against its hinges. "You!" She whirls around to look at Spike. "And *you!*"

"Bye-bye, Leonora." Spike slips the band from her ankle and hurls it at the Silver. "Nice knowing you."

They sprint down the path that sits aside the saline lake, sirens blaring behind them, the sound of drones in the far distance. They run in silence, ducking behind every bush and tree to shield themselves. Around them, always, is the reek of brine shrimp.

After twenty minutes or so, Harp feels his mind cloud over, his brain slow down. He grips Spike's hand and can tell that she knows what's happening.

"I'll get us the rest of the way."

"The rest of the way to *where?*"

"Just follow me," Spike says. "Pretend I'm the red."

He squeezes her hand, and nods.

The house beside the dead city on the lake. Certainly the Goddess wasn't talking about Leonora's house. There were no people there working together against the mist. Another lake? Another city? Spike has no idea where she's supposed to go, but she doesn't let Harp know that. It would freak him out. It would *destroy* him.

They press on.

She knows it's dangerous to be out here with her Platinum plates exposed. Aside from the risk of plate theft, there might be some enterprising people who would just kill her for the hell of it. Not that her people didn't deserve everything that was coming to them, even if she didn't individually merit any violent acts.

Maybe I do deserve it, she thinks. But she can't give herself up. She has to remain alive for Harp. To find that place the Goddess said they both belonged.

She keeps the lake always in sight out of the corner of one of her eyes, and Harp in the corner of the other one. "Doing okay?"

He just grunts, the pain of his regression already wearing on him. He didn't get a chance to tell her what it was like, being unaffected by the mist and then returning to his natural unnatural state, but she could read it all in his face.

"We'll stop in a few minutes. Just let me get my bearings." She stares out over the lake. Was that some sort of cloth tied to a tree near the coastline? She makes Harp stay where he is, and goes over to inspect it.

It *is* cloth. She unrolls it, revealing a pair of triangles intersecting a round sphere. It's the fucking Channel Only symbol, screenprinted onto a rag. She tosses it into the water with a sigh. "Nothing," she yells over her shoulder.

She doesn't know how to hunt, and doesn't want to eat anything that comes from the lake, which is probably full of mist residue. Platinums never ate seafood for that reason. So instead of having a meal, they sit next to each other on a decaying log and think about food.

"Ham sandwiches," Harp says, licking his lips.

"Blueberry ice cream."

"Fried chicken. With mashed potatoes."

"Roast beef in wine sauce." But their bellies still rumble, and Spike knows that even if they're not caught, they're toast. And not the edible kind.

They press on. And on.

When the sun is halfway down the sky, Spike finds the Channel Only logo chalked on a tree. Not chalked. Engraved. *A lot of Channel Only fans out here in the hinterlands*, she thinks.

Harp touches the carving. "What is it?"

"I don't know. We must have gone halfway around the lake

by now." She ransacks her externalized memory for the rough circumference of the Great Salt Lake. "Maybe not."

Harp just gapes at it with his mouth open. She reminds herself that it's not his fault. It's *hers*.

They continue on. And on.

When dark nears they find a cabin. Weeds have overrun the front yard. They step over the mess, picking their way along the broken stones of the front walkway. Hesitantly, Spike swings opens the unlocked door and surveys the wreckage of the living room, long picked over by scavengers and animals. She sniffs the air, but doesn't find the telltale odor of rotting bodies. The original owners must have fled long ago, when their minds did.

She nudges him forward. "Come on, Harp." Dazed, he follows her inside.

Spike directs Harp to lie down on the threadbare couch while she prepares the bed for herself. She finds several guns in a hidden cache under the bed, but quickly conceals them again. She strips out of the ruined taffeta dress and lies down on her back, almost instantly falling into sleep. And that's when she sees it.

A tiny Channel Only logo, painted in red near the upper corner of the ceiling.

She punches sleep away with invisible fists and goes over to inspect the logo. There's a line of coordinates nearby, which she logs into her plate-memory. Only then does she let herself fall into the world of dreams.

The next day, she rouses Harp from his sleep—he sleeps deep, like a bear—and sets out for the coordinates logged in her memory. She doesn't know where they lead. But they're *something*.

"Where are we going?" Harp says, still groggy.

"I'm following the red," she replies.

"No red around here." He shakes his head. "Nothing around here."

Oh, there's something all right, she thinks.

She leads him away from the lake and the occasional siren she can still hear echoing over the flat, barren land. Toward the scrub. The ground is unbroken by human feet, and she wonders if there's anyone at the end of this string of directions. Some rogue group of Channel Only enthusiasts?

The mist is wearing off, the Goddess had told her.

Finally, they arrive at another cabin, nearly as dilapidated as the place where they spent the night. It makes Leonora's house look like a palace. Tentatively, Spike knocks on the door. "Hello?"

The door creaks open.

Harp rears back, but Spike grabs his forearm and drags him closer. "It's okay," she says, though she can't even convince herself. He goes passive—a feature of his plate—and trudges after her.

The inside of the house is filled with computers, floor to ceiling. Spike has never seen so much tech before, not even at her father's factories. At every console sits a woman or man with a determined expression on their face. Some are manipulating shapes into different places, while others tinker with audio cues. Nobody turns to greet them.

"Does someone want to tell me what's going on here?" Spike asks.

Harp doesn't say anything. He's drawn to the screens, mesmerized by them. He kneels in front of one of the consoles, nearly knocking the woman at the controls out of her seat.

The woman smiles and lets him sit down. She walks over to Spike, her expression frostier. "I see you've found us."

"Who are *you*?"

"The real Channel Only. The ones bringing everything down." She tosses her hair and Spike glimpses pure Platinum. "Welcome to the revolution."

*

Harp doesn't watch Channel Only anymore. They'd told him that was because it wasn't *for* him, that only people affected by the mist were susceptible to its underlying message. Still, he misses its soothing patterns and syncopated rhythms.

"How's the wiring going?" Spike asks. She looks a lot more like herself, dressed in jeans and a T-shirt, her orange hair back in reverse icicles.

"Almost got it," Harp says as a spark jumps from one of his tools to the circuit board. "Maybe not." He'd shown no talent as a programmer, but Channel Only was in need of a good electrician. *We need those even more than we need programmers,* they'd said.

Spike groans as she lowers herself onto Harp's bench. The cabin had been only the tip of the iceberg, most of the headquarters buried deep underground. "Don't these fuckers know how to clean up after themselves?"

"We couldn't do what we do without a janitor to keep everything tidy."

"Oh, spare me the 'everyone has an important role here' line. I should just go back East. You don't need me here."

Harp ignores her. It's not the first time she's cried about her relative mediocrity. "We have a new pattern premiering tonight. Splicing it in at 8:07 EST."

Five years ago a splinter group of eight programmers broke away from the official state television channel when they discovered that certain combinations of shapes and sounds could influence human behavior, even in minds clouded by mist dust. The rogue Platinums recruited others from all six of the other plate castes, choosing people who had once been artists, or musicians, or writers. They replaced their plates with ones stolen from hospitals that served Platinums, or that were ripped from the temples of people that they'd assured Harp were really, really evil and deserved it.

Harp had been a Plastic. He remembered what it was like. Nobody deserved it.

Harp was told they were doing good work, and as he came out of the mist's neural fog, he saw it was true. This secret cabal spent their days developing "pulses" of programming to insert into normal broadcasts, subliminal messages that would influence the lower castes to rise up in revolution . . . and eventually find their way here.

"We have an outreach team at each of the gathering points," one of them had said. "When the people arrive, we'll be there for them."

Harp finishes up his work and fits the chassis back over the machinery. "All set." He wipes his hands on his pants.

Spike pouts at the clean walls of Harp's underground lair. "Do you really think we're *doing* anything?"

"It's a slow process, Pamela. We can't incite change too quickly. The Platinums will notice if half their workforce suddenly disappears."

"That's not my name," she says, scowling. "Maybe I can help from D.C. Work *within* the system."

"There's no such thing as working within the system, Spike. We need you *here*." Harp knows that if Spike did try to leave, the guards at the front door will shoot her in the back. The splinter group can't risk some punk kid spilling their secrets.

"Don't you miss the Goddess?"

Harp's face reddens. "Don't make fun of me, girl." The Salt Lake technicians had explained it to him. The manifestation of the Goddess of the Highway was the result of amphetamine psychosis mixed with sleep deprivation mixed with a faulty wire somewhere in his Plastic plates. He'd fashioned the whole mythology through a sort of temporary madness. He'd chopped off his fingers himself. He'd boosted his own capabilities there at the end, his last wish. None of it had been her. "There's no Goddess of the Highway."

"Yes there is," says Spike with a smile he can't interpret.

Harp moves on to the next machine. "Besides, you don't want to go back there. Isn't this what you wanted? To bring down the system, make everyone a Platinum?"

"I'm too good for this," she mutters.

"Excuse me?"

"What I mean is," she says, "I just didn't think it would take so long."

"It'll be over sooner than you think," he replies.

"Not soon enough," she says before flouncing out of the room.

When he knows nobody is watching, Harp kneels next to the terminals that line both sides of the room. He pictures *her* in his mind. The unreal woman with asphalt skin and signpost hair. And he prays.

As Harp's mind returned, so did his memories, images of a family living in the shadow of some mountain range. Lots of families were disrupted in the post-mist panic, not just his. Families scattered to different castes, different lives. *We'll find them*, the other operatives had said. *If we can, we'll bring them here. Or they'll find us.* In a fractured world, he knows it's the longest of shots.

Find them for me, Harp thinks to the being that doesn't exist.

He knows it's pointless. She was wishful thinking spun into a personal mythology to help him survive thousands of miles traveled along desolate highways across the gutted continent. She isn't real, and never was.

But hey, it's not going to *hurt*.

STORY NOTES

STATES OF EMERGENCY

I used to have a shower curtain with a cartoon rendition of the United States with each state's most recognizable image doodled within its borders: credit cards for Delaware, Starbucks for Washington, etc. That's the inspiration for this vignette story where each state has a distinctive element except that in this case all of them are nightmare worlds (or at least moderately awkward ones to live in). You could read a narrative about political polarization into this story if you want, but to paraphrase a well-known tweet, it's really just about a fucking shower curtain.

HUMAN RESOURCES

The first of many stories here that have to do with income inequality and the evil authoritarian governments trying to perpetuate it. Though it's perhaps a bit on the nose, once I came up with the central idea and the punny title, I couldn't not write it. With limb transplants becoming more advanced, it's potentially a look at our own terrifying future.

DAYS LIKE THESE

When I lived in Baltimore, most nights the shadiest ice cream truck imaginable would rumble down our street, even during Hurricane Sandy. No children ever ran up to it. My husband/editor Rob and I called it the Meth Cream Truck. "Days Like These" is about finding a temporary salvation in the back of a shady vehicle, and also about people being sad that they live in a virtual reality suburban prison. I think this is the only non-flash story I've ever written that has been completed in one sitting, though I don't know that this means anything about the story in particular.

THE BIG SO-SO

I rarely fall in love with my own characters, but I've written multiple stories involving these guys, including another one you've already read if you're reading this book in order (if you haven't, please disregard). For this story, the first one in the series, I set out to write something fun and light with a quirky, easily-distractible first-person narrator, and what's more light-hearted than aliens slipping the entire world a mickey and kicking back in their flying saucers to see how it all goes down? Enter Syl: a woman who wasn't as affected as other people but still has to deal with the fallout of a world suffering from a permanent hangover, including a roommate who's fiendishly searching for the recipe to the alien love drug. It's been interesting to see how throwaway concepts I wrote into what I expected to be a one-off story have paid off in later tales of my "magic band."

A CHILD OF THE REVOLUTION

2020 was a surreal year to live through for many reasons, but one of the most head-spinning is that it's the year when "socialism" was mainstreamed, or at least an ideology that calls itself socialism. Some people cheered this on and see it as a sign that progressives are winning, but I'm a cynical asshole. In my view, corporations (and to a large extent, political organizations) stand for nothing more than making money, and allowing them to drape themselves in the mantle of progress cheapens whatever cause they've decided to infect. You might get a bigger microphone if you choose to align yourself with Amazon or McDonald's, but you'll be cut off the moment such revolutionary talk becomes unprofitable. The feudal society in "A Child of the Revolution" doesn't really have money, but they do have power, and they're naïve enough to think that enlisting the help of the very cause they've vowed to fight is going to turn out well for them. But it doesn't, any more than promoting a glitzy media-friendly version of socialism is going to achieve the material goals of universal healthcare, basic income, or any other concrete economic programs. The first person plural voice, while tricky to write, was necessary to show the co-optation of the Revolution from many different viewpoints.

LUCKY GIRL

I'm a big fan of a band called the Eels, whose frontman is the son of physicist Hugh Everett III, the originator of the many-worlds interpretation (MWI) of quantum physics. The MWI states that every decision we make creates a different reality, and that there are an infinite number of parallel universes, some with only the tiniest of differences. Everett postulated—and you can't exactly prove him wrong—that due to the MWI there must always be a world where he was immortal. From that point on he began chain-smoking and drinking to excess, because fuck it, right? In our universe he died at the age of 51, but if his interpretation is correct there's still a universe where he's alive. Natalie in "Lucky Girl" is also a believer in quantum immortality, and takes part in thrill-seeking adventures which, from everyone else's perspective, look like an increasingly bizarre string of suicide attempts. This story was originally published in *The Dark*, and it's probably my most horrific tale despite the fact that it's basically two women talking about physics for like ten pages. The use of a move to Portland as a framing device reflects the fact that I wrote this shortly after moving to Portland in 2014. There are also an infinite number of universes where this is not true. Maybe.

BUCKET LIST FOUND IN THE LOCKER OF MADDIE PRICE, AGE 14, TWO WEEKS BEFORE THE GREAT UPLIFTING OF ALL MANKIND

This is by a wide margin the story of mine that got the most attention/fan mail/kudos. I hope that's not only because it's the shortest! Like much of the flash in this collection, this started out as a prompt in a Codex Writers Group contest. The original story didn't really have a through-line, and I'm grateful for an editorial comment that convinced me to emphasize the budding and doomed relationship between Maddie and Sandra, neither of whom is long for the corporeal world.

CAN YOU TELL ME HOW TO GET TO APOCALYPSE?

We're living in the age of reboots, and personally I'm not too happy about it. But you can't really blame the people in this story for going to extraordinary lengths to keep a children's show running, since it's the only way any of them can ever see children at all. This is a world of adults, and while the #girlboss narrator prides herself on being all business, she too secretly grieves for her dying world. Considering that some of the first movies to be released after a year of coronavirus lockdown were a *Tom & Jerry* reboot, a *101 Dalmatians* prequel, and sequels to films that were themselves rehashed stories, I guess I wasn't too far off in postulating that post-pandemic audiences would seek out comfort food, even if ours is far less grisly than *Gumdrop Road*.

AFTER WE WALKED AWAY

Everyone gets to write one Omelas response story, and this one is mine. Le Guin's story ends by describing the titular "ones" walking away, unable to be happy at the expense of an innocent child. My story begins where hers leaves off, as the nameless couple departs their magical village forever and tries to make a go of it in the world outside—our world, full of misery. While I'm a huge fan of Le Guin, I've always had a problem with "Omelas," namely that leaving doesn't fix anything. It might make the leavers feel righteous, but the child doesn't get any less tortured. Save a full-scale assault on Omelas (and I hope someone writes that story someday) the only effect of leaving is that the leavers downgrade their life while witnessing far worse tortures inflicted upon far more people. If Omelas is rotten (and it is), then our world is a hundred times more so. And as the nameless main characters quickly discover, there is no real option to walk away.

SEA CHANGES

Aside from space, we've run out of frontier. So what's a person who wants to live life on the edge of civilization to do? In this story, the solution is to build a dome home under the sea and fuck up your daughter enough that she writes a tell-all short story about it sometime in the future. Like many of my stories, I started with the first line and moved on from there. This is the first of three stories I published in the sadly-defunct *Ideomancer*, one of the first fiction magazines to be published entirely online (speaking of frontiers).

LOVING GRACE

I'm a proponent of universal basic income (UBI) as a way to replace wages lost due to increasing automation and subsequent job losses as we lurch towards a post-scarcity economy that may never come. But what if you had all the scientific ability to create a post-scarcity utopia but still couldn't get out of your capitalist mindset? That's the world of "Loving Grace," where people are forced to participate in employment drafts. Everyone in the story, including the main character whose wife is caught in the draft, knows that this program is nothing more than a way to keep the rabble in line. But what can they do? Shouldn't they be grateful for whatever the government gives them, even if they know they deserve way more, that society would actually work better if help was universal and generous rather than means-tested and kept to a bare minimum? That's right, this is a story about neoliberal austerity politics and I am Not A Fan. Automation is unavoidable, but it only has to be terrible if we allow it to be.

THE SPECIES OF LEAST CONCERN

In 2013, the Supreme Court ruled that the Monsanto Corporation had the right to limit how many crops a farmer was allowed to plant with their patented weedkiller-resistant seeds. Usually, farmers save seeds from previous plantings, but due to the copyright, the rhythm of a job that has existed since the beginning of human civilization was disrupted for profit. (The weedkiller-resistant seeds also had a habit of spreading into neighboring farms, which led to additional legal battles about whether the farmers had to compensate Monsanto or the other way around, a real mess.) This is the inspiration for "The Species of Least Concern," in which an evil agribusiness attempts to replace nature with products they can market. Yet, genetically engineered life is still life, something that the genetically damaged narrator knows all too well.

THIRTY-SIX INTERROGATORIES PROPOUNDED BY THE HUMAN-POWERED PLASMA BOMB IN THE MOMENTS BEFORE HER IMMINENT DETONATION

From 2011 to the start of the pandemic, my day job has been as a file clerk for two separate law offices. I got to read a lot of depositions and court pleadings over the years, and noticed how the plain, clinical legal language stripped harrying situations of all emotion. In this story, the "plaintiff" is a woman wronged by a powerful alien race, humanity's sole survivor who has been transmogrified into an interplanetary missile in order to take out another doomed species. If the aliens ever responded to her, it hasn't been recorded, but at least the plasma bomb got to register her complaints before becoming a massive explosion.

A SLOW, CONSTANT PATH

For someone who's owned a lot of cats over the years, it's kind of surprising that this is my only cat story. (I told my cats this, and they were not impressed.) It's also a generation ship story, and what's always fascinated me about generation ships is the idea of human language, culture, and mores diverting so far from any sort of pre-existing human civilizational construct that the humans would cease to be recognizable to us as human. Such is the case in this story, where robotic cats are tasked to be the "constants" for the thread of humanity imprisoned on the generation ship. But the cats can't keep the humans from realizing their worth forever, and in the end it's the more stand-offish, gruff robo-cat Eberling who decides to let humanity off its leash.

SASQUATCH SUMMER

The year is 1899, and robber barons and lasseiz-faire economic policy have created a level of income inequality only slightly better than the present level of income inequality. One rich asshole sets up a company logging town in the Pacific Northwest, only to find that people are unnecessary costs when sasquatches are proven to be real, trainable, and effectively free. While the townsfolk point their rage at the wrong species, a ragtag bunch of anarchists from New York City arrive to "save" the cryptids that most humans in town see as nothing more than big furry scabs (eww). This is the only short story I've ever written that takes place at a specific point in the real past, and like many of the stories in this collection, the setting was inspired by my move to Portland. And look at me, writing an actual happy ending for once.

THE FATE OF THE WORLD, REDUCED TO A TEN-SECOND PISSING CONTEST

This story was written for a flash contest on the Codex Writers forum, its title supplied by an unknown member. Another story about asshole aliens, though at least this time they've only taken one bar instead of the entire world.

SIGNS FOLLOWING

Snake handlers in space. I've been fascinated with snake handlers for ages and the absolute conviction in one's beliefs one must have to not only give God the wheel to your life but also tamper with the car a little first. The short-furred, always-damp alien with an unusual number of eyes was based on my one-eyed kitty Pistol, though unfortunately she didn't have the power to answer prayers with bitterly ironic solutions. Just to make things damp by licking them.

ACT OF PROVIDENCE

This story takes place in the setting of my novella *Busted Synapses*, a very near future dystopia that's slowly starting to become reality. "Act of Providence" revolves around a VR gaming platform that exists in this world, showing the creation of one of the digital playgrounds from the production side. It's also a story about which victims actually get listened to. In *Busted Synapses*, a climate catastrophe takes out the Eastern Seaboard, and given Rhode Island's small size it wasn't hard to imagine that state in particular suffering heavy losses. There are millions of climate refugees in this world, but Rhode Islanders get a "privileged" position since there are so few of them that they can be seen as individuals, which Hailey correctly identifies as unfair. Hopefully the future victims of the real climate crisis won't have their survival rest on how solid their social media game is.

AUTOMATIC

My first professional sale! Like many of my stories, this one came to me in the shower, or at least the first line did. I turned it over in my brain like a rock tumbler for most of a day and then wrote the story at like three a.m. It was also the first story I ever submitted for publication (other than a story that got published in a local anthology in 2005), and I submitted it to the then-fledgling *Clarkesworld*, not based on the pay—I was not aware at the time that one actually could be paid for short fiction—but because some of my writer friends at the time were complaining about getting really mean rejections and I wanted one too. I didn't get the rejection, but the "mean" editor has since become a friend and wrote the introduction to this collection.

WHERE YOU LEAD, I WILL FOLLOW: AN ORAL HISTORY OF THE DENVER INCIDENT

I got into *Pokemon Go* about three years too late. But once I did, I became absolutely obsessed with it for like four months. This period happened to coincide with my deadline for a solicited story about a fictional conflict between the United States and Russia, and I decided to write what I know and was spending hours playing every day. It's also, obviously, a story about misinformation and its role in fueling conspiracy theories, particularly those of the bipartisan "some other country is screwing with us" variety. In reality, no human or group of humans could have directed Follow the Leader in such a way as to produce maximum carnage, and it's also irrational to blame humans for misinformation fueled by algorithms and the relentless march of capitalism. I wrote this story at the 2019 Rainforest Writers Retreat, and it's probably the most experimental story of mine that's been published so far.

TRIAL AND TERROR

This is, in a roundabout way, the story that introduced me to the joy of writing sequels. When this story was solicited for *A Punk Rock Future*, the editor mentioned liking "The Big So-So," and he asked if I wanted to write something in that vein. That's when I realized I not only wanted to write something in the same vein but also in the same world. In addition to this story, in which Syl, Frank, and Clem hit the road in hopes of healing the strung-out land beyond Pittsburgh, I'm also working on a novella with these characters. So if you like Syl and company as much as I do, make sure the publishing world knows so I can write more for you!

USEFUL OBJECTS

One last little bit of flash, again written for a Codex contest. This commentary on "rise and grind" culture was fun to write, and despite its lack of scientific accuracy, it was published in *Nature*, which is really cool.

THE GODDESS OF THE HIGHWAY

"The Goddess of the Highway" is a reaction story. In this case, a reaction to the movie *Idiocracy*. While the movie is funny and quotable, the science couldn't be more wrong. I set out to write a story where oligarchs would do pretty much anything to dumb down the poor, up to and including physically hobbling their brains. It's also a story about faith, namely believing in a spiritual force (like a road goddess who gives you a sandwich if you hand over your fingers) without any hard evidence to back it up. Harp's decision to believe in the Goddess of the Highway gives him the strength to use his clever mind to fight through the engineered fog and earn a tasty, if costly, lunch.

ACKNOWLEDGMENTS

THIS COLLECTION IS THE culmination of a life-long dream. Unlike many science fiction readers, short stories were my portal into genre fiction. Instead of a fat trilogy, I wished for (and now have) a list of published stories as long as my arm. While this feat was partially assisted by some ridiculously long story titles, it's still an accomplishment. I've written and published longer work since then, but short stories are where my writing heart truly lives—and where most of my creations go to live out their bleak little existences.

Thanks to all the editors who have published me over the years, including but not limited to Neil Clarke, Andy Cox, Nick Mamatas, Leah Bobet, Jonathan Laden and Michele Barasso, Jason Sizemore and Lesley Conner, Kelly Link and Gavin Grant, Elise Tobler, Silvia Moreno-Garcia and Sean Wallace, Colin Sullivan, Elektra Hammond, Hayden Trenholm, Edmund Schubert, Sigrid Ellis, Scott Gable, Sean Patrick Hazlett, Brian White, Edmund Schubert, Brian Lewis, and Steve Zisson. I appreciate you pulling me out of the slush pile!

Props are also due to the Codex Writers Group, whose prompt-based contests were the starting place for about a quarter of the stories in this collection, and whose deadlines got those stories finished.

And of course, this book wouldn't exist without my publisher, Patrick Swenson. We've known each other for a long time now, and I can honestly say that Fairwood was my dream press for a short story collection. Thank you so much, Patrick!

But the biggest shout-out of all goes to my spouse and editor, Rob McMonigal, who's spent countless hours reading, revising, and hashing out these stories with me. I couldn't have asked for a better critique partner, and I couldn't have done this without you, babe.